EVASION
Fernsby's War Book 5

J.C. JARVIS

WHERRY ROAD PRESS

Get a FREE Book!

Before John Howard found sanctuary on the streets of Henry VIII's London, Andrew Cullane formed a small band of outlawed survivors called the Underlings. Discover their fight for life for free when you join J.C. Jarvis's newsletter at jcjarvis.com/cullane

Evasion

By J.C. Jarvis

To my wife, Glenda, who is my biggest supporter and my bedrock. Without her support and encouragement none of this would ever have happened.

My editor, Melanie Underwood, who patiently and expertly wove her magic through the pages of the manuscript and turned it into the thrilling book you see today. The deft touch and the care she poured into each page has made the book far better than it could have ever been on its own.

My cover designer, Jane Dixon-Smith, who far exceeds my expectations with the masterpieces she creates every time we work together. Jane is a true master of her art, and I am extremely grateful to be able to work with her.

To our beloved daughter, Tiffany Lattimore, whose memory inspires us every day. Though she is no longer with us, her spirit and love continue to guide and uplift us. Tiffany's bright light and boundless joy remain in our hearts, providing the strength to carry on and find hope in every moment. This book is a testament to her enduring presence in our lives, and we dedicate it to her memory with all our love.

WHERRY ROAD PRESS

Evasion

Fernsby's War Series Book 5

© 2025 by J.C Jarvis

Edited by https://melanieunderwood.co.uk/

Cover Design by http://www.jdsmith-design.com/

This book is a work of fiction. Names, characters, businesses, organisations, places and events, other than those clearly in the public domain, are either the product of the author's imagination, or are used fictitiously. Any resemblances to actual persons, living or dead, events or locales are purely coincidental.

No part of this book may be reproduced, stored in a retrieval system, or transmitted by any means without the written permission of the author and publisher.

Foreword

Welcome to *Evasion*, the fifth novel in the Fernsby's War Series, which continues to chronicle the remarkable odyssey of Michael Fernsby through the harrowing yet inspiring years of World War II.

Set against the backdrop of the Battle of Dunkirk and the fall of France, *Evasion* delves into themes of resilience, sacrifice, and the human cost of war. Michael's story takes him into the heart of Nazi-occupied Europe, where survival depends not just on courage and cunning, but also on trust—an elusive commodity in a land brimming with collaborators, spies, and soldiers.

As with the previous instalments, this novel stays rooted in historical authenticity. The story captures the desperate fight to hold the line near Dunkirk, the chaos of retreat, and the heartbreak of betrayal. Through meticulous research, I have sought to recreate the atmosphere of Europe in 1940, from the tense streets of France and Holland under siege to the quiet heroism of those who resisted.

In keeping with the series' tradition, *Evasion* reflects

British English usage, ensuring fidelity to the characters' voices and the time period. The narrative continues to embrace Michael's personal and sometimes fragmented perspective. His observations are grounded in his understanding of the unfamiliar landscapes and equipment he encounters, and his memories are coloured by exhaustion, grief, and moments of fleeting triumph.

One example is his description of the Lysander aircraft, a symbol of both peril and hope in this tale. His impressions of the machine—half awe, half trepidation—underscore the precariousness of his missions and the sheer audacity of the efforts to undermine the Nazi regime.

As always, historical figures and events are woven into the narrative with great care. Deviations from the historical record, where they occur, are minimal and serve only to enhance the emotional and thematic integrity of Michael's journey.

In *Evasion*, Michael faces new challenges that force him to confront his deepest fears and moral dilemmas. His choices, and the sacrifices of those around him, will resonate far beyond the borders of occupied Europe. This is not just a story of survival, but of how the flickering light of hope can endure even in the darkest times.

Thank you for continuing this journey with Michael Fernsby. His path is fraught with danger, yet it is also paved with humanity, courage, and the promise of redemption.

Enjoy the adventure.

J.C. Jarvis

Evasion

By J.C. Jarvis

Chapter 1

Wormhoudt, France. May 28, 1940

Twenty-two-year-old Lieutenant Ben Townshend of the 2nd Battalion Grenadier Guards squinted against the pale morning light as he led his battered squad into Wormhoudt, the distant thunder of artillery punctuating the eerie silence of the village streets as they moved slowly towards the chaos.

Just days ago, they'd been holding the line at La Bassée, but now their orders were clear: reinforce the Warwickshire and Cheshire Regiments at all costs. The Waffen-SS was pushing hard, and if they broke through there, the extraordinary evacuations taking place at Dunkirk would be jeopardised.

A mere ten miles from Dunkirk, Wormhoudt was the last obstacle between the Waffen-SS and the mass of British and Allied troops on the beaches, waiting for evacuation back to England.

"Stay sharp, lads," Ben murmured, his voice carrying quiet authority through the eerie silence of the village despite his young age. "Remember, we're all that stands between the Krauts and Dunkirk."

As if to punctuate his words, a distant explosion sent tremors through the ground and Ben instinctively steadied Private Will Cullen, still nursing his wounds from their difficult journey from La Bassée.

"You alright, Cullen?" Ben asked, concern etched across his face.

Cullen nodded, wincing as he clutched his side. "I'll manage, sir."

Ben squeezed his shoulder reassuringly before turning to Sergeant Dave Thompson. "Sergeant, how's our ammo situation?"

Thompson's grave expression said it all. "Down to our last clips, sir. It's not looking good."

"How about you, Private Harris?"

"Never better, sir."

Ben's mind raced, weighing their dwindling resources against their critical mission. He knew his men were putting on a brave face. Deprived of sleep and food, all four had barely survived the dangerous forty-mile journey from La Bassée, and now here they were, expected to reinforce the beleaguered troops defending the road into Dunkirk.

"Right, lads," he said after a long pause. "We find our boys, assess the situation, and make every bullet count. Don't do anything stupid and keep your heads down."

As they rounded a corner, the crack of nearby gunfire sent them scrambling for cover.

"Bastards!" Ben roared as he pressed himself against a partially collapsed wall. He glanced at his men, saw the fear in their eyes, and knew he had to be their rock.

"Stay calm," he said, forcing a reassuring smile.

"Remember why we're here. Every minute we hold is another life saved at Dunkirk."

Suddenly, a frantic voice called out, "Over here!"

They spotted a haggard soldier from the Warwickshire Regiment waving urgently from a bombed-out building. Ben led his men in a dash across the exposed street, sporadic rifle fire spurring them on.

Once inside, the soldier, Corporal Jenkins, briefed them breathlessly. "The Germans are advancing, sir. Mostly infantry, but they've got some armoured support. Word is there are Panzer divisions not far behind."

"Who are we facing, exactly?" Ben asked.

"Waffen-SS soldiers from the 1st SS Division Leibstandarte SS Adolf Hitler, sir."

Ben's brow furrowed. "What's our situation here, Corporal Jenkins?"

"We're scattered throughout Wormhoudt, sir. Holding, but barely. The Waffen-SS have been relentless, knowing how close they are to Dunkirk."

Ben quickly formulated a plan. "Cullen, set up the Bren gun to cover the crossroads. Sergeant Thompson, find us an escape route—we may need to fall back closer to Dunkirk if push comes to shove. Harris, you're on watch."

As his men moved to their positions, Ben turned back to Corporal Jenkins. "Any word from your commanding officer?"

"I don't know where he is, sir. Probably dead for all I know. As I said, we're scattered all over the town."

The weight of command settled heavily on Ben's shoulders. He thought fleetingly of his sweetheart in Edinburgh, but quickly refocused on the monumental task at hand.

"We hold this position," he stated firmly. "For those on the beaches, for those still trying to get there, and for everyone back home in Blighty. Stay sharp and give it everything you've got."

Suddenly, the distinctive sound of tracked vehicles reached their ears, growing louder by the second. Ben's heart raced, but his voice remained steady as he addressed his men.

"Listen up! We've got SS infantry incoming, likely with some armoured support. Remember your training and remember why we're here. Every second we hold them is another life saved on those beaches. Conserve ammo, aim true, and watch each other's backs."

The sound of German voices and the clatter of equipment grew closer. Ben checked his pistol one last time and looked at the faces of his men—tired, scared, but resolute.

"This is it, lads," he said, a fierce light in his eyes. "Let's show them what the Grenadier Guards are made of. For Dunkirk!"

As the first wave of SS troops came into view, followed by the ominous silhouette of an armoured car, Ben Townshend steeled himself for the fight of his life.

The next few hours in the small French village, just ten miles from Dunkirk, would determine the fate of thousands waiting on those beaches, and perhaps even the course of the war itself.

Chapter 2

As Ben took his position watching the crossroads, Sergeant Dave Thompson ran towards them with four more men behind him. The acrid stench of cordite hung heavy in the air, mingling with the choking smoke from smouldering buildings. Broken glass crunched underfoot as they moved, and the distant rumble of explosions sent tremors through the debris-strewn street.

One man, a captain, ran to Ben. The others took up defensive positions around them, their eyes darting warily across the shattered landscape of crumbling walls and overturned vehicles.

"Lieutenant, it's good to see you," the captain said, his voice hoarse from shouting orders. "James Lynn-Allen, Second Battalion, Royal Warwickshire's. How many of you are there?"

Ben threw Captain Lynn-Allen a quick salute, noting the man's dirt-streaked face and the dark circles under his eyes.

"I'm afraid there's only four of us, sir. We're taking a

terrible beating in La Bassée, and we're all that could be spared."

"It's better than nothing. Our job is to hold them off for as long as we can before retreating to Dunkirk."

"We'll do our best, sir," Ben replied, tightening his grip on his rifle.

Automatic gunfire erupted no more than a hundred yards away, cutting their conversation short. The rat-tat-tat of machine guns echoed off the walls of bombed-out buildings.

The bedraggled remnants of the British and French forces scattered around Wormhoudt returned fire, and for a moment Ben's world stood still, frozen in time as bullets whizzed past, kicking up small clouds of dust where they struck.

As Ben crouched behind a partially collapsed wall, movement caught his eye. A mangy dog, its coat matted with dust and blood, limped out from an alleyway. The animal's ribs protruded sharply, and it sniffed cautiously at the ground, searching for anything edible amidst the rubble.

Despite the chaos, Ben felt a pang of sympathy. He reached into his pocket and pulled out a small tin of bully beef. The metal was warm from being close to his body, and the acrid smell of cordite clung to it as he pried off the lid.

"Here, boy," he called softly, holding out a chunk of the preserved meat.

The dog's ears perked up, and it approached warily, its tail tucked between its legs. As it came closer, Ben could see a nasty gash on its side, crusted with dried blood and dirt. The animal snatched the meat from his outstretched hand and bolted it down in seconds, then looked up expectantly for more.

Ben smiled sadly and offered another piece. "Not much, I'm afraid. We're all struggling here."

As the dog wolfed down the second morsel, a nearby explosion rocked the ground. The animal yelped and darted away, disappearing into the maze of ruined buildings.

Ben turned his attention back to the battle, his moment of compassion swallowed by the brutal reality of war. The whine of an approaching Stuka dive bomber cut through the air, growing louder with each passing second. Ben and James Lynn-Allen instinctively ducked, pressing themselves against the cold, rough stonework of their meagre shelter.

The Stuka's scream reached a fever pitch before suddenly cutting off. Ben watched, heart pounding, as the plane pulled up sharply after releasing its payload. The whistle of the falling bomb seemed to last an eternity before it was engulfed by a deafening explosion. The ground shook violently, and a cloud of dust and debris billowed into the air three hundred yards down the street.

As the dust began to settle, revealing the skeletal remains of what had once been a sturdy building, Ben knew it was only a matter of time before they were forced to surrender. The air was thick with the smell of destruction—burning wood, melted metal, and the unmistakable, sickening odour of death.

A tug on his arm caught his attention. James Lynn-Allen was shouting at him, but his words were lost in the cacophony of battle. Instead, the captain pointed behind them, his grimy face etched with grim determination as he indicated they should fall back and regroup.

Ben nodded, his throat too dry to speak. He and Captain Lynn-Allen rounded up what was left of their men, their boots slipping on rubble-strewn streets as they dodged from one burned-out building to another.

The town centre, when they reached it, was a scene of utter devastation. They joined the remnants of the Warwickshire, Cheshire, and Royal Artillery units, a ragtag group of exhausted, soot-stained soldiers grimly holding their position at a crossroads leading to Dunkirk.

The realisation sank in like a stone: they were surrounded, with nothing left to offer except annihilation. The Germans pressed their advantage, their overwhelming firepower forcing the British farther and farther into their trap.

The air was filled with a constant barrage of noise—the crack of rifles, the chatter of machine guns, and the screams of the wounded—all underscored by the relentless rumble of approaching German armour.

An hour passed, by which time it was obvious they had lost the battle. All they could hope for was that the Germans had been held up long enough to allow as many Allied troops as possible to escape the beaches at Dunkirk.

"It's over, Ben," Captain James Lynn-Allen, the senior British officer present, said. "We need to tell the men to lay down their arms and surrender. We've lost enough lives and there's nothing to gain by continuing to fight."

Ben nodded. There was no other way. "Yes, sir. You're right."

He followed Captain Lynn-Allen by raising a white handkerchief in the air and laying down his rifle.

"Lay down your weapons, lads," Captain Lynn-Allen shouted. "You've fought valiantly, but it's over."

Murmurs and shouts followed as the British men lowered their weapons one by one. Those that had them raised white hankies in the air and waved them to signify their surrender.

At first, the Germans advanced tentatively, their weapons aimed and ready. They surrounded the one hundred strong British soldiers and ordered them to drop their weapons.

With their weapons aimed at the British men, one of the English-speaking Waffen-SS soldiers shouted at them.

"Drop your weapons and gather in the town centre. Hands in the air, and if anyone makes a move, you will be killed."

The British soldiers stopped talking as they assembled amidst the debris of the devastated town. The firing stopped, and silence fell over Wormhoudt.

Chapter 3

Leaving their weapons and helmets behind, the men were marched west out of the town. Cold droplets pelted their faces as dark clouds rolled in, turning the muddy path into a treacherous slick. After a gruelling kilometre, they reached a dilapidated farmhouse where they rested, muscles aching, as the Germans deliberated their fate.

The rain intensified, drumming against tin roofs and transforming gutters into miniature waterfalls. A group of Waffen-SS soldiers, their field-grey uniforms glistening wet, barked orders and gestured with their rifles towards a narrow, puddled road.

Captain Lynn-Allen and Ben Townshend led the weary column. Ben's sodden uniform clung to his skin, each step squelching in his waterlogged boots. Behind him, a soldier's voice cut through the patter of rain.

"We'll be well treated. The Jerries treated us right in the last war, and they'll do the same now."

Ben caught James Lynn-Allen's eye. The captain gave a slight nod, a flicker of hope in his tired eyes. Ben wanted to believe it, but a knot of unease tightened in his gut.

Scanning the bedraggled troops, Ben spotted Dave Thompson and Sam Harris a few paces back. The absence of Will Cullen sent a pang through his chest.

"Stay close, lads," Ben called, his voice barely carrying over the wind and rain. "We don't want to get separated if we can help it."

As they trudged on, Ben noticed several soldiers lagging behind, their faces contorted with pain from untreated wounds. He was about to speak up when two Waffen-SS soldiers fell back to flank them.

Or so Ben thought.

Ben's momentary relief evaporated as guttural shouts pierced the air. The SS men shoved the wounded brutally, rifle butts thudding against flesh and bone.

Captain Lynn-Allen turned to protest, only to be met with a torrent of German invective and a violent push that sent him staggering.

Ben's heart lurched as two badly wounded men collapsed into the mud. In a horrifying instant, the SS were upon them. Bayonets flashed in the grey light, accompanied by sickening thuds and strangled cries, quickly silenced.

James Lynn-Allen's face flushed crimson with fury. He bellowed at the nearest German, only to be answered by a vicious blow that sent him sprawling face first into the mud.

Ben hauled him up, feeling the captain's frame trembling with rage beneath his soaked uniform.

"This is unbelievable," Ben muttered, the words tasting like ash in his mouth. "I never thought the Germans would—"

"Not all Germans," James spat, wiping mud from his lips. "This is the SS. They're known for their cruelty. Mark my words, they'll pay for this."

Ben nodded grimly, the rain mingling with cold sweat on his brow.

After another agonising kilometre, they approached a weathered barn squatting in a rain-lashed field. Its timbers groaned in the wind, and the sickly-sweet smell of wet hay drifted from the gaping doorway. The SS herded them all inside, the press of bodies providing little warmth in the damp, cramped space.

"Perhaps they're just sheltering us from the rain," a hopeful voice suggested, but the words rang hollow in the tense silence.

Ben leaned close to James, his whisper barely audible over the drumming rain. "They might be holding us until transport arrives for POW processing."

"Let's hope so," James replied, his eyes darting to the door. "The sooner the regular Wehrmacht gets here, the better it will be for us."

A moment later, their world exploded into chaos. Ben, James, and a young private found themselves at the entrance as stick grenades arced through the air. The private's agonised scream cut through the din as shrapnel shredded his arm.

In a blur of motion, Captain Lynn-Allen grabbed the wounded man, shoving through the panicked crowd. Ben's eyes widened as he spotted their destination—a gap in the barn's rear wall, just large enough for a man to squeeze through.

Heart pounding, Ben whirled to find Dave and Sam. The air filled with acrid smoke and the metallic tang of blood. Soldiers shouted in confusion and terror, some cursing the SS, others scrambling for the escape route.

He spotted his men huddled in a corner, their faces pale with shock. As Ben fought his way towards them, more grenades sailed in. With gut-wrenching clarity, he watched a sergeant-major and a sergeant he'd only just met throw themselves onto the explosives. Their bodies jerked violently as they absorbed the blasts, their sacrifice saving countless lives in that moment.

Bile rose in Ben's throat as he reached Dave and Sam. "They're going to slaughter us all," he choked out. "We have to move now!"

Grabbing them, he shoved through the press of bodies towards the gap. The air filled with German shouts and the crack of gunfire as the SS began executing prisoners.

They burst into the rain-soaked field just as machine-gun fire erupted behind them. The staccato bursts mixed with screams of the dying, a hellish cacophony that would haunt Ben's dreams for years to come.

They sprinted through mud and long grass, lungs burning, until they reached a pond. Captain Lynn-Allen was there, struggling to help the wounded private across.

As Ben moved to assist, movement caught his eye. A lone SS soldier appeared at the pond's edge, his rifle raised.

Time seemed to slow. Ben watched in helpless horror as two shots rang out. Captain Lynn-Allen's body jerked and fell, lifeless, into the murky water. The private followed a heartbeat later.

Rage coursed through Ben's veins as he dragged Dave and Sam into a ditch, their ragged breathing deafening in the sudden quiet. Ben pointed to a cluster of trees by the pond, and they moved in a crouch, every snapping twig sounding like gunfire in their ears.

They scrambled up the tallest tree, the rough bark scraping their hands. Huddled in the branches, soaked to the bone, and shaking with more than cold, they waited.

The sounds of slaughter drifted on the wind, a grim

reminder of how close they'd come to sharing that same fate. Ben's eyes met those in the ashen faces of Dave and Sam, seeing his own shock and disbelief mirrored there.

And so they waited, praying for salvation, as rain dripped through the leaves as the world they'd known crumbled around them.

Chapter 4

The repulsive stench of distant smoke hung in the air as nineteen-year-old Michael Fernsby stumbled into Versailles, his legs aching and his mind foggy from nine days of relentless travel.

Racing against the Nazi advance towards Paris, he'd navigated treacherous terrain, evaded countless patrols, and pushed through adrenaline-fuelled nights with only the briefest moments of restless sleep.

The sun dipped below the horizon, casting long shadows across the cobblestone streets. In the distance, a muffled explosion rumbled, the earth convulsing visibly through the haze. The city held its breath, bracing for the advancing German forces.

Michael's hand instinctively went to the Walther PPK concealed beneath his borrowed jacket. The weight of it was reassuring, a grim reminder of the perilous journey that had brought him there.

As he made his way through the eerily quiet streets, his mind drifted back to his harrowing escape from Rotterdam in what seemed a lifetime ago.

The farmer's cart taking him away from the beleaguered city had rattled beneath him as he lay hidden under sacks of potatoes, every bump sending a jolt of fear through his body. The pungent smell of earth and vegetables had filled his nostrils, mingling with the sickly tang of his own sweat.

"Godspeed, Englishman," the farmer had whispered as he dropped Michael at the outskirts of Dordrecht, his weathered face etched with a mix of concern and determination.

From there, it had been a gruelling trek to get across Belgium and reach the border. Michael had stuck to forest paths and abandoned barns, relying on the kindness of the local people for scraps of food and whispered directions.

He remembered one night, huddled in the hayloft of a derelict farm, when the distant sound of German voices froze him in place. He'd barely dared to breathe, every muscle taut, as heavy boots crunched on the gravel below. The voices had faded, but sleep had eluded him that night.

Near Brussels, he'd lain in a muddy ditch, heart pounding, as a German patrol passed mere metres away. The squelch of boots in mud, the metallic clank of military equipment, the guttural sound of German orders—each noise amplified in Michael's hyper-alert state.

He'd pressed his face into the damp earth, willing himself to become invisible, as the beam from a torch swept agonisingly close.

Crossing into France brought little relief. He'd hitched a ride with retreating French soldiers, their eyes hollow with defeat.

"We're finished," one had muttered, passing Michael a cigarette with trembling hands. Although he didn't smoke, Michael accepted the soldier's act of kindness with deep gratitude, the smoke creating a bond between them; a common enemy once again joining France and England in arms. Michael knew the machine they faced only too well.

The shared moment of quiet desperation had forged a fleeting connection with men he'd never see again. As they parted ways, he raised his palm outward in a quiet salute.

The train to Paris had been packed with refugees, everyone pushing and straining to get anywhere but where they were. Michael had kept his head down, grateful for the borrowed clothes that helped him blend in.

A young mother, clutching a wailing infant to her chest, caught his eye. For a moment, Mina's face superimposed itself over the stranger's, and Michael's heart clenched with a mixture of longing and fear.

Was she safe? Had Jeroen kept her and Senta out of harm's way? The uncertainty gnawed at him, a constant ache that no amount of mission focus could entirely dispel.

Now, as he approached 37 Avenue de Sceaux, Michael's instincts kicked in. He doubled back twice, weaving through narrow alleys and side roads.

His eyes scanned rooftops and windows, searching for any sign of surveillance. Satisfied he wasn't being followed, he slipped into the shadows of a nearby alley. He watched the building for ten long minutes, cataloguing every movement, every flicker of light behind curtained windows.

A cat yowled nearby, making him jump. He took a deep breath, steeling himself. This was it. Either he was walking into the arms of allies, or he was about to step into a trap. Either way, there was no turning back now.

He approached the apartment block and knocked on the door of apartment 204. A moment of tense silence followed, during which Michael's hand hovered near his concealed weapon. Then came the click of a lock. The door opened a crack, revealing a sharp-featured man in his fifties.

"Marcel Bertrand?" Michael asked, his voice barely above a whisper.

The man's eyes narrowed, scanning Michael's face with piercing intensity. "Who's asking?"

"Aquila."

Aquila was Latin for eagle. This was the codeword he'd been directed to use, and his fingers trembled slightly as he spoke.

Marcel's gaze flicked over Michael, his posture relaxing fractionally. He stepped back, allowing Michael entry, but Michael noted how the Frenchman's hand lingered near his own pocket. Trust, it seemed, would not come easily on either side.

As he stepped into the apartment, Michael's eyes quickly took in his surroundings. The space was sparsely furnished, with a worn leather couch against one wall and a single armchair opposite.

A battered radio set sat on a small table near the window, its dials glinting dully in the fading light. The walls were bare save for a faded map of France, its corners curling with age.

Marcel, a grizzled man in his fifties, gestured for Michael to sit. His hawkish grey eyes, set deep in a weathered face, scanned Michael with sharp intensity. A neatly trimmed moustache and small grey beard framed his thin lips, while his long, grey hair was swept back from his forehead. Standing at about five feet eight inches, his slender frame moved with a wiry energy that belied his age.

"You look like hell," Marcel said, pouring two glasses of cognac. His voice was gruff but not unkind.

Michael accepted the drink gratefully, sinking into the couch. Its springs creaked in protest, hinting at the discomfort that likely awaited him in the spare bedroom.

"Sounds about right," he replied, taking a sip.

The amber liquid burned pleasantly down his throat, warming him from the inside out. He savoured the moment; such small luxuries were as welcome as they were scarce.

As Marcel settled into the armchair opposite, Michael caught a glimpse of the apartment's two bedrooms through partially open doors.

He could make out a narrow bed in one, its frame looking as worn and tired as he felt. A grey blanket was folded at its foot, threadbare but clean. Michael suppressed a sigh, knowing that his coat would likely serve as his pillow for the night.

"How much do you know about the situation here?" Marcel asked.

Michael shook his head. "Not much. Information's been hard to come by on the road. I know the Germans are advancing, but beyond that..." He trailed off, letting the unspoken question hang in the air.

Marcel's face darkened. "France is falling," he said bluntly. "The Germans will be here within days, a week at most. Our armies are in disarray, the government is paralysed. It's a disaster."

Michael nodded grimly, processing the information. "What about the British forces? The last I heard, they were still holding the line."

Marcel let out a bitter laugh. "Holding the line? They're scrambling to evacuate from the beaches at Dunkirk. Your country sent every fishing vessel and small boat they could muster to pick up as many soldiers as they can."

Marcel sighed and let out a deep breath. "It's all that's left now—get as many men off the beaches as possible before the Germans overrun them."

The news hit Michael like a physical blow. He'd known things were bad, but this… this was catastrophic.

"Christ," he muttered, draining his glass.

As if to punctuate Marcel's words, a sudden, thunderous explosion rocked the building. The windows rattled ominously, and both men instinctively ducked, months of wartime reflexes kicking in.

"Bloody hell!" Michael exclaimed, his heart racing. "That was close."

Marcel rushed to the window, pulling back the heavy blackout curtains and peering out into the gathering dusk. His face, illuminated by the fading light, was a mask of grim determination.

"The Germans are getting closer," he muttered. "We don't have much time."

The distant wail of air raid sirens filled the air, a haunting reminder of the approaching danger. Michael felt a renewed sense of urgency coursing through him, but exhaustion clouded his thoughts. The long journey, the constant vigilance, the emotional toll—it was all catching up to him now.

Marcel seemed to sense Michael's fatigue. "We'll talk more in the morning," he said, his tone softening slightly. "You're pale and need rest. There's a spare room down the hall. It's not much, but it's safe."

Michael nodded gratefully, suddenly aware of just how bone-tired he was. Marcel showed him to the small, sparsely furnished room. A single bed, a rickety bedside table, and a lone candle were all it contained, but to Michael, it looked like paradise.

"Thank you," he said, turning to Marcel. "For everything."

Marcel clasped his shoulder briefly. "Get some sleep. Tomorrow will come soon enough."

Evasion

Left alone, Michael sank onto the bed, his body crying out for rest. Yet his mind continued to race, replaying the events of the past weeks. He thought of Mina, her tear-stained face as he'd left Rotterdam seared into his memory.

Had he done the right thing, leaving her behind? The doubt gnawed at him, mingling with the ever-present fear that he might never see her again.

He pictured Senta with her fierce determination and loyalty. Would her quick wit and special talents be enough to keep her safe in occupied Holland?

And Jeroen, the stalwart leader of the Dutch resistance. Michael could only hope that his resourcefulness and courage would see him through the dark days ahead.

The candle flickered on the bedside table, casting Michael's face in a dance of light and shadow. He watched the flame, mesmerised by its constant motion.

Light and dark, hope and despair—the dichotomy seemed to mirror his own internal struggle. Part of him longed for the simplicity of his life before the war, before he'd been thrust into this world of violence and espionage.

Memories flickered through his mind of better times when he ran to classes at Cambridge, and the evenings with his brother David at the local pub.

But he knew there was no going back. The world was changing, and he had to change with it.

He closed his eyes, forcing himself to steady his breathing. Whatever the next day brought, he'd face it head-on. For Mina, for all those he'd left behind, and for the hope of a future free from Nazi tyranny.

He thought of Jeroen and the Dutch resistance fighting against overwhelming odds. Of the French soldiers he'd met, their spirits broken but still clinging to a shred of hope. Of the countless civilians caught in the crossfire of a monstrous war.

As sleep finally began to claim him, Michael felt a release, a resolve surge through him. He would see this through, no matter the cost.

He would fight, not just for his country, but for all those who couldn't fight for themselves. And somehow, someway, he would find his way back to Mina.

As consciousness slipped away, Michael's last thought was of Mina. Her comfort, her strength, the feel of her around him while they slept; the memories were his talisman, his reason to keep going when all seemed lost.

The candle flickered one last time, then went out, plunging the room into darkness. Outside, the distant rumble of explosions continued, a grim lullaby for a world at war. But inside the small room, for a few precious hours at least, there was peace.

Chapter 5

As dawn broke, painting the sky in hues of pink and gold, Michael stirred. For a moment, disoriented, he didn't know where he was. Then reality came crashing back—the fall of Rotterdam, the perilous journey, the looming threat of the German advance. He sat up, running a hand through his dishevelled black hair.

The distant sound of explosions had faded, replaced by the more mundane noise of a city waking up. But the tension in the air remained, a constant reminder that the tranquillity could shatter at any moment.

Soon, Marcel would brief him on whatever mission Sanders and Dansey had planned for him. For a little while, though, he allowed himself a few moments of quiet reflection.

He thought of home, of Britain standing alone against the Nazi tide. Of his parents and his sister, worried sick no doubt, not knowing if their son was alive or dead. He thought of his colleagues in Unit 317, scattered across Europe on their own dangerous assignments. And always, always, his thoughts returned to Mina.

"I'll make it back," he whispered to the empty room. "I promise."

With a deep breath, Michael swung his legs over the side of the bed. Whatever the day held, whatever challenges lay ahead, he was ready to face them. He had to be. Too much depended on it.

Marcel was sitting at the small, rickety table in the kitchen. A radio set took up the entire space on the table, and Michael noted the wire antenna sticking out of the window.

"I radioed London last night and told them you had arrived," Marcel said matter-of-factly. "They sent a message back telling us to await further orders."

"They'd better hurry, or Paris will be in German hands."

"There's bread and cheese over there." Marcel changed the subject and pointed towards the kitchen counter. "Did you sleep well?"

"Like a baby." He meant it too.

Marcel rose to his feet and poured two cups of coffee, handing one to Michael.

"That's good, because I don't think London will want you to stay here for too long."

"I thought I'd be coming here to discover how I'm getting back to England," Michael said. "I wasn't expecting to be sent on another mission."

"There's a war on. What *did* you expect?"

Michael shook his head but didn't answer. Instead, he sat on the worn couch and sipped on his coffee.

Thirty minutes passed with neither man uttering a word. Michal ate in silence while Marcel stared at the radio as if waiting for an important message.

Perhaps he was.

Michael sat lost in thought, his mind going over and

over the events in Rotterdam. The face of his arch nemesis, Albert Kreise, flooded his mind, though he was grateful because Mina, Senta, and Jeroen's lives were a lot safer now that he was dead.

Michael never dwelt on any of the lives he'd taken, but Kreise was different. He was the one man who'd deserved his fate, and Michael was glad it was he who'd delivered the fatal blow.

As he pondered, a sound outside the front door of the apartment caught his attention. He rose to his feet, his hand grasping the handle of his trusty Walther PPK. He moved rapidly to the side of the room, away from the arc of fire, should someone start shooting through the locked door.

Marcel heard it too, and he took a position on the opposite side of the door to Michael. Both men crouched, ready to return fire at a moment's notice.

Michael had decided long ago that he was never going to be taken alive. He knew his life wouldn't be worth living if the Gestapo or SD ever got hold of him.

Any member of Unit 317, the top-secret operational division of Britain's Secret Intelligence Service that was tasked with carrying out dangerous, deniable missions both home and abroad, often alone and without support, would be interrogated beyond the point of sanity if they were captured. Death was guaranteed, and Michael knew it would be a painful one.

So, whatever else happened, he was steadfast in his conviction that he would never be taken alive.

The two men watched as a large envelope was slid underneath the apartment door. As soon as it appeared, footsteps could be heard scurrying away as fast as they'd appeared.

By the time Marcel opened the door, the dark, damp corridor was empty.

Michael picked up the envelope and turned it over in his hands. One word was handwritten on the front of the envelope:

Fernsby.

Marcel shrugged his shoulders and returned to his radio set. Michael took the envelope to his bedroom and closed the door, then tore open the envelope and pulled out a handwritten note that was stuffed inside.

Pièce d'Eau des Suisses. All du Potager opposite rail tracks. Noon.

The note wasn't signed, and there was nothing else in the envelope. Michael studied the handwriting, but didn't recognise it. Nobody he knew had written the note.

Feeling uneasy, he left the bedroom and approached Marcel.

"Do you have a street map of the area?" he asked.

Without asking any questions, Marcel rose from his chair and pulled a folded street map from a drawer in the kitchen. Michael went back to his room and spread it out on the bed.

Frustrated at not being able to understand French, he had no clue what he was looking for. Eventually, he gave up and went to Marcel with the note.

"Do you know where the note is referring to?" he asked, passing the note and the map to Marcel.

Marcel smiled and tapped his finger on a small lake close to the Palace of Versailles.

"This is the Pièce d'Eau des Suisses. It's a large pond."

He traced his finger to a set of railroad tracks on the southern edge of the pond.

"The All du Potager is a single-track road between the

rail tracks and the Pièce d'Eau des Suisses. Once you get there, you can't miss it."

He looked up at Michael. "Do you need backup?"

Michael shook his head. "I doubt it's a trap. If it were the Germans, they'd have burst in here and taken both of us already. It's genuine, I'm sure."

Marcel nodded. "I think you're right. Beware, though, because the palace is well known for clandestine meetings. There are spies everywhere."

Michael bowed his head and tapped Marcel on the shoulder. "Perhaps an extra pair of eyes wouldn't be a bad thing after all."

"Consider it done, my young English friend."

They spent the next thirty minutes poring over the map and making plans as to how and from where Michael should approach the meeting place.

At eleven o'clock, they were ready. Michael groaned when Marcel pointed at a bicycle leaning against the living room wall.

Chapter 6

Twenty minutes later, Michael dismounted from the bicycle, glad to separate his cheeks from the rock-hard seat that still gave him nightmares after his legendary three-hundred-mile trek through Nazi Germany to Denmark seven months earlier.

He hadn't been sure what to expect, and from Marcel's description, he'd been expecting to find a small duck pond on the outside edge of the grounds of the palace, so he was pleasantly surprised to see that the pond was, in fact, more like a small lake than a pond.

Oblong in shape, it reminded Michael of a big cigar, not unlike the ones his father was so fond of.

At the thought of his father, Michael quickly shook them from his mind. Now was not the time to dwell on family, no matter how much he missed them.

He pushed the bike around the corner at the southern edge of the pond and hid it in the thick trees that separated it from the railway lines he knew were there because he heard a train pass by not far from where he stood.

He was early, so he walked the length of the All du

Potager, which, it turned out, wasn't very long. When it curved around to the right at the far end of the pond, the name of the single-track road changed to All du Mail.

A bench faced the gap in the trees halfway down the All du Potager. The pond could clearly be seen through the gap, and Michael imagined families sitting on the bench while their children played on the grass between the bench and the pond.

But now, with the threat of Paris falling any day, the pond and its surrounding area were quiet. A woman walked her small dog on the palace side of the pond, and Michael noted that she kept her eyes firmly on a man wearing a wool suit and a fedora sitting on a bench feeding the ducks.

Using a few trees as cover, Michael kept out of sight, sitting on the edge of the empty bench in front of the pond.

He pretended to while away the morning reading the newspaper he'd brought with him as a man strolled by. Although the two didn't make eye contact, Michael knew he was being scrutinised as the man walked past.

Not wanting to begin any conversation with the man, Michael kept his eyes on the newspaper. He couldn't speak French, so even the slightest sentence would give him away, which was the last thing he needed.

The man turned right to follow the path down the side of the pond and vanished from view. Michael wasn't sure where Marcel was, but he knew he'd be keeping an eye on anyone who got too close to his location.

Rustling in the trees behind warned him that someone was approaching. He rose from the bench quickly and reached for his weapon.

"Put that away, Michael."

Michael froze in disbelief. He'd recognise that voice anywhere.

"Tony Sanders!" he exclaimed in a whisper. "What are you doing here?"

Michael spun around, shocked to his core that Major Tony Sanders, the head of Unit 317 and the man responsible for every agent in the unit, was there in person.

"It's good to see you, Michael," Sanders whispered in his strong Kent accent.

Michael sat down on the bench, stunned. His jaw dropped as Sanders sat next to him. At thirty-eight years old, Major Sanders had always looked young for his age. But now, with dark lines under his eyes from lack of sleep and fatigue, he was beginning to look older.

"You've lost weight," Sanders said as they shook hands.

"You look tired," Michael retorted. "It's so good to see you, Tony. I wasn't expecting this at all."

"Alison Turnberry, our unit secretary, received the message last night from Marcel that you had arrived in Paris. We all feared that you'd been captured, or that you'd been killed somewhere. When Marcel told us you were in Paris, I had to come to see you myself."

"How is everything back home?" Michael asked.

"Worrisome." Sanders got right down to business. "I'm sure you've heard by now that France is about to fall. Britain is about to stand alone against the full might of Hitler's Germany, and it's more important now than ever that we focus and deliver some much-needed success to our shores."

"Why are you here, Tony?" Michael asked. "Am I going home?"

"No such luck, I'm afraid." Sanders glanced at Michael, his friendly blue eyes tinged with sadness; perhaps even loneliness. Michael couldn't say for sure, knowing little about Sanders' personal life, though the long hours he'd been putting in likely didn't leave much room for one.

Michael bowed his head. He knew he wasn't going home anytime soon.

"What would you have me do?" he asked.

"After you left Rotterdam—where you performed splendidly, I must add—we received a communication from the leader of the resistance there. His name is Jeroen, and I believe you know him."

"Jeroen?" Michael asked, dumfounded. "Yes, I know him. He's an exceptional leader, and we should be doing all we can to help his cause."

He paused for a moment before adding: "Why did he contact you?"

"He told us about your bravery and how you helped them during the invasion. He had extremely high praise for you, Michael."

"Then why do I feel as though I'm in some sort of trouble?"

Sanders sighed and looked around. Nobody was near them, and they were free to talk.

"Jeroen told us what happened to his resistance group. He said that he'd be dead if it wasn't for you."

"That's not true," Michael refuted. "If anything, it was the opposite way around."

"Either way, you two stopped Zobart and saved countless lives in the process."

Michael shrugged.

"Why are you here?" he asked again.

"Jeroen told us about the German girls who worked for him." Sanders stared at Michael, his rounded features staring through him.

Michael gulped as he realised where the conversation was heading.

"He said he was worried that SS-Sturmbannführer Albert Kreise was closing in on them, and although he wasn't concerned for his own welfare, the German girls were too important to fall into his custody."

Sanders stared at Michael. "One of them, at least."

Michael took a deep breath and considered his reply.

"He doesn't need to worry about Kreise anymore. He's dead."

"Kreise is dead?" Sanders' shoulders shot upright. "When did this happen? Are you sure he's dead?"

"I killed him myself right before I left Rotterdam. So to answer your question, yes, I'm sure he's dead."

"That's one man who won't be missed." Sanders tapped Michael on the shoulder. "You never cease to amaze me, Michael. You are one amazing man."

"I didn't do it for praise. He was a direct threat to Mina, Jeroen, and Senta. He was a threat to the Dutch resistance, and he was a threat to me and all of us in Unit 317."

"I can't argue with any of that. Heydrich will be furious, I'm sure."

"Sod Heydrich. Sod all of them. All I want is for this war to be over."

"We're a long way from that, I'm afraid. We know all about Mina and her sister, Michael, and we know that you placed yourself and your mission at risk in order to see her and to be with her."

Michael felt his neck turning red. His nostrils flared, and for the first time, he felt an intense anger rising inside him at his commander.

"If you think I'm going to stand by and watch the woman I love die because of lowlifes like Harrington, Zobart, and Kreise, you can think again. If that's what you want from me, then you have the wrong person. I'll resign here and now, if that's the case."

Michael's mind momentarily cast back to the dark waterways of Rotterdam where he'd watched Edward Harrington, the British traitor, being killed by Kreise's men after being betrayed by Wilhelm Zobart, the Dutch Minister of Defence and Maritime Affairs.

"Calm down, tiger. That's not what I'm saying. However, I will say that Colonel Z is furious with you, and he wanted me to reprimand you when you returned to England."

"In that case, my offer of resignation stands. I did my best, and if that isn't good enough, then I'll transfer to a regular army unit where I might better serve His Majesty."

"That's not going to happen, Michael. I argued your corner. Dansey wasn't mad because you saved Mina. He was mad because you didn't tell us about her sister."

Michael closed his eyes. Why did Jeroen tell Dansey about Senta's special gifts? He must have known it would cause a stampede to get to her.

"I'm beginning to realise why you're here in person and didn't want the French involved," Michael said, staring at Sanders. "You want Senta, don't you?"

"Do you know how rare it is for someone to have an eidetic memory?" Sanders asked. "We still don't know yet whether we believe Jeroen or not. From your reactions, I'm starting to believe it's true."

Michael sat in silence, not wanting to face the fact that Senta was probably the most wanted commodity in Europe. Or at least she will be when word of her eidetic memory spilled out, which it surely would.

"Is it true?" Sanders asked. "And if so, why didn't you tell us? You've known her for quite a while now, and yet you decided to keep that from us?"

"Now we're getting to the reason why Dansey is so mad at me." Michael pulled a face at Sanders. "He… you… all think I withheld it. Well, I didn't. I had no idea until we were together in Rotterdam, and when I was there, I had no way of telling you without Senta herself or Mina knowing about it."

"So you left her there, knowing the Nazis would be after her as soon as they found out about her talents." It was a statement more than a question.

Sanders shook his hand at Michael. "Someone like her can change the course of the war, Michael. You know that. Why didn't you bring her back here with you?"

"I tried. I tried to bring both her and Mina with me, but neither would come. They lost everything, including their parents, in Germany. They wanted to stay and fight, and short of kidnapping them, I wasn't going to change their minds."

"Well, that's what you are going to have to do." Sanders gave Michael a withering look.

"You want me to go back to Rotterdam and kidnap Mina and Senta?" He'd been expecting it, but when Sanders spoke the words, Michael could scarcely believe his ears.

"How am I going to do that, exactly?"

Sanders lowered his head. "Only Senta, Michael. I'm sorry. I know what Mina means to you, but only Senta is to be rescued and brought to London."

Michael jumped to his feet.

"Sit down and don't make a scene," Sanders ordered. "Don't think I didn't argue for all my worth on this, Michael. Because I did. Frankly, I felt that putting you in charge of this mission was wrong. It's too personal for my liking, but you're the only one who can pull it off, so I had no choice."

Sanders paused for breath. "I told Colonel Z that you would refuse to do it if Mina wasn't included, but he wouldn't relent. Those are his orders, and there is nothing I can do to override it."

Michael snorted at Sanders. "Dansey can go to hell. If I'm going back for Senta, then I'm bringing Mina as well. If that isn't acceptable, then you'll have to find someone else to do it. Dansey can court martial me if he wants, but if I take Senta to London, then Mina's coming too."

Michael glared at Sanders, his face deep red. "And that's not negotiable."

Sanders sighed. "I told Dansey you'd say that."

"And?"

"He said that your family would have to be responsible for Mina if you defied his orders."

"Now that I can do." Michael immediately calmed down.

"That's what I told him." Sanders smirked at Michael.

Chapter 7

Michael spent the next fifteen minutes briefing Sanders on the Rotterdam mission. He left nothing out, and his breath hitched as Tony's eyes clouded over when he told him about Sofie Meijer, the little girl he'd pulled from the wreckage of the bombing.

Sanders covered his mouth with his hand when Michael revealed the true nature of Wilhelm Zobart after he and Jeroen discovered him in the wardrobe with Margriet, the other little girl they'd rescued from the orphanage.

"Zobart was sub-human," he said after a moment's silence. "War brings out the worst and the vilest. Always remember that, Michael. I'm glad you killed him."

Michael ended his briefing by revealing how Albert Kreise had died, and he watched with satisfaction as Tony Sanders smiled at the way he'd dealt with him.

"And then you travelled almost four hundred miles through enemy territory and made it all the way to Versailles. You never fail to amaze me."

"And yet I'm a failure in Dansey's eyes."

"No, you're not." Sanders shook his head. "He doesn't know the entire picture. He'll be recommending you for more awards after he hears all this."

"I don't want any more awards. All I want is for Mina and Senta to be safe."

He stared at Sanders for a long moment.

"And I want our government to do all they can to help Jeroen and the Dutch resistance. He is as brave a man as I have ever met, and he needs all the help we can give him."

"I'll pass it up the chain. It's in our own best interests for us to help the resistance, and I'm sure Downing Street will agree."

"Did Richard Keene ever make it back from Denmark?" Michael asked.

He was referring to his friend and fellow Unit 317 operative, who had been in Denmark when the country fell to the Nazis. The last he'd heard, Richard was evading the Nazis and trying to make his way back to England.

Sanders nodded. "You know Richard as well as I do. He's very resourceful, and I'm happy to tell you he's safe."

Michael pursed his lips. He knew Keene was probably on another dangerous mission somewhere in Europe, but Sanders would never tell him, and he would never ask. The less the unit's members knew about each other, the better it was for operational security.

"Does Senta know anything about this?" Michael changed the subject.

Sanders shook his head. "Not yet. Jeroen told us that she refused to leave with you, and he warned us that she wouldn't go willingly. And certainly not without her sister."

"If Jeroen told you she wouldn't leave with me, then why is Dansey angry at me?" Michael furrowed his brow.

"Because he thinks you should have told us about her and dragged her along with you, regardless."

"It doesn't work like that," Michael snapped. "I'm not in the habit of kidnapping innocent people on the off chance that Dansey would approve."

Sanders went to say something, but changed his mind and remained quiet. He gave Michael a few moments to calm down.

"I understand the situation, and I'll explain everything to Dansey when I get back to London. Don't take it personally, Michael. Dansey is all about winning the war, and he doesn't care what he has to do to win it."

Michael sighed. "I can't make any promises that Senta will go to London. I'll try, but as I said before, I'll only bring her if Mina comes as well. Even then, they will probably refuse, and I won't force them."

"I can't," he added after a pause.

"You have to, Michael. She is too important. Not only for us, but it's vital that she doesn't fall into the Nazi's hands. Can you imagine the damage she could inflict on us if they take Mina and force her to spy on us?"

"You're effectively asking me to do the same thing."

"No, we're not. Hitler and his cronies killed their father and probably their mother as well. They stole their farm and forced them out of Germany. We're their friends, Michael, whether they see it that way or not."

"How do I do it?" Michael asked, trepidation at the thought of trying to convince Senta to go to England mingling with the thought of seeing Mina again bouncing around inside his head.

"Everything you need will be delivered to Marcel's apartment by the end of the day tomorrow. You will leave and bring Senta back to London."

"What happens to her once she's in London?"

"She will be trained in counter intelligence techniques

and then she'll be used to strike at the heart of the Nazi war machine."

Sanders placed his hand on Michael's shoulder. "We'll take good care of her, Michael."

"I seriously doubt that!" Michael pulled away. "She's just another expendable asset, just like I am. The big difference is that I signed up for it. She hasn't."

"I disagree. She signed up for it when she joined the Dutch resistance. I'm sure she'll take every opportunity to help bring down the Nazis."

"Do me a favour." Michael changed the subject before he lost his temper completely with his boss. "Tell my mum and dad that I'm alive and in good health. They're probably worried sick about me by now."

"Consider it done." Sanders softened his tone. "I'll call them as soon as I get back to London."

Sanders rose from the bench and grasped Michael's hand. "I know you don't want to do this, but it's vital for the war effort. Senta is a high value asset for both us and the Germans, and we can't allow her to fall into their hands. Surely even you can see this."

Michael nodded. He did, but he didn't want to admit it.

"Take care, Michael. If anyone can do this, it's you. Get Senta and yourself back to London safely and as fast as you can. The situation in Europe is going to rat shit and we need you back home."

"And Mina," Michael reminded him.

"I didn't hear that," Sanders answered. "But if she was to come with you, I wouldn't object."

The two men shook hands and then Sanders was gone, heading back into the trees towards the railway lines. Michael waited five minutes and then retrieved his bicycle.

Chapter 8

When Michael awoke early the next morning, Marcel pointed to a large envelope sitting on the kitchen counter. His face remained neutral, in contrast to the flash of curiosity in his eyes as they lingered on the envelope.

"That was pushed under the door during the night," he said, pouring them both a hot cup of coffee. "I tried to get English tea for you, but coffee it is."

"Thanks." Michael grabbed the coffee and the envelope and took them back to his room, coffee spilling from his trembling hands in anticipation of his new orders.

Once the door was closed, he inspected the envelope to see if anyone had tampered with it, in particular Marcel, who Michael didn't know well enough to ascertain if he was fully trustworthy or not.

I suppose he must be if Sanders and Dansey trust him. But his loyalty is to the French, not the British.

The envelope was still sealed and once inside, another envelope, also sealed, gave way to yet a third that was also sealed. As much as Sanders trusted Marcel, he obviously wasn't taking any chances.

Michael tore open the third envelope and pulled out a one-page report that was typewritten and signed by Sanders himself. Along with the report, Michael found two hand-drawn maps in pencil. One gave directions to what looked like an empty field somewhere south of Orleans, and the other looked like a similar field on the outskirts of Rotterdam.

A fresh set of identification papers came next, and Michael set them aside for later.

Also present was a code book containing the code words he was to use in all correspondence with London, both written and transmitted. He spread the letter out on the bed and read the typed words, which, after decoding, read:

The unit's Lysander will leave a remote airstrip south of Orleans at 11pm tomorrow night. It will take you to an airstrip close to Rotterdam, where the resistance will meet you and take you to your contact.

You have seventy-two hours to make contact, extract the package, and make it to the airstrip at the place shown on the map. The Lysander will be waiting for you. Don't be late because it won't wait.

Marcel will take you to the rendezvous point in France. He is unaware of the true purpose of your mission, and he is not to be told. This is top secret, and it remains within Unit 317.

A new ID is enclosed. For your protection, and to allow safe passage throughout the occupied territories, you will take the name of a Wehrmacht officer. Memorise the details before leaving France.

Whatever you do, the package must be on that plane when it leaves Rotterdam. If you miss the rendezvous, you will be on your own. Use the enclosed funds along with the ID papers and get back home with the package any way you can.

If anyone can pull this off, it is you. You will be doing the Allies a great service, and I wish you Godspeed.

Tony Sanders.

Michael took the code book and placed it inside one of the hidden compartments of his well-worn and abused rucksack. Then he took the envelope full of French and Dutch money and stuffed it in a second hidden compartment.

Next, he studied the identification papers. If necessary, he would become Leutnant Hans Keller of the 16th Air Landing Regiment, which was one of the units involved with the invasion of Rotterdam.

Keller's birthdate was the same as Michael's, which was perfect should he be stopped and questioned over his papers. He was from Hanover, and before the war he'd been studying engineering at a military academy.

He was assigned to oversee the repair and reorganisation of critical transportation hubs, including the port of Rotterdam, to ensure efficient ongoing logistical support for German operations.

Michael put the papers down. That was enough for the moment. He'd study his family history later, but for now at least, he knew enough to get by in most situations.

He lay back on his bed and closed his eyes. Images of Mina washed over him, comforting him like a warm blanket. Her long blonde hair flowed over her shoulders, and her deep blue eyes melted his heart as he imagined staring into them.

His shoulders twitched at the thought of her embrace, and for a moment, he was lost in her love. A bang on the bedroom door shattered his peace, and he jumped to his feet to answer Marcel's yells.

"We leave at three pm," Marcel said as Michael threw open the door.

Michael nodded and returned to his new orders. He had a lot to do between now and the time Marcel wanted to leave.

Chapter 9

Marcel led the way through several back alleys until he reached a remote vehicle repair garage on a quiet side street in Versailles. Neither man spoke during the fifteen-minute walk, both feeling the tension of what was ahead of them.

Although Marcel didn't know the details of Michael's mission, he knew it was important to the British government. He never asked Michael for any details, and none were offered. Even so, he'd given Michael enough dried meats, cheese, and bread to last several days should his mission require it.

Michael made sure to bring along a gallon of water, which weighed down his bulging rucksack even more.

This summer weather…

Marcel pulled a set of keys from his pocket and opened the garage doors and Michael's jaw dropped when he saw the gleaming black vehicle parked inside.

He gave a low whistle and looked at Marcel in surprise. The elongated bonnet seemed to go on forever, and the black leather seats gave off a hint of luxury.

"I wasn't expecting this," he said to Marcel as he walked to the vehicle's rear. "What is it?"

Although he enjoyed driving, Michael wasn't too interested in the different makes and models of motor vehicles. His passion was more directed to architecture and ancient buildings, not modern modes of transportation. As far as he was concerned, if it got him from A to B, then he was satisfied.

"It's a 1939 Citroën Traction Avant," Marcel announced proudly. "I only bring it out for special occasions, and it's good for long journeys."

"I'm honoured."

"So you should be. Now get in. We've got a long drive ahead of us."

Michael jumped into the passenger seat on the right-hand side of the car, which still felt strange after being used to everything being on the opposite side in England.

Marcel pulled the vehicle out of the garage and locked the doors behind him. The engine purred as they took their time getting out of Versailles.

"I want to avoid driving through the blackout if I can help it," Marcel explained as they sped up on the open roads. "It's dangerous enough as it is with the army everywhere and the Germans expected to arrive any day. Add in the thousands of refugees, and it's a recipe for disaster, especially at night with no lights."

Michael knew exactly what he meant. He remembered the dangerous journeys he'd made in England during the blackout, and that was without the Wehrmacht advancing and thousands of refugees fleeing the area.

"Luckily, it doesn't get dark until past ten, so we have plenty of daylight left."

"What about roadblocks?" Michael asked. "You know I can't speak French."

"Hopefully, we won't run into any, but if we do, we'll handle it when we get there. Whatever you do, don't say anything in German."

"Obviously."

"Or English."

"I'll just shut up then."

Marcel laughed, breaking the tension inside the vehicle. "Yes, that would be preferable."

It didn't take long for them to encounter their first unit of weary looking French soldiers. Dust and dirt kicked up from the sides of the road as an endless stream of horses pulling wagons full of supplies and injured soldiers clattered past their vehicle, which Marcel had pulled over to the side as far as he could.

An infantry unit marched behind, their faces streaked with dirt. Michael felt sorry for them as they gave haunted, despairing looks as they filed past.

A few miles farther on, the smell of food wafted in the air as the two men drove by a field canteen, feeding the army as it made its way to the next destination.

Hundreds of men sat on upturned ammunition boxes in a field at the side of the road as the makeshift kitchen did its best to feed a starving, defeated army.

Refugees were interspersed with the army, hundreds upon hundreds heading in the opposite direction, trying to flee the advancing Nazis. Michael's heart broke at the sight of families pushing and pulling carts with all their worldly belongings along the narrow roads, their faces displaying a mix of fear and hopelessness.

The sights revealed in vivid detail what a defeated, proud nation looked like, and Michael felt incredible sympathy for the people of Western Europe. He closed his eyes at the thought that his beloved Britain could be next.

The roads were busier as they entered Orleans. Several

vehicles, interspersed with horses and carts, lined up ahead of them, forcing Marcel to stop.

Horses stamped their feet as they waited to proceed and people passed by on bicycles. If it wasn't for the worried, harried looks on their faces, it could have been a scene from any European city in more peaceful times.

But it wasn't. Doom and gloom hung over the city like a dark cloud, touching everyone with its presence.

Marcel nudged Michael with his elbow, bringing him back to the present.

"There's a roadblock ahead."

French policemen and soldiers were checking the ID papers of both drivers and passengers, no matter the form of transport. Michael felt a knot forming in the pit of his stomach as he watched a soldier drag one man out of the rear seat of a vehicle not too dissimilar to their own.

The soldier was screaming at the man as he grabbed him by the hair and roughly manhandled him to three more soldiers, who dragged him away and out of sight.

"They're searching for deserters," Marcel explained. "And probably German spies. You can't be seen, Michael, or they will arrest you."

As they'd discussed in Versailles, Michael grabbed his rucksack and opened the door. The roadblock was about three hundred yards ahead, so he had time to slip away before they noticed him.

"Wait for me on the other side." Michael didn't wait for an answer.

He jumped out of the Citroën and melted into the bushes at the side of the road. The plan was to find a parallel street and box around the roadblock, rejoining Marcel on the other side.

He groaned when he realised where the roadblock was.

He hadn't been able to see the river from where they were stopped, but as he got closer, he couldn't miss it.

The soldiers and policemen had set up the roadblock on the main bridge crossing the River Loire, and it would be a far from simple task to reconnect with Marcel.

It was still around a hundred miles to the rendezvous point with the Lysander, and he had no easy way to get there. The knot in his stomach tightened as he realised his mission was in danger of failing before it had even begun.

The thought of seeing Mina again stirred something inside him, and he hurried his steps in search of an alternate way over the river.

Mingling with the locals going about their daily lives, Michael hurried as much as he dared towards another bridge he hoped would be clear of soldiers.

He marched for a mile or more along a small lane alongside the river, keeping his head down and his wits about him. There weren't many people on this narrow track, which suited Michael perfectly.

A bridge appeared ahead, and Michael swallowed hard when he saw a smaller roadblock on his side of the river. He couldn't see the opposite side, but he'd worry about that if and when he got there.

He reached the bridge and took notice of what he was facing. Although it was blocked, this roadblock was nowhere near as big or as well manned as the one he'd just avoided. He joined a group of five other pedestrians waiting to cross and watched as a group of soldiers approached a truck.

As soon as they were occupied, he made his move. The other civilians waiting with him followed his lead, and together they pushed past the roadblock without being stopped.

Breathing a sigh of relief, Michael took notice of what

was on the opposite side of the bridge. His heart dropped when he saw the road was manned by three more soldiers.

At least the soldiers faced the other way as they stopped vehicles entering the bridge. He hung back while another group of pedestrians ahead of him approached them. One of the soldiers turned around and barked orders at them, obviously telling them to stop and show their identification.

Michael grimaced and looked for an exit. He knew he couldn't allow himself to be stopped because he'd be arrested for being either a deserter from the British Expeditionary Force or a German spy. Either way, he couldn't let it happen.

The soldier checked the pedestrians and turned to speak to his comrades. He hung back from the five civilians he'd crossed the bridge with, and leaned against the side of the bridge to make sure none of the soldiers were looking his way.

After waiting for the right moment when the soldiers on both sides were occupied, he climbed over the side of the bridge. Clinging to the rusty steel stanchions, he climbed down to the ground and hid underneath the bridge in the middle of thick, overgrown bushes.

The ground was damp, but he was far enough away from the edge of the river to be on firm land.

Around five minutes later, the coast seemed to be clear. No shouts or alarms were raised above his head, so he gathered his rucksack and sauntered into the narrow lane as if he'd been strolling along it all morning.

Although the hackles were up on the back of his neck, he resisted the urge to look back. Instead, he fixed his gaze ahead of him and hoped for the best.

Nobody said anything, and Michael hurried away as fast as he dared, heaving a big sigh of relief once he'd cleared the area. Now all he had to do was to find Marcel, who was hopefully still waiting for him somewhere.

Twenty minutes later, he saw Marcel's vehicle stopped at the side of the road. Marcel was standing on the pavement, deep in conversation with a passerby. Michael had no clue what they were talking about, but he didn't care. He'd found him and that was all that mattered.

"I was wondering if you were going to make it," Marcel said as Michael climbed into the passenger seat. "I had to ask a local his advice on the best café in Orleans as a diversion because I'd been waiting too long."

"Did you find one?"

"A café? Yes, but that's for the way back. We're not stopping anywhere until we reach the drop-off point."

Feeling a little disappointed, Michael sat back in the seat and reached for a sandwich inside his rucksack.

"Were you stopped?" Marcel asked, looking at Michael's muddy boots.

"No." Michael didn't want to elaborate, and as he'd already discovered, Marcel didn't probe or ask any further questions.

"Good," was all he said in reply.

They drove in silence for over an hour, the city giving way to the French countryside, and they made good time as they sped down the open roads.

More army units trundled past forcing them to slow down occasionally, and they encountered more refugees heading away from Orleans, but otherwise they drove unhindered.

Chapter 10

Marcel stopped in a small town called Vierzon to refuel, and Michael used the time to buy fresh sandwiches from a shop next door. He bought enough to share, and both men ate and drank in silence as they once again entered the serene French countryside.

As they left Vierzon behind, the countryside stretched wide under the June sun, a vast mosaic of golden wheat fields rippling in the breeze and lush green meadows where cattle grazed lazily.

High hedgerows and clusters of oak trees provided shade, while the occasional orchard, heavy with unripe apples, hinted at the promise of summer's bounty.

In the distance, a farmer and his mule plodded along a dirt path, while smoke rose in thin wisps from the chimneys of scattered farmhouses. It was a scene of pastoral serenity, the kind that felt timeless and untouched, even as the Nazi war machine crept ever closer.

It was almost eight pm by the time they reached Chateauroux, another small town in the Loire region.

Being summer, it was still daylight, and Marcel turned off the main road and through a series of side streets before eventually coming to a stop outside a lone house on the edge of the small town.

Four men immediately ran outside, and Marcel hugged them as if they were long-lost friends.

They probably are, Michael mused as he watched through the windshield of the Citroën.

After the greetings were over, Marcel indicated for Michael to join them. Each man shook hands with him, and although no names were either offered or asked for, they all had warm smiles that put Michael's racing pulse at ease.

Like Marcel, all the resistance men looked to be in their early fifties. Two wore berets, and all seemed to be in good physical shape for their age.

Michael assumed they were old comrades from World War One who were still active in the intelligence community. Otherwise, how would Sanders and Dansey know about them? Michael shrugged his shoulders. As long as they got him onto the Lysander later that night, he didn't care.

"Come." The burliest of the four men clapped Michael on the shoulder. "You must be hungry. We eat and then we leave."

He spoke in broken English with the French accent that Michael enjoyed hearing so much. It reminded him of happier days when he'd visited Paris with his family.

David! Images of him and his brother running towards the Eiffel Tower made him wince.

The house sat alone in the middle of a field at the end of a narrow lane. Bushes and trees hid it from prying eyes in the village; it was the perfect place for resistance members to hide out and make their plans to disrupt the Nazis as they took control of France.

He followed the men inside to what Michael assumed was once a farmhouse living room. All it contained now was a large rectangular table that was cleared and empty of everything except four flickering candles that cast shadows around the room. The walls were full of maps of France with red markings covering the areas where the Wehrmacht was advancing.

The smell of food filled his nostrils, and Michael realised he was starving. It had been a few hours since they'd eaten the sandwiches, and his stomach rumbled at the aromas wafting in the air.

Blackout curtains blocked daylight from entering, and the candles danced in the sway of the wind as the men filed past the table towards the kitchen, where it was lighter because the curtains were not yet drawn.

"We made you our specialty," said the solid, grizzled veteran who seemed to be in charge as he squeezed Michael's shoulder. "Pot-au-feu, or French stew, as you would say in English."

"Thank you," Michael said. "It smells delicious."

"Please, sit."

Michael did as the man asked, and the next thing he knew, a bowl of piping hot stew was sitting in front of him. Hearty chunks of beef, mixed with carrots, onions, leeks, potatoes, and cabbage sat before him, and Michael couldn't wait to dig in.

The rest of the men joined him, and one of them tore off a piece of a baguette and handed it to Michael.

The candles flickered, their gentle glow adding to the homely, serene ambience that sat in complete contrast to what was happening to the world outside. Michael savoured the moments of peacefulness, knowing full well that this was probably the last time he would experience it for a long time.

If ever.

Wine was served with the meal, but Michael declined, preferring instead to take a glass of water. He had a dangerous journey ahead of him, and he needed to keep his faculties about him.

The men ate in silence, and only spoke once every dish had been emptied.

"That was lovely," Michael said, soaking up the last of the stew with his bread. "I really mean that."

"You're welcome, Englander. We hope that wherever you are going, it strikes fear and confusion into the hearts of our enemy."

"I hope so too." Michael bowed his head as the importance of his mission hit home once again.

The five men conversed in French, leaving Michael to his thoughts. Although it was still daylight outside, he only had a couple of hours before the Lysander would meet him.

"It's time," Marcel announced in English. "We have much to do before your aircraft gets here."

Daylight was fading when the men, all dressed in dark overalls, steered Michael towards a large shed at the rear of the house. Inside, they headed to what looked like an old French army truck with an enclosed rear bed.

The stocky leader jumped into the driver's seat and one of the others took the passenger seat next to him. The rest, along with Michael, jumped into the back of the truck.

As he climbed in, his eyes stung at the heavy stench of aviation fuel. Two fifty-five-gallon drums sat in the middle of the floor, surrounded by hoses and what looked like hand pumps.

"Your Lysander needs to refuel before taking off,"

Marcel explained. "One of us is an experienced aircraft mechanic, and we regularly assist Dansey with his operations."

That's why Sanders and Dansey are so familiar with him! The realisation hit Michael like a ton of bricks. It made perfect sense now. He didn't ask where they got the aviation fuel from.

The truck rattled and rolled for fifteen minutes until it came to a stop and Marcel waited until the two men in the front opened the back before beckoning for Michael to jump down.

Dusk had settled over the landscape and it wouldn't be too long before everywhere was blanketed in darkness. They appeared to be stopped in the corner of a field in the middle of nowhere, which was perfect for what they were about to do.

The leader and Marcel turned the heavy barrels onto their sides and rolled them off the truck. Two others ran into the field armed with flares, which would aid the Lysander as it landed.

"What do you need me to do?" Michael stood ready to assist the operatives of the French resistance.

"Stay out of sight and wait," the burly leader answered. "We know what we're doing."

Not wanting to get in the way, Michael walked a few feet to a series of trees and bushes and sat underneath the canopy, out of sight from the lane they'd driven up.

The three remaining men rolled the barrels of aviation fuel to where Michael sat, and satisfied they were hidden from view from both the air and the road, the burly man, as Michael had named him, went back to the truck to remove the pumps and hoses.

Once they were with the drums, he drove the truck away from the lane and parked it underneath a group of trees a hundred yards from where Michael waited. The men produced a camouflage net from the rear of the truck and set about covering it so it wouldn't show up if a German reconnaissance aircraft flew overhead.

Then they waited.

Chapter 11

At ten thirty, the four Frenchmen lit the flares, their red flames lighting up the night sky to create a landing strip in the middle of the barren field.

Moments later, Michael heard the faint sounds of an aircraft as it approached in the darkness. He rolled his shoulders to release the tension that was building.

What if it was the Luftwaffe? They often flew reconnaissance missions over the occupied countries, and if they'd spotted the flares, they would be sure to come and check it out.

To be safe, burly man had them all assemble at the edge of the field, hidden in the trees. Although the Germans did not yet have men on the ground that could intercept them, the aircraft was more than capable of spraying them with machine-gun fire.

All five men lay flat on the ground, silently waiting to see if it was friend or foe. If it were the enemy, they'd leave the truck where it was, as it would be an easy target for the Luftwaffe to attack.

Instead, they would split up and go their separate ways.

Michael's stomach tensed, the familiar feeling of butterflies doing their impression of *Swan Lake* inside his body. He wiggled his fingers to stop them from shaking and held his breath as the aircraft circled one time overhead.

After circling, it rapidly lost altitude, and Michael breathed a sigh of relief when its wheels touched down in the middle of the field. The flares burned themselves out, and the field once again fell into darkness.

Burly man jumped to his feet and ran to the barrels of aviation fuel. Once there, he turned on a battery-operated lantern. The green light guided the Lysander towards the fuel, and as soon as it was within range, burly man extinguished the lantern.

As the aircraft got close, Michael recognised the unique shape of the Westland Lysander. Its sturdy, high-wing design and oversized, bulbous canopy glowed at him in the dull light, and once he'd got a glimpse of the fixed landing gear and the RAF circular decal on the wings, his tension vanished, replaced with a renewed sense of purpose.

He was ready for whatever lay ahead, especially as it gave him the opportunity to spend more time with Mina.

As soon as the propeller stopped rotating from the single-engine plane, the well-trained resistance men leapt into action. Using just a single light from a handheld torch, the men rolled the first barrel of aviation fuel towards the Lysander.

Two of the men pumped the fuel, and the other two rolled the second heavy drum close by. As soon as the first drum was empty, they switched over and began pumping again.

While the Lysander was being refuelled, the pilot pulled Michael to the side, out of earshot of the Frenchmen. Tall and thin, he looked to be in his late twenties.

"This might get a bit rough, I'm afraid," he said in an

upper crust accent that Michael knew all too well from his days at public school. "We're flying over enemy held territory the whole way, so I'll be staying at a low altitude in the hope that we aren't spotted."

The pilot paused. "We're in trouble if we are. There's no backup."

"I'm aware," Michael whispered back.

"We'll leave as soon as they're finished, so be ready." The pilot went back to oversee the refuelling of his aircraft.

Forty minutes after the pilot cut his engine, the well-practised French resistance men were done. They rolled the empty fuel drums out of the way and coiled up the hoses.

Michael shook hands with the men as the pilot fired up the engine.

"I don't know where you're going," Marcel shouted above the sound of the engine. "But wherever it is, I wish you godspeed."

"Thank you for everything," Michael shouted back.

He made sure his rucksack was firmly in his grasp and jumped aboard, closing the door with a final wave. From the window, he watched as the pilot expertly turned the aircraft around and used the Lysander for what it was famous for—short take-offs in less-than-ideal conditions where space was at a premium.

Moments later, the plane was in the air and Michael settled down in the modified rear and closed his eyes. He'd been over everything multiple times, and he knew everything that was in his control to know.

What he didn't know was the uncertainty of warfare behind enemy lines, and he was experienced enough to understand that things could, and would, go wrong.

He wasn't about to sit and worry about things that were outside his control, so he closed his eyes and rested. It was going to be a long night, and he didn't know when he would be able to rest again.

The steady drone from the Lysander as it smoothly made its way into the heart of enemy territory soothed his frayed nerves, and although sleep was impossible, at least he could conserve his strength and resilience for later.

He sighed as he contemplated the enormous task ahead of him, and hoped he could convince Senta and Mina that it was in their best interests to travel back to England with him.

Somehow, he knew that would not be as easy as Dansey and Sanders may think it was.

Chapter 12

The Lysander wound its way through France and Belgium before crossing the border into Holland. At the border, the pilot took a detour to avoid a battery of anti-aircraft guns he'd spotted guarding the River Meuse.

Michael sat in the back of the aircraft with sweat pouring down his forehead as the pilot flew as low as he dared around the battery of deadly guns and altered his course towards Rotterdam.

Three hours later, the pilot turned to Michael and gave him the thumbs-up sign. They'd made it, and it was time to land.

Michael watched as the pilot made a circle, and on the second approach, a set of red flares went up, just as it had in France. This time it was the Dutch resistance who were risking their lives, and as the Germans did have men on the ground, Michael knew they would have to act swiftly once they'd landed.

Michael's skull throbbed with every jolt as the pilot expertly landed the Lysander on the bumpy field. The plane quickly slowed, and Michael tensed, his fingers clamped around the door handle, waiting for the signal.

As soon as the pilot turned on the green overhead light in the cockpit, Michael sprang into action. Making sure his rucksack straps were tight around his shoulders, he swung open the door and jumped out of the barely moving aircraft.

He closed the door as quietly as he could and returned the thumbs-up sign the pilot was giving him. Then he ran for cover. Seconds later, the Lysander turned around, revved its engines, and used the short landing strip to take off again and vanish into the night.

Michael knew the pilot didn't have enough fuel to make it all the way to England, but for security reasons, he didn't know where he was going to refuel.

Silence fell over the dark field as the sound of the aircraft's engines faded and the flares burned themselves out. Michael lay still at the edge of the field, the damp grass seeping through his clothes, soaking him to the skin.

Thick clouds made visibility poor, and he knew rain was expected. The sound of rustling grass to his right caught his attention, and Michael gripped his Walther PPK in case the reception party wasn't friendly.

It was almost pitch black, and although his eyes had adjusted, he could barely see anything. The rustling got closer until it stopped a few feet away from his position.

There wasn't much Michael could do if it was the Gestapo, so he closed his eyes and gulped in a lungful of air. Above all else, he wanted Jeroen to be one of the men greeting him. Outside of Mina and Senta, who he hoped hadn't been placed in such grave danger, Jeroen was the only person in Rotterdam he knew.

Two men emerged from the darkness, both pointing guns at Michael, who remained prone on the wet ground.

His own weapon was ready, just in case he had to fight his way out.

Michael had long since resigned himself to the fact that he wouldn't live to see the end of the war. His job was on the extreme edge of danger, and he wasn't naïve; his life expectancy was low.

As much as he dreamt of a life after the war with Mina, he knew the chances of it actually happening were slim to none. With that in mind, he felt no fear as the men aimed their weapons at him.

"Where do the tulips grow?" a gruff, heavily accented voice asked.

This was the phrase Michael had been expecting, though it still didn't guarantee it was the Dutch resistance, as the Gestapo could have tortured them and discovered it that way.

At least it can't be Kreise!

SS-Sturmbannführer Albert Kreise was the only man in Rotterdam who could positively identify Michael, Jeroen, Mina and Senta, so his death at Michael's hands a few weeks earlier had removed the greatest threat to them.

For now, at least.

"In the land of freedom," Michael replied. He took another deep breath and waited with bated breath for the response, his finger ready on the trigger.

"Jeroen sends his regards, Englander. He is sorry he couldn't be here to greet you himself."

Michael let out a sigh of relief. Although he'd hoped to see Jeroen, these men appeared, on first contact at least, to be genuine.

"It's good to be back," Michael replied. "I trust he is doing well?"

"As well as can be expected. Come, we must get away from here before it is swarming with Germans."

Michael rose to his feet and shook hands with the two men. It was dark, so he couldn't get a good look at their features, but from what he could tell, both men appeared to be in their thirties, and both were taller than he was.

"I'm Geert, and this here is Henk."

"Michael. Nice to meet you."

"Now let's get out of here," Geert said.

Michael kept his hand on the Walther PPK in his pocket as they trudged around the edge of the wet field. He thought they were genuine, but he still wasn't one hundred per cent sure, and until he was, he'd be extra cautious.

The three men climbed over a gate onto a narrow lane. No lights were visible anywhere, so Michael knew they must be several miles outside the city.

A truck emerged out of the shadows, parked under a tree at the side of the lane. Michael immediately recognised it from the distinctive front grille. It was a Mercedes L-3000 truck, the workhorse of the Wehrmacht, and a vehicle that would blend in perfectly in occupied Holland.

A third man stepped out from behind the truck, joining Geert and Henk as Michael hung back, taking in the situation.

The three men conversed in Dutch before turning to Michael, who stood by a large tree several feet away.

The third man stepped towards him, removing his woolly hat to reveal himself. His pock-marked face and close-cropped dark hair gave him away, and although it was dark, Michael knew who it was instantly.

"Jeroen!" he exclaimed, stepping forward to greet his old friend. "I thought you weren't coming."

"I couldn't miss greeting my most trusted friend," Jeroen said, his mouth wide open in a smile. "Come, it's too dangerous to remain here and we have much to discuss."

Now fully at ease, Michael relaxed his grip on his gun and shook hands vigorously with Jeroen.

Geert and Henk removed their coats to reveal the uniforms of the Wehrmacht, and when Jeroen did the same, Michael realised what they were doing.

"If we're stopped, we can talk our way out of it," Jeroen explained. "We're a supply truck taking fuel to the vehicles. Jump in the back and remain hidden until we tell you it's safe."

Michael jumped into the rear of the truck, something he would have refused to do had it not been for Jeroen showing his face. The truck was full of fuel drums, so he squeezed between two near the front of the truck and settled down for the ride.

He was desperate to see Mina, and couldn't wait to hold her in his arms again.

Chapter 13

Thirty minutes later, the Wehrmacht truck pulled to a stop, and the driver turned the engine off. Michael put his ear to the canvas, listening for the harsh barks of a German soldier at a roadblock.

All he heard were the doors of the truck slamming shut. Moments later, Jeroen's voice broke the tension as he slapped the canvas walls.

"We're here."

Michael didn't know where here was but, relieved they had avoided any roadblocks, jumped down from the rear of the truck, and stretched his back.

From what he could make out, the truck was parked inside a barn. As his eyes adjusted, he made out dull shapes off to the side, which he recognised as bales of stacked hay going almost all the way to the roof.

Jeroen waited for him outside the barn. "Welcome to our new home."

"Where are we?" Michael asked, following him towards a farmhouse he could just about make out.

"It's Geert's farmhouse, which is near Schoonhoven, about twenty miles east of Rotterdam."

"Are we safe here?"

Jeroen shrugged his shoulders. "As safe as can be. The Nazis are everywhere, and they're always looking for me. So you tell me how safe we are."

Goosebumps attacked Michael's body as he watched for Mina bursting through the door and run to his waiting arms. It was all he had thought of on the journey from France, and now he was there, the jitters exploded into life.

Struggling to control the shaking in his hands, he put them into his coat pocket so Jeroen wouldn't notice.

The farmhouse wasn't large, but as Jeroen led them inside, it was welcoming and homely. The small porch was big enough to store muddy boots and wet jackets, and beyond that, an open door led into what looked like a comfortable living room.

Michael followed Jeroen, disappointed not to see Mina waiting for him. Two men stood beside Geert and Henk, acting as the reception party as Michael entered the room with Jeroen.

"Welcome to my humble farm," Geert said as they entered. "It was left to me when my father died in the last war."

"I'm sorry to hear that." Michael scanned the room as he entered. A three-seater couch made from sturdy wood sat against the wall underneath the heavily curtained windows with two matching chairs positioned opposite.

A worn rug covered the stone floor, and the walls were adorned with black-and-white photographs of a family of three young boys and two girls.

"Those are my parents. I'm this one here." Geert proudly pointed to a young man in his late teens. "The rest are my brothers and sisters."

In the light, Michael got his first good look at Geert and the other resistance members. Geert was in his mid-thirties, strong and masculine, with short dark hair and a prominent, chiselled chin.

Henk looked similar, and Michael realised they might be brothers. A few years younger than Geert and much stockier and more muscular, he had the same granite chin. They were two strong young Dutchmen.

"Henk and I are brothers," Geert said, watching Michael compare the two.

"What happened to the rest of your family?"

"As I said, our father died in the Great War. Mother died just after the war, leaving me as the oldest to take care of my brothers and sisters. Arjen, our youngest brother, is standing right there."

He pointed to one of the two men Michael hadn't met. On closer inspection, the resemblance was similar, but Arjen lacked the chiselled chin. He was in his late twenties and had a much softer complexion than his older brothers.

"Arjen." Michael nodded at the younger brother.

"Englishman." Arjen answered.

"The other is our brother-in-law, Gerrit. He operates our radios and is good at forging documents."

Michael's ears pricked up at the mention of a radio operator. Mina was an expert at operating radios, and she'd broadcast on the airways in both German and English for months before the German invasion in May.

Gerrit stepped forward to shake hands with Michael. "I have heard so much about you from Mina," he said, offering his hand. "It is a pleasure to meet you."

Gerrit was in his mid-twenties and had blond hair and blue eyes. If he hadn't been told differently, Michael could have mistaken him for a Nazi.

"He looks like a perfect Aryan," Jeroen spoke up,

noticing Michael's gaze. "It works for us because he can pose as a German soldier much better than we can."

Michael was about to open his mouth to speak, but Jeroen cut him off.

"Gerrit is married to Elska, Geert's sister. I'll tell you about her later."

Jeroen threw Michael a look that told him not to ask any questions.

"And that's all of us," Jeroen said. "We had to rebuild after they killed nearly all of us last month, but if it wasn't for you, we'd all be dead. I owe you, Michael, and I will do my best to help you with your latest quest."

"Where's Mina and Senta?" Michael asked the burning question.

The five men exchanged glances, and Michael felt the tension rising in the room.

"I'll make the tea." Geert vanished into the kitchen, which from what Michael could see from where he stood was spacious and well laid out, with plenty of cupboard space.

The others followed him, leaving Jeroen alone with Michael. Jeroen closed the door to the kitchen and turned to Michael.

"Sit down, Michael. A lot has happened since we last met."

Chapter 14

Michael fixed his gaze on Jeroen as he sat in a chair opposite him on the couch. Sweat dripped from Jeroen's forehead, and Michael knew something major had happened.

"Where are they?" he asked again. "Tell me they're alright."

Jeroen shook his head, his eyes never leaving Michael's. "After you left, things got really hairy for us. The resistance was broken, and all that was left was myself, Mina, and Senta."

"I know. I was here," Michael said curtly. The familiar feeling of dread rose from the pit of his stomach as he stared at Jeroen.

Are they alive? Have the Germans captured them?

"Where are they?" he repeated, hissing as he spoke.

Jeroen shook his head once more. "I knew I couldn't protect them. Especially Senta, who has the gift of a generation. If she fell into enemy hands, there's no telling how much damage she could do to our cause. I had to do it."

"What did you do?" Michael's face turned red. "Where are they?"

"Geert and I used to work together in the Dutch intelligence, so I reached out to him for help. We were desperate, and we had nowhere else to go. Geert took us in and allowed us to use his farm as a base for our new resistance movement."

"Where are they? I won't ask again."

"I'm getting to it, but you have to know the backstory to understand why I did what I did."

Michael groaned. All he wanted was to know what happened to them.

"On my orders, Geert radioed London and told them about Senta and her unique gifts. They told us to hold on to her and someone would be sent to get her. I assumed it would be you, and I was correct."

Jeroen looked down, his gaze focused on the floor. "Senta was on an observation mission for us, and Mina was supposed to be resting. A message came from London telling us that Senta was about to go to London, but Mina wasn't included. I knew you wouldn't accept that, and I told them."

Michael stared at Jeroen, his eyes ablaze.

"They said you would understand and follow orders. Unfortunately, Mina was the one who received and decoded the message." Jeroen sighed. "She was distraught, but she understood. Or at least she said she did."

"So, what happened to them? Where are they?"

"Senta never returned from her mission. The Germans arrested her and took her into custody. As far as we know, they have no idea what she's capable of, and she'll be better off if she keeps it that way."

"And Mina? Did they capture her as well?"

"No." Jeroen shook his head. "She never knew Senta had been captured. She ran away before any of us knew."

"Ran away where?" Michael was on the verge of full-blown panic.

"She left a note."

Jeroen pulled a piece of crumpled paper from his pocket and handed it to Michael.

Jeroen,

Believe me when I say that I understand why Britain wants Senta and not me. Her gift is unique and can win the war for us if she's given the chance. Radio operators like me are not hard to train, so there is no reason why they'd want me as well.

Senta will refuse to leave without me, and it is far too dangerous for her here. So, I'm leaving before she gets back. This way, she will have no choice other than to leave with whoever they send for her.

I hope it's Michael, and if it is, please tell him I love him with all my heart. I will wait for him at Anna's family farm in France.

Do not worry about me, as I will either make it or I won't. My fate is unimportant. What is important is that Senta makes it to London, where she will be safe and her skills can help win the war against the Nazis.

Take care,

Mina Postner

PS Don't forget to tell Michael that I love him and not to worry about me.

Michael clutched the note to his chest. "When?" he gasped, the words almost choking him.

"Two days ago. We've searched for her, but so far we haven't found her. Do you know the place in France she refers to in the note?"

Michael shook his head. "I tried convincing Anna and her father to leave Rotterdam before the invasion. Anna mentioned the family farm in the South of France, but I don't know where it is."

A sense of hopelessness washed over him. He knew from personal experience how dangerous it was to get to France, and that was for him, a trained operative of British intelligence. For a beautiful blonde-haired German girl travelling alone, it would be all but impossible.

"I've got to find her."

"What about Senta? I thought your orders were to take Senta to London?"

"You told me she's been captured. She's beyond our reach." Michael wasn't thinking of anything other than finding Mina before it was too late.

Jeroen pulled a second piece of paper from his pocket. "She left this too."

Michael snatched it from him and unfolded it impatiently. The page contained just a few words and a hand-drawn map.

Anna's family. Les Vans, France.

The map depicted what looked like an isolated farmhouse in a small town somewhere Michael had never heard of in the South of France. He stood up and grabbed his rucksack.

"Where are you going?" Jeroen asked.

"I'm going to find Mina before it's too late."

Jeroen stood to his feet and touched Michael's shoulder. "You could do that, and I won't try to stop you. However, we have another very important task that we need your help with first."

"What's that?"

"We know where Senta is being held, and we're going to bust her out."

Michael stared at Jeroen as if he'd gone mad. "That's suicide. We won't be able to get anywhere near her."

"Not while she's in custody, but we have it on good

authority that she's about to be moved, and that's when we can rescue her."

Michael tilted his head and pursed his lips. "Where did you hear this?"

"Remember when I said I'd tell you about Elske? She works at a hotel in Rotterdam that's frequented by senior Nazis. She flirts with them and risks her life every day, but she picks up valuable intelligence for us. Michael, she's saved many lives already."

"What did she tell you about Senta?"

"She discovered that a group of women prisoners are to be sent to Germany on a train in the next few days. The women are all being held at the police station and they need the cells for other prisoners. We believe Senta is going to be on that train."

"Why are they being sent to Germany?" Michael asked.

"We believe they are being sent for forced labour, but we can't be certain."

Michael mulled it over for a few minutes before answering. His heart screamed at him to find Mina, but if he could rescue Senta and get her on the Lysander, he'd have carried out his orders. Then he could concentrate on finding Mina.

"When does the train leave?"

He only had a brief window to find her and get her to the rendezvous point, so time was of the essence.

"June ninth. Two days from now."

Chapter 15

Michael woke from a deep sleep and rubbed his eyes. It took a moment to get his bearings, and as he stretched and brushed his teeth, his mind focused on what lay ahead.

Time was of the essence, and he didn't have a minute to spare. The Lysander would leave without him if he weren't at the rendezvous point, and every minute that Mina was alone, was another minute she was in extreme danger. He had to find her quickly, but before that, he had to give his undivided attention to the audacious plan Jeroen had come up with to rescue Senta.

At first, Michael thought he'd lost his mind, but the more he thought about it, the more it made sense. Senta literally was that important to the war effort, and he chided himself for not paying more attention to her abilities before he'd left for Paris.

No wonder Dansey was angry at him. Now that he thought about it, Dansey was correct. His love for Mina had clouded his judgement, and as much as he loved her, he couldn't allow that to happen again.

War effort first, personal feelings later. That would be his motto from now on he decided.

A grandfather clock chimed as he descended the stairs, telling him it was six am. Everyone else was already up and about, and Michael could smell fresh coffee brewing in the kitchen. Even though it would be made from chicory extract because of the shortage of coffee in Europe, he would savour every drop.

Eggs were simmering in boiling water, and a loaf of rye bread stood ready to be sliced on the table. It was about as close to being at home as Michael had felt in ages, and the warmth and camaraderie in the farmhouse kitchen relaxed and comforted him.

The only people missing were Mina and Senta.

"Good morning, Michael," Jeroen greeted him as everyone stared at the new guest entering the kitchen.

"Morning," Michael replied, his eyes fixed on a pretty woman in her mid-twenties with dark, shoulder-length hair and deep, green eyes that sparkled with life, even at that early hour of the morning.

She smiled at Michael and waved at him. Her eyes lit up even brighter when she smiled, her soft, delicate features drawing him in.

"This is Elske," Jeroen said, noticing the two staring at each other.

It was obvious why the German officers enjoyed her working in the hotel. Even without knowing her, Michael could tell that she was friendly, disarming, charming, and, obviously, incredibly pretty, a deadly combination for a resistance spy.

"Good morning, Elske." Michael bowed his head slightly. "I heard a lot about you last night, and I think you are very brave to do what you do."

Elske snorted. "It's the least I can do for my country.

The Nazi pigs have killed the people I love, and they have taken over my beloved Holland. I gladly give my life in service."

Elske sounded fierce, and Michael had no doubt that she was backing up her harsh words with equally dangerous actions.

Gerrit massaged her shoulders, and she placed her hand on his in a show of affection. Michael could see they were a close-knit family, which reassured him because it meant loyalty, not only to the cause, but more importantly, to each other, and in times of war, that could be the difference between life and death.

Michael took one of the boiled eggs from the pan with a spoon and took a place at the table. He grabbed a couple of slices of bread, and for the next ten minutes, nobody spoke as they ate, each no doubt lost in their own thoughts about what they faced.

Once breakfast was over, Jeroen stood up and told everyone to clear the table. They did so, and with coffee in hand, Michael watched as a map was spread out, covered with notes and arrows.

Two hours later, they were ready. Everyone knew what they were supposed to do, which was to gather the equipment they needed and to make sure they were at their designated positions ahead of time.

Michael looked around the kitchen table at the defiant faces staring back at him. This was a heavy blow the resistance would strike at the Nazis, and he knew that each and every one of them was prepared to give their lives to the cause.

"Let's go." Jeroen strode out of the kitchen. It was time to do some serious reconnaissance before dark when the real action would begin later that night.

Chapter 16

Virtually unscathed from the Rotterdam blitz bombing raid, the Hotel Atlanta stood proudly in the centre of the city as a beacon of Dutch innovation.

The hotel boasted centrally heated rooms, with telephones and radios in every room, and an upmarket restaurant that offered hard-to-get food and beverage choices to discerning residents.

The hotel had a glass dome on the roof that allowed for sweeping views of the city, and this is where Elske spent most of her time when she was at work, serving the clientele with cognacs and cigars.

Because of its unique location in the heart of the city, the Hotel Atlanta was a favourite retreat for senior Nazis, who treated it as their own personal living space while they confiscated and renovated properties from the locals.

Men of the Dutch Collaborators, the NSB, stood alongside German soldiers on the steps of the hotel, restricting access to only senior Nazis, other hotel guests with appropriate credentials, and hotel staff. Everyone else was turned away.

The streets around the hotel, Coolsingel and Aert van Nesstraat, were blocked from all directions, and checkpoints stopped all foot traffic before it got close.

The Hotel Atlanta was well guarded, and its VIP clientele were well protected.

It was against this backdrop that Michael nervously approached one of the checkpoints. Jeroen had dropped him off a half mile away after a nervy journey over the Nieuwe Maas River. They'd been stopped twice, but each time they'd been allowed to pass when they showed their hotel worker's identification created by Gerrit.

"Halt!" the soldier barked his orders at Michael, who stopped and nervously handed his hotel staff credentials to the soldier.

The soldier studied the identification papers and compared the picture to Michael. He handed the papers back and pointed at his rucksack.

Michael complied and handed it to the Wehrmacht soldier, his stomach churning and his body clammy as the soldier opened the rucksack. This was it, the key moment in the entire operation. If the soldier found what was inside, it meant certain death for Michael and Jeroen, who was somewhere close by in case of trouble.

The soldier rummaged through the top of Michael's rucksack, pushing aside the loaf of bread and hard cheese he'd brought for his night shift dinner.

His hand hovered on the hardbound book cover, and Michael watched with his heart pumping as the soldier pulled it halfway out of the rucksack.

He pointed his torch deeper inside and saw only work overalls underneath the book. With a grunt, he pushed everything back inside and handed the rucksack back to Michael.

Evasion

"I haven't seen you here before. Are you new?" the soldier asked in German.

With great relief, Michael grabbed his rucksack and placed it over his shoulder.

"Yes, this is my first night. I've been called in to work on the heating system, as I hear some of the rooms are having problems."

He knew that, because he'd spent most of the previous afternoon with Elske, going over the plans for the evening. She'd given him all the details of how the hotel operated, and she'd planned everything down to the smallest detail.

All he had to do was show up and do what he'd been trained to do.

Easy, he thought as the soldier beckoned him past.

Once through the final checkpoint, Michael heaved a huge sigh of relief. He'd done the hard part, and as long as Elske had done her job properly, the rest should be plain sailing.

Michael rolled his eyes. He'd been in this job too long to know that nothing ever went to plan, but Elske had done all she could to make the operation go as smoothly as possible.

Michael skirted around to the rear of the hotel. It was pitch black when he got there, but he knew from the drawings Elske had made where the parking garage was located.

As directed, he kept to the side of the building and located the door on the rear right side, close to a street entrance. The valet was sympathetic to the cause, and he'd agreed to unlock the door at eleven o'clock for twenty minutes.

After that, he would lock it again so that everything was back to normal the next morning when the senior Nazis returned to their vehicles along with their drivers.

Tension rose in Michael's chest as he tried the side door. The handle turned, and the door opened easily. He stepped inside and took a moment to allow his eyes to adjust, listening intently for any signs of movement close by.

The valet had assured Elske that the garage would be empty at that time of night. His own office was at the front of the garage, where the vehicles entered and left, and his door was closed.

Michael was alone.

Using his torch, he scanned the luxury vehicles that stood in sharp contrast to the devastation their owners had caused outside. He scowled at the array of opulence on display as the light bounced off Mercedes after Mercedes.

He found the one he was looking for at the rear of the garage. Gleaming after a fresh wash and polish, the black Mercedes 320 convertible was a sight to behold.

The long, sleek bonnet covered a powerful six-cylinder engine, and although he wasn't a vehicle enthusiast, Michael could tell just from the torchlight that he was looking at an engineering wonder.

Scanning the licence plate, he confirmed that it was the correct vehicle: SS-3214.

This was the vehicle owned and driven by SS Standartenführer Karl Schneider, the senior Sicherheitsdienst, or SD as it was better known, commander in Rotterdam and its surrounding districts.

Schneider, unlike many senior Nazis, preferred to drive himself rather use a chauffeur.

Amongst other duties, the SD was the arm of the SS responsible for dealing with resistance units.

From what Jeroen had told him, Schneider was brought in days after Michael had killed Kreise, and for all intents and purposes, he was even more ruthless and vindictive.

Schneider ordered the execution of another resistance unit that included Geerts youngest sister Femke, and Elske, as a Dutch employee of the hotel, had been forced to watch as they were shot by the side of the river.

Schneider didn't know about the family connection, and Elske used her hatred cleverly, silently gathering intelligence while pretending to be a friend and collaborator.

As planned, the valet left the key to the car underneath the front right wheel arch. Michael quickly found it and opened the door, being careful to make as little noise as possible.

He unpacked his rucksack and took out the book the soldier had nearly opened. The book had been hollowed out, and Michael carefully removed the pressure plate, setting it aside for the moment on the driver's seat.

He went back into his rucksack and pulled out the overalls. After unfolding them, he gently removed six sticks of TNT from their protective wax wrappings and bundled them together with string.

He inserted the detonator into one of the TNT sticks, he placed them directly underneath the driver's seat. Then he wired the detonator to the pressure plate and put that under the seat alongside the TNT.

Returning the empty wax paper inside the hollowed-out book, he put everything back in his rucksack, carefully locked the door, and replaced the key underneath the wheel arch.

The entire thing had taken less than ten minutes, and a relieved Michael quickly left the garage by the unlocked door. He took a different route away from the hotel to avoid running into the same guard, and met Jeroen a mile down the street, parked underneath a tree.

Phase one of the operation was complete, and it was a case of so far, so good. Now it was time to begin phase two.

Chapter 17

Geert and the others were waiting at the farmhouse when Jeroen pulled into the barn. They surrounded the vehicle, eager to find out what had happened.

"Well?" Geert asked. "How did it go?"

"Did you plant the bomb?" Henk asked more directly.

"Did you get in okay?" Gerrit asked.

Jeroen threw his hand in the air to stop the questions. "Stop talking all at once," he commanded. "If you give us a chance, we'll tell you."

Jeroen turned to Michael, his look suggesting that he should be the one to tell the story.

"Everything went well," Michael said. "The pressure plate is set, and as soon as the SS officer sits on the seat, the car will explode, killing him and anyone near him."

Geert clapped Michael on the shoulder. "Good. He killed our sister, so I hope he rots in hell."

Michael took a more serious tone. "The explosion will create the diversion we need, but I hope you're all prepared for the reprisals, because believe me, they will be severe."

"As long as they aim their ire at us and not the general population, we can live with that," Jeroen replied.

"There's no guarantee that will happen," Michael responded truthfully. "You must be prepared for whatever they throw at you."

"Is Elske safe?" Geert asked.

Everyone looked at Gerrit. His face blushed a deep red, and he shook his head slowly from side to side before he spoke.

"I hope so. Knowing Elske, she's covered her tracks very well, but there's no guarantee that any of us are safe, let alone her. She works in the heart of the enemy's lair, and nobody is safe in there."

He closed his eyes for a moment. "If anyone can pull this off, it's Elske. She should be home soon, so she'll be far away when the bomb goes off."

"Go watch for her," Jeroen told Gerrit. "We'll load the truck."

By 1.15 am, the Mercedes L-3000 truck was loaded and ready to go. Elske had returned, and stood next to Gerrit as Arjen positioned the fuel drums at the rear of the truck in case they were stopped.

"Was everything quiet at the hotel?" Jeroen asked Elske, in English so Michael could understand.

Elske nodded. "The valet will leave at the end of his shift and never go back. He's going to his brother's place in Amsterdam. Schneider works like clockwork. He'll go to his vehicle at almost exactly six thirty, and he'll be dead before his cruel hands touch the steering wheel."

She spat the last sentence out, her hatred for the Nazi on full display.

The Mercedes truck trundled out of the farmyard, full of resistance fighters and explosives. Arjen was the only one left behind to listen to the radio and keep up with the latest news about the car bombing.

They had chosen a remote section of the railway lines near a small town called Nunspeet, which was perfect for clandestine operations such as the ones they were about to undertake.

The area was heavily forested, sparsely populated, and, more importantly, bereft of the Nazi patrols that swamped the busy streets of Rotterdam.

The journey northeast took a little over two and a half hours, which gave them plenty of time under cover of darkness to lay the explosives and get out of the way before daylight left them exposed to being spotted by Nazi patrols, especially from the air.

After an uneventful drive, Jeroen pulled the truck off the main road a few miles east of Nunspeet. Michael and the others bounced around in the back as the Mercedes drove down narrow forest roads full of potholes.

Five minutes later, they pulled to a stop, silence suddenly filling the air as Jeroen killed the engine. Michael jumped down from the back of the truck, and in a well-rehearsed drill from the previous day, each of them grabbed a bag before gathering together at the side of the truck.

Silence fell, and for a few minutes, nobody spoke as they allowed their eyes and brains to adjust to the terrain. They were parked on the side of a narrow lane in a deep forest. Trees blocked out the moon and the stars, leaving them in almost total darkness.

"Are we ready?" Jeroen's whisper echoed off the trees, making him seem louder than he actually was. Michael closed his eyes tight, shutting out the memories of previous forays in the Black Forest of Bavaria, where he'd barely escaped with his life.

"Let's go," Jeroen whispered. "Remember, keep close and remain quiet. No torchlight until we reach the railway line."

They followed in single file for ten minutes until they emerged from the forest onto a railway line in the middle of nowhere. Michael glanced at the luminous dial on his watch: 4:12 am.

He needed to hurry if he was going to set up the explosives before dawn. Jeroen held the torch while Michael worked, setting up the TNT underneath the railroad tracks and running the wire to a plunger hidden behind the trees.

Dawn was breaking as Michael finished, and the small group of exhausted resistance fighters took a moment to rest, hidden in the depths of the forest. They checked their weapons and waited.

The one good thing about the Nazis was that they were uber efficient, meaning that normally, the trains ran on time. The one carrying Senta and the other women was slated to leave Rotterdam at five am, which meant it would reach the ambush point around eight.

"The car explosion should give us the diversion we need," Michael said. "I just hope you're prepared for the retaliation afterwards."

The devastation the Nazis would unleash on the people of Rotterdam in the wake of the assassination bothered Michael, and he wished they had considered a different option.

But this was personal, and the resistance group, especially Elske, wanted revenge on Schneider, and Michael couldn't blame them after the cruelty inflicted on their sister and many others by the evil SS officer.

Jeroen and the others ignored him. They knew what was at stake, and if it meant giving their lives in defence of their beloved country, then so be it.

"Now we wait," Jeroen said, leaning back against a tree.

Chapter 18

SS Standartenführer Karl Schneider adjusted his uniform as he strode through the Hotel Atlanta's lobby, the single oak leaf insignia displayed on both collars reminding anyone who saw them of his importance to the Reich.

He paused to look in the full-length mirror by one of the lifts, and frowned at his expanding waistline. Since his transfer to Rotterdam after the unfortunate death of Albert Kreise, Schneider had enjoyed the trappings of victory a little too much, and now, just a few short weeks later, his normally trim figure was starting to show the effects.

At five feet eight inches, Karl Schneider was not the tallest man in the building, but his rank and his ego more than made up for it.

Neither was he the most Aryan, which bothered him more than it should have. After all, hadn't he already proven his family's lineage all the way back to 1750?

He'd considered dying his dark brown hair blond, but decided against it when he realised how much it was receding as he aged. At the rate it was going, he'd be completely bald by the time he reached his mid-forties.

Schneider exchanged pleasantries with two senior officers, ignoring the rest as he made his way towards his vehicle in the parking garage.

The early morning sunlight glinted off the polished marble floors, casting long shadows across the room. He nodded curtly at the NSB collaborators standing guard, their eyes following him with a mixture of fear and reverence.

Schneider's lips curled into a thin smile as he turned his attention to the day ahead. The transports of women to Germany were proceeding smoothly, which was another step forward in the grand plan to cleanse Europe of its undesirables.

But it was the upcoming interrogation that truly excited him.

They'd captured a suspected member of the Dutch resistance, a stubborn man who'd thus far refused to divulge any information.

Schneider's pulse quickened at the thought of breaking him, of hearing his screams echo through the cells. He'd developed quite a reputation for his creative methods, and he intended to live up to his reputation that day.

As he entered the parking garage, the valet jumped to attention, his face notably paler than usual. Schneider's ego swelled at the sight of the young man's trembling hands as he handed over the keys to his sleek Mercedes 320 convertible.

"Is everything alright?" Schneider asked, his voice deceptively soft.

"Y-yes, Herr Standartenführer," the valet stammered, sweat beading on his forehead. "Your vehicle is washed and polished as you ordered."

"Very good."

Schneider's eyes narrowed, drinking in the man's fear.

Evasion

This was how it should be—the inferior cowering before their superior. He dismissed the valet with a wave of his hand and strode towards his vehicle.

The garage was quieter than usual, with several spaces already empty. Punctuality was a virtue, after all. Schneider glanced at his watch—6:28 am. He was early, eager to begin what promised to be a productive day.

As he approached his Mercedes, Schneider focused on the interrogation ahead, visualising the array of tools at his disposal, considering which would be most effective in breaking the prisoner's will. Perhaps he'd start with the pliers, always a classic.

Schneider opened the car door, the familiar smell of leather greeting him. He savoured the moment, drawing in a deep breath as he slid one leg into the vehicle. This was his domain, his seat of power from which he would continue to crush the pathetic resistance movement and its leaders.

He'd promised his superiors the head of Jeroen, and he was close to delivering it.

Time seemed to slow as he lowered himself onto the seat. The leather creaked softly beneath his weight, and for a split second, Schneider thought he heard an odd click.

In that infinitesimal moment between sitting and settling, a deafening roar shattered the stillness of the garage. A blinding flash erupted from beneath Schneider, engulfing him in a maelstrom of fire and twisted metal.

The explosion ripped through the Mercedes, sending shrapnel tearing into nearby Nazis and their vehicles. The shockwave shattered windows and cracked concrete, the confined space of the garage amplifying the sound of the destruction.

In those last, agonising seconds of consciousness, Schneider's world became nothing but searing heat and unimaginable pain. His body was thrown violently, limbs torn apart and flailing uselessly against the inferno that consumed him.

As darkness closed in, Schneider's fading thoughts turned to the resistance fighters he'd hunted so ruthlessly. In his final moment of clarity, he realised with bitter irony that they had got the better of him.

Jeroen had won.

Then, mercifully, everything went black. SS Standartenführer Karl Schneider, the terror of Rotterdam, was no more.

The explosion's echoes faded, leaving behind the crackle of flames and the screams of the wounded and the dying. The valet watched from across the street, his lips formed into a cold smile.

As everyone ran towards the carnage, the valet scampered away in the opposite direction. His work for the resistance, at least in Rotterdam, was over.

Chapter 19

The acrid smell of burning rubber and melted metal filled the air as flames licked the twisted remains of what had been SS Standartenführer Karl Schneider's prized Mercedes.

Thick, black smoke billowed from the wreckage, obscuring visibility, and making it difficult to breathe in the confined space of the Hotel Atlanta's parking garage.

Amid the chaos, a young Wehrmacht soldier stumbled through the haze, his ears ringing from the force of the explosion. He coughed violently, struggling to catch his breath as he surveyed the scene of devastation before him. The soldier's eyes widened in horror as he spotted a severed arm lying amidst the debris, the sleeve of an SS uniform still partially intact.

"Mein Gott," he whispered, fighting the urge to vomit.

The sound of groaning metal echoed through the garage as parts of the ceiling threatened to give way. Concrete dust rained down, coating everything in a ghostly grey powder. The soldier's training kicked in, and he shouted towards the entrance, his voice hoarse from the smoke.

"Medic! We need medics in here now!"

As if in response to his call, a team of Wehrmacht medics rushed into the garage, their faces covered with makeshift masks to filter out the worst of the smoke. They fanned out, moving swiftly from one victim to the next, assessing the carnage with practised efficiency.

One medic knelt beside a badly wounded SS officer, whose leg had been torn off just below the knee. The officer's face was contorted in agony, his screams piercing through the din of crackling flames and falling debris.

"Hold still, Herr Obersturmbannführer," the medic said firmly, applying a tourniquet to stem the flow of blood. "We'll get you out of here as soon as we can."

Nearby, two more medics worked frantically to free a trapped Wehrmacht colonel from the wreckage of his staff car. His vehicle had been caught in the blast radius, its frame crumpled like tissue paper. The colonel's body was wedged between the seat and the dashboard, his breathing laboured and eyes unfocused.

"Stay with us, Herr Oberst," one of the medics urged as they carefully extracted him from the mangled car. "Just a little longer."

Outside the garage, the sound of breaking glass had drawn a crowd of onlookers. Several civilians lay on the sidewalk, cut by the shower of razor-sharp shards that had exploded outward from the garage's windows.

Dutch police officers, working alongside NSB collaborators, struggled to maintain order as curious bystanders pressed forward, eager to catch a glimpse of the destruction.

"Get back!" shouted an NSB officer, his face flushed with exertion. "This area is now under military control!"

A convoy of military trucks roared down the street, screeching to a halt in front of the hotel. Soldiers poured out of the vehicles, their boots pounding on the pavement as they rushed to secure the perimeter. Among them was a group of SS men, their black uniforms standing out starkly against the sea of field grey.

SS-Obersturmführer Erik Stadtler, a young, mid-thirties rising star in the Rotterdam SD, took charge of the scene. His piercing blue eyes scanned the area, taking in every detail as he barked orders to his subordinates.

The SD were responsible for counterintelligence operations, and Stadtler wanted to stamp his authority on the situation right from the start.

"I want this entire block locked down," he commanded. "No one in or out without my express permission. Understood?"

"Jawohl, Herr Obersturmführer!" his men chorused, saluting crisply before dispersing to carry out his orders.

Stadtler turned to the man beside him. "I want all the Dutch personnel who work here to be found and brought to the police station, especially those who worked last night."

"Jawohl, Obersturmführer. Consider it done." The junior officer scurried away.

Stadtler turned his attention to the garage, where rescue efforts were underway. He watched as a group of soldiers carefully manoeuvred a stretcher bearing the remains of what he assumed was Standartenführer Schneider. The body was barely recognisable, charred beyond recognition, and missing several limbs.

A lump formed in Stadtler's throat as he realised the implications of the attack. Schneider had been his mentor, a man he both feared and admired. Now, in the blink of an eye, he was gone, reduced to a smouldering heap of flesh and bone.

As Stadtler contemplated the loss, a staff car pulled up, and a harried aide jumped out. He rushed over to Stadtler, snapping to attention before delivering his message.

"Herr Obersturmführer, I've just received word from The Hague. Reichskommissar Seyss-Inquart and General Rauter have been informed of the situation. They're demanding immediate action and a full report."

Stadtler nodded grimly. "Of course they are. Tell them we're conducting a thorough investigation and I'll update them as soon as we have something to give them."

The aide hesitated, shifting nervously from foot to foot. "There's more, sir. General Rauter is personally overseeing the response. He's ordered an immediate crackdown on all suspected resistance activities."

A cold smile played across Stadtler's lips. "Good. It's about time we showed these Dutch rats the true meaning of the Führer's wrath."

As the morning wore on, the full extent of the attack became clear. In addition to Schneider, two colonels, one Wehrmacht and one SS, had been killed in the blast. Their bodies, along with those of several unfortunate chauffeurs, were carefully removed from the scene and taken to a makeshift morgue set up in the hotel's ballroom.

The wounded SS Obersturmbannführer, identified as Heinrich Kramer, was rushed to the nearest military hospital. His prognosis was grim; even if he survived, he would never walk again without the aid of a prosthetic.

By noon, the immediate crisis had passed, but the atmosphere in Rotterdam remained tense. Word of the attack spread quickly, and the city's inhabitants watched with a mixture of fear and grim satisfaction as the occupiers scrambled to respond.

Chapter 20

The distant whistle of an approaching train pierced the early morning silence, sending a jolt of adrenaline through Michael's body. His eyes snapped open, instantly alert after hours of tense waiting. He glanced at his watch—7:58 am. Right on schedule.

The small group of six resistance fighters rose to their feet, exchanging nervous glances as the steam train full of Dutch women, as well as Germans returning home, approached.

"It's time," Jeroen whispered, his voice barely audible over the growing rumble of the locomotive.

Michael nodded, his jaw set with grim determination. He tightened his grip on the plunger, feeling the rough wood beneath his sweaty palms. The lives of countless women, including Senta, hung in the balance. There was no room for error.

The ground vibrated beneath their feet as the train drew nearer. Through gaps in the dense foliage, they caught glimpses of steam billowing from the engine. The distinctive black-and-red livery of the Deutsche Reichsbahn came into view, a stark reminder of the Nazi occupation that had engulfed their country.

"Wait for it," Jeroen murmured, his eyes fixed on the approaching train.

Michael's heart pounded in his chest, each beat seeming to echo the rhythmic chug of the locomotive. He could see the engineer now through the gap in the trees, a middle-aged man with a cap pulled low over his eyes, oblivious to the danger that lay ahead.

Behind the engine, a line of drab, age-worn passenger cars stretched into the distance, their windows dark and forbidding. Somewhere in those cars, they hoped, was Senta.

"Now!" Jeroen hissed, his hand squeezing Michael's shoulder.

Michael didn't hesitate. He slammed down on the plunger with all his might, feeling the mechanism give way beneath his hands.

For a split second, nothing happened. The train continued its inexorable approach, the rails groaning beneath its wheels. Then, with a deafening roar that seemed to shake the very earth, the world exploded.

The ground heaved as multiple explosions ripped through the railway line. Dirt and debris shot skyward, engulfing the front of the train in a roiling cloud of smoke and shrapnel. The locomotive lurched violently, its wheels leaving the twisted tracks in a shower of sparks.

Time seemed to slow as the massive engine tipped to one side, momentum carrying it forward even as it began to topple. With a screech of tortured metal that set Michael's teeth on edge, it ploughed into the soft earth beside the tracks, digging a deep furrow as it slid.

Behind it, chaos unfolded in a nightmarish ballet of

destruction. The passenger cars jackknifed, slamming into each other with bone-jarring force.

Windows shattered, showering the ground with a deadly rain of glittering shards. The sound of twisting metal and splintering wood filled the air, punctuated by the terrified screams of those trapped inside.

Elske covered her ears with her hands, and Michael watched in horror as car after car left the tracks, each adding to the growing pile of wreckage.

The train's momentum carried it forward relentlessly, cars crumpling and folding like accordions. Some tipped onto their sides with a groan of protesting metal, while others remained upright but were crushed between their neighbours, their frames buckling under the immense pressure.

After what felt like an eternity, but was, in reality, only minutes, the last car came to a shuddering halt. An eerie silence fell over the scene, broken only by the hiss of escaping steam and the screams of passengers trapped in the wreckage.

Smoke billowed from the wreckage, obscuring parts of the train from view. Michael strained his eyes, searching for any sign of movement among the twisted cars. His heart raced as he thought of Senta, praying that she had somehow survived the impact.

Gerrit squeezed Elske's hand tight, and they looked at each other with wide eyes and pale faces.

"I hope we did the right thing," Geert said nervously, his face as white as a ghost.

Henke closed his eyes and took a deep breath. "I hope so too."

"We need to move," Jeroen said urgently, snapping the bedraggled group back to reality. "The guards will be recovering soon. We have to find Senta before they regroup."

Michael nodded, pushing aside his shock and the sickening realisation of what they had just done. They had known this would be violent, but the reality of it was still overwhelming. He took a deep breath, steeling himself for what lay ahead.

"Let's go," he said, his voice steady despite the turmoil in his gut.

As they emerged from their hiding spot, the full scale of the devastation became clear. The locomotive lay on its side like a fallen giant, steam still escaping from its ruptured boiler in angry hisses. Behind it, a tangle of wreckage stretched for hundreds of yards, a twisted monument to the brutality of their desperate act.

Some cars had split open like overripe fruit, spilling their contents onto the forest floor. Others remained largely intact but were wedged at odd angles, their doors jammed shut by the force of the impact. Everywhere, there were signs of the human cost—personal belongings scattered across the ground, and the distant sounds of people crying out for help.

Michael and Jeroen exchanged a grim look. Somewhere in this chaos was Senta, if she had even been on the train at all. They had gambled everything on this moment, and now they would face the consequences of their actions.

With a nod to the other resistance members, they separated and moved towards the wreckage. It wouldn't be long before Nazi reinforcements arrived, and when they did, the forest would become a war zone.

Chapter 21

The foul smell of smoke and burning metal filled the air as Michael and his fellow resistance fighters approached the wreckage. As they drew closer, the full extent of what they'd done became painfully clear.

Michael's stomach churned as he took in the scene before him. The locomotive, a massive beast of steel and steam, lay on its side, still hissing and groaning as if in its death throes.

"Remember," Jeroen's voice cut through the chaos. "Senta is our target. Don't allow yourselves to be distracted by anyone else. Point them in the right direction and tell them to get as far away as they can. That's all we can do for them."

Michael nodded grimly, steeling himself for what lay ahead. They split into teams, each taking a section of the train. Michael and Geert headed for the front carriages, while Jeroen and Henk moved towards the rear. Elske and Gerrit took the middle carriages.

As Michael approached the first carriage, the sounds of human suffering became impossible to ignore. Cries for help in Dutch and German mingled with pained moans and terrified sobbing. Michael swallowed hard, pushing down the guilt that threatened to overwhelm him. He'd known there would be casualties, but the reality of it was far worse than he had imagined.

The door was jammed shut, so Geert smashed the window of the carriage with the butt of his rifle. "Anyone who can move, come to the window!" he shouted in Dutch. "We're here to help!"

Faces appeared at the shattered opening, some streaked with blood, others pale with shock. Michael and Geert worked quickly, helping passengers climb through the narrow space. Many were injured, sporting cuts, bruises, and what looked like broken bones.

"Head for the woods," Geert pointed towards the direction the escaping prisoners should follow, instructing each person as they emerged. "Make for Nunspeet if you can. Don't go back to your old lives, the Nazis will be looking for you."

Some of the freed prisoners nodded in understanding, while others seemed too dazed to fully comprehend. A few of the stronger ones stayed behind to help, forming a human chain to help free more of their fellow captives.

Michael remained silent, searching every face for signs of Senta.

As they moved to the next carriage, the sight that greeted him would haunt him for years to come. Bodies lay strewn about the compartment, some clearly dead, others moaning in agony. Blood painted the walls and seats, and the sickly-sweet smell of death mingled with the acrid smoke.

"Oh God," Geert whispered, his voice cracking. "What have we done?"

Michael placed a hand on his shoulder. "We did what we had to," he said firmly. "Remember why we're here."

Shaking off his horror, Michael pushed the images to the back of his mind and got back to work. They moved from carriage to carriage, freeing those they could and offering comfort to those too injured to move.

In the fourth carriage, they found a group of women huddled together, their faces a mixture of fear and hope. As Michael helped them through the window, one of them grasped his arm.

"Thank you," she said in Dutch, her eyes brimming with tears. "You're heroes, all of you."

Geert translated what she'd said, and as he spoke, Michael felt a lump form in his throat. Hero? He didn't feel like a hero. He felt like a man with blood on his hands, even if it was for a just cause.

As they worked, shouts in German echoed across the wreckage. The Nazi guards and returning soldiers were regrouping, and the sound of sporadic gunfire filled the air.

"We need to move faster," Michael urged. "They're coming."

They redoubled their efforts, smashing windows and pulling people to safety as quickly as they could. The freed prisoners who had stayed to help now fled into the woods, the threat of recapture spurring them on.

Suddenly, a burst of machine-gun fire tore through the air, sending splinters of wood flying from the carriage next to them. Michael ducked instinctively, pulling a woman down with him as bullets whizzed overhead.

"Get down!" he shouted. "Take cover!"

Geert returned fire, his rifle cracking sharply in the morning air. Michael joined him, aiming at the muzzle flashes he could see through the smoke and debris. The resistance fighters and the Nazis exchanged a fierce volley of gunfire, the sound deafening in the confined space of the wreckage.

Through the chaos, Michael caught glimpses of the brutal reality of their situation. A man who had been helping them free others suddenly jerked backwards, a red stain blossoming on his chest. He crumpled to the ground, his eyes wide with shock and pain.

A woman screamed as a bullet caught her in the leg, sending her spinning to the earth.

The air was thick with gun smoke and the metallic tang of blood. Shell casings thudded against the ground as Michael reloaded his Walther PPK.

A Nazi guard outside the carriage shot a woman in the back of the head as she ran for the trees. As he turned his rifle towards his next victim, Michael let loose, dropping the Nazi like a stone.

A shout from farther down the train brought him back to reality. "Michael! We need help here!"

It was Jeroen's voice. Michael turned to Geert. "Can you handle things here?"

Geert nodded grimly, firing off another round. "Go! Find Senta!"

Michael sprinted down the length of the train, ducking and weaving to avoid the ongoing gunfire. As he ran, he saw more of the carnage they had wrought. Bodies lay scattered on the ground, some moving, many still, the cries of the wounded mixed with the sharp reports of gunfire, creating a hellish cacophony.

He found Jeroen and Henk pinned down behind an overturned dining car, exchanging fire with a group of Nazi soldiers who had taken up a position close by.

"What's the situation?" Michael asked, sliding into cover beside them.

Evasion

"We've cleared most of the rear carriages," Jeroen reported. "But we haven't found Senta yet. The Nazis are shooting at anyone who's trying to escape. I've seen at least twenty men and women shot before they could reach the cover of the trees."

Michael grimaced, his hatred for the Nazis and everything they stood for searing his mind. As if to emphasise his point, a hail of bullets peppered their position, sending splinters flying. Michael returned fire, his shots forcing the Germans to duck behind their own cover.

"We need to flank them," Henk suggested. "I'll provide covering fire, you two circle around."

Before they could argue, Henk popped up and let loose a barrage from his rifle. Michael and Jeroen seized the opportunity, sprinting towards a better position off to their left.

Three women lay on the ground as they ran. At least two of them had blood oozing from bullet wounds, and the third sobbed as she clung to the ground.

They had almost made it when a cry of pain rang out behind them. Michael turned to see Henk slump to the ground, blood seeping from a wound in his chest.

"Henk!" Jeroen shouted, moving back.

"No!" Henk waved them off. "Keep going! Find Senta!"

With heavy hearts, they pressed on, leaving their wounded comrade behind. The gunfight intensified as they closed in on the Nazi position.

A German soldier appeared suddenly from behind a piece of wreckage. In a flash, Michael squeezed the trigger. The man's chest erupted in a spray of red, his face frozen in a look of surprise as he fell.

There was no time to dwell on it. They pushed forward, systematically eliminating the German resistance.

As the last soldier fell, an eerie quiet settled over the scene, broken only by the moans of the wounded and the distant sounds of escapees fleeing through the woods.

"We need to hurry," Jeroen said, his voice tight with urgency. "Reinforcements will be here soon."

They split up again, each taking a carriage. Michael's heart raced as he peered into compartment after compartment, dreading what he might find but desperate to locate Senta.

In the third carriage from the end, Michael saw a teenage girl with long blonde hair kneeling beside a badly injured woman, trying to stem the flow of blood from a nasty gash on her leg.

"Senta!" Michael called out, relief flooding through him.

The girl looked up, and recognition spread over her face as she recognised the man speaking to her in her native German language.

She looked up, her face streaked with dirt and tears. "Michael! What are you doing here? We need to help these people!"

Michael's heart sank as he took in the scene. The carriage was full of injured women, many of them in critical condition. He knew they couldn't possibly evacuate them all.

"Senta," he hissed, moving towards her. "We can't. We need to go."

She shook her head vehemently. "We can't just leave them!"

"We have to," Michael insisted, his voice thick with emotion. "More Germans will be here soon. If we stay, we'll all be captured or killed."

Senta looked at him, her eyes filled with anguish. "But…"

"I'm sorry," Michael said, addressing the wounded women in English. "Help will come for you soon. The Germans will take care of you. But we have to go."

He gently took Senta's arm, guiding her towards the shattered window. She resisted for a moment, then seemed to deflate, the fight going out of her.

As they climbed out of the carriage, Michael struggled to block out the cries for help behind him.

"Jeroen!" he shouted. "I've got her! Where are you?"

He saw him, along with Geert, Elise and Gerrit, kneeling by the side of Henk. Michael grabbed Senta's arm and dragged her along as he ran to their aid.

His heart dropped when he saw blood trickling from the corner of Henk's mouth. Although covered in dirt and sweat, his face was as pale as a moonlit sky.

Jeroen worked on the wound to his chest, trying unsuccessfully to stem the flow of blood. Henk's eyes grew wide when he saw Senta, and for a moment, a smile formed on his lips. Then his eyes rolled towards the top of his head, and with one last gasp of air, he was gone. His body fell limp in Jeroen's arms.

Jeroen took a deep breath as he lowered his friend to the ground. Elske sobbed in Gerrit's arms, and their tears fell together, dampening the ground where he lay.

Senta stared at Henk's lifeless body, her face wracked with guilt and sorrow. Michael had seen this too many times, and he forced the ghastly sight from his mind.

"We can't leave him here. Help me carry him to the truck."

Elske hugged Senta while the men picked up their fallen comrade. Jeroen led the way as they retreated towards the forest and the truck that was hidden in the foliage.

Michael took one last look at the scene behind them.

The once-peaceful stretch of railway had been transformed into a nightmare landscape of twisted metal and broken bodies. Smoke still rose from the wreckage, and the cries of the wounded hung in the air like a sorrowful requiem.

They had accomplished their mission. Senta was safe, and dozens of prisoners had been freed. But the cost had been high. Perhaps too high. As they melted into the shadows of the forest, Michael couldn't shake the feeling that this day would mark a turning point for the resistance.

The battle for the Netherlands had entered a new, more brutal phase. There was no going back now. This was total war, and they were committed to seeing the fight through to its bitter end.

No matter the cost.

Chapter 22

In The Hague, SS-Obergruppenführer Hanns Albin Rauter paced his office, his face a mask of barely contained fury. As the highest-ranking SS officer in the Netherlands and chief of police, Rauter held the lofty title of Höhere SS- und Polizeiführer Nordwest und Reichskommissariat Niederlande.

Whichever way he looked at it, the attack at the Hotel Atlanta was a personal affront to his authority.

"This is unacceptable!" he roared, slamming his fist on his desk. "How could this happen right under our noses?"

His aide, a young SS-Untersturmführer, stood rigidly at attention, trying not to flinch at Rauter's outburst. "The Rotterdam SD is still investigating, Herr General. They believe it was the work of the Dutch resistance, possibly with help from British intelligence."

Rauter's eyes narrowed dangerously. "Whoever was behind this will pay with their lives. Their lives and the lives of all their loved ones."

He turned to stare out of the window, his hands

clasped behind his back. After a moment of tense silence, he spoke again, his voice low and menacing.

"We must respond swiftly and decisively. The Dutch need to understand that such actions will not be tolerated."

The aide cleared his throat nervously. "What are your orders, sir?"

Before he could reply, the shrill ring of the telephone interrupted their conversation.

"Leave me," Rauter ordered.

The young officer snapped his heels together and threw his right arm in the air in the Nazi salute. He turned and hurried out of the office.

"Yes?" Rauter barked into the telephone receiver.

"Herr General, my name is SS-Obersturmführer Stadtler. I'm from the Rotterdam SD office. I'm told you wanted to speak to me?

"Are you in charge of the operations in Rotterdam?" Rauter asked.

"Yes, Herr General. SS Standartenführer Schneider was tragically killed in the attack, so I am the senior officer in charge."

"Good. I am led to believe that Schneider was the target of the attack. Can you confirm that?"

"That's correct, Herr General. It appears that the bomb was attached to Standartenführer Schneider's vehicle, so we think he was the one they were after."

"Do you know who was responsible?" Rauter asked.

"We're not certain yet, but we believe it was the work of a well-known leader of the Dutch resistance called Jeroen. He's a former member of the Dutch intelligence services, and so far he's managed to elude us."

"I've heard this name too many times." Rauter mopped his brow with a handkerchief. "Listen to me carefully, Obersturmführer. I want that man, and everyone associated with him, captured, do you hear?" Rauter was shouting now, his voice growing angrier by the second.

"Yes, Herr General. We are working on it right now. He had to have had help from inside the hotel, so I'm rounding up all the Dutch workers. One of them will reveal the whereabouts of this Jeroen. We'll get him, sir."

"To make sure, I want you to let everyone in the city know there is a reward on offer for his capture. I want this man caught by nightfall."

"How much is the reward?"

Rauter paused for effect. "Fifty thousand guilders."

Stadtler gave a low whistle. "That should get them talking, sir. I'll get word out immediately."

Rauter stared straight ahead, a cold gleam in his eye. "First, I want every known or suspected resistance member in Rotterdam rounded up and brought in for questioning. Use whatever means necessary to extract information."

He paused, contemplating his next move. "Second, we'll make an example of some of these terrorists. Choose five of the most prominent suspects, beginning with the one they call Jeroen, and have them publicly executed. Make sure it's well-publicised. I want every person in Rotterdam to know the price of defiance."

"Consider it done, Herr General." The order was music to Stadtler's ears.

Rauter continued, his voice growing more animated as he outlined his plan.

"Increase patrols throughout the city, especially around key installations. I want checkpoints at every major intersection. Anyone without proper papers is to be detained immediately."

He glanced at a large map of the Netherlands pinned

to the wall, his finger tracing the outline of Rotterdam. "And finally, I want a complete lockdown of the city. No one enters or leaves without express permission from my office. Is that understood?"

"Completely, Herr General," Stadtler replied crisply. "It will be done exactly as you ordered."

"Report back to me directly," Rauter ordered.

"Jawohl, Herr General."

Rauter replaced the receiver and called his aide back into his office.

"Contact Reichskommissar Seyss-Inquart. He's in charge of the civilian administration for Holland. Tell him I recommend implementing a curfew for all of occupied Holland. It's time the Dutch learned their place in the New Order."

"I'll see to it immediately, Herr General."

The young SS-Untersturmführer hovered, shifting uneasily from foot to foot.

"Well?" Rauter yelled. "What is it?"

"Herr General," the aide stammered, not wanting to give his ruthless boss more bad news. "I'm afraid there's more. I just received word from a field telephone that one of our trains has been attacked and derailed outside a town called Nunspeet, which is to the northeast of Rotterdam."

Rauter sat back in his chair, his face pale. "Tell me that again," he said softly.

The aide repeated his words.

"Who was on that train?" Rauter asked.

"As far as I know, it was carrying male and female prisoners from Holland to Germany, as well as a few of our soldiers returning home for either leave or to have their injuries treated."

"Do we know if it was related to the car bombing?" Rauter asked.

"We don't know yet, sir. The reports are only just coming in. Units have been dispatched to the scene, and we'll know more once they are on the ground."

Rauter tapped his pen on the desk, deep in thought. "Someone on that train was important to the resistance. Perhaps even more important to the British or the French. Someone important enough to derail a train, and, I suspect, carry out the bombing in Rotterdam earlier this morning."

Rauter was thinking aloud more than conversing with his aide. He looked up, his face now flushed with the blood returning to his cheeks.

"I want a full report on my desk by nightfall. I want to know who was on that train, who was so important that the resistance would risk everything for it. And I also want to know if this Jeroen I keep hearing about was behind both attacks."

"Every available resource has been allocated to this task, Herr General. I'll get a full report as soon as I can."

"You'll do better than that," Rauter snapped. "You'll get whoever is in charge of the train derailment to call me direct as soon as he's done his initial assessment. This is to be our top priority, and nobody may rest until we know who is behind it and why."

"Jawohl, Herr General."

"I want to know *who* was on that train."

The young aide threw his arm in the air. "Heil Hitler," he bellowed. Then he turned and marched out.

Rauter reached for the telephone as his aide left the office. "Get me SS-Obergruppenführer Heydrich in Berlin," he said to the switchboard operator as soon as she answered.

"Tell him it's urgent."

The thought of speaking to the Blond Beast sent shivers down Rauter's spine, but he knew he had no other choice than to keep him updated on the situation. The last thing he wanted was to get on the wrong side of SS-Obergruppenführer Heydrich.

Chapter 23

The battered Mercedes L-3000 truck rumbled down the muddy lane, its suspension groaning under the weight of the resistance fighters and their grim cargo.

Michael sat in the back, his clothes still damp from the morning's exertions, cradling Senta as she drifted from remorse to anger.

"Where's Mina?" she asked, looking up at Michael. "And why are you here? I thought you were supposed to be back in England by now."

Michael closed his eyes momentarily, trying to find the words he didn't want to say.

"Mina isn't here," he said after a long pause. "A lot happened after you were captured, and there's a lot you don't know."

"Then tell me." Senta pulled away from Michael. Her words, shouted above the din of the noisy truck, caught the attention of Elske sitting opposite her.

Elske reached forward and touched Senta's hand. "We'll tell you everything once we're back at the farmhouse," she said in English.

"I want to know now!" Senta shouted. "Where's Mina? Is she alright? And why is he here?" She pointed at Michael.

"Jeroen should be the one who tells you," Michael replied. "But as he's in the front with Geert, we'll have to wait until we get back to the farmhouse."

"Where is my sister?" Senta demanded, her voice louder and hardening.

Michael sighed. "You know how much I love Mina. Nobody is more concerned about her than me, but we don't know where she is. I asked the same questions when I got back here, and nobody knows where she is."

Senta glared at Michael, her eyes boring into his.

"Please, Senta. Wait until we get to the farmhouse and then we'll explain everything. As far as I know, Mina is safe, but once this is over, I'm going to find her."

"Not without me, you're not." Senta fell into a brooding silence, her face as deep red as the dried blood spread across Henk's chest.

Nobody spoke for the rest of the three-hour journey back to the farmhouse, their eyes looking anywhere except at the lifeless body of Henk lying on the floor near their feet.

Michael spent the time working on his plans in the aftermath of the train derailment and the bombing attack on the Nazi stronghold in the hotel car park.

Whatever else he did, Senta had to be on the plane the next evening. Her importance to the Allied war effort couldn't be underestimated, and Michael berated himself for not recognising it before. He'd placed both her and Mina in grave danger by his lack of foresight, and it was a mistake he wouldn't make again.

Although he was desperate to find Mina, she would have to wait until he'd completed his mission.

Tension was high as the returning resistance fighters arrived back at the farmhouse. Although weary from the events of the last twenty-four hours, they showed no signs of fatigue as they traipsed in single file into the kitchen.

Arjen sat hunched over the small radio, the grim look on his face a reflection of the bleak news crackling through the static. His fingers tapped anxiously on the table as he adjusted the dial, trying to catch every word.

Looking up from the radio set, his eyes scanned the room. "Where's Henk?" he asked, his eyes wide open, as if in fear of the answer he was about to receive.

Elske hugged his neck, soft tears falling down her face. "He's gone, Arjen. He died saving all of us."

Arjen turned his gaze back to the radio set. "Did you at least bring him back with you?" he asked.

"He's in the truck outside," Elske answered.

After a lengthy pause, Arjen changed the subject, his voice breaking as he spoke.

"They've locked down Rotterdam," he said in broken English before going into a two-minute spiel in Dutch as he updated them on what was happening after the car bombing.

Jeroen leaned against the doorframe, his face drawn and pale from fatigue, stress, and loss. He translated Arjen's words for Michael.

"Reprisals are underway. The SD and Gestapo are rounding up everyone suspected of helping the resistance. Every Dutch worker from the hotel is to report to the SS headquarters by five o'clock today, and any that don't are to be considered enemies of the state and executed immediately."

Jeroen paused before looking Michael in the eye, his face a picture of resignation. "They're offering a reward of fifty thousand guilders for information that leads to my capture. My days are numbered, Michael, because not many will turn down a sum like that."

"Fifty thousand?" Michael gave a low whistle.

He did a quick calculation in his head and worked out that the Germans were offering a sum of over five thousand pounds for the capture of Jeroen. That was a life-changing amount of money, enough to buy an entire street full of houses in most towns in England.

Jeroen's chances of survival had just taken a downward turn to somewhere near zero.

"That's an enormous sum of money," he said after a lengthy pause, when the two men just stared at each other. "They must really want you."

"This is not about me," Jeroen answered. "I need to get Elske and everyone else here out of Rotterdam before it's too late."

"What did you expect would happen?" Michael asked, his face flushed. "You knew the Germans would react like this after you blew up the car and killed Schneider. This was always going to happen. I warned you, Jeroen, but you wouldn't listen."

"It was worth it," Elske butted in. "Schneider was a monster who killed our sister, along with many more Dutch men and women."

She paused for a second as if to add weight to her words. "If it costs everyone here's life, including mine, it will be worth it, because Schneider wouldn't have stopped. Who knows how many more of us he would have killed before the war ends if we didn't stop him?"

"It won't stop," Michael argued. "Before him, they had Albert Kreise, and you don't need me to tell you how evil he was. All they'll do is send someone else, who is probably far worse than either of those two. The killing won't stop, Elske, not until we defeat the Nazis."

"We might not be able to match them on the battleground," Jeroen said. "But we'll never surrender our country to these animals. Whatever happens to us, there are thousands more like us out there, waiting for a chance to strike at them. They will never win."

The small group of Dutch resistance fighters huddled together around Jeroen, each showing defiance in the face of a mighty enemy. Michael couldn't help but feel inspired by their courage and determination, and he was surprised by a sudden surge of energy spreading through his body.

Whatever patriotic resistance they were feeling, he was feeling it too.

As if reading his mind, Jeroen spoke up. "Imagine how you would feel if it was in the British Isles, Michael. You, and thousands like you, would never give up. You would gladly lay down your lives for the freedom of your country, and we are just the same."

Michael nodded, his eyes never leaving Jeroen's. As crazy as it was, Michael knew he would embrace the exact same madness if it were in Britain.

"What about Mina?" Senta, who had been sitting at the table opposite Arjen, spoke up. "Where is she?"

Elske placed her hand in Senta's and sat beside her. "London knows about your special abilities, Senta. When you left here on the mission that got you captured, we received a message informing us that someone was coming to take you back to London."

Senta shot Michael a dirty look, as if to blame him for telling the British government about her eidetic memory.

"What does that have to do with Mina?" she asked. "Where is she?"

"The message clearly stated that only you were to go. Not Mina." Elske spoke gently, rubbing her hands.

Senta's eyes were wide open. "I'm not going without Mina, and you all know that. Michael knows that."

"Mina was the one who took the radio message," Elske said softly. "She knows how important your talent is, and she also knew how you would react. She left to go to somewhere she would be safe in France, knowing that if she stayed, you would refuse to go."

"She's gone to France?" Senta pulled her hands from Elske's. "Why haven't you gone to find her? She'll never get there on her own."

"All this happened so quickly, Senta," Jeroen said. "We haven't had time to do anything other than carry out our mission to remove Schneider and rescue you before the Nazis found out how important you are. Mina was next on our list."

"I'm going to find her." Senta jumped up, but Michael stopped her.

"Nobody is more important to me than Mina is, and you all know that to be true," he said. "But you have to listen to me, Senta. You are vital to our chances of eventually defeating Hitler. Henk willingly gave his life for you, and all these people here risked everything to get you to safety. This has to be everyone's priority."

He paused, making sure Senta understood what he was saying.

"I promise you I will find Mina and bring her with me to England. I've already had this argument with my superiors, and I refused this mission unless they allowed Mina to come with us. They reluctantly agreed, as long as it was my family that took care of her once she was there."

Senta's eyes filled with tears, and Michael watched as they dripped down her face. "Let's go find her then," she sobbed.

"You and I have an appointment with a plane

tomorrow evening that will take us home. Then I'm coming back for Mina, and I don't care what the British government says about it."

"I'm not leaving witho—"

"Yes, you are," Michael said firmly. "Millions of lives, and potentially the fate of the entire war, rests in the hands of people with abilities such as yours. Senta, you have a gift that is as rare as anything I have ever heard of before, and it's my fault that I didn't recognise it sooner. If I had, all three of us would be safe in England by now."

Senta pulled a face, but she didn't object. How could she? Everyone in the room knew that every word Michael had spoken was true, and the sacrifices they were making for the war effort were worth it for the ultimate victory that had to come eventually.

Especially as Henk lay dead in the rear of the truck parked in the barn.

Chapter 24

Gerrit, who had been quiet so far, broke in. "You and Mina are important to us, and I promise I will do all I can to find her once you leave with Michael, which you surely must. You do not need to worry about her, Senta. I'll find her and keep her safe until Michael comes back for her."

Gerrit had a way with words. Michael couldn't put his finger on it, but when he spoke, he seemed to put everyone at ease, which was a great comfort right then.

Senta rose from her chair and threw her arms around Gerrit.

"Now that's settled, we have other important matters to discuss," Jeroen said, taking over the conversation. "We need to bury Henk and then discuss what we're going to do about the ultimatum the Nazis gave regarding the hotel workers. Elske will be on the top of their list when she doesn't turn herself in, and we've got to be prepared for what they might do."

"I have another idea," Gerrit spoke again. "We all know what will happen if she turns herself in, so I took the precaution of obtaining some hair dye in case I had to alter her appearance after the Schneider bombing. I think we should cut and dye both her and Senta's hair and I'll create new documents for them. That way, they will be safer."

"That's a good idea," Jeroen agreed. "Can you take care of that while we bury Henk?"

Gerrit nodded, looking at Senta and Elske for permission. They both nodded their heads in agreement.

"There are shovels in the barn." Geert spoke for the first time. He was a man of few words, but Michael could tell the loss of his brother had hurt him deeply.

Geert led the way, leaving Gerrit to work with Senta and Elske in creating their new identities.

Michael was glad of something to do. At least he could be physically active, which took his mind away from the huge task ahead of him.

As they filed outside in what they expected to be the mid-morning sun, Michael was shocked to see the weather had turned. It was as though Mother Nature herself had witnessed the carnage and the losses that day and was mourning with them.

A storm had rolled in during their kitchen conversation, and the dark clouds hung over the farmhouse like an oppressive blanket. Rain poured down, sending splashes of mud in every direction as it hit the ground.

"We can always wait and do this later," Arjen muttered, although Michael could tell from the tone of his voice that he didn't mean it.

"No," Geert answered. "We might not get time later, and Henk deserves a proper burial."

Nobody argued, and Michael followed the others outside, the driving rain soaking him to the skin within seconds. They each grabbed a shovel and opened the rear of the truck to retrieve Henk's body.

They carried him to a corner of a field he loved to stand in and set about the painful task of burying him.

As they dug, a fierce, heavy emotion set about Michael, forcing him to dig furiously without regard to either the weather or his own fatigue.

Memories of another burial consumed his mind, and he allowed the guilt of yet another good man lost for his mistakes to join the ever-growing list of others who had laid down their lives for him.

Except that first one was personal and the most difficult of all for him to accept.

The faces of those lost haunted his dreams at night, but none more so than his brother, David, who'd died after a shootout with the Gestapo in Munich. Michael blamed himself for David's death, and the memories of burying him in the pouring rain consumed him now as he dug.

Sometimes, he would have full-blown conversations with his dead brother, but those moments were usually when he was alone and wracked with guilt.

David didn't appear today, but Michael felt his presence, and it comforted him as they laid Henk to rest.

Once the sodden soil was replaced on top of Henke's body, all the men took turns to say something to their fallen brother and comrade.

Once they'd finished, Jeroen turned to Michael. "Is there anything you would like to say?" he asked.

Without hesitation, Michael clasped his hands together and recited the same prayer he'd spoken at David's grave after he'd laid him to rest. The others bowed their heads as he began to speak.

Our Father, who art in heaven,
hallowed be thy name;
thy kingdom come;
thy will be done;

on earth as it is in heaven.
Give us this day our daily bread.
And forgive us our trespasses,
as we forgive those who trespass against us.
And lead us not into temptation;
but deliver us from evil.
For thine is the kingdom,
the power and the glory,
for ever and ever.
Amen.

"Amen," the others replied in unison.

After a final, long look at Henk's resting place, Michael turned and silently followed the others back to the farmhouse.

Chapter 25

A hot bath worked wonders for Michael's fatigued body. He lay in it until the water went cold, enjoying the solitude and using the time to plan his next move, which would be to get Senta safely to the rendezvous with the Lysander the next evening.

The consequences of failure were too great to consider, so he was determined that, come what may, he was making it to that aeroplane with Senta.

Although not a perfect fit, Henk's clean clothes fit well enough, and while he felt uncomfortable about wearing them, he didn't have any other choice. His own clothes were torn, filthy, and beyond salvage.

The welcome smell of potatoes boiling on the stove wafted into his nostrils. He hadn't realised how hungry he was, but now his stomach rumbled and groaned.

Finishing dressing quickly, he ran down the stairs to join everyone at the kitchen table and stepped back in surprise when he saw Senta's and Elske's new looks; he had to look twice to make sure it was them.

Senta's long blonde hair had gone, replaced by a neck-length brown that altered her looks completely. At seventeen, she retained her youthful appearance, and her deep blue eyes still reminded Michael of Mina, but someone searching for Senta Postner would never recognise her in her new guise.

Gerrit had done a magnificent job on her, and if Michael had to look twice to recognise her, the Germans would have no chance.

Elske too, looked completely different. Her shoulder-length brown hair had changed to black and was cut to just below her ears. Gerrit had styled it with her parting over her left eye, and although not as flattering as her natural look, she wasn't easily recognisable.

Elske was more at risk, because some of the senior Nazis who frequented the Atlanta Hotel knew her quite well, but as long as she stayed away from them, her new identity should hold.

"You both look amazing," Michael said approvingly. "You did a great job, Gerrit."

"Thank you," Gerrit replied. "I called it the Henk look in respect for Elske's brother."

Michael bowed his head. Words weren't necessary, because he knew exactly how they were feeling, even if they were holding it in very well.

"What name do you have, Senta?" he asked. "If we're stopped, I'll need to know who I am travelling with."

"My name is Johanna Visser, and I'm an eighteen-year-old Dutch girl working for you as an interpreter."

Michael bowed his head in approval. As a Wehrmacht officer repairing critical transportation hubs, a Dutch translator would be useful, so her alias was perfect if they were stopped by a German patrol.

He didn't ask Elske, because the less he knew about her, the safer it was for all of them.

A plateful of boiled potatoes was thrust in front of him, which he received gratefully. His stomach groaned at the sight, and he relished the thought of devouring every single morsel.

Rations were scarce in occupied Europe, and luxuries like butter and meats were a rare luxury, so Michael was more than happy when Geert produced a slab of butter big enough for all of them to enjoy.

"Don't ask where I got it from, so I won't have to tell you any lies," Geert announced after grabbing a forkful and throwing it onto his plate.

Nobody spoke while they ate, and once they were finished, they worked together to wash the dishes and clean up the kitchen.

Everyone had a full stomach, fatigue soon set in. They'd been on the go flat out for twenty-four hours, and they were feeling it. Jeroen stood up, taking charge of the small group of brave men and women.

"Today is a day we can celebrate, because not only have we rid Rotterdam of the evil stain of SS Standartenführer Karl Schneider, but we also rescued Senta, who will prove vital to our eventual victory over the Nazis."

He looked around at the faces staring back at him. None of them shone with the afterglow of success; the price had been high.

Perhaps too high.

"The cost of our success has been high," Jeroen continued. "Losing Henk is a tragedy from which we will never recover, but we cannot allow his loss to distract from what lies ahead. We must continue striking the enemy at every opportunity, no matter the cost to ourselves and our loved ones."

Nodding heads and garbled sounds followed his words, and Michael felt even more respect for the Dutch resistance leader than before. What he was saying was true, but the words didn't come easy. Truth never did.

"Rescuing Senta was vital for not just us, but for everyone in the world who rejects Hitler and his fascist ideologies. The tragic losses we saw on the train will serve as a reminder that until we defeat them, the violence against our people will never stop. Our sacrifices will continue to grow, but eventually we will overcome the fascist stench and regain our freedom."

"And when we do, we will remember everyone who has fallen at the hands of our great enemy." Gerrit spoke up, raising his coffee mug in a toast to the fallen.

"To Henk and the countless other brave souls who died today, so we can be free." Jeroen offered a toast, which everyone accepted and raised their mugs.

"It won't end there, either," Jeroen continued. "Our victories today will not go unpunished. The Nazis will retaliate with brutality to both punish and frighten us into submission, but we will never surrender, no matter the cost. We can't, because if we do, we will never walk the streets in freedom again."

Jeroen sat down, his words echoing around the room as if amplified. There was no doubt that the road ahead would be troubled and bloody, but they could not lose sight of the end goal, which was the ultimate defeat of Hitler and his Nazis.

"We are all tired, yet we still have much to discuss," Jeroen continued from his chair. "I propose that we rest for the afternoon and meet here later tonight to discuss what we are going to do next, because believe me, the reprisals will be swift as well as brutal."

Nobody objected, and Michael was fast asleep as soon as his head hit the pillow.

Chapter 26

Back in Rotterdam, the effects of Rauter's orders were felt almost immediately. SS and Gestapo units, backed by regular Wehrmacht soldiers, began conducting raids across the city. Doors were kicked in, and families torn apart as suspected resistance members were dragged from their homes.

In the working-class neighbourhood of Crooswijk, a terrified woman clutched her young son to her chest as SS men ransacked their small apartment. Her husband, a dock worker with loose connections to the resistance, had been snatched from his bed after working a night shift.

"Please," she begged, her voice trembling. "We've done nothing wrong. Where are you taking him?"

The SS officer in charge, a hard-faced man with cold eyes, barely spared her a glance. "Your husband is a traitor. You are lucky you aren't being arrested with him."

As the sun set over Rotterdam, an eerie quiet settled over the city. The usual bustle of evening activity was replaced by the sound of military vehicles patrolling the streets and the occasional burst of gunfire in the distance.

In a small, nondescript farmhouse twenty miles outside the city, Jeroen sat huddled around a radio with Michael and the other members of the resistance cell. They listened in grim silence as a Dutch collaborator read out the new restrictions imposed by the occupation authorities.

"A curfew is now in effect from eight pm to six am," the announcer's voice crackled through the radio. "Anyone found on the streets during these hours without proper authorisation will be subject to immediate arrest."

Jeroen clicked off the radio, his face a mask of determination. He translated the message for Michael.

"They're scared," he said quietly. "This proves we've struck a real blow against them."

Michael nodded, but his expression remained troubled. "Yes, but at what cost? How many innocent people will suffer because of our actions?"

Jeroen placed a hand on Michael's shoulder, his voice firm but compassionate. "We knew there would be reprisals. It's the nature of the fight. But remember why we're doing this—for freedom, for our country, for all those who can't fight back themselves."

As the resistance members contemplated their next move, the streets of Rotterdam echoed with the sound of jackboots and the cries of the innocent.

Chapter 27

Early the next morning, SS-Obergruppenführer Hanns Albin Rauter sat at his desk, concentrating on the report his aide had just handed to him. It was the passenger list for all those aboard the derailed train, and Rauter studied it carefully, noting the highlighted names as he ran his finger down the list.

Nothing stood out to him, so he turned to the typed notes at the end of the report that had been written by the officer Rauter had handpicked to lead the investigation.

SS-Obersturmführer Erich Falken was a career SD officer based in The Hague that Rauter trusted implicitly. He had an exemplary record in leading sensitive political investigations, and a long history of friendship and trust with Rauter. Falken was renowned for his attention to detail, and had a reputation for picking up on minor details lesser men would easily miss.

If anyone could get to the bottom of why the train was derailed, Falken was the man who would do it.

He picked up Falken's report.

On the face of things, the passenger list does not reveal anyone that appears important to the Dutch resistance. The list is mainly men and women who have demonstrated their resistance to the Reich by their actions. None caused us any significant harm, and none were suspected of being of any importance.

Upon further inspection, an interesting, and presumed overlooked name came up. There was a situation a year or so back when a suspected British spy who is well known in the Fatherland escaped with the help of a German girl from Bavaria.

The spy's name is Michael Fernsby, and the girl who helped him was Mina Postner. Their family was proven to be traitors to the Reich, and although the parents were apprehended, the two sisters escaped Germany.

They emerged in Rotterdam, where Mina Postner made radio broadcasts, spreading lies and propaganda against the Führer. Fernsby was known to be in Rotterdam during the occupation, and it is believed the two worked together before Fernsby escaped yet again.

Postner and her sister, Senta, were about to be arrested by Sturmbannführer Albert Kreise when he was tragically killed. We believe it was Fernsby who killed him in order to protect the two German girls.

Interestingly, the passenger list contained the name of Senta Postner, who, if the name is correct, is one of the two sisters who escaped with Fernsby.

While the inclusion of Senta Postner's name does not prove anything, it is surely beyond coincidence that her name appears on the manifest of the train that was derailed by a resistance unit suspected to be led by Jeroen, who we know had close ties with both Fernsby and the Postner sisters.

There was no sign of Postner at the scene of the derailment, but several passengers told us they saw a blonde-haired girl leaving the scene with the group that attacked the train.

They also told us that one of the attackers spoke in English, which leads me to my initial conclusion that Fernsby was involved, as well as Jeroen.

We do not yet know why Senta Postner is so important to the resistance, and we can safely assume that if Fernsby was involved, then she is important to the British as well.

I believe that if we can establish why the girl is so important to them, we will discover the true reason for the derailment. For some reason, Senta Postner is considered vital to the Dutch and British, and we need to find out why.

It is too early to conclude if the derailment and the earlier car bombing at the Hotel Atlanta are connected, but it is my firm belief that they are.

I'll provide a more detailed report as soon as I have more information.

SS-Obersturmführer Erich Falken.

Rauter put the report down and clasped his hands together, deep in thought.

Fernsby! He knew that name. Heydrich himself raged at the mere mention of the man. If Fernsby was involved, then it was more imperative than ever that the perpetrators were caught quickly and interrogated.

Michael Fernsby, the hated British spy, wasn't getting away this time. Even if he had to round up and kill every resistance member in Holland, it would be worth it.

Chapter 28

The shrill ring of the telephone interrupted Rauter's thoughts. He glared at it, and for a moment considered ignoring it. Deciding against it, he grabbed the handset and snatched it from the cradle.

"Rauter," he snapped.

"Good morning, Obergruppenführer Hanns Rauter."

Rauter's face turned ashen at the sound of the all too familiar icy cold voice on the other end of the line. Of all the senior Nazis he dealt with, Reinhard Heydrich was the most fearsome of them all. One small misstep could bring about untold agonies and even death to anyone that crossed him.

Rauter hated dealing with the Blond Beast as he was known, although nobody dared utter those words in his presence.

"Good morning, Obergruppenführer Heydrich. I'm sure you've heard about the incident yesterday morning in Rotterdam, that was followed by a train derailment?" Rauter got straight to the point.

"I'm aware. I can tell you that the Führer is furious,

and he's demanding immediate retribution. Tell me what happened, Obergruppenführer."

Rauter cringed at the thought of Hitler ranting about the assassination of SS Standartenführer Karl Schneider the previous morning. He knew that heads would roll, and he was determined it wouldn't be his own on the chopping block.

"That's why I requested a call to you, Obergruppenführer. I have an update that I thought you might find interesting."

"I'm waiting."

Rauter gathered himself together and spoke rapidly into the mouthpiece.

"Rotterdam has been locked down. Nobody can come in or out without our express permission, and all known and suspected resistance members are being rounded up as we speak. We think we know who was behind the bombing, and we'll have them in custody very soon."

"I hear it was the work of the one they call Jeroen. Is this correct?"

Rauter looked up to the heavens. *How does he know this already? I'm supposed to be the only one who reports directly to him.*

Clearly, Heydrich had spies everywhere.

"Our initial investigations lead us to that conclusion, Obergruppenführer. We'll know for sure when we have him and his people in custody, but all the signs point to him."

"Did he have help from anyone else?"

Heydrich was fishing, waiting for verification that the British spy was involved.

"We believe he was helped by someone else, Obergruppenführer Heydrich." Rauter swallowed, knowing how angry the mere mention of Fernsby's name made him.

"We believe he was helped by the British spy, Michael Fernsby."

The silence was deafening.

"There's more, Obergruppenführer." Rauter swallowed hard. "I received a report this morning from a trusted source regarding the train derailment."

"Are they linked?"

"We believe they are, sir. Not only that, I believe we know who they were trying to rescue. Questions still remain as to why this person is so important to them, but I'm sure we'll find out."

"Who is it?"

"Senta Postner, Obergruppenführer Heydrich. She and her sister are known associates of Fernsby."

"I want your trusted source in my office first thing tomorrow morning, and I want a full personal briefing. I know who it is, so make sure it is this person you send. In the meantime, I want updates as soon as they happen. Send them via secure channels, and address them to me personally."

"Consider it done, Obergruppenführer Heydrich."

Heydrich was notoriously cautious when it came to matters of intelligence and secrecy. He never spoke about sensitive issues on open telephone lines, instead preferring to use trusted couriers or encrypted transmissions. Rauter knew this and had been expecting it.

"I want all of them in custody, Rauter, do you hear?" Heydrich's voice was raised, and Rauter could almost see the piercing blue eyes down the telephone line.

"I've allocated every resource we have to it, Obergruppenführer. We'll get them."

"There's a reason the girl is so important, and I want to know what it is."

"So do I, Obergruppenführer Heydrich. I will find out."

"Make sure you do."

The telephone line went dead. Rauter took a moment to gather himself before calling his aide into the office.

"Get Obersturmführer Erich Falken in here immediately. Tell him it is of the utmost importance."

The aide threw his arm in the air to acknowledge his orders.

"There's one more thing." Rauter glared at his aide. "I want my vehicle waiting for me outside as soon as I've seen Falken."

"I'll get on it immediately, Herr General. Shall I tell him where you are going?"

"We're going to Rotterdam."

Chapter 29

Gerrit ran the radio antenna out of the farmhouse window and transmitted the message Michael had encrypted to London. It was a risk, but a necessary one, as they needed to verify the coordinates for the Lysander aircraft pick-up later that evening.

Michael hovered, pacing around as Gerrit sent the transmission. This was perhaps the most risky time for the resistance group. The Germans were constantly monitoring the airways for signal transmissions, and it was accepted that a radio operator was one of the most dangerous jobs a resistance operator could undertake.

Unencrypted, Michael's message was simple and to the point. He read it again as they waited for a response from London.

Package is secured. Awaiting confirmation for collection. MF

The air crackled with intensity as they waited. Michael paced up and down behind Gerrit, barely able to contain the beating of his heart inside his chest.

He imagined Alison Turnberry running to Tony Sanders' office in the underground War Rooms with the transmission. Sanders was even now jumping into action, calling Dansey, and getting the Unit's RAF Lysander to give the go-ahead for the evacuation later that evening.

All that would take time, and each second seemed like a lifetime to Michael and Gerrit. Michael hardly dared breathe, such was the intensity of the moment.

Fifteen minutes passed. Then thirty. At forty-five, Michael couldn't take it anymore. He was about to go outside for some fresh air when the radio burst into life. Gerrit wrote down the message, his hand skating across the page as he formed each coded word.

When he finished, he handed Michael a piece of text that meant nothing to anyone, especially the Germans. Michael was the only one who could decipher the message, and he ran to his room to do it as quickly and securely as he could.

Gerrit waited by the radio set in case Michael needed to send a confirmation that he'd received his orders.

Michael closed the door and grabbed the codebook from one of the hidden pockets inside his battered rucksack. He spread the message on his bed and scanned the page.

QXGTC F ZK. IVZSLRVX XFGV BO VM TXVVIYYMZ QYBMRQZRXBQI BX 02PZ. JU YPVT OPEZ ZZV 15 UYMHMWPM, VXJ XMYZ IY QTX VFQ PNE VFF MTC ZOXA. PQL EFF KYZGRD BMB JOZXQ, OTV SFR ALZWXSE SOAD YH VJZZ NMDHX TLUSFYSZ.

Using the onetime pad, he decoded the message one syllable at a time. When he'd finished, he looked at the orders that had come from Sanders and Dansey.

Operation a go. Lysander will be at the following coordinates at 2am. It will wait 15 mins before leaving. If not there, extract the package by any means necessary.

Evasion

A series of map coordinates ended the message, so Michael ran to the living room, where a map of the area was pinned to the wall.

"Well?" Jeroen asked impatiently. "Is it a go?"

"I need to find these coordinates." Michael showed the message to Jeroen, who took it to the map and helped Michael find the location Sanders was sending the Lysander to.

What they found was a field near a small town called Polsbroekerdam, which was a little less than twenty miles from their location.

"Tell them we'll be there," Jeroen said.

Michael encoded his reply, and he checked it over before handing it to Gerrit for transmission.

Orders confirmed. Will be there.

Gerrit turned the radio off and went outside to retrieve the antenna wire. Michael returned to the living room and spoke to the gathered resistance group, waiting with bated breath to hear what London had to say.

"The extraction is a go. The RAF is picking Senta and myself up at two am tomorrow in a field about twenty miles from here."

He looked at Senta. "We will be on that plane, Senta, and I promise you I'll return to find Mina and somehow get her back to England. You know my feelings for her, and I won't rest until I find her."

"We'll find her." Jeroen spoke up from the back of the room. "We can't stay here much longer anyway, so after you've gone, we'll pack up and move somewhere else. While the rest of us do that, I'll find Mina and bring her back here, so she'll be waiting for you when you return."

"You'll do that for us?" Michael asked, genuinely surprised. "That's a lot to ask, especially as there is a huge price on your head."

"That's why I'm doing it," Jeroen answered. "I don't have long left, and it's the least I can do after all the help you and the sisters have given me."

Michael grabbed Jeroen's arm, and they grasped each other for a long moment. No words were spoken because none were necessary.

Chapter 30

A low murmur filled the dimly lit communications room in the basement of the SD headquarters in Rotterdam. A few desks down, an SS radioman on direction finding, or DF duties as it was known, stiffened, his headphones suddenly bursting with static.

The faintest trace of a signal cut through the interference, but it was just enough to catch his attention. He quickly scribbled some notes, marking down the frequency.

The message, whatever it was, was sent with speed and precision. Thirty seconds and it was over. But it was enough for the radio operator to lock onto.

The operator jumped up, signalling to his superior sitting at the desk at the front of the room.

"Herr Obersturmführer, I intercepted a brief transmission." He held his arm in the air while he shouted out the bearings.

The Obersturmführer, following the strict new orders passed down from none other than SS-Obergruppenführer Hanns Albin Rauter, grabbed the paper from the radioman and narrowed his eyes at the hastily scribbled notes.

"Has it been picked up elsewhere?" he asked.

"Likely, sir. The signal is strong enough," the radioman responded, his expression tense.

The Obersturmführer nodded, then reached for the telephone on his desk. He dialled the number for the special operations room set up to deal with the recent bombing and train derailment. As the line connected, he straightened in his chair.

"This is Obersturmführer Landers. We've intercepted a transmission here in Rotterdam. We need to know if other DF units in The Hague and Amsterdam picked it up during the transmission."

The voice on the other end was immediately alert. "Understood. Give me the bearings, and we'll confirm triangulation as soon as possible."

Landers knew that at least two other DF units needed to have picked up the signal so that triangulation could be performed.

In the special operation room set up in the SS headquarters at the seized City Hall, SS-Obersturmführer Erik Stadtler, who was in charge of the operation on the direct orders of SS-Obergruppenführer Rauter, felt the heat rise on his flushed cheeks.

Finally! The resistance had made a mistake. Stadtler bit his bottom lip as his mind whirred at a hundred miles per hour.

He paced up and down while he waited for the triangulation results. Within minutes, confirmation would come through, narrowing the search area.

He composed himself, closed the door to his office, and reached for the telephone. Then he dialled the number for SS-Obergruppenführer Rauter.

Evasion

"Sir," he spoke calmly, in complete contrast to how he felt inside. His innards jumped all over his body, and he forced back the urge to throw up.

"Do we have a breakthrough?" Rautin asked.

"It appears we may have, sir. So far, none of the captured resistance members have been able to give us any information regarding the bombing or the derailment, but my men have located the valet who was working the garage when the bomb went off. He will know more, I'm sure of it."

"He's here?" Rauter asked.

"He was picked up in Amsterdam early this morning, sir. He, and everyone in the house he was hiding in, have been arrested and are on the way here as we speak."

"Make sure he tells you where Jeroen and Fernsby are hiding. I want them arrested and brought before me."

"Yes, sir. I'll break him personally as soon as he gets here."

"Good. Is that all?"

"No, sir. There is more."

"Well?"

"One of the radio operators in Rotterdam picked up a radio message a few minutes ago. It was heavily encoded, and we believe it was sent by Fernsby to London. It has to be somewhere close by, and I have a team working on the triangulation right now. As long as other DF units picked up the signal, we'll be able to locate them."

"Good work, Stadtler. Let me know the instant you get the triangulation results. I have Wehrmacht, SS, and Gestapo units on standby, ready to leave at a moment's notice under your command. Fernsby and Jeroen are not to be harmed, at least not until I speak to them personally before anyone else does."

"I understand, Obergruppenführer. I'll call as soon as we get the triangulation results."

Stadtler sat back in his chair, his hands clasped together behind his head.

Chapter 31

Late in the afternoon, Sjoerd Koopman tilted his head to the side at the sound of approaching vehicles. Apart from the occasional truck or car driving either in or out of the nearby town of Schoonhoven, his rural farm was a haven for peace and tranquillity.

Although only twenty miles from Rotterdam, he'd rarely seen or heard any German patrols in the area, and if it weren't for the radio broadcasts and the Luftwaffe pounding the city with bombs before his beloved country surrendered, he and his family would have never known there was a war on.

Sjoerd shrugged and returned to his primary concern of the day, which was fixing the wobbly wheel on his hay cart.

A few seconds later, he stopped again, this time paying more attention. The sounds of the approaching vehicles were getting louder, and although the main road to Schoonhoven was close by, he could tell by the dust in the air that the vehicles were heading up the narrow lane leading to his farm.

Koopman dropped his tools and ran to the house he shared with his wife and adult son. His brother, an accountant from Amsterdam, and his wife were also staying with them to help out during these difficult times.

At forty-nine years old, Sjoerd Koopman was strong and healthy, reflecting a life of hard manual labour on the farm. At seventeen, his son, also named Sjoerd after his father and grandfather before him, was the spitting image of his father, and he too, bore the signs of a hard life as a farmer.

Sjoerd reached the rest of the family in the kitchen as the lead vehicle entered the farmyard.

"Quick!" he yelled at all four as they huddled around a radio set. "The Germans are here! Get rid of that radio now."

"What do the Germans want with us?" Maria, Sjoerd's wife asked. Her face was pale, and Sjoerd's breath hitched as he saw the concern lining her face.

Sjoerd threw his hands in the air. "I don't know, but whatever it is, it won't be good."

Bastiaan Koopman, the younger and wiser brother of Sjoerd, snatched the radio and hid it in a cupboard behind a row of pots and pans.

The family had no sooner reached the living room when a loud rap on the front door sent their pulses racing. Sjoerd took a deep breath and looked at his frightened family. They'd all heard the stories of how the Nazis treated the locals if they suspected any of them were helping the resistance.

"Everything will be alright. We're not part of the resistance, so just do as they say, and they'll leave us alone."

A second, more violent bang on the door grabbed Sjoerd's full attention, and he gulped for air one last time before opening it. Four or five men wearing field-grey uniforms shoved the door open, knocking Sjoerd backwards. The soldiers rushed past and began searching the farmhouse, their weapons ready to fire at the first sign of any resistance.

"Sjoerd Koopman?" A soldier appeared after the initial rush with three more surrounding him. Although he was wearing the same field-grey uniform, Sjoerd got a closer look at the insignia on his collar.

He gulped again when he recognised the distinctive SS insignia. These were not Wehrmacht soldiers—they were the SS.

"I won't ask again. Are you Sjoerd Koopman?" The officer, clearly in charge of the operation, whatever it was, stood impatiently, his deep blue eyes penetrating Sjoerd's feeble defences.

"Y-Yes, sir. I am he."

A soldier said something in German that Sjoerd didn't understand. The officer in charge, a slender man of average height and in his late thirties, pointed towards the living room.

"Go," he ordered.

Sjoerd did as he was told. His heart skipped a beat when he saw his wife and son clinging to each other on the couch, their faces drawn and their eyes wide with fear and dread.

Bastiaan and his wife, Neeltje, sat together in a single armchair, their arms wrapped around each other.

Bastiaan's white knuckles demonstrated the tension everyone was feeling. At least eight soldiers surrounded them, making the already small living room seem incredibly cramped.

Two more joined them and said something in German. Both Bastiaan and Neeltje spoke German, but nobody else did.

"Is there anyone else here?" the lead officer asked, with a sneer that sent shivers all the way to Sjoerd's toes.

"No, sir. We are all that is here."

"It will be better for you if you tell us the truth. My men are searching your farm, and if they find anyone else, they—and you—will be killed. So, I'll ask again. Is there anyone else here?"

"We are all that is here." Sjoerd's voice trembled, but he held himself together for the sake of his family.

The SS men spoke in German. Bastiaan listened, blinking hard when he realised what they were searching for.

Sjoerd too, understood what the SS were searching for. One word they'd spoken was understood by all, and all of them prayed silently as the realisation sank in as to why the SS were there.

Jeroen!

Everyone knew that name. It was the name of hope for the Dutch people of Rotterdam and its surrounding areas. It was a name synonymous with resistance and victory.

It was also a name that brought fear by association.

Nobody spoke for several minutes, a tactic Sjoerd was convinced was deliberate to intimidate them even more. It worked, because Maria sobbed gently on his shoulder.

The sight of his wife so scared forced the fear from Sjoerd's body. It was replaced with anger and a new boldness to stand up to the Nazis and show them that he wasn't scared.

He was, but he wasn't going to give them the satisfaction of showing it.

"What do you want with us?" he asked, breaking the silence.

"I think you know why we're here," the officer in

charge replied. "We're looking for someone, and we think you know where he is."

"Who?" Sjoerd asked. "We're hard-working, innocent farmers. Everyone who lives here is present in this room right now. So, whoever it is you are searching for, he isn't here."

"Allow me to introduce myself." The SS officer stepped forward, his granite features glowering in the late afternoon gloom. "My name is SS-Obersturmführer Erik Stadtler, and I have been tasked with finding a man known as Jeroen. I'm sure you've heard of him, and we believe he is here. So, make it easy on yourselves and tell us where he is."

The Koopman family glanced at each other, their faces drawn with trepidation.

"We know the name," Bastiaan spoke up. "Everyone in Holland does. But we've never seen him, and he's never been here.

"I thought you'd say that," Stadtler answered. "That is most unfortunate. Perhaps I can convince you to remember where he is before I am forced to hurt you."

The Germans spoke amongst themselves, but Stadtler's eyes never left the Koopman family. He was clearly enjoying the terror his words had provoked.

Chapter 32

"You are aquatinted with the Hoogland family?" It was more of an accusation than a question.

Sjoerd tensed his shoulders, trying to control the dread rising in the pit of his stomach.

"Of course. They own a farm not far from here. We help each other out from time to time, and we meet up for drinks now and again in the evenings."

The SS men glared at Sjoerd, their faces set in stone. Stadtler nodded slightly.

"Good. Now that we've established that you know each other, tell me what you discussed when you met for drinks?"

"We talked about farm equipment, and how we could help each other." Sjoerd sat upright, frustrated at the pointless questions. "What does that have to do with anything?"

"We paid them a visit before we came here." Stadtler's expression changed. His eyes narrowed, the corners of his lips turned downward in a snarl.

"In fact, we paid several farms and households a visit. You are the last ones on our list."

Evasion

"What do you want from us?" Sjoerd struggled to stop his voice from shaking. "We're not involved with the resistance, and there's nobody here except us."

"I'm tired of your lies," Stadtler shouted the words. "Your friends had to be persuaded, but they told us what you discussed over drinks, and it wasn't farm equipment!"

The last sentence was virtually screamed. Spittle foamed at his mouth, and at that moment, Stadtler was the most frightening man Sjoerd had ever encountered.

"I-I don't know what you're talking about," Sjoerd stammered. "I swear, that's all we talked about. We're not involved with the resistance. I beg you to believe me."

Stadtler nodded at his men stood behind the couch. Two of them grabbed Bastiaan by the hair and neck and threw him onto the floor. They stood over him, menacing and threatening in a way Sjoerd had never seen before in his entire life.

"Stop this madness," he pleaded. "I swear to you, we are not involved with the resistance."

Sjoerd was careful not to make any mention of Jeroen's name, so he wouldn't antagonise the Nazis any more than they already were.

Stadtler ignored Sjoerd and stood over Bastiaan.

"Does your brother know what you were up to with the Hooglands? Didn't you ever tell him what you were doing here?"

Bastiaan's face was pure white, his eyes as wide as a teacup. He glanced at Sjoerd before turning back to look up at Stadtler.

"They told us everything," Stadtler sneered. "They told us that you stored weapons here for Jeroen, and you used your vehicles to smuggle him in and out of Rotterdam."

Stadtler glowered down at Bastiaan. "You did all this,

risking the lives of your brother and his family, and didn't even tell them? What kind of brother are you?"

Bastiaan missed the slight tilt of Stadtler's head. They all did. He screamed as the butt of a machine gun smashed down on his nose, shattering bone, and showering the family with blood.

Maria and Neeltje screamed at the sight, and Sjoerd shrank back in shock. His son trembled beside him and, for a moment, an anger the likes of which he'd never known rose inside Sjoerd.

He quickly suppressed it, because there was nothing he could do against the SS thugs who were terrorising his family. In any case, he didn't believe a word they were saying.

Another SS man grabbed Bastiaan's right hand and lifted it into the air.

"I'll ask this only once," Stadtler said, his voice menacing. "Tell me where Jeroen is and spare your family. That's the only choice you have."

Bastiaan's cloudy eyes glanced at his brother, who stared back in fear and defeat.

"I don't know what your talk—"

He never finished his sentence. The SS officer holding his hand jerked back his little finger, snapping it with a sickening crack. Bastiaan howled, sending Sjoerd and his family into fits of uncontrollable sobs.

"That's enough," Neeltje pleaded through clenched teeth. "Please stop. For the love of God, please stop."

"Tell me where Jeroen is, and we'll stop. It's really that simple." Stadtler spoke as if he was in casual conversation.

Sjoerd rose from his seat, but he was shoved roughly back down again. The SS officer grabbed Bastiaan's wrist, ready to continue the torture.

"Believe me, it gets far worse than this," Stadtler threatened.

Bastiaan clenched his teeth, but didn't say anything. The SS officer grabbed his index finger.

"Stop!" Neeltje screamed. "I'll tell you where Jeroen is if you stop hurting him."

Stadtler nodded at the SS officer, who relaxed his grip.

"I'm waiting," Stadtler said.

"Promise you won't hurt him anymore."

SS-Obersturmführer Stadtler stared at Neeltje for a long moment. Sjoerd watched, unable to believe what he was witnessing.

"He won't suffer any more pain if you tell us where Jeroen is," Stadtler said finally, his eyes never leaving Neeltje's.

"Don't do it," Bastiaan croaked.

Tears dropped onto Neeltje's blouse, and she bowed her head in dismay. After a few moments, she raised her head high and glared defiantly at Stadtler.

"What I am about to do, I do for my family. Let Bastiaan go, and I'll tell you."

Stadtler nodded his head at the SS men holding him down.

"Speak," Stadtler ordered.

"Jeroen is hiding at Geert's farm on Bovenberg, across the field from here." Neeltje's voice cracked as she spoke, but she held Stadtler's gaze throughout.

"You'll show us where." Stadtler turned to his SS men. "Grab her."

Two SS men grabbed Neeltje and hauled her to her feet. She neither complained nor resisted.

The men dragged Neeltje out towards the vehicles waiting outside. Stadtler barked his orders to the remaining SS men.

"Take this one. I'll question him myself once we've got Jeroen." He pointed to Bastiaan, who was almost unconscious with pain.

"The rest?" One of the SS men asked.

"Kill them."

The SS officers opened fire.

Chapter 33

Geert threw a handful of papers into the metal barrel and soaked them with paraffin oil. Elske handed him the map from the living room wall, and he added that to the growing pile of incriminating evidence that had to be destroyed before they could leave the farm for good.

They rolled the barrel to the doorway of the barn so they were just inside in case it started raining again, and threw more paraffin oil onto the map.

Arjen stood by with another handful of papers, and they all stood back as Geert threw a lighted match into the metal barrel.

The inferno roared into life, and Geert stoked the fire as Arjen added his armful of notes. Elske left to check for anything else that needed to be destroyed.

"Where are we going?" Arjen asked. "I'll be sorry to leave this place. It's been home for all of my life."

"We'll be back when it's safe," Geert reassured his younger brother. "We've been here too long already, and it's time to move on before the Nazis find out that Jeroen has been here."

"So, where are we going?"

Geert laughed and prodded Arjen. "Somewhere safe. I'll tell you when we're on the road."

Arjen shrugged and prodded the fire with a stick he'd found propped up at the side of the barn door.

A rumbling sound caught Geert's attention, and he poked his head outside to see what it was. An army truck and three smaller vehicles were driving along Bovenberg, the main road that connected the farm with the outside world.

Geert squinted, trying to get a better look at the vehicles. They were approaching the area where the farm was located, but there was no cause for concern.

There were several small farms along Bovenberg, and the junction at the end of the road connected with Schoonhoven, so it wasn't unusual for vehicles to pass them by on their way in and out of town.

What was unusual was the fact that these were military vehicles, and from the look of them, they weren't Dutch. An uneasy feeling spread through Geert's body, and he poured more paraffin on the burning documents to hurry their destruction.

The lead vehicle turned into the farmhouse lane, and at the sight of this, Geert's pulse quickened.

"Quick!" he yelled at Arjen. "The Nazis are here. Go grab Elske and get to the hiding place."

"What about you?" Arjen looked scared, but there was no time to waste.

"I'll be right behind you. Go now."

Arjen ran to the farmhouse, leaving Geert to watch for the approaching Nazis and stall for time if he had to. They had rehearsed this a hundred times in preparation for a Nazi raid, and he knew Elske and Arjen would be well hidden by the time the first vehicle pulled to a stop.

During the initial occupation, Geert and Gerrit had constructed a safe room behind a false wall in what used to be a storeroom at the rear of the house. The Germans would never know it was there, and he heaved a sigh of relief when Arjen disappeared out of sight.

Geert turned his attention to the approaching vehicles that were now too close for him to be able to join Elske and Arjen in the safe room.

His thoughts drifted to Jeroen and Gerrit, who were enroute, with Michael and Senta in the truck, to the rendezvous with the British aeroplane later that evening.

Thank God they're not here.

The silence was deafening when the vehicles ground to a halt in the farmyard and they killed their engines. Geert furiously poked at the burning mass of papers in the barrel, hoping they were completely destroyed before the Nazis got their hands on them.

The door of the lead vehicle opened, and a man wearing an immaculately pressed field-grey uniform stepped out. Geert immediately noticed the SS insignia on his collar, and he gulped down a lungful of air to calm the butterflies raging in the pit of his stomach as the man approached.

Chapter 34

A dozen SS men jumped out of the truck, some running to the farmhouse and others towards the barn. They kicked over the barrel and stamped on the papers, trying to put out the fire.

Geert looked down in satisfaction as the papers turned into ash before him. Whatever the Nazis were hoping to find, they wouldn't find it there.

Two SS men grabbed Geert and forced him to his knees. He watched as the man in charge beckoned towards the truck, and closed his eyes in horror when he saw who they dragged out of it.

Neeltje! How did they find her?

Neeltje's face was swollen and red. She didn't make eye contact, but Geert knew she'd been beaten into submission. They'd all heard the stories of how cruel the SS were, and his stomach cramped as he realised he was about to find out for himself how true it was.

"Who are you?" Geert spoke calmly, in contrast to the fear inside him. "What do you want with us?"

Evasion

"What were you burning?" the SS officer in charge stared at Geert, his cold blue eyes penetrating his soul.

"Just some old papers I was clearing out. Why are you here?" Geert asked again.

A rifle butt smashed into his midriff, knocking him face first into the dirt in agony. He gasped for breath and grasped at his stomach, shockwaves spreading through his body.

"I'll ask the questions," the SS officer snarled. "What were you burning?"

"Just some old papers," Geert gasped, struggling for air.

The SS officer turned to Neeltje. "Is this Jeroen?"

Neeltje shook her head. "No. That's Geert. He owns this farm."

"Where is Jeroen?" The SS officer reached down and grabbed Geert by the hair.

"I don't know Jeroen. I've never seen him, and I don't know where he is."

Neeltje screwed her eyes tight together at Geert's words and looked away.

Two SS men yanked Geert back to his knees before the officer in command.

"My name is SS-Obersturmführer Stadtler, and I have neither the time nor the patience for your games. I know Jeroen is hiding here, and I know you are a part of the resistance unit that murdered my SS colleague and derailed the train yesterday morning."

Stadtler stepped forward and grabbed Geert's jaw. "You can either tell me where he is or die. I don't care either way."

He stepped back and kicked Geert hard in the groin, sending white-hot pain shooting through his body. He lurched forward, but the SS men held him firm.

"Well?" Stadtler asked. "Where is he?"

There was no point denying it, so Geert gathered what was left of his courage and stared up at the evil man before him.

"Jeroen isn't here. He left earlier today, and I don't know where he is. He moves around a lot, and he's gone."

Stadtler's face turned bright red. "I don't believe you. Is the British spy with him? Who else is he with?"

Geert stared back defiantly and said nothing.

The two SS men holding him let go, and as he fell to the floor, they launched into him with rifle butts and feet.

Geert lost consciousness, but awoke with a start when a bucket of water was thrown over his face. Agony immediately engulfed him, and he yearned for the darkness to come back and claim him.

"Where are the rest of your group?" Stadtler asked.

Geert shook his head.

The SS men attacked again. In his semi-conscious state, Geert heard Neeltje crying and pleading for them to stop.

"There's nobody in the house, Obersturmführer," said one of the SS men who'd raided the house. "What would you like us to do?"

"Did you search it for any evidence?" Stadtler asked.

"Jawohl, Obersturmführer. We've collected every piece of paper we could find."

"Good. Burn it to the ground."

"No!" Geert yelled through his broken jaw and cracked teeth. He knew Elske and Arjen were in there, but he wasn't telling the SS.

Stadtler grabbed Geert's hair again. "You are going to the SS headquarters where I will question you myself. You'll tell me everything I want to know, and by the time I'm finished with you, you'll be begging to die."

Evasion

Through his pain, Geert knew Stadtler wasn't lying. He closed his eyes and wished for death to come quickly.

Flames rose from the old farmhouse, and Geert watched in horror and dismay as he saw what was happening. He wanted to shout out, to save them, but he knew what fate awaited, and as horrid as it sounded, they were probably better off burning to death in there than they were facing torture and death at the hands of the SS.

Stadtler stood and watched the farmhouse burn as if some sixth sense told him the house was holding more secrets yet to be revealed. And he was right.

Fifteen minutes later, Elske and Arjen staggered out of the inferno, covered in soot, and gasping for oxygen.

"Who do we have here?" Stadtler asked. "Grab them!"

Neeltje, who was back in the truck, was dragged out again, and forced to her knees beside Geert.

"Now we have you all here, one of you will tell me where Jeroen is." Stadtler strode around them triumphantly.

Nobody spoke, but Stadtler looked twice at Elske. He ordered one of his men to clean her up, and after a bucket of water had been thrown over her head, he grabbed her jaw and inspected her face closely.

"You!" he yelled. "I know you. You look different, but you're one of the women who worked at the Atlanta Hotel. What's your name? Elske, that's it. We've been looking for you."

Elske spat on the floor, splattering Stadtler's feet with her spittle.

"Now we know which one of the workers planned the murder of Standartenführer Schneider. Perhaps you know where Jeroen is as well?"

Elske glared defiantly at Stadtler and said nothing.

"Your tongue will loosen by the time I've finished with you." Stadtler's face was beetroot red.

"Who are you?" he asked Arjen, who was on his knees next to Elske.

Arjen looked at Elske, who shook her head, telling him to remain quiet.

"I wouldn't listen to her if I were you," Stadtler yelled. "I won't ask you again."

"His name is Arjen," Neeltje shouted. "He is innocent in all of this. Please let him go."

Stadtler pulled his revolver from his holster and pointed it at Arjen. "Tell me where Jeroen is, or he dies."

"No!" Neeltje screamed. "He's not a part of this, I swear. He's Geert's younger brother, and that's all he is."

"Silence!" Stadtler ordered. "You say too much. Why don't one of you two say something?" He glared at Elske and Geert, daring them to remain silent.

They both stared straight ahead and said nothing. All of them knew the consequences of their involvement with Jeroen and the resistance, and they'd promised each other to say nothing, regardless of the repercussions.

"Last chance!" Stadtler screamed the words, his face a mask of fury.

Silence.

Tears streamed down Geert's broken face, and he closed his eyes so he wouldn't see what was happening. Elske sobbed next to him.

"Please, don't kill me," Arjen begged for his life. "Jeroen left earlier, but they wouldn't tell me where he was going."

"Who was he with?" Stadtler asked.

Arjen sobbed and trembled. "Fernsby, Senta, and Gerrit." His voice was high-pitched, and he struggled to get the words out.

"Stop, Arjen," Elske shouted. "Stop, or we die for nothing."

"Where did they go?" Stadtler asked.

"I swear I don't know," Arjen answered. "They didn't tell me."

Stadtler looked at Elske and Geert. "Last chance. Where are Jeroen and the British spy?"

Silence.

"What is so important about the German girl that you would go to all that trouble to rescue her?"

Silence.

Stadtler, his face flushed, aimed his pistol at Arjen's head and fired.

Chapter 35

The Mercedes L-3000 truck rumbled along the late afternoon back roads towards Polsbroekerdam and the remote field where they would prepare for the Lysander later that evening.

Michael and Senta sat in the back, behind several barrels full of diesel fuel. Jeroen and Gerrit travelled in the front of the truck, both wearing their Wehrmacht uniforms in case they were pulled over.

The noise in the back of the truck was too loud for conversation, so the two of them remained silent, deep in their own thoughts.

Daylight exposed the Wehrmacht truck too much for Michael's liking, and he constantly worried they'd be spotted at any moment. He couldn't wait for darkness, but that was hours away yet.

He was relieved not to be at the farmhouse any longer. Remaining static made him nervous, and he was glad to be on the move. Geert and Elske would make sure all evidence of their involvement with Jeroen and himself would be destroyed before they left for wherever their new hideout was going to be.

Michael didn't know where it was, and he didn't ask. It was safer that way.

His thoughts turned to Mina. Thoughts of seeing her again were the motivation to carry out his duties and stay alive, but he didn't know where she was or even if she was still alive.

For all he knew, the Gestapo could have arrested her, and she might even now be facing torture for information about her British boyfriend, the enemy of the Reich.

He didn't know, and his heart yearned to see her, to hold her, and to see that she was alive and healthy.

Senta too, worried about her sister, and Michael knew she carried the guilt of knowing that the British wanted only her and not both of them.

Michael caught Senta staring at him, and as he locked eyes with her, he couldn't help but see the resemblance to her older sister, even if her appearance was totally different now her hair was shorter and brown instead of blonde.

Her deep blue eyes still looked the same, and when he stared into them, he saw Mina, and for a moment, he was back in her arms in the apartment in Rotterdam before the Luftwaffe bombs destroyed it during the blitz a few weeks earlier.

Senta's face blushed at Michael's intense stare, and she looked away. Michael could see the worry on her face, and he knew that she too, was worried about Mina's safety.

"I'll find her," he shouted over the din of the truck. "If it's the last thing I ever do, I'll find her and get her to safety."

Senta nodded. She knew he meant it.

The truck slowed suddenly, dragging Michael's thoughts back to the here and now. He braced himself for the sound of German voices, and then relaxed as the truck took a sharp left turn and picked up speed again.

The canvas cover over the truck was fastened down, so neither Michael nor Senta could see where they were going. As a result, the slightest change to their speed worried them, and they exchanged nervous glances at the alteration in their direction.

A few minutes later, they slowed again, and Michael braced himself in case they'd been stopped. The truck made a right turn, and then another right turn almost immediately after.

Five minutes later, the truck lurched to the left, jerking violently from side to side. Michael and Senta grabbed hold of the sides of the truck so they wouldn't be thrown around like rag dolls.

The truck came to a stop, and the silence was deafening when the engine was turned off. Doors slammed, and Michael strained his ears to listen for any shouts or signs they'd been pulled over by a Nazi patrol.

Michael held his Walther PPK steady as someone opened the back of the truck, and he let out a sigh of relief when Jeroen's smiling face greeted them in the dismal early evening gloom.

He helped Senta out of the truck and jumped down. They were parked along a narrow, bumpy lane in the middle of a large copse of trees.

"Where are we?" he asked.

"Your aircraft will meet us here later tonight." Jeroen pointed through the trees. "For now, we wait until dark."

Chapter 36

Darkness came late, and Michael spent the time sitting on a branch up a tree, under heavy foliage, and planning his next move once he'd got Senta safely into the hands of Tony Sanders and Unit 317.

He daydreamed of a scenario where Sanders gave his blessing for Michael to be dropped back into Rotterdam so he could find Mina and whisk her back to his home in Sandwich, where she would be safe.

Reality bit, and he pulled a face as his vision crumbled in his mind.

"What are you thinking?" Senta asked, climbing to sit next to him. "You look worried. Is something wrong?"

"No." Michael shook his head and smiled, trying to reassure Senta that everything was fine. "I was imagining the look on my boss's face when I tell him that I'm coming back here for Mina."

"Will they let you?" Senta looked stressed.

"They won't have a choice," Michael answered. "I'm coming whether they like it or not."

"What should I expect when we get there?" Senta

asked. "Will they like me? Or will I be treated like the enemy because I'm German?"

"The British government wouldn't go to all this trouble just to treat you like the enemy," Michael answered. "I don't know what their plans are, but you have a special gift, Senta. Whatever it is, they know you will help them win this war. They'll take good care of you, I promise."

Senta looked at Michael, her eyes never leaving his.

"I hated you when I first met you."

Michael bowed his head. He knew his actions had been the cause of all the Postner family's troubles.

"I blamed you for everything. I thought that if you'd never stumbled into our barn, that everything would be fine, and that we'd still be all together, Mama, Papa, Mina, and me, all working the farm."

"I know, and I'm sorry." There was nothing else he could say.

"But the more I think about it, the more I realise that I was being naïve. What really happened was that you showed us what we should have been doing from the beginning—saving Jews, especially our friends and people we'd known all our lives."

Michael stared at Senta, marvelling at the maturity the seventeen-year-old girl was showing.

"Mina is obviously smitten with you, and it's clear you feel the same."

Senta reached forward and touched Michael's leg. "I couldn't ask for a better future brother-in-law, and I'm glad our lives crossed when they did. I'm only going to England because I know you will do everything you can to find Mina. If they'd sent anybody else, I would have refused to go with them."

"I promise I'll go to my grave before I'll give up on her," Michael said.

Senta gave a rueful smile. "I know," she said, before climbing back down the tree to rejoin Jeroen and Gerrit.

Darkness fell around eleven, and as soon as it was dark enough so they wouldn't be seen, Jeroen signalled to everyone that it was time to get ready for the Lysander.

He pulled one of the barrels from the back of the truck and opened the lid. Inside, instead of fuel, were numerous flares and a few lanterns. They each grabbed an armful of flares and followed Gerrit and Jeroen out of the trees and into the field.

Jeroen and Gerrit led the way, showing Michael and Senta how to lay out the flares so the aircraft would know where to land. When they'd finished, they gathered at the edge of the field, Jeroen holding a single lantern that he'd use when the Lysander landed.

"What happens now?" Senta asked.

"We rest," Michael said. "It's going to be a long night, and who knows when we'll be able to get some sleep. I'll take first watch."

Senta insisted on taking her turn on stag duty, and between them, they took turns resting and keeping watch for German patrols until Jeroen woke them all up at 1:45 am.

"It's time," he whispered in the darkness.

Michael wiped the sleep from his eyes and jumped up and down to wake himself up before scanning the night sky for any signs, but heavy clouds blocked the moonlight, making it difficult to see anything.

Rain fell, and the small group was soaked to the skin as soon as they left the shelter of the foliage. But nothing deterred them. After another check of the area for enemy activity, Jeroen and Gerrit lit the flares at exactly two am.

Red flames shot in the air, lighting the way and turning the field into a temporary landing strip.

In the distance, Michael made out the dull drone of an approaching aircraft. This was the moment of truth. If it were the Lysander, they would be aboard and on their way to safety in a matter of minutes, but if it were a Luftwaffe patrol, they would all be dead in a matter of seconds.

He waited anxiously to see which it was. His watch told him it was 2:02 am.

Heavy clouds obscured the aircraft from view, so the drenched group hid under the cover of the trees until they knew if they were facing friend or foe.

The single-engine aircraft circled overhead. Michael couldn't see it, but he pressed himself farther into the wet ground to make himself as small a target as possible.

The aircraft approached, and Michael relaxed as he heard it getting closer and closer, dropping from the sky and preparing to touch down.

He marvelled at the pilot's skill in finding a remote field in the middle of nowhere in a foreign country surrounded by the enemy on such a terrible night. The pilot's view of the ground would have been obscured all the way, and Michael felt renewed respect for the RAF pilots who risked their lives on a nightly basis.

The atmosphere around the group of resistance fighters palpably lifted when the aircraft wheels hit the ground. They rose from their hiding places and prepared for the landing.

Michael made sure his rucksack was secure on his back and turned towards Jeroen, who was holding the lantern high in the air above his head. Deep green light illuminated the night, casting strange shadows in the trees and foliage.

Gerrit and Senta were holding each other, speaking words only they could hear. As the aircraft reached their position, Jeroen turned off the green glowing lantern and grabbed Michael's arm.

They hugged for a long moment, neither man speaking. Jeroen pulled away and gripped his arm tightly.

"I won't forget what you've done for us. I promise I'll do my best to find Mina and keep her safe until you return."

"Thank you." A lump formed in Michael's throat. He really cared for Jeroen and his resistance team. They were the bravest men and women he had ever encountered, and he was proud to be associated with them.

"Be careful, and stay out of sight," he said, his voice cracking slightly. "The Nazis will stop at nothing until they find you, so get away from Rotterdam for a while, at least until things calm down."

Jeroen nodded. "It's time, Michael. Your aircraft won't wait."

Michael bowed his head and turned towards Gerrit. Senta threw herself into Jeroen's outstretched arms, and after one last hug and a handshake, Michael grabbed Senta and ran for the recognisable hulking shape waiting for them. He quickly helped Senta into the rear and jumped in after her.

The pilot had already turned around and was gathering speed by the time Michael had closed the door and sat down next to Senta.

The floor of the Lysander was cold, hard, and uncomfortable. But it was carrying them to safety. Michael sighed and relaxed, happy that his mission was over.

Senta looked pale in the dim light streaming through the cockpit window. Her eyes were wide, and Michael could see the fear in them. He realised that this was the first time she'd ever flown, so he grasped her arm to reassure her. She gripped tightly, smiling to cover her fear.

Michael sighed and allowed his thoughts to drift to his family in Sandwich, Kent. A lot had happened since he'd last seen them, and he missed them. He couldn't wait to see the look on his mother's face when she ran down the stairs to see him waiting for her in the sitting room.

The pilot took off, and Michael breathed another sigh of relief. The next stop was an RAF base in southern England, where Sanders would no doubt be waiting for them.

Chapter 37

The Lysander quickly disappeared into the heavy clouds, obscuring them from the ground. Driving rain lashed into the fuselage, sending reverberations through the small aircraft.

Senta scooted nearer to Michael, and they held each other tight as the rain battered the Lysander from all angles. It sounded as though bullets were ripping through the fabric of the aircraft, and with the fierce winds buffeting the plane from side to side, Senta lurched forward and threw up, trying her best to avoid their feet.

Michael wasn't far behind, and a moment later, he joined Senta, violently dispatching the contents of his stomach over the rear of the aircraft.

The pilot turned around and shouted something that nobody heard above the loud cracking of the storm. Michael shuffled to the cockpit and got close to the pilot so he could hear what he was saying.

"It's going to be rough," the pilot shouted. "Sit tight and hope that we make it."

Michael recognised the pilot as the same one who'd

dropped him off just a few days earlier in Rotterdam. His words were not comforting at all, and by his wide-eyed, pale-faced expression, Michael could see that he was as worried as they were.

"What did he say?" Senta asked once he was safely back beside her.

"He said to hold on tight because it's going to be a bumpy ride."

Michael squeezed Senta's arm. "He told us not to worry, because he does this sort of thing every night."

Senta looked a little reassured, and placed her head on Michael's shoulder, a gesture that somehow felt comforting in the dark, stormy night.

Although the storm provided cover from enemy eyes, the pilot was forced to fly low and use dead reckoning as best he could for navigation. He zigzagged constantly in an attempt to throw off any flak guns that may be trained on them.

Once Michael recovered from the initial shock, he gathered himself and approached the pilot once again.

"What's the plan?" he shouted in his ear. "How are we getting home?"

"We're flying inland to avoid coastal defences. I'll skirt south, around Antwerp, and then we'll head for the coast somewhere west of Ostend."

The pilot tapped his instrument panel. "I can't be sure of our exact location because of the weather, but that's the plan. Hold tight and let's hope we make it."

"I owe you a pint once we're back in Blighty."

"I'll hold you to that." The pilot smiled up at Michael. "Now, sit down and let me concentrate on getting us home."

Forty-five minutes later, the pilot turned due north, indicating to Michael that they were turning towards the coast. Senta stiffened beside him, so he leaned into her ear and shouted.

"He's turning towards the coast. We'll be safe once we get past the coastline and over the North Sea."

They fell silent as the Lysander was buffeted by the wind, and zigzagged from side to side, skirting around the defences in Bruges and Ostend, but Michael couldn't see anything outside the cockpit window to give him a reference point.

How the pilot knew where he was remained a mystery to Michael, and he sat with his back against the cold fuselage in awe of his skills.

Fifteen minutes later, their world was shattered. Thick clouds forced the pilot lower and lower so he could get his bearings, and by so doing, they must have been spotted by searchlights positioned around the coastline.

Anti-aircraft guns engaged, their missiles booming as they exploded close by, the shockwaves rocking the tiny aircraft ever more violently as they tried to avoid them.

The pilot jerked the Lysander upwards in an attempt to gain altitude, but it was too late.

A flak shell exploded just off the right side of the fuselage and shrapnel ripped through the thin fabric, tearing a jagged hole that sent a howl of wind into the Lysander.

Michael ducked instinctively as debris flew past his head. The plane lurched violently, the right wing dipping as the pilot fought to control it.

Smoke billowed from somewhere behind them, and Michael caught a glimpse of the pilot's bloodied face as he turned back, eyes wide with unspoken urgency.

"Brace yourselves!" he shouted, before the Lysander pitched downward in a final, desperate descent.

The plane spiralled downward, the pilot fighting to maintain control as the right wing tilted downward violently. The howling wind rushed into the cockpit, ripping at Michael's hair and clothes.

The ground blurred into a dark smear beneath them as the pilot pulled back on the stick, teeth gritted, muscles straining against the unresponsive controls.

The plane jolted, shuddering with each gust of wind, and the acrid smell of smoke filled their nostrils and made their eyes water.

A scream tore through the chaos—Senta's voice, raw and terrified, cutting through the roar of the wind. She clung to Michael, their hands white-knuckled, locked together in a desperate grip.

Michael's shoulder slammed against the side of the cockpit as the plane bucked, tossing them like rag dolls. The pilot's eyes flicked back once more, blood streaming down his face, and for a heartbeat, Michael caught a glimpse of pure determination, a silent promise to get them down alive.

The ground surged up at them, details sharp and sudden—the blurred streak of a field, the skeletal outline of trees ahead. The pilot dipped the left wing, levelling the descent with incredible finesse, guiding the crippled plane in one final arc.

They skimmed the field, the Lysander's wheels slapping against the ground, bouncing once, twice, each impact jarring through the frame like a sledgehammer blow. For a fleeting moment, it seemed as if they might make it.

Then came the sickening crunch. The right wing caught the top of a fence post, snapping like a brittle twig, spinning the plane sideways. A tree loomed up, a shadowy pillar against the stormy night, and the fuselage slammed into it with a bone-rattling thud.

The cockpit crumpled in an instant. The pilot's head

snapped forward, then fell slack, pinned against the shattered controls.

Michael and Senta were flung forward, crashing into the back of the pilot's seat. It buckled under their combined weight, absorbing the brunt of the impact as metal and wood splintered around them. Pain exploded across Michael's vision, a blinding white flash, and then there was nothing.

Chapter 38

Silence settled, broken only by the patter of rain and the slow hiss of smoke escaping the wreckage. Cold air rushed in through the gaping holes in the fuselage, carrying with it the sharp, metallic tang of blood and the heavy smell of aviation fuel.

The cockpit was a shattered shell, rain streaming in through the cracks, pooling on the floor around their limp bodies.

For a moment, everything was still, the night holding its breath as if unsure whether anyone had survived. Then Michael stirred, a shallow gasp escaping his lips as his eyes fluttered open.

White-hot pain seared through his left arm and shoulder, and he groaned when he tried to raise himself. His head swam, and he shook it to gain control of his senses. A sense of urgency hit him when he realised the severity of their situation.

"Senta!" His voice sounded distant and hoarse.

Senta was slumped on the floor of the Lysander, face

down. In a panic, Michael ignored his protesting body and shook her.

"Senta!" he shouted again, shattering the eerie silence that had descended on the wreckage.

Senta groaned and shifted slightly. Michael raised his eyes skywards and thanked God that she was alive.

"I thought you were dead." He raised her head, instantly feeling warm blood run down the back of his hand as he did.

"You're hurt," he said, cradling her in his uninjured right arm.

He tried to lift Senta, but the sharp, stabbing sensation in his shoulder made him gasp, forcing a groan to slip through his clenched teeth.

The pain was unlike anything he'd felt before—deep and intense, like a grinding pressure beneath the skin. His arm hung uselessly at his side, the angle unnatural, as if it no longer belonged to him, his fingers were numb, tingling slightly, and every slight movement sent a jolt of agony up through his neck. He realised what it was. He'd dislocated his shoulder.

He'd seen it before on the rugby field back in Cambridge, the way a player's arm would hang limply, the joint visibly out of place, the pain etched on their faces.

It was a grinding, hollow ache that pulsed with each beat of his heart, worsened by the chill of the rain seeping into his jacket.

He couldn't stay like that. Not with the Germans already searching for the crash site. Gritting his teeth, he forced himself to his knees, breathing hard through the pain. He'd seen this done before, had even helped a mate with it once. Now it was his turn.

He lowered Senta's head gently, softly speaking to her all the way down.

"Don't move. I'll be right back."

"Where are you going?" Senta murmured. "Don't leave me here."

"I'm not." Michael was relieved to hear her speak coherently. "I'm just checking on the pilot, and I'll be right back."

The pilot was dead, but he'd double-check once he'd sorted his arm out. The pain was unbearable, and he couldn't think about anything else other than relieving the agony.

Forcing himself to his feet, breathing hard through the pain, and ignoring the rest of his body for a moment, he braced himself for what he was about to do.

He stumbled out of the gaping hole in the side of the fuselage and staggered to one of the trees. Sweat poured from his forehead as he sank into a sitting position, using the tree as a brace for his back. The cold, wet bark dug into his spine, but he ignored it, focusing on the task ahead.

He took a deep breath, forcing himself to relax the muscles in his shoulder and arm. The pain was excruciating, but he knew tensing up would make it worse, so he exhaled slowly, willing his body to go limp.

With his good hand, he grabbed his left wrist and slowly, steadily pulled his arm outwards—away from his body. The pain was white-hot, nearly unbearable, but he couldn't stop and almost passed out as he angled the arm slightly upwards, feeling for the moment when the bone would slip back into place.

He twisted his left arm gently, rotating it outward as he pulled. There was a sickening pop and a deep stab of pain that made him cry out, the sound echoing through the forest. But then, the pressure released, he felt the ball of the joint slip back into the socket with a dull, grinding sound.

He gingerly moved his arm, testing it. The pain was still there, a raw ache, but it was no longer the blinding agony of a dislocation. He'd managed it. His shoulder was back in place.

Gasping for breath, Michael leaned against the tree, his left arm cradled against his chest. The joint felt raw and inflamed, but it was functional. He knew he couldn't use it much; it would still be weak, possibly prone to slipping out again. But it would do. For now, it had to do.

He glanced over at the wreckage, where Senta was beginning to stir. They didn't have long, so he braced himself once again and rose to his feet.

He quickly checked himself for any other injuries, but except for a few cuts and bruises, he was okay.

After jumping up and down on the spot a few times to get his circulation going, he hurried back to the wreckage of the Westland Lysander.

The pilot was still, slumped over the damaged cockpit controls that had smashed into him on impact. Michael shook him, but he knew the pilot was dead.

He knew the pilot would not be wearing his dog tags, or anything that would identify him, as it was a standard operating procedure for any special operations behind enemy lines to make sure that the operative couldn't be identified in case of capture.

Or death, in the case of the brave young pilot.

Michael closed his eyes for a moment and then turned his attention to Senta, who was now sat up and shouting for Michael.

After helping her outside, Michael assisted her to stand up fully and check herself for any injuries.

"You've got a nasty gash on your head, but are you hurt anywhere else?" Michael asked.

Senta shook her head, raindrops running down her face and neck. "No, I think I'm alright."

"Good. Listen, Senta, we've got to get as far away from here as we can. The Germans will be all over the wreckage soon, and we don't want to be here when they find it."

"What about the pilot?" Senta asked.

Michael shook his head. "He's gone."

He took Senta's hand in his and bowed his head.

"God, receive this man whose courage and skill saved our lives tonight. He faced the darkness without hesitation, giving everything so that we might live. I swear I'll make sure his family knows the truth—that he was a hero who flew into the storm with a steady hand and an unbreakable spirit. May he find peace in Your arms, and may his loved ones find comfort in his sacrifice. Amen."

"Amen." Senta echoed Michael's final word.

"Let's go."

Michael checked his rucksack was still secure, and after one last look at the pilot, he grasped Senta's hand and pulled her away.

They trudged through the wet, muddy field in the stormy darkness, heading somewhere, anywhere, that would take them away from the wrecked RAF Lysander.

Chapter 39

Dawn was little more than an hour away, and the Germans would be swarming all over the area once the wrecked plane was discovered.

Wet mud clung to their ankles, sucking them deeper and deeper into the quagmire, slowing them to the point to where they were barely moving.

Every step was a battle, each pull of their boots a struggle that left them breathless. Michael's shoulder throbbed in time with his heartbeat, and the mud splattered his trousers and crept up Senta's legs as they pressed on, desperate to put distance between themselves and the twisted wreckage behind them, smouldering in the dark.

Michael's breath came in short gasps, each step an effort as he hauled Senta up from another sinking patch of mud. The rain had eased, but the wind still whipped through the trees, carrying with it the distant sound of engines—vehicles moving fast, heading in all directions. The Germans were already searching.

"We need to get out of this mud," Michael muttered, his eyes scanning the darkened woods for higher ground.

He tugged Senta forward, feeling her shiver through her soaked clothes. Her head wound was no longer bleeding, but a dark stain still marred her temple, smeared by the rain.

Fields gave way to narrow lanes, and they kept to them as much as they could, as long as they headed southwest towards what Michael hoped was France.

When the roads changed direction, they re-entered the fields and resumed their general direction. Some fields were muddy, and others not so much, but each step was a race against the dawn, and they didn't have much time left.

Daylight came later than normal because of the heavy clouds. Michael, who had been cursing the nasty weather all night long, now welcomed it as it gave them precious time to put more distance between themselves and the wreckage.

Shadows started to appear in the distance, and it was time to find somewhere to lie low. They would be sitting ducks in the daylight, and they wouldn't make it through the morning before they were captured and handed over to the SS.

The outline of trees appeared in front of them, and Michael sighed in relief when he realised he was looking at a wood. He didn't care how dense it was; the wood would provide enough cover for them to hide high in the trees until the following evening.

He just hoped the rain would hold off so they could dry out and warm up.

Fifteen minutes later, the gloomy morning made its appearance. With it came more rain, but this time not as heavy.

The lights of a nearby town off to their left faded, and the sounds of men and women starting their daily routines disturbed the silence.

Evasion

The woods thickened, branches clawing at their clothes as they pushed forward in silence, scanning the shadows ahead for any sign of shelter.

Then, through the trees, Michael spotted it—a faint outline in the dim light. A crumbling structure, barely visible through the shifting mist and steady drizzle, perched at the edge of a clearing, shrouded in the gloom of dawn.

They edged closer, staying low. The place was old, its brickwork scarred and pitted, with sections of the roof caved in. Weeds choked the pathway, long untamed, and the remnants of a stone wall crumbled under the strain of ivy and age.

A stray bomb may have struck it, but by the look of things it had been abandoned long ago. The structure had fallen in on itself in places, the upper floors having collapsed and the windows shattered.

Michael motioned to Senta to stay put and crept forward, moving silently around the perimeter, ears straining for any hint of movement within. The place was silent and abandoned. At least as far as he could tell.

Satisfied, he waved her over. Together, they entered through the doorway, the wet squelch of their shoes echoing loudly in the silence.

The air was damp and smelled of mould, the kind of place abandoned in a hurry, left to rot and collapse into decay. Michael glanced around, spotting a rusty sink in the corner. Outside, beside a pile of broken beams was an old well.

Leaving Senta inside, Michael ran out to check the well. It was now light enough to see, so he was glad of the remote location.

A rusted metal pump leaned precariously over the stone rim of the well and he tested it, gripping the handle and pumping hard. With a groan, the pump sputtered, and a trickle of clear water poured into his cupped hand.

Looking up to the heavens, Michael let out a guttural sound as relief spread through his body. At the side of the house, he found a bucket, so he filled it with water and carried it inside.

By some miracle, the plug for the kitchen sink was still there, so he plugged it and poured the bucket of water into the sink.

Four more trips and the sink was full enough for them to get cleaned up. He made one more trip and left the clean water in the bucket.

They took it in turns to drink from the bucket, the cold water reviving them and quenching their deep thirst.

"We need to clean ourselves up," Michael announced. "All this mud will give us away if we're seen like this."

He recalled a house in Denmark a year earlier when he'd faced a similar situation, except that time he'd been alone. He searched the only other room that was accessible, which looked to have been the living room, and he picked up a dusty old curtain that was lying on the floor.

He shook it off and handed it to Senta.

"I'm sorry, but that's the best I can come up with. We need to strip off these clothes and clean them as best we can. They'll be wet, but at least they won't be caked in mud."

Senta threw him a look of disgust, but she knew he was right. She turned her back on Michael and stripped down to her underwear.

"I'm not wearing that." She pointed at the filthy curtain on the floor. "It's dirtier than my clothes! Who knows what diseases are on it?"

Michael didn't blame her, and ignoring his own

Evasion

discomfort, he stripped to his underwear and gathered their clothes together.

In the sink, they washed themselves, and then Michael scrubbed their clothes as best he could. When he was done, he pulled them from the dark brown water, and Senta took them and hung them over broken cupboard doors to air dry.

Michael then took their boots and scrubbed the mud off them. It wasn't perfect, but it would do until they could find something else.

Once that was done, Michael grabbed a three-legged chair and indicated to Senta to sit down, saying, "I need to clean your wound." The chair wobbled as she sat.

Michael gently dabbed the dirt away from the wound on Senta's temple, the water tracing pink streaks down her pale skin.

"That'll have to do," he murmured, wishing he had more than his damp handkerchief to offer. "It's deep, but it's not as bad as it looked."

It was cold in their underwear, and they both shivered in the early morning gloom, so they collapsed in the corner of the ruined living room, and huddled together for warmth.

"I bet you wish I was Mina," Senta said, looking away, her face deep red in embarrassment.

"As much as I wish Mina was here, I'm glad it's you, Senta. I'm sorry this happened, but I'm going to do all I can to get us back to England safely."

Senta turned and looked at Michael. "That poor pilot had no chance, did he?"

Michael shook his head. "No. He was dead the moment the plane hit the ground. He gave his life trying to save us."

Senta placed her head on Michael's shoulder, sending

ripples of pain down his arm but he said nothing, wanting to comfort her as much as he could. They shared the scant provisions they'd brought with them, which amounted to a piece of dried bread and a tin of sardines.

"What are we going to do?" Senta asked, her voice rising. "How are we going to get to England from here? The Nazis will be looking for us everywhere, and we'll never make it to France, never mind England."

Michael squeezed Senta's hand. "The Nazis don't know who was on that plane. They certainly don't know it was us, so we have an advantage over them there. We'll find some supplies and travel by night. It might take us a while, but if we're careful, we can make it to the coast, and from there we'll try to find a boat to England."

"You've done this before, haven't you?" Senta asked.

"Once or twice."

The raw ache of exhaustion overcame them, and they fell asleep, shivering, huddled together in the corner.

Chapter 40

SS-Obersturmführer Erik Stadtler rubbed his tired eyes and glanced at his watch. He pulled his boots off and lay back on his bed, frustrated, and yet happy with the progress he'd made into the investigations of the recent resistance attacks.

It was two thirty in the morning, and after a few hours of sleep, he'd continue interrogating the men and women he'd arrested over the last two days.

The SS officers on night duty had been ordered to keep all the prisoners awake, but under no circumstances were they to allow the Gestapo or anyone else in the SD anywhere near them.

He knew they'd try, because it was something he himself would do.

As he drifted off to sleep, he thought about what he was going to do the following morning. The valet they'd arrested along with his brother in Amsterdam was weak, so he'd start with him.

After a sleepless night and plenty of threats, Stadtler was sure the valet would crack and confess.

The resistance members he'd personally arrested near Schoonhoven were going to be harder to crack, especially Elske, the woman he knew from the Hotel Atlanta.

But he'd worry about them tomorrow. Right then, he needed to sleep.

One and a half hours later, a loud bang on the door stirred Stadtler from a deep sleep. Another, even louder bang half woke him up, and by the third bang, he was fully awake.

Angry, Stadtler rolled off his bed and staggered towards the door.

"What is it?" he demanded as he opened the door, shielding his eyes from the blinding light from the well-lit corridors.

"SS-Obersturmführer, I'm sorry to disturb you." The junior SS guard's eyes were wide, and his face pale.

"Well?" Stadtler barked.

"Sir, I have an urgent report for you. They say it cannot wait."

Stadtler tore the sealed report from the terrified guard's hands and slammed the door in his face. He took a moment to compose himself and turned on the overhead light.

Begin message

Single-engine enemy aircraft intercepted by anti-aircraft guns in Bruges, Belgium, heading west towards the coast. Aircraft believed hit by flak and was last seen losing altitude, veering southwest. Wehrmacht units have been dispatched to locate the wreckage. Aircraft suspected to have been used by British intelligence for reasons unknown.

Report made on the orders of Höhere SS- und Polizeiführer Nordwest und Reichskommissariat Niederlande Rauter. Incident to be investigated further.

End of message.

Evasion

Stadtler's thoughts immediately turned to Geert's mumbled words earlier.

"You'll never find Fernsby or the girl. They'll be long gone by now, safe from your grasp."

Was that what he meant when he said they'd be long gone? Had they boarded an aeroplane to take them to England?

All thoughts of sleep gone, Stadtler quickly dressed and raced out of his bedroom.

Chapter 41

The heavy, damp air in the basement of the seized City Hall clung to SS-Obersturmführer Erik Stadtler like a shroud as he descended the final steps.

The dim, flickering, overhead lights cast long, restless shadows that seemed to reach out for him, dancing on the rough stone walls. His boots echoed sharply, the sound swallowed by the oppressive gloom of the place.

The converted basement was nothing like the pristine offices above. Down there, it stank of mildew, sweat, and fear. A faint metallic tang lingered, unmistakable to those who had spent enough time in rooms like those.

The holding cells lined one side of the corridor, their barred doors dull and rust streaked. In the distance, muffled coughs and faint whispers filtered through the gloom, the prisoners' voices barely audible over the steady drip of water from a cracked pipe.

As Stadtler entered the small interrogation room, he took a deep breath, steadying himself. Even now, after countless hours spent in rooms like this, he felt a flicker of excitement. The power, control, and the raw intensity of what unfolded never failed to exhilarate him.

The room was cramped and stark, lit by a single overhead bulb that swayed slightly, casting erratic shadows on the crumbling, bare stone walls.

A heavy wooden table dominated the centre of the room, its surface scarred with knife marks and cigarette burns. Two metal chairs flanked it, one bolted to the floor. Against the far wall stood an iron ring fixed to the wall, its purpose unmistakable.

Leaning against the table, smoking lazily, was SS-Unterscharführer Dietrich Keller, the man Stadtler relied upon for the more physical aspects of his interrogations.

Keller's blunt features were impassive, his eyes as cold and grey as the iron tools he carried in his kitbag. His knuckles were bruised and swollen, as they often were after interrogation sessions.

Stadtler glanced at him briefly before sitting down at the table.

"Bring him in," he said curtly.

His voice carried the weight of authority, but inside, his nerves tightened. Time was slipping through his fingers, and whoever was on that aircraft could already be out of reach.

∼

DOWN THE CORRIDOR, the scrape of keys echoed sharply. Two SS guards stood outside Geert's cell, one tapping his baton against the iron bars.

"On your feet," one of them barked.

Geert didn't move immediately. He sat on the filthy floor, his back against the wall, his head tilted upward, as if he hadn't heard them.

The guard unlocked the door and strode in, grabbing him roughly by the arm and hauling him to his feet. Geert stumbled, his bruised, aching body stiff from hours in the cramped, damp cell.

"Get moving."

The guard shoved him into the corridor, where the flickering lights made him squint. The cold air hit his face like a slap, but it didn't wake him fully from the fog of exhaustion and hunger.

As they dragged him past the neighbouring cell, his eyes briefly met those of Neeltje, who sat on the cold floor, clutching her knees. She didn't speak, but the fear in her eyes cut through him like a blade.

He gave her a small nod, a gesture that said nothing but tried to mean everything, before the guards yanked him forward.

∾

THE DOOR CREAKED OPEN, and two guards shoved Geert into the room. He stumbled and fell to his knees, the cold concrete scraping his palms. Keller strode forward, grabbing him by the back of the neck and hauling him into the chair, where leather straps hung loosely at the sides.

"Sit still," Keller growled, yanking the straps tight around Geert's wrists and chest.

The prisoner coughed, his breath ragged, but he met Stadtler's gaze with a defiance that hadn't yet been beaten out of him.

Stadtler leaned forward, interlinking his hands on the table.

"You look tired, Geert," he said, his tone deceptively

calm. "Perhaps we can make this easier for both of us. I ask the questions, you answer them. Quickly. Honestly."

Geert said nothing, his lips pressed into a thin, bloodless line. Stadtler sighed, rubbing his temple as though the silence were an inconvenience.

"Let's start simply," he said, his voice low. "We know about the aircraft Jeroen and his friends were meeting with."

He leaned forward, his face almost touching Geert's.

"That's where they went after they left you at the farm, wasn't it?"

Geert remained silent, staring at the wall ahead.

"The plane was shot down over Belgium. Everyone aboard is dead."

Stadtler noticed a glimmer of shock on Geert's deadpan face.

"You didn't know that, did you?" Stadtler rammed home his advantage.

Still, Geert said nothing.

"You told me earlier that Fernsby and the girl would be long gone. Were you talking about the plane?"

Geert's silence lingered a moment too long. Keller stepped forward, slamming a fist into the table beside him. The sharp sound made Geert flinch, but he kept his eyes fixed on the far wall.

"Was Fernsby on that plane?" Stadtler repeated, his voice colder now. "Was the girl with him? Jeroen? Answer me!"

When Geert finally spoke, his voice was hoarse but steady. "I thought you said everyone aboard was dead. Surely then, you know who was on it."

Keller smashed a huge fist into Geert's midriff, sending him into jerky spasms in the metal chair.

"You didn't find them, did you?" A thin smile emerged

on Geert's lips. "You won't find them. Not you, not anyone."

"The bodies were so badly burned that we couldn't tell who was on the aircraft," Stadtler lied. "We just need to know so we can identify them and close our files on the matter."

Geert smiled and stared straight ahead.

Stadtler's jaw tightened. He gestured to Keller, who grabbed a bucket of water from the corner. Without hesitation, he threw its contents into Geert's face, the icy shock wrenching a gasp from the prisoner.

"Where were they going? England?" Stadtler leaned forward, his eyes boring into Geert's. "Why is the girl so important to them? Answer me, or you'll wish you had."

Geert spat blood onto the floor. "You'll never understand."

Stadtler slammed his palm onto the table, the sound reverberating through the small room. "Do not test me. Was Jeroen with them?"

Geert's breathing quickened, his resolve faltering as Keller stood over him, a length of rubber hose dangling ominously from his hand.

"Tell me where Jeroen is and why the girl is so important," Stadtler demanded, his voice sharp and cutting. "And the names of the others who helped with the attacks. If you cooperate, you might still see daylight again."

Geert's head slumped forward, the straps digging into his shoulders. He muttered something under his breath, too low for Stadtler to hear.

"What did you say?" Stadtler snapped.

Geert raised his head slowly, blood trickling from the corner of his mouth. "You will never win," he whispered.

Stadtler's expression darkened. He turned to Keller and nodded his head.

Evasion

Keller pounded on the closed cell door, and another heavy-set SS officer joined them, leaving the cell door open after he entered. Stadtler stood back, ready to watch a master go about his work with ruthless efficiency.

Geert's body stiffened as he was unfastened from the chair and thrown face down on the ground. The two SS interrogators tore off his boots and socks and positioned his body so his feet lay over the edge of the chair, exposing the soft flesh on the underside of his feet.

Keller's partner pinned Geert to the ground so he couldn't move.

Stadtler knew what they were doing because he'd seen it many times before. They were using the ancient bastinado, or foot whipping technique that was popular with the SS.

Keller got to work, striking Geert repeatedly with the rubber hose on his soles. Geert screamed in agony, and Stadtler watched as Keller's cold grey eyes lit up and filled with raw excitement with each strike.

The foot whipping technique was not designed to cause permanent damage to the victim. Rather, it was used to inflict severe pain, which it did very successfully.

Geert screamed louder and louder with each strike, begging Keller to stop.

After five minutes of repeated whipping that Stadtler knew would have felt like hours to Geert, he ordered Keller to stop.

Keller looked disappointed, but obeyed Stadtler's orders. Geert was pulled to his feet, and immediately collapsed to the ground in agony.

The bastinado method caused deep internal damage to the feet, and the victims wouldn't be able to walk for a long time afterwards.

Geert was disabled, and escape would be impossible.

Most victims would have crumbled by now, and Stadtler felt respect for this tough Dutchman who was holding out longer than most.

But he'd break down, eventually. They all did.

Stadtler's gaze settled on the terrified figure standing at the doorway, forced to watch by the SS guards holding her there. Neeltje shook, visibly terrified by what she'd just witnessed.

At the raising of his head, the SS guards dragged Neeltje into the cell as the moaning, semi-conscious Geert was dragged out.

Neeltje stared at Stadtler as she was strapped into the metal chair, her eyes wide with terror.

Stadtler sighed. "You can save yourself a lot of pain if you tell me what I need to know."

Neeltje stared at the wall, just as Geert had done before her.

Stadtler raised his hand at Keller, who vanished out of the cell for a moment. When he came back, he led two SS officers into the cell, dragging Geert along with them.

They tied Geert to the iron ring attached to the wall and let him hang there, his shoulders and arms taking all his weight because of his damaged feet.

He moaned and closed his eyes with the agony of his ordeal.

"You may not talk for yourself," Stadtler spoke to Neeltje. "But you might for your friend."

He gestured towards Geert. "What he's been through is a drop in the bucket compared to what's coming next. Unless you cooperate and answer my questions, Geert will suffer like no man has ever suffered before. And you will watch every blow, knowing that each strike is your fault because you refuse to speak."

Silence followed, filling the room with tension and fear.

Evasion

Stadtler enjoyed watching the look on Neeltje's face as his words sank in. Geert was out of it, and the words probably didn't register.

But they did with Neeltje.

"And once we've finished with him, we'll do it to you."

Tears rolled down Neeltje's cheeks. She was beaten.

"May God forgive me."

She looked up at Stadtler. "What happens to us if I tell you?"

"You'll be sent to a POW camp in Germany where you will be well treated until the end of the war."

"Senta is a very special girl." Neeltje began to speak.

Chapter 42

The sounds of creaking timbers and water dripping onto the floor stirred Michael from his restless sleep. Senta was huddled next to him, her bare arms cold to the touch.

Each sound in the mid-afternoon gloom made his spine tingle, and he half expected a squad of Wehrmacht soldiers to rush in at any moment to arrest them at gunpoint.

Or worse, the SS.

He was deathly cold, and his limbs were stiff and frozen. Damp seeped through the crumbling walls, and every surface seemed to carry the chill deeper into his bones.

He moved, trying to get some circulation going in his body. Senta opened her eyes, and at the sight of Michael so close to her, she jerked herself to her knees, and on unsteady legs, she stood up and moved away.

Michael knew she was embarrassed, and he felt sorry for her. She was exposed in just her underwear, as he was himself. He looked away, allowing her a modicum of modesty as she put distance between them.

"What happens now?" Senta asked, gingerly touching the wound on her head. Her hair, damp and unkempt, stuck to her head, and she pulled at it, trying her best to make herself as presentable as possible.

"We're close to a town. We need to wait until after dark, and if we can, we need to find food and clothing that will get us to the border. A map will be useful too, so we'll know where we are."

"What about our clothes?" Senta indicated with her hand at the soaking wet clothes hanging over a cupboard door.

"They're wet, but it's all we have," Michael answered. "At least until we can find some more."

Senta picked up her wet clothes, and without a word of complaint, she dressed herself. Michael followed suit, buttoning up his soaked, mud-stained shirt over his clammy skin.

It felt terrible, making them both even colder and more miserable than they already were. Michael bit his top lip in frustration at the dire situation they faced. He'd much rather be alone, where he would be responsible for only his own life, but he had to make sure Senta survived as well.

He jumped up and down to get his circulation going. Senta did the same, and after a few minutes, the colour returned to her face.

They finished the last of the stale bread in Michael's rucksack and drank from the filthy bucket.

"I'm going to check the lie of the land," Michael said. "Wait here for me."

"I'm going with you," Senta retorted. "You're not leaving me alone in here. It's creepy."

"We need to be careful. They'll have found the wreckage by now, and they'll be swarming all over this place soon."

Senta nodded. She knew.

Michael's shoulder throbbed, but he clenched his jaw, blocked out the pain, and led the way out of the derelict house, glad to see the back of it.

They ran to the trees and hid in the wood, the dripping leaves and wet ground immediately soaking them to the skin again. But at least the rain had stopped.

Heavy clouds hung in the air, which lightened Michael's mood because they would be harder to track once it got dark.

They sat and listened for an hour, but all they heard were the sounds of occasional patrol vehicles driving up and down the nearby road.

Michael left Senta in their hiding place in the trees while he searched the perimeter of the abandoned house. The road was off to the west, and the clearing extended about a hundred feet in all directions around the house.

When he returned to Senta, she placed her finger to her lips, telling Michael to be quiet. She pointed towards another road that intersected with the one Michael had found on the other side of the woods. She cupped her ear, telling him to listen.

He didn't need any encouragement. The sound of barking dogs was getting louder as they approached. From the sound of them, they were some way away, but there was little doubt they were heading in their direction.

Michael whispered into Senta's ear. "We've got to get away from here now."

Senta bowed her head in agreement, and the two of them rose to their feet and headed towards the nearby town, Michael leading them through the woods until they reached a small stream that ran north to south. As awful as the option was, Michael knew what they had to do if they were to survive the night.

Evasion

Senta looked at him and shook her head as if she knew what he was about to say.

"I'm not going in there," she whispered. "It's freezing and probably muddy."

"We don't have a choice," Michael answered. "If we don't, the dogs will track us, and we'll be arrested before the night is out. At least this way we stand a fighting chance."

Senta pulled a face, but she knew he was right. She stepped forward, but Michael held her back.

"It's too exposed," he whispered. "It's better to wait until it's dark and then we'll make a move."

Senta pulled back, probably glad of the reprieve. They re-entered the woods and climbed a tree to a stout branch that hid them underneath its canopy.

Darkness was less than an hour away, and then they would make their move.

Chapter 43

The safety of darkness couldn't come fast enough. Minute by minute, the sound of barking dogs got louder as they closed in on their location.

Heavy clouds blocked the stars, which worked to their advantage, and as the shadows faded into darkness, Michael indicated to Senta that it was time to move.

With stiff limbs, they climbed down from the branches and approached the stream, which looked more like a river after the heavy rainfall over the previous twenty-four hours.

"Are you ready?" Michael asked, knowing full well that it was the last thing either of them wanted to do.

"No."

Michael grasped Senta's hand, and together they waded into the deep, freezing cold water. Michael gasped as the water shocked his body into spasms, and he gripped Senta tighter, as she too, went into shock.

Thick mud clawed at their legs, sucking them deeper and deeper into the riverbed, making it difficult to move.

They held onto each other, taking one step at a time in the deep, soul sucking mud.

When they were waist deep, the current took over, whisking them off their feet downstream and leaving them no choice but to let go of each other as they struggled to keep their heads above water.

The stream, that had become a raging mini river after the storm, widened at the end of the woods and the current slowed to almost a standstill, allowing Michael to swim to the bank and exit.

He threw his rucksack onto dry land and reached into the water to help Senta. They climbed out and lay momentarily on the riverbank, taking deep, lung-filling gasps of air while their bodies shivered and shook.

"Are you alright?" Michael asked, concerned at how cold her hands felt when he touched them.

"I'm fine," Senta answered sharply, telling Michael that she wasn't.

Michael's feet were frozen, and he couldn't feel anything below his knees. His hands too, were numb, and his fingers didn't want to obey his commands.

Senta must be feeling it too, so he helped her to her feet, and together they jumped up and down on what felt like lumps of ice until a modicum of circulation returned, sending pins and needles up and down their limbs.

Five minutes later, still shivering, Michael led the way towards the town a short way to the east. He hoped against hope that their incursion into the raging stream would at the very least throw the dogs off long enough for them to find some supplies and get out of the area.

They trudged over a field and crossed a road, their soaking wet feet making squelching sounds as they walked, following the road towards the town centre.

The faint outline of a sign loomed in the distance,

barely visible against the darkened shapes of hedgerows and empty fields. Michael wiped his dirty face with the back of his hand, squinting through the murky darkness.

As they drew closer, the letters came into view, black and bold against the weather-beaten wood: Heuvelland.

"Well," Michael whispered. "At least we know where we are, although it doesn't help because I've never heard of Heuvelland."

"We're in Belgium," Senta answered. "I saw it on one of the maps Jeroen had on the wall at the farm. It's not far from the French border if my memory serves me right."

"If your memory says we're close to the French border, then I'll believe it," Michael said. Senta's memory was fast becoming legendary, and he didn't doubt her accuracy for a moment.

Michael sighed with relief. They'd been fumbling in the dark, unsure of exactly where they were, but now they had a name and a rough location.

He traced the letters with his eyes as though committing them to memory before nudging Senta forward. "We're closer to France than I thought," he murmured, trying to sound optimistic.

They moved forward, the town eerily silent in the oppressive gloom of a full blackout. Not a single light shone from any window or streetlamp, making Michael feel both grateful and unnerved.

They moved cautiously, skirting the edge of the main road that cut through the heart of the town. A distant rumble of engines echoed off the buildings, and Michael crouched, motioning for Senta to follow.

Ahead, faint voices reached his ears, muffled and clipped. As they crept closer, the source of the sound became clear—a roadblock had been set up in the town centre.

Evasion

Michael peered around the corner of a wall, trying to get a better view of what was going on. His worst nightmares were realised as at least eight soldiers moved back and forth under the dim glow of a handheld lamp, blocking the road to anything that dared to approach.

"They've found the wreckage," Michael whispered as he retreated behind the wall."

"What do we do now?" Senta asked, her face ashen in the dim light. Behind her bravery, Michael knew she was reaching the limit of her endurance. He needed to find some relief for her, or she wouldn't be able to continue much longer.

Leading the way, Michael retraced their steps, crossing fields and roads in an attempt to enter the town from the opposite side. He needed to reach the main road where the shops were located, and to do that, he needed to be on the other side of the roadblock.

Senta followed, uncomplaining and silent. She was struggling, and Michael was beyond proud of how brave and determined she was. Many others would have given up by now, but Senta seemed as resolute as ever to evade the Nazis and live to fight another day.

They cautiously crossed another main road and followed a series of alleyways and backyards that eventually dissected the road to the shops.

On the opposite side, Michael could make out a large group of trees, and it was there where he led Senta. He triple-checked the main street to make sure they weren't being watched, and held Senta's hand as they ran across as fast as they could.

On the opposite side, they ran into the trees and hid behind a thick tree trunk, panting for breath, their hearts racing in fear of being arrested or shot. The sound of barking dogs still lingered faintly in the distance, a haunting reminder that their pursuers weren't far behind.

Ten minutes later, Michael made his move.

"Stay here where it's safe," he whispered in Senta's ear. "It'll be quicker and safer if I do it alone. If I'm not back in an hour, run for the border and try to find some help in France."

"You're not going without me." Senta pursed her lips and stared at Michael.

"Please, Senta, we don't have time to argue. It's safer for both of us if I go alone. There's less chance we'll be seen if we're not together, and if I'm caught, it's much more important that you get away. If what they say is true, you could be the difference in this war, and it's vital that you get away."

"Even if I don't," he added after a pause. "Please, Senta."

Senta stared at Michael, and although he could tell that she didn't agree, she tilted her head in acknowledgement.

"Good. I'll get us some food and new clothes if I can. As I said, give me an hour, and if I'm not back, get out of here as fast as you can."

Senta gripped Michael's hand, her frozen fingers a message to Michael that time truly was of the essence. He made sure his rucksack was strapped firmly to his back, and without a second backwards glance, he was gone.

Chapter 44

The row of shops came into view as he emerged from another alley. Being careful not to make any noise, Michael scanned the darkened buildings, looking for any signs of what they contained inside. All he saw were blacked-out windows and locked doors.

He was less than a hundred yards from the roadblock, and his temples pulsated at the thought of being so close. He was about to move away when his nostrils caught the distinct aroma of freshly baked bread.

Well, bread at least.

His eyes followed the scent, and he groaned inwardly when he realised the bakery was even closer to the soldiers than he was right then. Ignoring the inner voice that told him to run, he inched towards the smell with a renewed determination.

The rear door of the bakery was hidden in the shadows of a narrow passageway, which was a mild relief. Taking a moment to make sure he was completely alone, Michael tried the handle, but the door was locked.

He moved to a window that was big enough for a man

to climb through, removed his still soaking wet jacket and wrapped the sleeve around the hilt of his knife. Then, he struck the windowpane with a short, sharp jab that smashed the glass with as little noise as possible, reached inside and opened the latch. The window swung open and Michael climbed inside.

The stale scent of flour and yeast invaded his senses, and his stomach growled from the realisation that he was starving. The glow from the red filter on his torch revealed a row of loaves stacked on a shelf, presumably from earlier in the day. He grabbed five of them, tucking them into his rucksack.

On another shelf, he pulled back a cover to reveal a large block of hard cheese wrapped in wax paper, grabbed it, and stuffed it next to the loaves.

He was about to leave when he noticed a set of stairs. He cautiously climbed them, hoping against hope that nobody was sleeping in the flat above the bakery.

At the top, his dim red light revealed a single bedroom. The door was open, and he peered inside, ready to bolt at the first sight of another human.

The room was empty, but it was obvious that it was occupied by someone. Whoever stayed there was untidy, with clothes and empty cigarette cartons strewn across the floor.

Michael picked through the clothes and determined they belonged to an adult man, albeit a smaller man than he himself was.

He took a pair of trousers and a shirt from the floor, and, ignoring the bile rising in his stomach, he changed from his sopping wet, energy draining clothes into the dirty, but dry ones he'd picked out.

Then he searched again and found another set for Senta. They'd look stupid on her, but it was the best he

Evasion

could do. At least she wouldn't freeze to death in the dry clothes.

On the way out, he rinsed his face and filled his flask with water from the sink, and when he was ready, he unlocked the rear door of the bakery and cracked it open.

Happy he was still alone, he made his escape and headed back to the trees to find Senta.

"Senta," he whispered as he got close to the tree trunk where he'd left her. Panic rose in his chest when he realised she wasn't there.

He dropped to the ground and pulled the Walther PPK from his waistband. If the Nazis had found Senta, then he would be next, and he wasn't going to be caught alive.

Silence reigned for several minutes, allowing Michael's heart rate to slow down a little. If the Germans hadn't caught her, then where was she? Had she left on her own?

Surely she hadn't. Despite what he'd said, they both knew she wouldn't get far without him. Escape and evasion was his speciality, and although unpleasant, he was good at it.

"Psst."

A noise above his head caught Michael's attention.

"Michael."

Another whisper. This time, he pinpointed the source. Senta was high up in the tree above his head.

He rose to his feet. "Senta, get down here. You scared me to death."

Senta slowly climbed down, joining Michael on the ground next to the thick tree trunk.

"I heard a noise after you left, so I hid up there. When you came back, I had to make sure it was you before I said anything."

Her fingers were still frozen solid, and Michael feared

that hypothermia would set in if he didn't hurry and do something about it.

"Here, put these on." He passed her the clothes he'd taken from the bakery. "They won't fit well, and they're men's clothes, but at least they're dry and they'll keep you warm."

Senta pulled a face, but didn't say anything and once she'd changed, she handed Michael her wet clothes, which he added to his own, wrapped inside a dry shirt from the bakery in his rucksack.

"I look terrible," Senta whispered.

"You look great, and you'll be a hell of a lot warmer," Michael countered.

They shared a block of cheese, one of the loaves, and then set off for France, heading back the way they'd come. Michael sighed in relief when they crossed the street and headed away from the roadblock.

The relief didn't last long.

As they approached the larger road that headed north to south, the sounds of approaching vehicles disturbed the peacefulness. Michael grabbed Senta's arm and pushed her over a hedgerow into someone's back garden.

They watched from the hedgerow as the convoy of vehicles got nearer. Michael's stomach churned when he recognised them as Volkswagen Kübelwagens, or bathtubs, as he called them.

He'd run into the vehicles several times before, and every time nothing good had come of it. Their long, boxy frames were shallow and narrow, and both doors opened outwards, side by side. They were the ugliest vehicle Michael had ever seen, and yet the Wehrmacht seemed to love them.

They resembled a bathtub on wheels, which was why

Michael had christened them with that name the first time he'd clapped eyes on them back in 1938.

They lay on the ground as low as they could until the convoy passed, and Michael breathed deeply once they'd gone.

"I hate those vehicles," he whispered to Senta.

As they skirted to the south of the derelict building they'd sheltered in the previous day, dogs could be heard barking to their north, which probably meant they were at the building right now searching for them.

Michael shook off the feeling of dread and led Senta deeper into the middle of the woods, heading southwest, away from Heuvelland.

"How are we going to get out of here?" Senta asked when they stopped for a break. "We can't walk to the coast from here. It's too far, and we'd never make it past the patrols."

"We're going to Versailles," Michael answered. "I know a man there who can help us."

Chapter 45

Jeroen and Gerrit had been waiting at the remote farmhouse half a mile north of the Oude Rijn, a branch of the Rhine delta close to Alphen aan den Rijn for two days.

Two nights earlier, after watching Senta and Fernsby leave on the British aircraft, they'd made the thirty-kilometre journey north as Gerrit's home in Bovenberg was no longer safe after the recent attacks by their resistance group.

The two men were initially ecstatic at the success of their missions. Not only had they successfully rescued Senta Postner—the girl the British deemed important enough to change the course of the war in their favour, but they'd also rid Holland of an evil Nazi SS officer who was responsible for the deaths of many Dutch citizens, including Gerrit's younger sister, Femke.

But now, two days after watching the British aircraft take to the skies, their mood was sombre. Elske, Geert, and the others should have joined them, and although they'd decided to give them two full days to make the short journey, they'd been expected to arrive the same night they had.

Now, so long after the attacks, they were worried that something had gone horribly wrong.

Gerrit, especially, was concerned. Elske was his wife, and Geert and Arjen were his brothers, so in his mind he had more to lose than Jeroen, although Jeroen insisted they were as much a family to him as they were to Gerrit.

Gerrit doubted that very much.

"Where are they?" Gerrit asked for the umpteenth time. "They should have been here by now."

He paced up and down the stone hallway in the dim light of early evening, in and out of the sparse living room and kitchen. It secretly drove Jeroen mad, but he understood Gerrit's concern and kept his thoughts to himself.

"Something obviously happened," Gerrit continued pacing. "Where are Bastiaan and Neeltje? They should be here as well. I'm telling you, Jeroen, something bad happened."

Jeroen looked up from the kitchen table, where he sat in front of a map of Holland. "Neither Bastiaan nor Neeltje knew the location of this place, so they couldn't be here, not without Elske or Geert picking them up first and bringing them here."

"Yes, of course." Gerrit continued pacing. "But then, where are they?"

"As we agreed earlier, if they aren't here by morning, we'll know that something has happened to them," Jeroen explained patiently for the millionth time that day. "They may have broken down and are having to walk here, or something may have happened to one of them and they are lying low for a few days. Until we know what happened, we can't speculate, Gerrit."

"No, no. It's something much worse. I can feel it in my

heart. Jeroen… something has happened to my wife and my brothers. I just know it."

"If they aren't here by daylight, we'll go find them," Jeroen said patiently but firmly. "I want to know what happened to them as much as you do, but we all knew the dangers coming into this, and after the car bomb and the train derailment, the Nazis were bound to come after us hard."

Gerrit glared at Jeroen. "It's easy for you to say. It's not your wife and family that are missing."

"I understand loss, Gerrit. You know I do. Elske and the rest mean as much to me as anyone, and I want to find them too."

"We'll go back to my farm and find them first thing," Gerrit announced, still pacing around the dimly lit ground floor.

"Too dangerous." Jeroen shook his head. "If they were captured, the SS and Gestapo will be waiting for us there. We'll walk right into their trap. We can't go back to your farm, not ever."

"Then where?" Gerrit shouted. "There's nowhere else they should have been except there or here. We have to start there."

Jeroen shook his head. "You're forgetting Bastiaan and Neeltje. They weren't at your farm. We kept them away on purpose, in case any of them were captured. That's why we never told them about this place."

Gerrit stopped pacing. "We go to Koopman's farm?"

Jeroen bowed his head. "We go to Koopman's farm. That's where we'll find our answers."

Nobody arrived during the night.

After another sleepless night, Jeroen waited in the Wehrmacht truck for Gerrit. Wearing full German army uniforms and armed with MP 38 submachine guns, the two men hoped for a clear run, but they were ready for any eventuality.

Gerrit, normally so calm and calculated, was a nervous wreck, so Jeroen drove, taking the long way back to Schoonhoven and the Koopman farm, across the fields from Gerrit's farm at nearby Bovenberg.

Neither man spoke during the drive, both wrapped up in their own thoughts. Gerrit fidgeted with the strap of his MP 38, while Jeroen kept his eyes on the road, looking out for any German patrols that might get in their way.

Only a few miles from their safe house, Jeroen slowed the truck as they approached the bridge that crossed the Oude Rijn. This was the one spot that worried him, and he was proven right, as every vehicle crossing the bridge was stopped by a Wehrmacht patrol.

With their weapons well hidden, Jeroen wound down the window of the Mercedes truck.

"Good morning," he shouted in perfect German over the loud noise of the engine. "At least the rain's stopped." He pointed at the dreary, heavy clouds that hung over them like a shroud.

"It's done nothing but rain ever since we got here days ago," the young soldier complained.

Jeroen laughed along with the soldier. "Where are you going?" the soldier asked as he glanced at their military identification papers.

"We're heading back to Rotterdam to collect more fuel barrels," Jeroen lied. "They're sending us farther and farther away from the city ever since the savage attack on our men a few days ago."

"Yeah, tell me about it," the soldier answered, handing him back their IDs. "Ever since they caught that group outside Rotterdam, we've been on high alert. We haven't had any sleep for two days now!"

Jeroen's ears pricked up at the soldier's words. He took a deep breath to calm himself, and he pinched Gerrit, who was about to say something.

"We didn't hear about that. What happened? Did they catch the culprits?" Jeroen looked down at his new best friend. "I hope so, because we haven't seen our beds since the attack either."

"From what we heard, the SS caught them red-handed on a farm near Schoonhoven. They got in a firefight, and our men were lucky to escape with their lives."

"Goodness gracious!" Jeroen feigned sympathy for the SS. "Did they catch them, at least?"

"Better than that. From what one of the men who was there said, we killed all but two of them. They were taken by the SS for questioning. I'd feel sorry for them if they hadn't set car bombs and opened fire on our men."

Jeroen ground his teeth together to stop himself from shooting the young soldier on the spot, gripped Gerrit's knee to stop him from doing anything stupid, and looked down at the young man, who was now standing aside to let them pass.

"Thanks. I'm glad we caught them," Jeroen said through a clenched jaw.

He drove off, and when they were out of sight, Gerrit let out a loud howl.

"We don't know if they were referring to your farm or the Koopman's," Jeroen reminded him. "So let's not jump to conclusions."

"You heard him," Gerrit shouted. "The bastards shot and killed them."

Jeroen sighed deeply. He didn't know which was the better fate—being shot in cold blood or being arrested by the SS.

They made the rest of the journey in silence, Jeroen

coming up with a story as to why he was lost in Schoonhoven, and he didn't stop until he pulled into the farmyard at Koopman's farm.

He turned the truck around in case they had to leave in a hurry, and shut off the engine. The silence was deafening, and both men took a minute to gather their thoughts.

The front door to the Koopman residence was open, and the heavy, oppressive stench told them what was inside before they got there.

They covered their faces with their sleeves and ran inside.

Chapter 46

Flies attacked them as soon as they entered the house. The obnoxious smell was so strong that Jeroen thought he was going to pass out.

Gerrit pushed past him, seemingly oblivious to the heavy stench of death. He ran to the living room and stopped in his tracks when he saw what was there.

"No!" he howled, falling to his knees.

Jeroen caught up to him, and he too, momentarily forgot about the overwhelming stench when he saw the bodies sitting together on the couch, placed and left there as a warning to everyone else in the vicinity. Visual evidence of what happened when you worked with the resistance.

Sjoerd Koopman, his wife Maria, and their young son, also named Sjoerd Koopman, were sitting together on the couch, lifeless, shot to death by Nazi bullets.

Their crime? Unknowingly being related to members of the resistance.

"They weren't even in the resistance," Gerrit wailed. "They were innocent."

Evasion

"Where's Bastiaan and Neeltje?" Jeroen spoke out loud. "They must be the two they arrested."

Jeroen left Gerrit to his misery in the living room while he searched the house for signs of the two missing family members. When he returned to Gerrit, who was still on his knees, he threw his hands in the air.

"They aren't here, so they must have been taken."

"We need to go to our farm and see if Elske's there," Gerrit wailed.

"It's too dangerous. They may have set a trap for us."

"I don't care. I'm going, so you can come if you want or you can stay here. Either way, I'm going."

Jeroen sighed. He knew there was no talking Gerrit out of it.

Back in the truck, Jeroen tried reasoning with the distraught man. "I know Elske is your wife, but if we give ourselves up now, everything we've done, everyone who's died for us, has been for nothing. We need to be sensible about this or we're throwing everything away for no reason."

Gerrit sat silent, staring vacantly at the windshield. Eventually, after a long pause, he looked up at Jeroen. "What do you suggest we do? Because either way, I'm going back to my farmhouse."

"I suggest we leave the truck here, hidden inside the barn, so no patrols will see if they drive past. Then, after dark, we'll walk over the fields to your farm and see if they've set a trap for us."

Gerrit mulled it over for a few seconds and nodded his head. "Sounds like a plan, but I'm not going in wearing these." He pulled at the German uniform he was wearing.

"I agree."

Jeroen backed the truck into Koopman's barn, and once inside, they stripped off the uniforms and replaced them with the civilian clothes they'd hidden underneath the front seats.

Jeroen grabbed a couple of shovels and propped them against the barn door.

"What's that for?" Gerrit asked.

"The Koopman's. The least we can do is give them a proper burial."

The two men spent the next few hours digging three graves in the field behind the farmhouse. Hidden behind a wall where it was difficult for anyone to see them, they worked until their fingers were blistered and bleeding.

But they didn't stop, except for an occasional sip of water.

When the graves were deep enough, Jeroen and Gerrit carefully carried the bodies of the Koopman family outside and laid them to rest.

When the holes were filled, they stuck three crosses into the ground above their heads and the two men bowed their heads in prayer as Jeroen began to speak.

"Lord, we lay before You the souls of the Koopman family, taken from this earth in an act of senseless cruelty. They were innocent of any wrongdoing, yet their lives were cut short by evil men who sought to make them a warning to others. We pray You welcome them into Your eternal peace, far from the suffering and fear of this broken world.

"Give us the strength to continue on, to honour their memory by standing firm against the darkness that claimed them. May we find courage in their sacrifice and resolve in their tragedy, and may Your light guide us as we carry on the fight for freedom and justice. Amen."

"Amen," Gerrit said softly.

The two men waited in the barn until nightfall.

Chapter 47

Open fields stretched before them, an endless expanse of darkness broken only by the whisper of the wind through the grass. Clouds hung heavy overhead, blotting out the moon and stars, leaving the world submerged in darkness.

Jeroen pulled his collar tighter against the chill as he led the way, the faint squelch of their boots on the damp earth the only sound.

"Whatever happens, don't run in there like a farmer with a toothache. The SS might be there, hoping we come back for Elske and the others and we don't want to walk into their trap."

"I know," Gerrit whispered back. "You've told me a hundred times already."

Jeroen felt sorry for Gerrit. He was normally so stoic and reliable but after potentially losing his entire family in a single day, he was an emotional wreck.

"War is hard," Jeroen whispered. "Very hard."

Gerrit nodded, but said nothing. The weight of the situation was too much for him to contemplate.

They moved in silence, crouching low as they neared

the edge of Gerrit's farm. The outline of the house came into view—a jagged silhouette against the night sky, its roof collapsed in on itself. Jeroen slowed, holding a hand out to stop Gerrit.

The smell hit him first: acrid and sharp, the unmistakable stench of charred wood and ash. A faint metallic tang lingered beneath it, enough to make Jeroen's stomach churn.

"No!" Gerrit said far too loudly. "It's burned to the ground. They've burned it all."

"Keep your head," Jeroen warned, gripping Gerrit's arm. "We don't know if they're still watching. For the love of God, don't do anything stupid."

But Gerrit wasn't listening. He wrenched his arm free, his breathing ragged. "I need to see."

Jeroen swore under his breath but followed as Gerrit pushed forward, moving with a recklessness that made Jeroen's blood run cold.

They approached the ruins of the house, the scorched timber black and skeletal in the faint light. The ground crunched underfoot, brittle fragments of burned timber and shattered tiles scattered across the yard.

The barn was gone, reduced to little more than a smouldering pile of ash. Beside it, the house was barely standing, its walls buckled, the roof caved in entirely. The air still carried a faint warmth, as though the fire had only recently died out.

"They're gone," Gerrit said, his voice trembling. He stepped over a fallen beam, his boots stirring the ash. "Elske… Geert… Arjen… They're all gone."

"We don't know that," Jeroen said firmly, though the words felt hollow even as he spoke them. "There are no bodies here. They could have been taken alive."

"And then what?" Gerrit spat, spinning around to face him. "You know what they'll do to them. You know."

Jeroen didn't respond. He didn't have to. They both knew.

Gerrit stumbled back, his hands trembling as he stared at the ruins. His breath came in sharp, uneven gasps, and Jeroen realised that he was on the verge of losing control.

"Gerrit," he hissed, stepping forward. "Pull yourself together. We don't have time for this."

But Gerrit wasn't listening. He dropped to his knees, his hands clenching into fists as he let out a low, guttural cry. The sound was raw, primal, the kind of anguish that tore through the chest and left nothing but distressed silence in its wake.

Jeroen glanced around, his nerves alight with the fear that someone might hear. His eyes jumped from shadow to shadow, half expecting a squad of angry Germans to rush at them with rifles ready to open fire.

"Get up," he said, his voice low and urgent. "Now. If they're alive, you breaking down here won't do them any good. They're not here and we need to go."

When Gerrit didn't move, Jeroen grabbed him by the arm and hauled him to his feet. He hated to act like this after his best friend had just lost his entire family, but their own survival, and perhaps even the fate of the Dutch resistance, depended on them getting away.

Gerrit resisted at first, but eventually he staggered upright, his head bowed, his shoulders heaving with silent sobs.

"They're gone," Gerrit murmured as Jeroen dragged him away from the ruins. "They're gone, and it's my fault."

"It's not your fault," Jeroen snapped. "And we're not staying here to join them."

They crossed the fields as quickly as they could. Gerrit

continually stopped and looked back, but each time Jeroen urged him on, telling him that the time to grieve was later.

"We won't get back at them by giving up," he whispered harshly into Gerrit's ear. "Use this to harden your resolve to get even. We can't rest, not until the Nazis have been driven out of our country. What happened here is happening to families all across Europe, and it won't stop until we beat them into submission."

Gerrit scrunched his face, closing his eyes tightly. Whatever he did worked, because he turned away from the smouldering farmyard and walked with purpose towards the Koopman farm and the waiting Wehrmacht truck.

They reached the truck in silence, further words neither needed nor spoken. Jeroen climbed into the driver's seat and waited for Gerrit to join him.

With the doors shut, they sat in silence, contemplating their next move. Whatever it was going to be, it had to be vital and decisive.

"We shouldn't have done it," Gerrit broke the silence. "We should never have planted that bomb."

Jeroen remained silent, staring into the darkness in front of the windshield.

"Fernsby warned us," Gerrit continued. "He told us the repercussions would be too severe. We didn't listen, and now I've lost my entire family."

"We don't know that," Jeroen said angrily. "They must have arrested them, and are probably torturing them right now as we sit here. But they'll survive, and when we find out where they are, we'll get them out."

Jeroen softened his tone. "We'll find them, Gerrit, and when we do, we'll get them back."

"Then we'll kill them all," Gerrit hissed through clenched teeth.

"We will. Carefully, and with great caution, so they

don't take it out on innocent civilians like the Koopmans. But yes, we'll get our revenge for what they've done to us."

Silence fell once again as both men considered their options. Jeroen worried that either Elske or Geert would give up their safe house, which would put him and Geritt in enormous danger, but he knew better than to blame them knowing how effective the SS were at interrogating their victims.

"We can't go back to the safe house," he announced after another long silence. "It's not safe anymore. If they've taken Elske and the others, the SS will know where it is. We need another plan."

Gerrit didn't respond and Jeroen glanced at him, noting the vacant look in his eyes and the way his shoulders sagged. It was as though the fight had been drained from him.

Jeroen clenched his fists together. "We'll figure it out," he said quietly, though he wasn't sure if he was talking to Gerrit or himself. "We have to."

He fell silent again, his mind turning over what their next move was going to be. It started with finding a new location to hide and lie low until the reprisals blew over.

But where? That was the burning question his mind was struggling to answer.

Chapter 48

The two men sat in silence for over an hour. A plan had formed in Jeroen's mind, and he mulled over whether to pursue it or not.

He didn't want to—the man in question wasn't entirely fond of Jeroen and they'd never seen eye to eye, not even back in the days when they were friends.

Jeroen sighed. He didn't see any other choices at that moment in time.

"Our operation in Rotterdam is blown." Jeroen broke the silence. "For now, at least. We need to lie low until the reprisals blow over, and we need somewhere where we can plan what to do about Elske and the others."

"Where would that be?" Gerrit answered. "There's nowhere left in Rotterdam. Nobody will take us in, not with that massive reward on your head."

Gerrit looked away. "Nobody we can trust, at least."

"I know, Gerrit, and that is why we need to get away from here for a while. We'll come back when the heat dies down, because I'll never give up on Rotterdam, no matter the cost."

"I'll be back, because I'm finding Elske if it's the last thing I ever do."

Silence fell again.

"Well?" Gerrit asked impatiently. "What are we going to do? We can't sit here all night or the Nazis will catch us for sure."

"I have an old friend in Den Bosch. We go way back, and he's the leader of the resistance there."

Den Bosch was the popular name for Hertogenbosch, which was about sixty kilometres south of Rotterdam. Jeroen had spent time there during his military career, and it wasn't a place that held good memories for him.

But right now, he couldn't think of anywhere else they could go.

"Den Bosch?" Gerrit's eyes widened. "Who do you know down there?"

"His name is Rinus Van der Hoek. We served together."

"Can we trust him? I mean, how well do you know him?"

"I know him well enough, and yes, we can trust him. I'm not saying he'll be delighted to see me, because he probably won't, but we can trust him."

"What happened? Why won't he be pleased to see you?"

"Let's just say we had a disagreement over a girl." Jeroen didn't want to dig up the old memories, although he knew he'd have to when he faced Rinus again.

If he's still there.

"Well, if that's our only option, then let's go." Gerrit sat up in his seat and indicated to Jeroen to get moving.

After changing back into the hated German uniforms, the truck rolled east for over an hour in an attempt to get away from the many roadblocks around Rotterdam.

Along the way, Gerrit sat facing forward and didn't utter a word. Jeroen knew he was trying to contain his grief, and yet the pure hatred etched on his face told of plans he was making that went far beyond grieving.

Jeroen left him to it, hoping he wasn't about to do something stupid.

In a town called De Klomp, he turned the truck south. A few German vehicles patrolled the town, but none of them bothered with the Mercedes truck.

Forty-five minutes later, they slowed as they approached a bridge crossing the Waal river. The one thing they'd tried to avoid was about to happen—the bridge was manned, and all vehicles and pedestrians were being stopped.

Jeroen wound down the window and passed their identification papers to the miserable looking soldier on duty. The soldier scrutinised the papers for a long time, which made Jeroen's stomach twitch in despair.

"Where are you heading?" the soldier barked.

"Hertogenbosch." Jeroen gave the town its proper name, as that would be how the Germans referred to it.

"What are you doing there?" The soldier's tone was harsh and questioning.

"We're a resupply truck, and we've been ordered to report to the barracks there. That's all we know until we get there."

"What's in the back of the truck?"

This was getting uncomfortable.

"Fuel barrels, most of them empty. That's what we do. We're a resupply vehicle."

"Show me." The soldier marched towards the back of the truck.

Jeroen and Gerrit exchanged nervous glances. "Wait here," Jeroen said softly. "If it gets ugly, open fire and drive off. I'll jump in the back if I can. If not, just get as far away as you can."

"I'm not leaving you." Gerrit's face was set in stone.

"We don't have time for this. Just do as I tell you." Jeroens' words were harsh.

He opened the door and jumped down. Gerrit clutched his MP 38 submachine gun out of sight of the soldiers.

Jeroen joined the soldier, who was already in the back of the truck, shining his torch on the barrels. He kicked some of them and seemed satisfied when he heard the echo of the empty drum answering back.

The soldier shone the light into Jeroen's face, forcing him to squint in the bright light. "Where did you come from?" he barked.

Jeroen had been ready for this. "We were based in Rotterdam, but we were sent to a field unit in De Klomp to resupply their vehicles before coming down here. That's why the barrels are empty."

Without another word, the soldier passed their identification papers back and jumped out of the back of the truck. Jeroen didn't know if he'd believed him or not, so he cautiously followed, keeping a slight distance behind in case he had to duck underneath the truck.

"Go," the soldier ordered, turning his attention to the vehicle behind the truck.

Jeroen sighed inwardly and hurried to the driver's door before the soldier changed his mind.

"That was close," he said as he drove off.

"Too close," Gerrit agreed, although from the look on his face, Jeroen reckoned he would have preferred to get into a firefight with them.

The remainder of the journey was uneventful, and an hour later, Jeroen pulled the truck close to some heavy trees on the side of a narrow lane in the middle of nowhere.

"Are we here?" Gerrit asked.

"Close," Jeroen answered. "We can't exactly pull up to his house in a German truck, wearing German uniforms. We'd be dead before we got out of the truck."

"Good point." Gerrit began stripping off the hated uniform.

The engine ticked as it cooled, and Jeroen took his hands from the wheel, flexing his stiff fingers. The air was damp and heavy with the promise of more rain.

"Are you sure you trust this man?" Gerrit asked. "I mean, enough for this?"

"I do." Jeroen sighed. "Rinus has good reasons to dislike me, but we're on the same side, and he's as loyal to Holland as we are. He'll help us."

The walk to Rinus's house was short but tense. The path wound through dense foliage, which in the darkness was the kind of place where every shadow seemed to move if you looked too hard.

Gerrit followed him, gripping his weapon as though his life depended on it.

When the house came into view, its outline faint against the trees, Jeroen raised a hand to stop Gerrit.

"Let me do the talking," he said. "Rinus won't shoot us, but his companions might if we surprise them."

"It's late. Won't they be asleep?"

"Someone will be on watch. Rinus was always cautious, which is probably why the Nazis haven't caught him yet."

"What's our excuse then?" Gerrit retorted. "We've hardly been cautious."

"Luck." Jeroen shut down the conversation and

concentrated on the meeting about to take place. He glanced at his watch. It was 2:20 am.

The path narrowed as Jeroen and Gerrit neared the edge of the woods. Beyond the trees, the house was shrouded in darkness and half-hidden by overgrown hedges.

Rinus's home was old, its tiled roof sagging slightly after years of neglect. The stone walls, once pale, were now stained and weathered, and the windows reflected nothing but the emptiness of the night.

To a casual observer, the house looked empty, but Jeroen knew better. Rinus had never been one for the fancy things in life, and the state of his house, on the outside at least, was everything Jeroen had been expecting.

Nothing's changed then.

Jeroen paused, his breath clouding in the chill air. The sight of the house brought with it a pang of unease, a sharp reminder of what lay ahead. Memories he'd tried to bury rose unbidden—late nights in smoky rooms, arguments that cut deeper than the world outside.

And then there was the incident. Jeroen winced at the thought of it being dragged into the open again after so many years.

Rinus had been a brilliant strategist in their days with Dutch intelligence, but he was also stubborn, with a temper that matched Jeroen's own. The two had clashed more often than not, their shared ideals clumsily wrapped in bruised egos.

And now, after everything, here he was, walking up to Rinus's doorstep in the dead of night, dragging with him a mountain of trouble.

"This is madness," Jeroen muttered, half to himself.

"What is?" Gerrit whispered.

"Coming here. Asking for help from someone I spent years butting heads with. It's... complicated."

Gerrit gave him a sidelong glance. "Complicated? The man's a resistance leader. He'll help us, you said so yourself."

Jeroen didn't respond. Gerrit couldn't know—couldn't understand—the rift that had formed between him and Rinus. It wasn't just about their operational differences.

It was about trust, about knowing that whatever their shared history, Rinus would look at Jeroen now and see more than just the most wanted man in Holland and the man he'd been friends with and hated more than any other at the same time.

He ran a hand through his hair, exhaling sharply. "Let's just hope he hates the Nazis more than he hates me."

Chapter 49

As they approached the ramshackle old house, Jeroen's eyes scanned the perimeter, noting the barricaded windows and the faint glint of wire near the ground.

It was a tripwire, likely connected to a warning bell inside. Rinus had always been meticulous, paranoid even, and it seemed the years hadn't changed that.

The house itself loomed larger now, the crooked shape of a weather-beaten shed visible to one side, while a long-forgotten wheelbarrow leaned haphazardly against the back fence. Everything about the place spoke of practicality—no frills, no comforts. It was a hideout, not a home.

Jeroen's stomach tightened as they reached the door. For all his experience, for all the risks he'd taken, there was something profoundly unsettling about standing there, knocking on the door of an old adversary and asking for help.

But what choice did he have?

He raised his hand to knock, but as his hand rose, he heard the distinctive sound of a rifle cocking behind him.

"Stand where you are and put your hands up!"

Both Jeroen and Gerrit did as they were ordered. Gerrit slowly turned around, but was stopped in his tracks.

"Stand still and don't move a muscle. Who are you, and what are you doing here in the middle of the night?"

Jeroen didn't recognise the man's voice, so whoever it was, it wasn't Rinus.

"We're here to see Rinus," he said, staring at the unopened front door. "We're old friends."

"Nobody with that name lives here. And who visits old friends in the middle of the night?"

"Old military friends with a lot in common." Jeroen was growing tired of the charade. "I know he's here, so please tell him Jeroen is here to see him. I'm sure he'll be delighted."

The man with the gun fell silent for a moment. "Jeroen?" he asked. "Did you say your name is Jeroen?"

"I'm Jeroen, and I'm here to see my old friend."

"If you're Jeroen, you've got a nerve coming here. Keep your hands up and move."

The gunman indicated with the barrel of his rifle that they were to walk around the side of the house. The two men from Rotterdam did as he ordered and walked into the darkness.

A door opened halfway down the side of the house, and for a moment they were flooded with light.

"He says his name is Jeroen," the man behind them said.

"Jeroen? Here?" the man at the door asked, surprised.

A third man pushed past from inside the house and stepped outside. In the light, he and Jeroen stared at each other for a long moment, neither saying a word.

"It's good to see you again, Rinus." Jeroen finally broke the awkward silence. "I'm sorry to show up at such a late hour."

"Come inside," Rinus said, his voice deep and gruff. "Pieter, check them for weapons."

The broad-shouldered, well-built man with the physique of someone used to hard labour, who was standing next to Rinus stepped forward. Jeroen threw his arms outwards in an act of submission.

Gerrit followed suit, and Pieter patted them down. From Jeroen, he removed the MP 38, two pistols, and three knives. Gerrit only had the MP 38.

Once their weapons had been removed, the man behind them indicated for them to go inside the house. With all the locks reset, they moved to a bare sitting room with no wallpaper. The only contents were a couch for two people against a wall, a table with a radio set, and four wooden chairs.

If Jeroen suspected that this was not a working farm before, now he had confirmation.

This was Rinus's safe place away from the Nazis.

Jeroen got a good look at his old friend. They hadn't seen each other for years, but apart from ageing, not much had changed.

Rinus was a wiry man, his frame lean and angular, as if every ounce of fat had been burned away by years of hardship and stress. His face, lined and weathered, bore the unmistakable marks of someone who had lived a life of constant vigilance.

His dark eyes were sharp and calculating, darting between Jeroen and Gerrit with a mix of suspicion and recognition. There was an intensity to his gaze, as though he could dissect a man's soul with a single look, his hair, streaked with grey, was cropped close to his scalp, and a neatly trimmed beard clung to his jawline, giving him a rugged but controlled appearance, and his hands, calloused and rough, hinted at a man unafraid of hard labour, though the way he carried himself spoke of someone used to giving orders.

Rinus caught Jeroen staring at him, and scowled. Gerrit, who had remained silent ever since they'd arrived, now spoke up.

"You must be Rinus?" he said. "I've heard a lot about you."

Rinus cast his gaze over Gerrit. "I highly doubt that. Jeroen would rather I didn't exist. Who are you?"

Jeroen threw Gerrit a dark look and took over the conversation.

"This is Gerrit, and he's loyal to the cause. He's a master forger, and he's just lost every member of his family to the Nazis."

"Ah, yes. I heard about your exploits in Rotterdam. You always were one for the grand entrance. I'm sorry for your friend's loss, but what did you expect? Why do you think we don't go around planting car bombs and derailing trains?"

Jeroen didn't answer. He waited for the inevitable from Rinus so they could get it out of the way.

"Why are you here? Has it got so bad for you in Rotterdam that you'd turn to the one man you hate more than any other to help?"

Jeroen's face turned red. "I never hated you, Rinus. We were always friends until…" He broke off, leaving the sentence unfinished.

"Until you took the one thing from me, that meant more than anything else." Rinus finished the sentence for him.

Jeroen bowed his head. "I've apologised for that many times, and I do so again now. I was young and stupid, and I'd do anything to turn the clock back and change what I did."

"What did you do, Jeroen?" Gerrit interrupted. "I can see that you two don't like each other, and I don't want any more trouble. We're in enough as it is."

Rinus looked over at Gerrit. "I'm assuming he never told you what he did? I doubt he would."

Jeroen sighed out loud. "When we were young, we worked together and were good friends. We drank together and did almost everything together. Rinus met a beautiful young lady, and they fell madly in love. They even set a wedding date."

"I can see where this is going," Gerrit said.

"I was drunk one night, which wasn't unusual in those days. Rinus was away on a job and had asked me to take care of Jannetje. Unfortunately, we were both drunk, and well, you can guess the rest."

Gerrit sighed. "That's a dirty thing to do to your best friend."

"I'm glad you agree," Rinus said.

"What happened after that?" Gerrit asked.

"Jannetje felt so guilty that she couldn't face either of us again. She told Rinus what we'd done and then she packed her bags and left. I never saw her again, and after that, well, Rinus and I drifted and went our separate ways. We worked together occasionally, but it was never the same again."

"I'm not surprised," Gerrit said. "I'd be the same if anyone had done that to my Elske."

With the thought of Elske, Gerrit's eyes filled up, and he looked at the ground to avoid any further eye contact.

"I apologise again, Rinus. What I did was wrong, and I'd do anything to put things right between us."

Rinus rose from his seat and walked towards Jeroen. With no warning, he lashed out, striking him on the side of the face with the palm of his hand.

Jeroen, caught off guard, rubbed his bright red cheek.

"I deserved that, I suppose."

"I've been wanting to do that for over twenty years," Rinus said with an air of satisfaction. "Now, tell me why you're here."

Chapter 50

Jeroen spent the next thirty minutes telling Rinus everything that had happened up to, and including the possible arrests of Elske, Geert, and Arjen.

Rinus tensed when he heard what the Nazis did to the Koopman family, and he gazed sympathetically at Gerrit during the final moments of Jeroen's explanations.

The one part Jeroen left out was the reason why they'd rescued Senta. As far as they were concerned, it was a request from the British government. No reasons were offered, and none were asked for.

Rinus, as an experienced operator, knew only too well how the world's intelligence agencies worked, so it came as no surprise to him.

"And now you're here wanting our help," he said after Jeroen finished speaking. "You do know that you are the most wanted man in Holland right now? There's a price on your head that's frankly, quite staggering. I doubt the Nazis will ever pay it, but it shows how badly they want you."

"Isn't he worth it?" The well-built man who'd frisked Jeroen spoke up.

Rinus gave the man a long, hard look. "Allow me to introduce two of my most trusted men. The one who just spoke is Pieter. He's blunt, and always to the point. But he can be relied on when things get rough."

Jeroen nodded at the young man, who was somewhere in his mid-twenties. A faint scar ran down his right cheek, giving him the aura of a man not to be messed with, and his pale blue eyes were cold, assessing everyone and everything with a dispassionate gaze, as though calculating whether they were a threat. Rinus had chosen wisely, which didn't surprise Jeroen at all.

"The other one is a genius with weapons and any kind of explosives." Rinus pointed at the man who'd met them at the door. "His name is Rogier, although we all know him as Fuse. Both of them love our country and can be trusted implicitly."

Rogier was shorter than Pieter but wiry, with a quick, restless energy radiating from him. His dark brown hair was slicked back, though a few strands had managed to escape, giving him a slightly dishevelled look.

His sharp nose and high cheekbones lent him a fox-like appearance, an impression only heightened by his quick, darting eyes. A thin cigarette dangled from his lips, its smoke curling lazily around his angular face.

"And this, gentlemen," Rinus looked at his men. "Is the infamous Jeroen. He needs no introduction from me. Everyone in Holland knows his name, and although our country needs a hero right now, it doesn't help that a leader of the resistance is the one that should be that hero."

"What do you want from us?" Pieter asked, staring into Jeroen's eyes.

Jeroen opened his mouth to answer, but Rinus waved him off.

"We are in this together, and even if we were enemies before, the Nazi invasion has changed everything. We work together to rid ourselves of the infestation, because that's the only way we are ever going to win."

"What does that even mean?" Pieter shot back. "What are we going to do? Blow up more Nazi vehicles? Endanger our families? Friends?"

"If that's what it takes to defeat them, then yes," Rinus answered, his eyes solemn. "Whatever resentments I hold towards this man, I will tell you that he is the best intelligence operator I ever worked with. If he is to be the face of the Dutch resistance, then we all need to band together behind him and support him as I would any of you."

"Right now, he needs to lie low," Gerrit butted in. "He's too hot for any of us to work with, at least until things die down. We have to keep him hidden where the Nazis can't find him."

Jeroen glared at Gerrit. "That's not what I want," he said. "There's a lot to do, and we can't achieve our goals if I'm hidden away somewhere."

"He's right, Jeroen," Rinus said. "You need to stay out of sight and let others run the show for a while."

Jeroen scowled, but Gerrit cut him off.

"I was hoping you would help me find out where they're keeping Elske and the others and, if possible, help me get them out."

"Finding out where they're at will be easy," Rinus said. "Getting them out will be impossible. I know you managed it with the German girl, but their security will be much tighter from now on. I'm afraid we won't be able to get your wife out, but we can help recruit and train new people to take their places. That's the fastest way to see your wife again, because the sooner we win this war, the sooner you will be with her again."

Gerrit frowned; it wasn't what he wanted to hear.

"He's right, Gerrit," Jeroen said. "There's no way we're getting anywhere near Elske now."

"Speaking of the German girl, there's something that you might not be aware of that I want to talk to you about."

"Senta? What about her?" Jeroen answered. "We told you everything we know about her. We don't know why the British wanted her."

"Not her," Rinus said. "The other one."

Chapter 51

Jeroen's eyes narrowed as Rinus leaned back in his chair, the scrape of wood on the floor echoing faintly in the quiet room. The two men studied each other, unspoken tension hanging heavy in the air.

Gerrit sat off to the side, his expression a blend of exhaustion and wariness, waiting for what would come next.

"Do you remember our old colleague, Adriaan Westerhout?" Rinus asked.

"Of course I do. He runs a cell close to the border with Belgium, where he gets people, Jews mainly, out of Holland. He's done a lot of good work, from what I hear."

"Adriaan sent a messenger," Rinus began, his voice low but deliberate. "One of his men found a girl—a blonde, German girl—hiding in a barn near the border with Belgium."

Jeroen felt his breath hitch, but said nothing. Rinus continued, his sharp eyes fixed on Jeroen's face.

"She claims her name is Mina Postner."

Jeroen's heart sank and Gerrit shifted uncomfortably, a mixture of shock and something unspoken passing between them.

"She said she knows you," Rinus added, watching their reaction closely. "Like everybody else, Adriaan knows about the German girls you were working with, especially the one who did the radio broadcasts before the Rotterdam bombings."

"Mina," Gerrit muttered, rubbing his face with the back of his hand.

"You've already told me that Mina ran away to France, so this more or less confirms what you said." Rinus chewed his bottom lip, deep in thought.

"She ran," Jeroen said. "As I told you before, she left for France because she knew Senta wouldn't leave her behind. Whatever the reason, the British want Senta, but not Mina. That's why she left."

Rinus leaned forward in his chair. "There's something you're not telling me about Senta. Why do the British want her so badly?"

Jeroen sighed and looked across at Gerrit. "Rinus can be trusted. He needs to know the truth."

Gerrit's head bowed, indicating his agreement.

"Senta has a special gift," Jeroen said. "She has a once-in-a-generation talent that can turn this war against the Nazis."

Rinus and his two comrades sat ramrod still, their eyes locked onto Jeroen.

"She has an eidetic memory, which means she can see something once and remember every little detail forever."

Rinus gave a low whistle. "No wonder the British want her. If word ever gets out, every intelligence agency in the world will be after her."

Evasion

"Including the Nazis," Jeroen added. "That's why we rescued her. The British sent Michael Fernsby to take her back to England. Mina knew this, so she left before Senta could object."

"Before you ask," Gerrit broke in. "Mina didn't know that Senta had been captured by the Germans when she left. If she had, she'd never have gone."

Rinus nodded grimly. "Her story fits, more or less. She claimed it was too dangerous for her in Rotterdam, and that she's trying to reach a family in France—friends of someone she lost, apparently. Says the family doesn't even know she's coming."

"That's true too," Gerrit said. "Mina's best friend from Germany was a Jew. Unfortunately, her and her father were killed in the Rotterdam blitz, but it's her family that Mina was trying to reach."

"What's Westerhout planning on doing with her?" Jeroen asked.

"You know Westerhout as well as I do," Rinus answered. "He's suspicious of his own mother. He doesn't believe her, and he thinks she might be a German spy. It's serious, because if the woman is a spy, their entire operation is in jeopardy."

"What's he going to do?" Jeroen asked.

"If they decide she's lying?" Rinus asked.

Jeroen nodded.

"She'll be executed."

A heavy silence followed. Gerrit stared at the floor, his jaw working as he tried to process the implications.

"What is he waiting for?" Jeroen asked. "Why did he send a messenger to tell you this?"

"He didn't. The messenger was here on other business and told me this as an aside. Westerhout wanted to find you and give you a chance to verify her story, but after the car bombing and train derailment in Rotterdam, he couldn't find you."

Rinus stared at his old friend and adversary. "He wanted to give her a chance, but he can't risk the lives of his operatives on the words of an unknown German girl."

"Her life is in your hands, Jeroen," Gerrit said. "You have to save her."

"How?" Jeroen asked. "I can't go anywhere. I'm needed here."

"It would be better for everyone if you left here for a while so things can calm down," Gerrit said

"You're the only one that can save her life," Rinus said. "Westerhout is only keeping her alive because he's heard her story and is sympathetic to her cause. If you don't go and verify it's really her, she'll be killed, and that will be on you, Jeroen."

The weight of the situation pressed down on Jeroen like a millstone. He ran a hand through his hair and glanced at Gerrit, whose face was etched with worry.

"What do you suggest I do?" Jeroen asked after a long pause.

"Go to Breda and verify it's her," Gerrit said. "If it is, keep her safe and take her to France. You owe her that much, at least."

"Are you coming too?"

"No." Gerrit shook his head. "I'm more useful here. With Rinus's help, I'll create us all new IDs, and we'll find Elske and the others."

Jeroen closed his eyes. He knew that what they were saying made sense.

"He's right," Rinus said. "Take Mina to where she needs to go. Get her out of harm's way, and yourself out of the SS's reach for a while. The resistance will hold without you."

The room fell silent, the tension palpable. Nobody spoke for several minutes.

Eventually, Jeroen rose to his feet and looked at everyone in turn. "I'll do it. I'll leave first thing in the morning."

Chapter 52

The following morning, Jeroen, bleary-eyed after very little sleep, entered the living room to find everyone else huddled around the radio.

A cultured voice from the BBC World Service was announcing the day's events to the world.

"This is London calling.

This is the BBC World Service. We regret to report that earlier today, German troops entered the city of Paris. After several days of intense fighting along the approaches to the French capital, the French government has declared Paris an open city in an effort to spare it from destruction.

German forces began their occupation early this morning, and reports indicate that the swastika now flies over many of the city's landmarks, including the Eiffel Tower. Civilians have been seen fleeing in great numbers, seeking refuge farther south.

Despite this significant setback, the French and British governments remain resolute in their fight against the enemy. Forces continue to regroup and reorganise in anticipation of future operations. We urge listeners to remember that this is but one chapter in a longer struggle.

Stay tuned for further updates.

This is London calling."

Jeroen wrung his hands together in desperation. The look he shared with Gerrit and Rinus said it all, and the radio was turned off to spare them from any further depressing news.

"It gets worse by the day," Rogier said.

"Britain will be next, and when that falls, Hitler will control all of Europe," Pieter said, his face a mixture of fury and regret.

"Britain won't fall," Rinus said. "It can't. If it does, it's over for all of us."

"Whatever happens, we'll never stop fighting for our freedom," Jeroen snapped. "They'll have to kill every last one of us, and then they'll have to fight the next generation. We'll never give up."

"You sound like Winston Churchill," Rinus said, bringing some much-needed relief to the dark atmosphere. "But I agree. The Nazis might have occupied us, but they'll never defeat us."

Pieter threw a set of keys at Jeroen. "I brought your truck here last night. It's in the barn, out of sight of prying eyes."

"Thank you."

Breakfast was eaten in silence, Jeroen's mind filled with thoughts of how he was going to get Mina to France. The others remained quiet to give him the time and space he needed to think.

Rinus produced a bagful of supplies that would get him to Breda, and everyone watched as Jeroen put on the Wehrmacht uniform that had served him so well on the dangerous roads of occupied Holland.

With a final handshake and words of encouragement from Gerrit, Jeroen slipped outside and set off to find Mina.

Chapter 53

SS-Obergruppenführer Hanns Albin Rauter ascended the stone steps of the RSHA building located at Prinz-Albrecht-Straße 8 in Berlin. The RSHA, as the headquarters of the feared security apparatus for Hitler's Third Reich, was the most intimidating building in the whole of Germany.

The RSHA was the central organisation responsible for security, intelligence, and policing under Heinrich Himmler, with Reinhard Heydrich as its first chief.

Even for someone as seasoned and high ranking as Albin Rauter, the RSHA building struck fear into his heart as he headed into the devil's lair.

The building loomed like a grey monolith, its stark façade exuding an aura of oppression. The chill seeped through the soles of his polished boots and into his spine, a reminder that the power within those walls was absolute—and often arbitrary.

The iron-framed double doors creaked open, revealing an atrium that smelled faintly of polish and paper, overlaid with the acrid sting of cigarette smoke.

Black-clad SS guards snapped to attention, their rifles gleaming under the cold electric light. Rauter returned their salute with a curt nod, his jaw set as he approached the receptionist.

"Obergruppenführer Heydrich is expecting me," he said, his voice clipped.

The secretary, a pale young woman in a tight bun, motioned silently towards the corridor leading to the Reich Security Main Office. Rauter knew the way; he'd been there before.

Too many times.

The journey to Heydrich's office on the top floor felt interminable. Rauter's boots clicked against the marble floor, the sound swallowed by the oppressive silence. Finally, he reached the heavy oak door marked with Heydrich's name and title on a gleaming brass nameplate.

SS-Obergruppenführer Heydrich.

The Blond Beast.

He knocked once, firmly.

"Enter." The voice was cold and devoid of humanity.

Rauter entered, bracing himself. Heydrich stood behind his massive, ornately decorated desk, a vision of controlled menace. Tall and lean, his SS uniform was immaculate, the silver insignia catching the light. His pale, hawkish features were inscrutable, save for the icy glint in his eyes that pinned Rauter like a specimen on display.

"Ah, Rauter." Heydrich's voice was as cold as the Berlin winter. "It's good of you to join us. Sit down."

Rauter obeyed, settling into the straight-backed chair opposite Heydrich's desk. The room was sparse but arranged efficiently, dominated by a large map of occupied Europe and a black-and-red swastika banner draped in one corner. A sheaf of papers sat neatly on the desk, flanked by a half-empty glass of schnapps.

Evasion

"Well?" Heydrich prompted, his gaze unblinking. "The visit from Falken was most enlightening. What updates do you bring me?"

Rauter took a deep breath. "Herr Obergruppenführer, I bring news of recent developments from Rotterdam. We have made good progress in our investigations, including the arrest of several members of the resistance group that carried out the attacks on the hotel and the train."

Heydrich leaned forward in his chair, his cold eyes menacing and brooding. "Did you find out why the girl is so important?"

"We did, sir. Two of the group broke down under questioning and told us everything. The girl, Senta Postner, has an eidetic memory, and is able to remember everything she sees down to the minutest detail. That is why the British hold her in such high regard."

Heydrich's eyes grew wider. "An eidetic memory? Do you know how rare that is, Rauter?"

"I do, sir, and so do the British. If they fully exploit her talents, it could shift certain strategic balances in their favour."

"Indeed." Heydrich stared at Rauter as a cat would stare at a mouse before it pounced.

"There's more," Rauter spoke rapidly in an attempt to quell the acrid sensation rising in his stomach. "I've prepared a detailed report for you, sir."

Rauter handed Heydrich a typed report detailing the events in Rotterdam. Heydrich pored over the report, occasionally looking up to glare at Rauter before delving deeper into the details.

"Who else knows about this?" Heydrich asked after finishing the report.

"SS-Obersturmführer Falken, who wrote the report, and SS-Obersturmführer Stadtler, who is in charge of the investigation and who conducted the interrogations. That's all, sir, besides the two of us, of course."

"Good, keep it that way."

Heydrich sat back in his chair and placed his hands behind his head. "So, Fernsby, who has been nothing but a thorn in our side, is potentially injured and on the run somewhere in Belgium."

"Yes, sir."

"He's babysitting the girl with the eidetic memory and is trying to get her to England. They are alone, without supplies, and they are desperate. Am I right so far?"

"Yes, Obergruppenführer, but I wouldn't underestimate the resourcefulness of Fernsby. From what I know of him, he's been in this situation before and got out of it. He's dangerous, sir."

"I know all about Fernsby and his fellow Unit 317 operatives. I have plans to take care of them, but for now, I want you to concentrate on finding Fernsby and the girl."

"All available units are searching for them. We found the wreckage of the aircraft, so we know the general vicinity where they are located."

"Good. Find them at all costs. I don't want all *available* units on this, I want *all* units on it. This is a top priority, Rauter, so find them. Find the girl."

"Yes, Obergruppenführer Heydrich."

"What about her sister, the one who did the broadcasts? Have you found her yet?"

"No, sir. We're concentrating our efforts on finding Fernsby and the girl, so we haven't looked for her. She's somewhere between Rotterdam and the South of France, from what I hear."

Heydrich slammed his fists on the desk.

"Find her!" he roared. "Don't you see? If we have her,

the sister will have no choice other than to cooperate with us. If we don't have her sister as leverage, she'll probably refuse and go to her grave resisting us."

Rauter thought for a moment. "That makes sense, Obergruppenführer Heydrich. I'll set someone on it right away."

"You'll do more than that, Rauter. This is an absolute top priority. I want you to put your best man on this. Task him with finding Fernsby and the two sisters. That is to be his only job, and he is to be given every resource available. Promote him if you have to, but he is to have full authority to do whatever needs to be done to find and capture the two girls."

"I understand, Obergruppenführer. What about Fernsby?"

"Kill him on sight. He's done enough damage to the Reich already, and he's no use to us."

"Consider it done."

"This is top secret, Rauter. Nobody other than those involved must know anything, especially about the girl. Do you understand?"

"Absolutely, Obergruppenführer."

"Wait outside my office with my secretary. I'm going to give you a signed document from myself that grants the owner of it full authority over all local resources and manpower. I want that girl, Rauter, so do not fail me."

"I won't, sir."

SS-Obergruppenführer Hanns Albin Rauter rose to his feet and threw his right arm in the air. With a deep-throated roar, he bellowed the two most popular words in Nazi Germany.

"Heil Hitler!" he roared.

"Heil Hitler," Heydrich replied.

Rautin left Heydrich's office and waited for the signed letter of authority from one of the highest-ranking men in the Reich.

And the most feared.

Chapter 54

The countryside stretched endlessly before them, a patchwork of green fields and quiet farmhouses basking under the summer sun. Michael and Senta trudged along a dirt path, their clothes stained with sweat and dust.

It had been three days since they crossed into France at Bailleul, slipping past the border unnoticed in the confusion of a nation on edge.

The heat was less oppressive now, both in temperature and in the pursuit. The Germans, focused on consolidating their search in Belgium, seemed to have abandoned their hunt for the fugitives.

For the first time in ages, Michael felt they could walk without constantly looking over their shoulders.

The weather had cleared up as well. Gone were the oppressive, heavy rain clouds from the night of the plane crash, replaced by wispy clouds that danced in a perfect blue sky.

Their clothes had dried, but both had blisters on their feet, making it difficult to walk. To that end, they'd rested for a day in a house in a small village that had been abandoned during the German invasion.

A well outside provided fresh water, and they boiled it on a wood stove to clean both their bodies and their clothes. After resting for a day, they felt refreshed and ready to continue their journey.

"Do you think Mina found a place like this?" Senta asked. "I've been thinking about her a lot ever since we crossed the border, and I hope she's safe somewhere."

Michael's heart dropped like a stone at the mention of Mina's name. He'd purposely avoided thinking about her because to do so broke his soul.

"I hope so. I worry about her every second of every day. She wasn't prepared for a journey like this, so the best I've hoped for was that she turned around and went back to Jeroen. At least she's safe there."

"Do you think that's what she did?"

"That's what I'm clinging to, at least until I know something different. I promised you I'd find her, and I will come back for her, no matter what my bosses say when I get you home safely."

"We are both very lucky to have you in our lives," Senta said, which was a complete change of tune from when they'd first met.

"No, Senta, I'm the lucky one. Without you, I'd be dead by now. You, Mina, you give me something to live for, and something to fight for other than just the evil of Hitler and his deranged Nazis."

Senta swiped at her eyes as she rose to her feet. "I think she's safe somewhere waiting for you to find her. I'll cling to that belief until we're together again."

Michael smiled. He wished he had the same optimistic outlook. In reality, he feared the worst for his beloved

Evasion

Mina, and the thought of her suffering drove him to the edge of insanity.

"Let's go." He donned his rucksack and tightened the straps, reached down to tie his shoelaces, and fastened the buttons on his shirt. Anything to avoid thinking about her.

They headed west in the general direction of Paris, which was still one hundred and fifty miles away, and he knew they would never make it on foot, not with the Germans advancing as rapidly as they were. The city could fall any day, although Michael hoped the French and British were defending it to the hilt.

If Paris fell, London would be next.

Their path took them through small villages and overgrown fields, where farmers gave them wary glances but asked no questions. Michael bartered for bread and cheese at a roadside stall, which was enough to keep them moving for the next few days if they were careful.

Later in the afternoon, they stumbled upon a railway line cutting through dense woodland near a town called Saint-Omer. The faint, rhythmic clatter of a train reached their ears, and Michael pulled Senta into the trees, crouching low to watch.

A crazy idea entered Michael's mind.

We'll take the train!

"If this is a goods train, we might be able to get a ride," he announced to incredulous looks from Senta. "It'll get us a lot nearer to Paris."

"Or we'll kill ourselves trying to jump onto a moving train!" Senta stared at Michael as if he'd gone completely mad. "The last time I was on a train, someone blew the line and derailed it."

Michael smiled and made a gurgling noise in his throat. "It's worth a try."

The train approached slowly, its engine a steady chug, and Michael's heart quickened. This wasn't the kind of freight they'd feared before, laden with soldiers. It *was* a goods train, and its pace was mercifully slow as it navigated a curve.

"This is our chance," Michael whispered, nodding towards the rear carriages.

Senta nodded in response, and they moved as one, darting from their hiding place and sprinting alongside the train. Michael leapt first, gripping the edge of a sliding door and hauling it open.

"Come on!" he urged, extending a hand. Senta grabbed it, and with one last effort, he pulled her aboard before slamming the door shut behind them.

Inside the darkened carriage, the air was heavy with the smell of grain and sawdust. Senta collapsed against the wooden crates lining the walls, her chest heaving as she caught her breath.

Michael struck a match, its tiny flame flickering as he studied the space. "Looks like this one's carrying feed," he muttered. "Not bad for cover."

Senta managed a faint smile. "As long as it's going south, I don't care what it's carrying."

Michael pulled out their map, squinting in the dim light. He traced the railway line with his finger, stopping at Amiens.

"This train won't take us all the way to Paris, but it should get us far enough to find another."

Senta leaned over, her eyes scanning the names of the towns. "Amiens," she murmured. "I remember reading about that in school. It's where a major battle took place in the Great War."

"It most certainly was," Michael agreed. "And we need to be careful this time too, because I guarantee you the Germans have a significant presence there right now."

Evasion

Senta didn't hear him. She was asleep.

Chapter 55

The train slowed hours later, the screech of its brakes pulling them from an uneasy sleep. Michael cracked the door open, peering out at the unfamiliar landscape.

The rhythmic chug of the locomotive echoed across the countryside, but what he saw set his heart racing.

A sign told them they were approaching Amiens, but Michael's attention was drawn to what was beyond the tracks.

A cluster of Wehrmacht bathtub vehicles were parked in formation, their hulking shapes illuminated by the late afternoon sun.

The telltale gleam of helmets and the faint murmur of German voices confirmed his worst fear—Amiens was crawling with troops. The train crept into the outskirts of the town, its brakes hissing as it approached a checkpoint.

Michael pulled back from the door and turned to Senta. "We have to get off. Now," he hissed urgently.

Senta, still groggy, rubbed her eyes. "What's wrong?"

"There are Germans everywhere," he said, his voice low but sharp. "If this train stops, they'll search it."

Evasion

Her eyes widened in alarm, and she scrambled to her feet. Michael opened the door slightly, letting in the cooler air. The train had slowed to a near crawl as it neared the checkpoint, giving them precious seconds to act.

"Follow me," Michael instructed, leaping from the carriage and landing in the soft grass beside the tracks. He turned, holding out his hand to steady Senta as she jumped down after him.

They crouched low in the long grass, watching as the train clattered on, the front of the train now just metres from the checkpoint. Soldiers with rifles slung over their shoulders moved towards the train, their boots crunching on gravel.

"Come on," Michael whispered, tugging Senta's arm.

They crept away from the tracks, slipping into the shadowy cover of a hedgerow. Buildings and roads spread out on the other side of the hedgerow, but their side opened up into a patchwork of fields bordered by lines of poplar trees, their silhouettes swaying gently in the breeze.

The checkpoint receded behind them, but Michael didn't stop. They moved quickly, darting from one clump of trees to the next, putting as much distance as they could between themselves and the German soldiers in Amiens.

The faint sound of engines and shouted orders carried on the wind, a grim reminder of the danger they were leaving behind.

Finally, after what felt like hours, Michael slowed. His chest heaved as he scanned the horizon, noting the faint outline of a farmhouse nestled at the edge of a wooded copse. Smoke curled lazily from its chimney, a sign of life.

Daylight was rapidly fading, and they needed a place to hole up for the night.

"We'll try there," he said, pointing.

"Someone's living there," Senta whispered. "I can see the smoke from the chimney from here."

"They'll have a barn," Michael answered. "As long as they don't have dogs, we'll be safe for the night."

"I don't like it," Senta said. "It's too dangerous."

"We don't have any other choices, unless you want to sleep in a tree again."

Senta pulled a face.

They approached cautiously, sticking to the shadows. As they neared the farmhouse, the soft glow of a lantern inside illuminated a modest kitchen.

Cautiously, peering through the window, Michael saw an older woman seated at a table, her hands folded in her lap as she stared into the fire. She seemed alone, but he couldn't be sure.

He ducked under the window and headed for the barn that was about a hundred feet away from the house. Senta followed, and once inside, they closed the door behind them.

The barn stank of animals and straw, but Senta took a deep breath as it reminded her of the family farm at Ryskamp. Michael's eyes stung, and he blinked rapidly to clear them.

He hesitated a moment, listening to the stillness. The faint crackle of the woman's fire reached them even there, carried on the cool night air seeping through the gaps in the wooden planks.

"We should stay near the back," he whispered. "Out of sight."

Senta nodded, her face pale in the dim moonlight filtering through the slats. Together, they moved deeper into the barn, their steps muffled by the dirt floor scattered with straw.

Michael's hand brushed against a wooden barrel, and

he crouched to inspect it. The faint scent of grain confirmed it held feed, perhaps for the pigs he'd spotted in a small pen outside.

"Over here," he murmured, motioning towards a pile of loose hay stacked against one wall. "We can hide behind this."

Time passed in tense silence. The barn creaked softly as the night wore on, only the occasional rustle of hay or faint cluck of a chicken breaking the stillness.

Michael leaned back against the wooden wall, keeping his ears trained for any sound of approaching footsteps.

It was Senta who first noticed the faint shuffle near the door. Her hand gripped Michael's sleeve, her eyes wide. He sat upright, his breath catching as the door creaked open, spilling a sliver of lantern light across the floor.

He reached for his trusty Walther PPK, placing his finger on the trigger, ready to strike at the first sign of danger.

The old woman stood in the doorway, her silhouette framed by the glow of the lantern she held aloft. She hesitated, her eyes scanning the barn until they settled on the pile of hay where Michael and Senta sat frozen.

"You can come out now," she said in French, her voice soft but firm. "I saw you earlier. There are no Germans here."

Michael didn't understand her, but Senta appeared to do so, at least the gist of it.

Michael's heart pounded as he exchanged a glance with Senta. Slowly, he rose, stepping into the light with his hands raised in a gesture of peace.

"Please," he said in English. "We mean no harm."

"Anglais?" the woman asked, startled.

"Yes, English," Senta answered in halting French.

The woman's gaze flicked to Senta, who had also

stood, her face pale but resolute. The old woman took a step closer, lowering the lantern slightly.

"You're not soldiers," she said, her tone laced with suspicion.

"She said we're not soldiers," Senta translated for Michael.

"Tell her that I am a British soldier and that we're trying to get to Paris for an important meeting."

Senta translated as best she could. The old woman seemed to understand, although she didn't seem to believe them.

"We're trying to get to Paris," Michael said again in English.

The woman studied them for a long moment before her shoulders relaxed slightly.

"Paris," she murmured, almost to herself. "I thought you might be French soldiers hiding from the Germans."

"British, not French," Senta answered. "And we are trying to hide from the Germans."

"Have you not heard?" the woman asked. "Paris fell to the Germans two days ago. The swastika now flies over the Eiffel Tower."

"Paris has fallen to the Germans," Senta translated. "Two days ago."

The woman's eyes filled with tears, and Michael felt incredibly sorry for her.

He was stunned. He should have expected it, but the news hit him like a fist to the solar plexus.

The old woman nodded slowly, noting their reaction. She set the lantern down on a nearby crate and reached into the folds of her apron, producing a bundle wrapped in cloth.

"Here," she said, unwrapping it to reveal a loaf of

Evasion

bread, a wedge of cheese, and a small flask of milk. "You look like you haven't eaten in days."

Michael hesitated, not wanting to take the food from the woman's table.

"You need this more than I do," she said to Senta. "Please, take it."

"She said to take it or it will offend her," Senta roughly translated.

"Thank you," Michael said. It was all he could think of to say.

The woman straightened, her expression guarded. "You can stay here tonight. But you must leave before dawn. It's not safe to linger."

Michael nodded after Senta translated.

"We will. Merci."

She gave a curt nod and turned, pausing at the door. "If anyone asks," she added, her voice low, "I haven't seen you."

Michael and Senta sat in silence for a moment, the weight of her kindness sinking in. Michael handed Senta the bread and cheese, and they shared the milk that tasted like nectar from heaven.

When they'd finished, they curled up in the straw. The barn settled around them, its creaks and whispers setting off alarm bells in Michael's ears all night long.

For that night, at least, they were safe, but Michael's mind wandered, not allowing sleep to overcome his brain. Now that Paris had fallen, Marcel would be gone. He was their only hope of getting back to England.

As he lay in the darkness, Michael decided that their only hope was to head for the coast and a boat out of France.

Chapter 56

SS-Obersturmführer Erik Stadtler adjusted his collar, his hand lingering for a moment on the silver insignia that marked his position within the SS ranks.

He'd been summoned to The Hague with no prior warning, so he knew that whatever SS-Obergruppenführer Rauter wanted with him, it was urgent.

Beyond urgent, even, and he knew it had something to do with the girl.

He stood outside the closed door to Rauter's office, flanked by two stoic guards who gave no indication they even noticed him. Stadtler drew a deep breath, trying to suppress the excitement bubbling beneath his calm exterior.

The guard to his left opened the door, nodding for him to enter. Stadtler squared his shoulders and stepped inside, his boots clicking sharply against the polished floor.

Rauter was seated at his desk, a massive thing of dark wood that seemed to swallow the man in its enormity. Papers lay in neat stacks, a black fountain pen resting alongside a small silver ashtray.

Evasion

Rauter's sharp eyes lifted from the document he was reading, locking onto Stadtler, adding to his unease with the weight of his gaze.

"Stadtler," Rauter said, his voice revealing his exhaustion and stress. "Please, sit."

Stadtler snapped his heels together, his right arm shooting up in salute. "Heil Hitler!"

Rauter returned the gesture with a curt motion before gesturing to the chair opposite him. Stadtler obeyed, lowering himself onto the hard seat with precision. He noted the lingering smell of cigars in the air, mingling with the faint metallic tang of the inkpot.

"I've just returned from Berlin," Rauter began, getting straight to the point. "I had a private meeting with Obergruppenführer Heydrich himself. Do you understand the significance of that?"

"Yes, Obergruppenführer," Stadtler replied, though his mind raced. He knew the recent attacks by the Dutch resistance were bad, but surely they weren't serious enough to warrant the personal attention of Heydrich himself?

It had to be about the girl and her amazing gifts. What else could it be?

Rauter leaned back in his chair, cupping his chin in his hands.

"The operation in Rotterdam, your operation, has taken on a level of importance you cannot yet comprehend. Heydrich has personally reviewed the reports on the girl and the British agent. He is particularly interested in the girl, Senta Postner. Her eidetic memory makes her an asset of unparalleled value, one that cannot be allowed to fall into British hands."

Stadtler's stomach tightened with anticipation. "I understand, Obergruppenführer."

"No, Stadtler, I don't think you do. This operation is

now a matter of Reich security. The Führer himself is following your progress. Therefore, absolute secrecy is paramount. You are to report to me and me alone. Not the Gestapo, not the local SD heads. Only me."

Stadtler gulped. "Yes, sir. It's an honour, sir."

Rauter leaned forward, pulling open a drawer in his desk with deliberate precision. From within, he retrieved a document, its top marked by the imposing Reichsadler crest, the black eagle clutching a swastika in its talons.

Beneath it, the letterhead bore the title SS-Obergruppenführer Reinhard Heydrich, Chief of the Reich Security Main Office, typed in crisp, authoritative script.

Heydrich's bold signature, underscored with a flourish, dominated the bottom of the page. As Rauter placed it before Stadtler, the weight of its authority was palpable, a silent reminder of the power and peril behind the orders it carried.

"This is an order signed by Obergruppenführer Heydrich. It grants you full authority over any and all military, SS, and Gestapo personnel in occupied territories. Should anyone question you, this document will silence them. Is that clear?"

Stadtler gulped again and stared at the paper for a long moment before meeting Rauter's gaze.

"Yes, Obergruppenführer." His stomach churned at the sight of Heydrich's name before him.

Rauter tapped the desk with one finger, his expression sharp. "Good. Effective immediately, I am promoting you to SS-Sturmbannführer. This rank will give you the authority you need to command respect and obedience from local units. Your insignia will be delivered by this evening."

The words landed like a hammer blow, and for a fleeting moment, Stadtler allowed himself the thrill of triumph. His eyes widened with the unexpected rush of ambition, the promotion marking not just recognition, but the promise of unparalleled authority in his mission.

"Thank you, Obergruppenführer. I will not disappoint."

Rauter nodded, his expression unreadable. "See that you don't. Now, to the specifics of your mission."

He leaned forward, his voice lowering. "You are to gather a small squad of your most trusted men. Men who will not hesitate, who understand the importance of discretion. I want you in France within three days, which is where I suspect Fernsby and the girl to be."

Stadtler stared at his superior officer, allowing his words and the importance of his mission to sink in.

"Your first priority is to locate Senta Postner and her handler, Michael Fernsby. She is to be taken alive and unharmed at all costs," Rauter said, his tone sharp and measured.

Then his expression hardened, a faint sneer tugging at the corners of his mouth.

"As for Fernsby, he is to be eliminated, but do not underestimate him. He is cunning and dangerous, and has a history of facing insurmountable odds and emerging victorious. Killing him will not be easy, Stadtler. It must be done with extreme care. He's cost the Reich dearly already, and I will not tolerate any more failures where he's concerned."

"Yes, sir," Stadtler said, his pulse quickening. "I understand."

"Furthermore," Rauter continued, "you are to locate the girl's sister, Mina Postner. She's critical to this operation. If we hold her, Senta will have no choice but to cooperate. She has evaded us thus far, but my sources indicate she is likely making her way towards France. Use whatever means necessary to find her."

Rauter stood, walking to the window and staring out at the bleak grey sky. "I've arranged for all the files Albert Kreise ever kept on Fernsby to be delivered to your office. Study them well. Fernsby is resourceful and dangerous. I'm repeating myself here, but do not underestimate him."

"I won't, Obergruppenführer."

Rauter turned back to him, his expression hard. "I want results, Stadtler. The girl, her sister, and Fernsby. Bring me success, and it will secure not just your career, but the future of the Reich. Fail, and…"

He let the words hang ominously in the air.

Stadtler rose to his feet, his chest swelling with determination. "I will not fail, Obergruppenführer."

"See that you don't. That's all, Sturmbannführer."

Stadtler jumped to his feet, the sound of his new rank music to his ears. He saluted sharply, his voice ringing with conviction.

"Heil Hitler!"

"Heil Hitler," Rauter replied, already turning back to his papers.

Chapter 57

The deep blue afternoon sky contrasted the mood of the people of Rotterdam, which was subdued and tense as they gathered at the city square under the grim watch of the occupying forces.

Posters plastered across walls and shopfronts declared the fate of three condemned men in bold black letters.

Justice for Traitors! they proclaimed, alongside an ominous warning: *To aid the resistance is to invite death. Only through obedience can there be peace.*

SS-Sturmbannführer Erik Stadtler had made sure the message was clear. Loudspeakers mounted on trucks had rolled through the streets the night before, repeating his announcement.

The executions would serve as a stark demonstration of the Reich's power and the futility of resistance.

The posters promised fifty thousand guilders to anyone who provided information leading to the capture of the resistance leader, Jeroen. This was a fortune to most people, and more than enough to tempt even the most loyal Dutch citizen to betray their neighbours.

A crude wooden platform had been hastily erected in the city square, flanked by Nazi banners that rippled in the stiff wind. Black-uniformed SS troops stood in a rigid line at the perimeter, their presence a silent, yet menacing reminder of the cost of defiance.

The crowd, numbering in the hundreds, was herded into place by barking German soldiers. Fear and tension rippled through the gathered civilians.

Parents clutched their children tightly, shielding their eyes from the gallows. Others stood with stoic expressions, unwilling to show emotion in front of their occupiers but unable to turn away.

Near the platform, Stadtler stood at the centre of a cluster of officers, his presence commanding and cold. His highly polished boots gleamed in the weak light, and the four pips denoting his new rank were prominently displayed on his right collar.

For anyone brave enough to glance his way, SS-Sturmbannführer Erik Stadtler cut an impressive, intimidating figure. He held himself with the confidence of a man who believed in the righteousness of his cause, or at least the necessity of it.

Stadtler took a final look at the square, noting the way the crowd shifted and murmured. The tension suited him. Fear was an effective weapon, and today's display would cement the authority of the Reich in Rotterdam.

The prisoners were dragged into view, their movements sluggish under the weight of chains and despair.

The valet from the Hotel Atlanta, his brother, and Geert were marched onto the platform, flanked by SS guards. Their appearances drew sharp intakes of breath from the crowd, who instinctively recoiled at the sight.

Battered and bloodied, the haunted looks on the faces

of the three men told of the cruel torture they'd endured at the hands of their SS captors.

Elske and Neeltje stood off to the side, guarded by four soldiers, their pale faces betraying the horror of what they were being forced to witness.

Stadtler allowed his gaze to linger on them for a moment. Their silent suffering would serve as yet another lesson for anyone considering defiance.

The crowd hushed as Stadtler stepped forward, his boots striking the platform with deliberate precision. His voice carried easily over the square, amplified by a microphone that crackled faintly in the wind.

"Citizens of Rotterdam," he began, his tone sharp and commanding. "These men before you, stand condemned for their treason against the Reich. They conspired with terrorists, endangered your lives, and sought to undermine the peace and prosperity we bring to this land."

He paused, letting the weight of his words settle over the crowd. "The resistance claims to fight for your freedom, but all they bring is destruction and misery. Their actions have led only to death. Your families' deaths, your neighbours' deaths, their deaths."

A murmur rippled through the crowd, swiftly silenced by the pointed glances of nearby soldiers.

"For those who remain obedient," Stadtler continued, his tone softening slightly, "there is nothing to fear. Obedience brings order. Order brings security. And security brings peace."

He gestured to the prisoners, who stood hunched, pained, and defeated.

"This is the fate of those who resist. Learn from their mistakes. Do not allow yourselves to be led astray by false promises and empty heroics. The Reich always rewards loyalty."

Stadtler's voice grew harder as he added, "A reward of fifty thousand guilders remains available for any information leading to the capture of the resistance leader known as Jeroen. That is enough to change your lives, enough to protect your families from the hardships of war. Think carefully about where your loyalties lie."

With a sharp nod, Stadtler stepped back, allowing the SS guards to take their positions. His eyes scanned the crowd one last time, noting the fear, the anger, and the resignation etched into their faces.

The gallows loomed, their stark silhouettes a grim punctuation to his speech.

Geert glanced one last time at Elske and Neeltje as he was shoved towards the noose. He gave a thumbs-up sign, an indication that he was ready for death, and that they shouldn't worry.

The two women held hands, tears flowing freely down their cheeks. Unbeknownst to the men, a train was waiting to take them to a concentration camp in Germany immediately following the executions.

The crowd fell silent, waiting for Stadtler's command.

Chapter 58

The forest hummed with birdsong as Jeroen stumbled over the uneven ground, the fading light casting long shadows between the trees.

The Wehrmacht truck lay abandoned behind him, smoke curling from the broken-down engine. He'd ditched the German uniform in a hollow under the truck, covering it with dead leaves, and now wore the plain, threadbare clothes of a regular civilian.

After five gruelling days of travel on foot, dodging patrols and sleeping under hedgerows, the outskirts of Breda finally came into view. Relief mingled with anxiety as he studied the hand-drawn map Rinus had given him.

Adriaan Westerhout was famously cautious, so Jeroen wasn't surprised to find that he lived in an isolated house on the edge of a dense woodland two miles south of the city.

A narrow road separated the house from the woods, and if it wasn't for a clearing at the rear, it would have been completely surrounded and hidden.

Weary and footsore after his travels, Jeroen sat high in a

tree, observing the house to make sure it hadn't been compromised. Dim light seeped from behind curtains, telling him that someone was there, but he had no way of knowing if it was friend or foe.

He waited until it was completely dark before making his move. With his limbs screaming in protest, Jeroen climbed from his perch and approached the rear of the house.

He'd just about reached the door when he heard the sharp click of a rifle behind him. He froze, and his pulse quickened as three men emerged from the shadows with their weapons raised.

In an instant, he was forced to the ground, his face pressed against the dirt. A feeling of déjà vu consumed him as the men patted him down for weapons. It was almost a repeat of what had happened with Rinus, and here he was again, visiting another old comrade and receiving the same treatment.

Can't blame them because I'd have done the same.

"Name!" one of the men barked, his accent thick with distrust.

"It's Jeroen!" he gasped, his voice muffled by the earth. "I'm here to see Adriaan Westerhout."

The men exchanged wary glances, their grips on their rifles unwavering. The tallest of them—a wiry figure with keen, suspicious eyes—reached into Jeroen's jacket and pulled out his identification papers. Without a word, he passed them to another, who nodded curtly and stepped back.

"These say your name is Lukas Vermeer," someone with a torch shouted.

"I'm hardly going to travel under my real name, am I?" Jeroen snapped back.

Unseen by those outside, a fourth figure had emerged

from the house, his gait deliberate and unhurried. Jeroen craned his neck upwards when he saw the feet coming towards him.

The tension melted from Jeroen's shoulders as he recognised Adriaan Westerhout's weathered face and piercing eyes.

"Let him up," Westerhout said, his voice calm but commanding. "I'd recognise that face anywhere."

The men hesitated for a second, then complied, hauling Jeroen to his feet. Westerhout stepped forward, a rare smile softening his stern expression.

"It's been a long time, old friend," he said, offering his hand. "I've been expecting you, or at least someone connected to you."

"Too long," Jeroen replied, his voice hoarse with fatigue.

Westerhout motioned towards the house. "Come. We've much to discuss."

Inside, the scent of tobacco and aged wood filled the air. Westerhout poured two glasses of whisky, handing one to Jeroen before settling into a high-backed chair.

The two men sat in companionable silence for a moment, the amber liquid warming Jeroen's throat while he got a good look at his old comrade and friend.

Adriaan Westerhout had the look of a man weathered by years of war and the toll of constant vigilance. His face, sharp and angular, sat in contrast to his grey eyes that sank back into their sockets as if they were permanently etched with worry and the heaviness of loss.

His thick, greying hair was combed back, though a few stubborn strands fell loose onto his forehead.

"You look tired, old friend," Westerhout said. "When was the last time you ate a good meal?"

"About a week ago," Jeroen answered. "My truck broke

down not long after leaving Rinus, and I walked the rest of the way here."

"You walked?" Westerhout's eyes sprang open. "How long did that take you?"

"Five days, give or take. I had to lie low for a day and a half while the Germans cleared the area. They were searching for something… or someone, and I had to be really careful. They almost found me twice."

"I heard you've been busy," Westerhout said, his tone laced with dry humour. "I guess you haven't heard the latest news since you've been on the run for the last week."

"I was hardly on the run, but no, I've not heard anything other than the fact that you might be holding Mina Postner. That's why I'm here, Adriaan, although it is good to see you again."

"I know that," Westerhout snapped at his old friend. "And it's good to see you again too, but there's a lot going on that you don't know about."

"What?"

"Eat first, and then we'll talk."

At Westerhout's direction, one of his men placed a plateful of cold food on the kitchen table. Jeroen, who hadn't realised how famished he was, practically ran to it and tucked in like a starving dog.

Although cold, the traditional Dutch meal of Stamppot, consisting of mashed potatoes and vegetables, tasted as good as a five-star dinner at the swankiest hotel in Rotterdam to Jeroen.

Adriaan Westerhout watched in amusement as Jeroen polished the plate clean in record time.

"That was delicious," he announced after he'd finished it all. "Now let's talk."

There were no signs of Westerhout's men as Adriaan

showed Jeroen to a sparse living room with a couch and a comfy chair.

"My men are taking care of some business for me, and others are on watch," Adriaan explained. "It pays to be cautious these days."

"Can't argue with that," Jeroen agreed. "Now, let's talk about Mina Postner. Where is she? I need to see her."

"All in good time. But first, there's a couple of things you need to know."

Tension rose in the room as Westerhout fell silent for a moment.

"Well?" Jeroen asked.

"Paris has fallen." Westerhouse looked at the floor and took a deep breath.

"Paris?" Jeroen closed his eyes. "I'm not surprised, but I was hoping against hope."

The two men fell silent for a few moments before Adriaan looked up at his friend. "There's more," he said.

"Tell me."

"Those soldiers you hid from that almost caught you. They were searching for someone."

"Who?" Jeroen's interest was piqued. "Me?"

"They'd have loved to have found you as well, but no, it wasn't you."

"Then who?"

"A British aircraft was shot down in Belgium a few days ago. From what I heard, it was trying to get to England when flak guns shot it down. Do you know anything about that plane, Jeroen?"

Jeroen's heart leapt out of his chest.

Fernsby and Senta!

"What happened? Were there any survivors?" He ignored Westerhout's questions.

"There must have been, because the Germans have

been searching ever since it went down. Whoever was on it, and assuming they survived, they're probably heading for the French coast, but the Germans are searching everywhere, just in case."

Jeroen sighed and took a deep breath.

"You do know who was on that plane, don't you?"

Jeroen shook his head. "I don't know anything about it, but I feel sorry for whoever it was."

Adriaan Westerhout stared at his old friend. He knew he was lying, but he also knew better than to delve any deeper.

"I thought you'd want to know about it, in case it changed anything."

"It changes nothing. I'm here for Mina Postner."

Jeroen's mind raced as he stared at Westerhout. *Did Fernsby and Senta survive? Are they hurt? Where are they? Have the Germans caught them?*

All those questions and more swirled in his brain as he listened to Westerhout telling him about the girl calling herself Mina Postner.

What do I tell Mina, assuming this girl is her?

Jeroen barely heard Westerhout's words as he struggled to come to terms with the news. If true, everything they'd gone through, and everyone that had died, had been for nothing.

"Are you even listening to me?" Westerhout shouted, red faced. "You haven't heard a word I've said."

"Sorry, tell me again."

"You *do* know about the British aircraft, don't you?"

"Some things are best kept secret, Adriaan. You know that as well as anyone."

Westerhout placed the tips of his fingers together. "You're correct, of course. Now, about this girl. She showed up in the barn of someone I know. He was going to hand her over to the police until she mentioned her name. Everyone in the resistance knows about the two German girls who worked for you, but we didn't expect one of them to show up here."

"What did he do with her? Where is she?"

"I'm still not convinced it is your girl, and I'm certainly not bringing her here in case she's a spy. As you know, I run a successful operation getting people across the border, and I can't jeopardise that for anyone, not even your German girls."

"I understand that, but where is she?"

"Some friends are taking care of her, but they are under orders to kill her if she tries to escape."

"Take me to her," Jeroen demanded. "I'll tell you in an instant if it's her or not."

"We'll go at first light. They're in Breda, and there's a curfew in effect after dark."

Westerhout showed Jeroen to a room where he could rest for the night. A single bed, a table, and a lamp were the only objects in the room, but that was all Jeroen needed.

As he drifted off to sleep, his mind spilled over with thoughts of an injured Michael Fernsby trying to protect Senta somewhere in Belgium. Wherever they were, they were out of reach of his help.

They were on their own.

Chapter 59

The following morning, the two men were joined by Westerhout's weary men, who looked as though they'd been up all night.

They probably have.

"There's something else I didn't tell you last night." Westerhout looked at Jeroen, sympathy etched all over his face.

"What else could possibly have happened?" Jeroen groaned. Ever since the car bomb and the train derailment, everything had gone wrong for them, and everyone close to him had either been killed or captured.

"I didn't tell you because you were exhausted and needed to sleep. I'm sorry, my old friend."

Blood drained from Jeroen's face as Westerhout told him what had happened in Rotterdam the previous day. He described the brutal executions of Geert and the valet, his voice thick with sorrow.

Jeroen listened, silent, overwhelmed with grief and guilt. He threw his hands to his head and screamed loudly.

"No! I should have been there, not here, chasing a

woman who might not even be who she says she is. I've lost so many people since the invasion, and I can't take any more."

He stood up and banged open the rear door to the house. Westerhout's men started after him, but Adriaan stopped them.

"Let him grieve. He's been through a lot."

When Jeroen returned thirty minutes later, his eyes were red and swollen, and his face set in stone, a picture of raw anger and hatred.

"I should have been there." He spat the words out.

"And what good would that have done?" Westerhout shot back. "You'd be dead too, and so would your cause. Jeroen, you're the most wanted man in Holland, and you're alive for a reason. You're alive because this country needs you like never before. We all know the risks when we sign up, and as sad as it is, it's only going to get worse before it gets better."

Jeroen slumped into a chair, head in hands. "Take me to her," he mumbled.

The morning sun cast a pale light over the cobblestones as Westerhout led Jeroen to the outskirts of Breda. A faint mist clung to the edges of the town, softening the outlines of buildings and fields, but Jeroen's nerves were anything but dulled.

Each step closer to the checkpoint tightened the knot in his stomach, his senses tuned to every sound—the crunch of gravel underfoot, the faint murmur of voices ahead, the bark of a dog in the distance.

A checkpoint came into view—a haphazard collection of sandbags and barricades, flanked by a small squad of German soldiers in grey-green uniforms. A black-and-white signboard posted nearby displayed an announcement in Dutch and German:

Reward: 50,000 Kroner for information leading to the capture of the Rotterdam terrorist, Jeroen.

Anger and resentment boiled over, leaving his cheeks hot to the touch. He'd wisely left his weapons behind, for if he'd had them with him right then, he'd have surely used them on the Nazis glaring at him as he approached.

He forced his gaze away, swallowing the bile rising in his throat. The poster didn't bear his photograph, instead giving only a vague description, but the weight of it bore down on him all the same. That amount of money was enough to tempt anyone.

"Stay calm," Westerhout murmured under his breath, his tone so low it barely carried.

Jeroen nodded, but didn't trust himself to speak. His heart thundered in his chest as they approached the barrier, where two soldiers stood with rifles slung over their shoulders.

"Halt!" one barked, his accent sharp and clipped.

The other soldier, a younger man with narrow eyes and a pale, almost sickly complexion, stepped forward. He held out his hand expectantly, and Westerhout reached into his coat, producing his identification papers.

"Lukas Vermeer," Jeroen said evenly, handing over his forged papers.

He forced his hands to remain steady, though every fibre of his being screamed to grab the soldier's rifle and mow them all down.

The soldier examined the papers, flipping through the pages with maddening slowness. His fingers lingered over the stamped endorsements, and his brow furrowed as if deciphering a code. Beside him, another soldier watched the exchange, his posture tense and alert.

"What brings you to Breda?" the younger man asked, his voice flat and suspicious.

Evasion

Jeroen spoke before Westerhout could reply. "We're visiting family," he said, injecting a tone of casual indifference. "My uncle is ill."

The soldier's eyes flicked to Jeroen's face, lingering for what felt like an eternity. Jeroen fought to maintain a neutral expression, though his heart thudded so loudly he was certain it must be audible.

The soldier turned his attention back to the papers, scrutinising the name and address with excruciating care. His gaze darted between Jeroen and the document, as if comparing him to an image that didn't exist. The seconds stretched into an agonising eternity.

Jeroen prepared himself for a fight. His days of running were over.

"Lukas Vermeer," the soldier repeated slowly, as though tasting the name. His eyes narrowed. "You're from Amsterdam?"

"I am," Jeroen replied, forcing himself to meet the man's gaze. "Born and raised." He hoped the lie sounded as effortless as it needed to be.

The soldier tilted his head, clearly unsatisfied. Behind him, another officer approached, a high-ranking man with an air of authority.

"What's the delay, Schreiber?" the officer demanded, his voice sharp.

"Routine check, sir," the young soldier replied quickly, snapping to attention.

The officer waved a dismissive hand. "Move it along. We don't have all day."

Reluctantly, the young soldier handed back the papers, but not before one final, probing glance at Jeroen. "You can go," he said curtly, stepping aside.

Jeroen's breath released in a slow, silent exhale as he accepted his documents and tucked them back into his coat. Westerhout, ever composed, nodded politely to the soldiers as they walked past the barricade and onto the narrow road leading into Breda.

It wasn't until they were out of earshot that Jeroen allowed his shoulders to relax. His palms were clammy, his heart still pounding with the residual fear of what might have been.

"They're getting desperate," he muttered, his voice tight.

Westerhout cast him a sidelong glance, his expression unreadable. "Desperate men make mistakes. We just have to make sure we don't."

Jeroen nodded, his jaw set. The sun broke through the mist, casting long shadows across the cobbled streets ahead, but the oppressive weight of danger lingered. He clenched his fists, ready to give everything in the fight for freedom.

Westerhout took them down streets and alleyways until they reached a colourful row of terraced houses on a street called Piet Heynlaan. The neat houses sat between a row of trees at the front and a hedgerow at the back.

As always, Westerhout had thought this through thoroughly.

He approached the bright yellow house at the end of the row and knocked six times. He paused and then repeated, knocking a further four times.

Jeroen understood that this was a sign, and he stood back, waiting or whoever was inside to let them in.

The door opened, and a woman in her late twenties with collar length brown hair smiled as she recognised Westerhout. Her smile dropped when she saw Jeroen standing behind him.

"Good morning, Clara," Westerhout said as he brushed past.

Clara stood aside, staring at Jeroen as she allowed them into her home.

"I know who you are," she said after closing the door. "You're Jeroen."

Jeroen nodded. "Nice to meet you, Clara. I'm here to see the German girl."

Clara exchanged glances with Westerhout, who lowered his head slightly as if to give consent.

"Follow me." She headed up the stairs.

Jeroen and Adriaan followed behind. Clara stopped at the door on the far end of a narrow corridor. She unlocked it and knocked.

"We're coming in."

Clara opened the door and stepped aside. Jeroen pushed past and entered the dark room with the curtains closed. Clara reached her hand around the side of the door and turned on an overhead light, revealing a forlorn looking blonde-haired girl with deep blue eyes sitting on the bed staring at the man entering her room.

"Jeroen!" she yelled, her eyes lighting up in recognition. The girl leapt from the bed and rushed to Jeroen, who caught her and held her shoulders to get a good look at her.

A smile broke out over his face as he turned to Westerhout and Clara.

"Adriaan, this is Mina Postner."

Mina buried her head in Jeroen's shoulder and cried.

Chapter 60

The tiny kitchen was dimly lit with the curtains drawn, the single bulb overhead casting long shadows across the peeling paint and scuffed wooden surfaces.

Jeroen sat at the table, Mina beside him, her hands trembling as she cradled a mug of tea Clara had insisted on making. Westerhout leaned against the doorframe, arms crossed, his keen eyes fixed on the two of them.

"It's her, Adriaan," Jeroen said, breaking the silence. His voice was steady now, though his face still bore the tension of the past days. "She's Mina Postner. I'd recognise her anywhere."

Westerhout gave a curt nod but said nothing. His scepticism lingered like smoke in the air, though he trusted Jeroen's judgement enough not to voice it.

Jeroen turned to Mina, his expression softening. "How did you get here?" he asked quietly.

Mina took a shaky breath, her gaze dropping to the table.

"I was lost," she began, her voice barely above a whisper. "I was alone and frightened, and I didn't know where to go. But I thought—..."

She faltered, gripping the mug tighter. "I thought I could find my way back to you. Or to someone who knew you."

She paused, and Jeroen waited, giving her the time she needed to collect herself.

"I never should have left. I wanted to get back to Michael and Senta and see them one more time before they left. The only reason I didn't was because I feared Senta would refuse to go without me."

"She probably would have," Jeroen agreed.

"I almost turned back," she continued. "I'd nearly been caught more times than I can count. Soldiers, collaborators. Every shadow felt like a threat."

She shuddered, glancing nervously at the window as if the memories might materialise there.

"I slept in a barn one night, thinking it was safe. I was so exhausted I didn't hear anyone coming."

Her hands tightened around the mug, her knuckles white. "When I woke up, there was a man standing over me with a rifle pointed at my head. I thought he was going to kill me... or worse." Her voice cracked, and Jeroen reached out, placing a reassuring hand on hers.

"At first, he shouted," she said, her voice trembling. "Asked me who I was, what I was doing there. When he realised I couldn't speak Dutch, he accused me of being a spy."

She swallowed hard.

"I told him my name. Told him I was looking for you. Something changed when I said your name. He stopped shouting and looked... confused, maybe."

She glanced at Westerhout, who gave a faint nod of recognition.

"That man was one of mine," Westerhout said. "He's cautious to a fault, which is probably why he didn't shoot you on the spot."

"He took me to his farmhouse," Mina continued. "Tied me up, though he didn't hurt me. I sat there for hours, waiting, wondering if I'd made a mistake." Her voice grew quieter. "Then that man showed up."

She pointed at Westerhout.

Adriaan Westerhout pushed off the doorframe and moved to the table, leaning his hands on its edge.

"You told me your story," he said gruffly. "I didn't believe you at first. I couldn't risk the lives of the good men and women who work for me."

He paused. "But we'd heard rumours about two German girls helping Jeroen in Rotterdam. Your name was enough for us to give you the benefit of the doubt and keep you alive until we could verify if you were who you said you were."

"If you hadn't come," Mina said, her voice trembling again. "They were going to kill me."

Westerhout's jaw tightened.

"As I said, we couldn't risk anything else. If you hadn't been who you claimed to be, the risk to the resistance would have been too great."

Jeroen glanced between them, a flash of understanding in his eyes. He turned to Mina.

"You're lucky to be alive," he said. "But it's not safe for you in Holland anymore."

Mina blinked, confusion crossing her face. "What do you mean?"

He leaned forward, his elbows on the table and reached over and took Mina's hand in his. Then he told her what happened after she'd left. He left nothing out, and Mina threw her hand over her mouth when she learned about Senta's arrest and subsequent rescue.

She cried when Jeroen told her about the Koopman family, and she sobbed when she heard about the arrests of Geert, Arjen, and Elske.

Jeroen ended when he got to the executions in Rotterdam, but hesitated when it came time to tell her about the plane crash, and the fact that Michael and Senta were probably dead. He didn't think she could handle any more at that moment.

"The resistance in Rotterdam has been crushed," he said softly. "The Germans are hunting down everyone connected to it. If they find out you're with me, they'll stop at nothing to capture you. I've already lost too many people, and I can't lose you too."

Tears welled in Mina's eyes, and she shook her head. "I don't want to leave you again, Jeroen, especially now that Michael and Senta are gone."

Jeroen and Westerhout exchanged glances.

"You won't be safe here," he said firmly. "I'm taking you to France. Your friend's family will keep you safe."

Westerhout cleared his throat. "There's another option," he said, his tone measured. "I have contacts in the French resistance. If you want, Mina, you could join them. Fight back."

Mina looked between them, her expression torn. "I don't know," she murmured. "I'm not like you or Michael. Not even Senta. I'm not strong enough."

"You are," Jeroen said, his voice soft but resolute. "You've already survived so much. You're stronger than you think. You are the voice of freedom to thousands, if not millions, of people across Europe. Your broadcasts are worth fighting for, whether you believe it or not."

Her lips trembled, and she nodded slowly, though

uncertainty lingered in her eyes. "What about Michael and Senta?" she asked hesitantly. "Where are they now? Did they make it to England?"

The room fell silent. Jeroen's chest tightened as he met her gaze. He glanced at Westerhout, uncertain if he should tell her or not. Could he lie, knowing full well that sooner or later she would find out the truth?

In the end, he couldn't lie. Regardless of the silence between them the previous evening, Westerhout knew Jeroen had something to do with the aircraft that had been shot down over Belgium. There was no point in holding back any longer.

"They're gone," he said, his voice low and pained. "Their plane was shot down."

Mina's hand flew to her mouth as a sob escaped her. She shook her head, tears spilling freely. "No. Not Michael. He… he promised…"

"I'm sorry," Jeroen said. "I'm so sorry."

Westerhout stepped away from the table, giving them a moment. "I'll arrange everything for you to leave," he said quietly. "You'll head out tomorrow."

Jeroen glanced up at Westerhout, his focus still on Mina as she wept. "Thank you, Adriaan."

Westerhout inclined his head and disappeared through the back door.

Chapter 61

After Westerhout's departure, Jeroen stood and paced the room, the weight of the recent tragedies weighing heavily.

After a while, Mina's sobs broke the fragile silence in the room, raw and unrestrained. She buried her face in her hands, her shoulders trembling as the weight of Jeroen's words crushed her.

"No," she whispered, shaking her head violently. "No, it's not true. It can't be true."

Her voice cracked with desperation, each word clawing at the air like a drowning soul grasping for something solid.

Jeroen reached out, placing a hand on her shoulder, but she pulled away, her anguish spilling out in a torrent of words.

"I should have been there!" she cried, her voice trembling with fury and heartbreak. "I never should have left them. I should have been with Senta. She wouldn't have gone without me. Maybe, just maybe, they'd still be alive if I'd stayed."

Her words hung in the air, heavy with blame and

sorrow. Jeroen tried to interject, his voice gentle, but she shook her head again, her pale face streaked with tears.

Jeroen's heart broke witnessing her pain, and he sat beside her, tears of anguish pouring down his face. Not just for Senta and Michael, but for all those he had lost since Hitler's armies invaded his beloved country.

The recent losses, raw and suppressed, broke through, consuming him in unbridled grief. Images of Esther laughing and singing at the hospital where she worked and died in the Rotterdam blitz drove him over the edge, and he held Mina tightly to his chest, both of them lost in their deep, agonising grief.

"They've taken everything from me," Mina said, her voice breaking up, and the fight draining from her as quickly as it had flared. "The Nazis have destroyed my life."

She pulled away and stared up at Clara, who was pouring glasses of whisky for all three of them. Clara, too, was sobbing, completely immersed in understanding what they were both feeling.

"They murdered my father in cold blood," Mina continued. "And they dragged my mother away to God knows where. And now Senta and Michael. They're gone. Everyone I've ever loved, gone."

Her breath hitched, her sobs turning to broken gasps. "I can't take it anymore," she said, her voice barely above a whisper. "I have nothing left. They've won, Jeroen. Don't you see? They've taken everything. What's the point of fighting when they just destroy everything we care about?"

She slumped forward, her face pressed against the table, her hands gripping the edge as though she might fall if she let go. The room was stifling, the air thick with unspoken sorrow.

Clara placed the whisky glass in her hands and did the

same for Jeroen. Then she held hers in front of her and forced her tears back long enough so she could speak.

"Drink," she said gently. "It won't fix anything, but it might help us breathe."

Mina's trembling fingers tightened around the glass, and she lifted it to her lips, her tears mingling with the amber liquid. She drank in small, shaky sips, the warmth spreading through her chest, though it did little to thaw the icy grip of despair.

Jeroen sat beside her, his voice low but firm.

"Mina," he said, reaching for her hand again. This time, she didn't pull away. "I know it feels like there's nothing left. I know the pain feels like it'll never end. But you're still here. You've survived everything they've thrown at you. That's something no one can ever take from you."

She looked at him, her eyes red and swollen, filled with a despair that cut him to his core. "What's the point?" she asked hoarsely. "What's the point of surviving when everyone else is gone?"

"The point," Jeroen said, his voice steady, "is that you're still here to fight. For Senta. For Michael. For everyone who can't. The Nazis haven't won, Mina. They can't win as long as people like us refuse to give up."

His words hung in the air, a faint glimmer of hope against the crushing darkness. Mina clung to the glass in her hand, her knuckles white, as her tears continued to fall.

"I don't know if I can," she whispered.

"You can," Jeroen said firmly. "And you will. Because that's one thing they can't take from us—our will to fight, even when it hurts, even when it feels like there's nothing left."

Mina's sobs quieted, though her shoulders still trembled. Slowly, she nodded, though the pain in her eyes remained as raw as ever. She raised the glass once more, drinking deeply this time, as though trying to summon the strength to believe him.

Nobody spoke for the rest of the morning. Mina, wanting to be alone, went to her room and lay on her bed. Jeroen sat downstairs with Clara, occasionally listening in on Mina's sobs from the bottom of the stairs.

"Leave her," Clara said. "Let her grieve."

Jeroen took the advice and left Mina alone, although it broke his heart to hear her cry alone.

By late afternoon, the shock had eased. Mina, her eyes red and swollen, and her face as pale as a winter ghost, rejoined Jeroen and Clara downstairs.

After a few minutes of silence, she gathered herself together to muster up some words.

"Tell me what happened in Rotterdam," she said.

Jeroen spent the rest of the day filling Mina in on the events in Rotterdam. She was especially interested in Michael's exploits when he planted the car bomb, and when he rescued Senta.

Jeroen's heart beat a little slower when he saw her expression soften at the mention of Michael's name, and it forced home the realisation of the deep love they'd held for each other.

Just like he had with Esther.

Later that night, after darkness fell over Breda, Clara and her husband, Jan, guided them out of the city through back alleys and backyards.

The journey to Westerhout's safe house was tense but uneventful. As they approached the secluded house, Jeroen cast a glance at Mina. Her face was pale but determined, her grief now tempered by a new, steely resolve.

Chapter 62

By the time dawn broke over the French countryside, Michael and Senta were already awake and ready to move. Their convoluted route to the coast was planned out, and with a bit of luck, they could be there within the next five days; less if they didn't have any problems with German patrols.

Michael gingerly flexed his left arm that still ached and hurt after the plane crash.

The silhouette of the woman filled the doorway to the barn, making her look large and menacing. She clutched a sack of food in her hands, and she held it out to Michael as they met at the doorway.

"Take this," she said, her face a mask of stern kindness. "You'll need it more than I will."

"Thank you," Michael said, his appreciation sincere.

As they walked into the morning sunlight, the woman's sharp eyes fell on Senta's head and she tutted loudly, stepping forward to grasp the younger girl's arm.

"Wait," she said, her tone brooking no argument. Her

fingers moved to Senta's hair, parting it slightly before recoiling with a hiss of dismay.

Senta yelped in pain, instinctively pulling away. "I'm fine," she insisted, though her pale face told another story.

The woman shook her head grimly. "You are not fine," she said, her voice low but urgent. "That wound is badly infected."

Michael frowned, stepping closer. "Let me see."

Senta hesitated, but finally relented, lowering her head slightly. Michael winced as he saw the angry red swelling beneath her hair oozing yellow pus. Guilt surged through him. How hadn't he noticed?

"She needs treatment," the old woman said firmly. "You won't get far like this. Stay until it's healed."

Senta sighed. "She's saying the wound needs treatment or we won't get far."

Senta opened her mouth to protest, but Michael silenced her with a look. "She's right," he said. "That's a nasty infection that will slow us down if we don't treat it."

The old woman pointed at her farmhouse and ushered them towards the door. Michael followed, his senses on high alert. Gaining his trust wasn't easy, not when every shadow could hide a German uniform.

He kept his weapon close, watching the doors and windows, ready for trouble that, thankfully, never came.

The old woman sat Senta down and pulled a selection of old bottles from one of her cupboards. She settled on one and held it up in triumph.

"Eau de Dakin," she said, showing the label to Senta and Michael.

"Dakin's solution," Michael needed no translation. "I know what that is."

Dakin's solution was an antiseptic liquid that was used for treating wounds and infections. It had been around since the Great War, and it was a popular and widely available solution all across Europe.

Michael's eyes watered when she opened the bottle, the strong smell of chlorine confirming the contents of the bottle.

Senta too, rubbed her eyes at the potent vapour.

The old woman bustled around the kitchen, muttering to herself as she prepared a makeshift workspace on the table. Senta sat stiffly in a wooden chair, her face pale and drawn as she winced at each movement of her infected scalp.

"Stay still, girl," the woman said brusquely, but not unkindly. "This won't be pleasant, but it's better than what you'll face if we leave it untreated."

She glanced at Michael, who hovered nearby, arms crossed, his weapon slung close. He seemed ready to intervene at the slightest provocation.

The woman's sharp gaze softened slightly as it met his.

"I'm Edith," she said, dipping a cloth into a bowl of steaming water. "And you'd best let me get on with this if you want her to live long enough to see the end of this war."

Senta translated, and Michael, racked with guilt over not seeing the infection, gave a small nod, his jaw tightening.

"Thank you, Edith. For helping her."

Edith snorted faintly as she wrung out the cloth.

"No need for thanks yet. This wound's in a bad state."

She tilted Senta's head gently, exposing the infected area.

"See this?" she asked, pointing to the angry red swelling. "It's heavily infected and already abscessing. If it's not treated, the infection will spread, and she'll end up fighting for her life instead of running from the Germans."

Again, Senta translated, her voice shaking. Michael's stomach churned at the sight, and guilt twisted inside him again.

"How long?" he asked.

Edith straightened, fixing him with a firm look.

"Two to three weeks, at least, if you want it healed properly. The solution will clean it, but it needs time to drain and recover."

"Two to three weeks!" Senta spat the words out in English.

"We don't have two to three days, let alone weeks," Michael protested.

Edith folded her arms, meeting his gaze head-on.

"You don't have a choice, unless you're willing to carry her half-dead through the countryside. This infection won't wait for your plans."

"She says you'll be carrying a corpse if you don't let her treat it." Senta's face was pale, and her eyes were heavy with worry.

"We haven't been through all this just for me to die of infection. We, that is I, have to take care of it."

"Can't she just give me the solution so I can treat you along the way?" Michael asked.

Senta asked Edith, who tutted and threw her arms in the air as if she was trying to catch flight.

"She said th—"

"I know what she said," Michael cut her off. "I don't need an interpreter for that."

He fell silent for a few minutes while he weighed up their options.

"Fine," he said eventually. "We'll stay for a few days, but last night, you said this place wasn't safe. What's changed?"

Senta translated, and Edith sighed, placing a hand on the edge of the table, her expression softening.

"I didn't want you here," she admitted. "It's true. I was frightened. You brought danger to my doorstep just by showing up." Her voice hardened slightly. "But I'm a nurse, not a monster. I can't turn you away, not with that wound as bad as it is."

"And I have my own reasons for hating the Germans," she added after a pause.

Senta translated, her voice faltering, and Michael studied Edith's face. He saw no deception there, only a weary determination.

"You were a nurse?" he asked.

Edith gave a curt nod. "In the Great War," she said. "I treated British soldiers at the Somme. Young boys with eyes too old for their years."

Her voice softened with the memory. "I know what wounds like this can do. And I know how to heal them."

Michael straightened slightly, his respect for the woman deepening. "Thank you," he said quietly, continuing to marvel at the generosity of people, even as they faced hardship and heartache themselves. All across Europe, he'd met men and women who risked their lives to help him, and it wasn't something he'd forget easily.

Edith waved him off as she got to work on Senta's wound.

Later, after treating Senta's wound for the third time that day and feeding them a hearty French dinner, Edith led them to a small room at the back of the house.

It was sparsely furnished but clean, with two narrow beds pushed against opposite walls.

"You'll stay here," she said. "Keep the windows shuttered and stay inside as much as you can. This place isn't as safe as it used to be."

Michael glanced around, noting the thick wooden door and the modest view from the single window. It wasn't much, but it would do.

"Thank you," he said again.

Edith gave him a long look before nodding. "Don't make me regret this," she said simply. Then she turned and left, her footsteps fading down the hall.

Michael looked at Senta, who was already lying on one of the beds, her face pale but composed. "I'm sorry, Senta," he said quietly.

"Not your fault," she replied. "In any case, it'll give your arm time to heal. Don't think I haven't noticed you wincing every time you use it."

Michael shot her a wry smile. "You don't miss much, do you?"

He cracked open the shutters to get a better look outside and was happy to see a nearby tree branch that was both close enough and strong enough to allow them quick egress if things got rough.

He closed the shutter and looked at Senta.

"That's our way out if the need arises."

"You don't trust her, do you?"

"I don't trust anyone I don't know. It's how we stay alive."

"Well, I like her. She's kind, and she is risking her life by doing this."

"I know, and that's what's worrying me."

Over the days and weeks that followed, the farmhouse became a strange sanctuary. Edith worked daily on Senta's wound that was now showing signs of being healed enough for them to finally leave, and Michael's shoulder, strained and painful since the plane crash, began to heal under Edith's excellent care.

In return, he and Senta helped on the farm, a task that

Senta felt completely at home with. If anything, farm work placated her mind, and she almost enjoyed herself.

Almost.

Slowly, Michael learned to trust Edith. Late at night, as he sat watch by the window, she would sometimes join him, her stories of the past weaving a picture of a life shaped by loss.

Senta translated, leaving Michael astounded at how quickly she picked up the language. What had started as broken and limited French had transformed into almost fluency. He could see how her gifts could help Britain and her allies in the war, and he felt more determined than ever to get her back to England.

"My husband died in the first war," Edith said one night, her gaze distant. "Barely a year after we married. We never had time for children."

Her voice softened, tinged with a sadness that felt almost too intimate to share. "This farm became my child. It's all I've ever known."

Michael said nothing, sensing that words would do little to comfort her. But her story stayed with him, deepening his respect for the quiet strength that had carried her through decades of solitude.

His thoughts turned to Mina and the deep love he held for her.

Where is she? Is she somewhere in France? Where? Or is she back in Rotterdam with Jeroen, sending radio broadcasts as Elise, allowing anyone who listened to know the truth of what Hitler's evil regime was doing to Europe?

Wherever she was, he hoped her heart still yearned for him as much as his did for her.

One day, Mina. One day when this is over.

Chapter 63

The farmhouse was never truly quiet. Men and women, young and old, came and went, their faces grim and their eyes sharp. They barely acknowledged Michael and Senta, and Edith offered no explanations.

But they didn't need any. They knew who they were—the French resistance. Edith was allowing them to use her farm as a safe house, and he was sure that if he searched the barn, he'd find a stash of weapons and explosives the resistance stockpiled for future operations against their oppressors.

Sometimes the visitors stayed the night, their presence a silent reminder of the war that loomed just beyond the farm's borders. Michael and Senta kept to themselves, watching from the sidelines as Edith patched wounds and provided food with the same loving care she had shown them.

They argued, the men in particular pointing at her foreign guests as though they were German spies. Edith argued back, telling her guests that the British were as welcome as any resistance member.

Evasion

They relented and the two groups ignored each other, exchanging no words, preferring instead to keep to themselves and act like the other wasn't there.

It took almost three weeks for Senta's wound to heal enough for her to be safe to travel. She and Michael had already decided that that day would be their last on Edith's farm, and they were working in the barn, waiting to tell her over breakfast, which was only a few minutes away.

From out of nowhere, the distant roar of vehicles grew louder, getting closer by the second.

"They're heading here," Michael yelled, pulling Senta instinctively towards the hayloft.

Seconds later he was proven right as car doors slammed, and feet crunched on the gravel outside the farmhouse. A truck pulled up after the car, and Michael knew they were in trouble.

They'd been careful. Every morning, they'd moved their meagre belongings to the barn and hidden them deep inside a barrel of animal feed. No sign of their existence was in the house.

"What are they here for?" Senta asked, her eyes wide with fear. "Us?"

"Possibly," Michael whispered back. "But I doubt it. I bet they got wind of the resistance being here."

He grabbed Senta's arm, pulling her towards the ladder leading to the hayloft. "Get up there," he said urgently.

"But what about Edith? We can't leave her like this?"

"We're not arguing. Go. Don't come out until I come for you."

Senta climbed quickly, her face pale. Michael turned back to the barn door, peering through a crack in the wooden planks. An army truck had pulled into the yard, its insignia unmistakable.

Gestapo, with a truck full of soldiers to do their dirty work.

The scene unfolded in a blur of movement and shouted orders. The four men and two women who'd stayed the night before ran out of the farmhouse, weapons blazing as confusion and carnage erupted.

A young man working near a hay cart leapt down and pulled a concealed weapon from underneath the hay. He crouched behind the cart and opened fire.

Michael didn't hesitate. The Gestapo would search every nook and cranny of the farm once they'd arrested the occupants. It was only a matter of time before he and Senta were discovered.

Cursing himself for overstaying their welcome, he ran outside, taking refuge behind a stone water trough. With his weapon in hand, he dropped two soldiers engaging with the man at the hay cart.

Shouts and screams erupted inside, and shots could be heard. Two of the six resistance fighters lay dead outside, and the other four fought for their lives.

Michael counted ten soldiers. Along with the Gestapo agents and other soldiers inside the house, they were outnumbered at least two or three to one.

Four more soldiers fell under the hail of fire, and the Gestapo agents ran from the house, back towards their vehicle. Michael caught one in the head, dropping him like a stone.

The rest reached their vehicle, and they sped off, gravel spitting in all directions as the vehicle raced away, leaving the soldiers to fight for their lives.

The resistance fighters ran into the house, and more shots were heard. Michael waited until the resistance fighters emerged, dragging dead bodies behind them.

He stood upright and ran to help, and was joined by

the man behind the hay cart. Between them, they dragged six soldiers from the house. They threw them into the back of the army truck, and the four remaining fighters jumped in without another word and drove off, taking the dead soldiers with them.

All that remained were the hay cart fighter and Michael. Plus Senta and Edith, of course. The two men ran to the house, both careful in case any enemy combatants were still in there.

By the time the dust settled, the farm was a scene of devastation. The Gestapo were gone, but the cost was staggering. Edith lay slumped against the doorframe of her house, her apron stained with blood. Michael dropped to his knees beside her, cradling her head gently.

"Edith," he said, his voice breaking.

Her eyes fluttered open, and she smiled faintly. "Take care of Senta," she whispered, her voice barely audible. "And... win this war for us."

Tears burned in Michael's eyes as her hand fell limp.

Behind him, Senta emerged from the barn, her face streaked with tears. She knelt beside Edith, her shoulders shaking as she wept.

The resistance fighter stood rigid, unable to look away. Tears fell down his face, and his expression said everything; no words were necessary.

"Thank you, Englishman," he said in halting English, his voice heavy with emotion. "You helped us."

Michael nodded, his throat too tight to speak.

The young man glanced at Senta, then back at Michael. "Come with us. It's too dangerous here because they will be back. Our leader will help you. We can get you to the coast. To a boat."

Michael knelt one more time and touched Edith's still warm hand. "I won't forget your kindness, Edith. I hope you find peace now that you're reunited with your husband."

He stood up and wiped his eyes. "Let's go."

He ran to the barn and retrieved his rucksack, and with one last look at the farm that had been their sanctuary, he climbed into the vehicle next to their new friend and they drove away.

Chapter 64

In the special operation room set up in the SS headquarters at the seized City Hall, SS-Obersturmführer Erik Stadtler stood up to address the three handpicked SD officers he'd chosen to work with him on the vital mission set for him by SS-Obergruppenführer Hanns Albin Rauter.

"Gentlemen, we have been tasked with carrying out a mission that is so vital to the Reich that none other than SS-Obergruppenführer Heydrich himself personally directed it."

He waited for the words to sink in. "I have a signed order from Heydrich, giving me authority over all branches of military and security to aid in this task. And you, gentlemen, have been handpicked by me to carry out this mission."

The excitement in the room was palpable, and the men sat facing Stadtler were completely taken aback by his opening words.

"The nature of this operation is top secret, and not a whisper can be made outside of the confines of our offices, wherever they are. Do you understand, gentlemen? If word of this gets out, Heydrich will hold us all personally accountable, and as none of us wants that, I'm sure we can agree to keep a lid on it."

It was more of a statement than a question, and all three acknowledged their agreement.

"Good. Open the files in front of you and read them. Study them. Know the faces inside as well as you know your wives or mistresses, because they are now your sole reason for being alive. We have to catch these people, and we don't have much time."

The three men Stadtler had chosen were the best the SD could offer. Two had been pulled from Berlin, and the third from The Hague. Stadtler beamed as he looked at their expressionless faces, their eyes focused on the files they were reading.

All were devout Nazis, ruthless and efficient, and they would follow Hitler's orders to their graves, no matter how dirty the missions got.

The first was a scar-faced officer named Albrecht Hauser. He was in his early forties and had been a close colleague of Albert Kreise, the man whose files Stadtler now possessed.

Hauser had proven his worth to the SD countless times, and he was a man to be relied on when investigations became vital.

The man next to him, Gerhardt Braun, had gone through university with Stadtler, and he possessed the sharpest mind Stadtler had ever seen. He was relentless, and he wouldn't stop until the job was completed.

The last was a man who Rautin had ordered Stadtler to include. He wouldn't be his first choice, but when the commander of all the forces in Holland tells you his man is in, then who was Stadtler to argue?

The man's name was Erich Falken, and he was a middle-aged, studious man who was a personal favourite of Rauter. Falken was known to be meticulous with details, and nothing, not even the smallest of details, ever seemed to slip by him.

Stadtler had to admit that Falken was a good addition to his team, but he couldn't help wondering if his primary role was to spy on him and report back to Rauter what he was up to.

All three men held the rank of Obersturmführer, so as a newly promoted Sturmbannführer, Stadtler held rank on all of them.

Erik Stadtler turned his attention to the files Kreise had amassed on Michael Fernsby, the young but elusive member of Britain's Unit 317, the secret department within MI6 that specialised in deniable operations behind enemy lines.

Like everyone else in the SD, Stadtler had heard of Fernsby, but he'd never known details of the missions he'd been able to pull off.

The man's a genius at escape and evasion, and he must be taken seriously, Kreise had written. Do not allow his youthful looks to deceive you. *He is as dangerous an enemy as we're ever likely to face.*

After reading the files, Stadtler was inclined to agree.

"What do we know about Senta Postner?" Falken asked. "There's not much in her file, and there's nothing that tells us why she's so important to the British."

Stadtler looked at each man in turn. "What I am about to tell you is top secret, so listen carefully, gentlemen. That young girl holds the key to winning the war, that's how important she is. She has an eidetic memory, which means that she can see something one time and remember every little detail forever."

Low whistles and incredulous stares followed Stadtler's words.

"Is that confirmed?" Falken pressed. "I mean, that is so rare a gift that I've never heard of anyone ever before who can do that."

"It's confirmed," Stadtler snapped. "Why else would the British go to so much trouble to get her?"

"I can see why she's so important," Braun said. "And I can see why we're going to so much trouble to find her."

Stadtler looked at Hauser. "Albrecht, I want you to concentrate on the other sister, Mina Postner. We believe she's somewhere in France, trying to reach her deceased best friend's family. The details, including their address, are in the file, so as long as she's going there, she'll be easy to find."

Hauser nodded, his eyes displaying no emotion, although Stadtler was sure he was disappointed not to be going after the main prize.

"Now that we know who we're up against, let's get on with it, shall we?" Stadtler turned towards the large map on the wall behind him.

"Fernsby and the girl were last seen near the crash site, which was here," Stadtler pointed at a circled point on the map.

"This derelict building here," he tapped the map with his finger, "was their last known location. From there, they would have gone south, into France."

"Do we have confirmation they crossed the border?" Braun asked.

"Not yet," Stadtler admitted. "But we will. Their trail went cold after the derelict building. But, if I were Fernsby, I'd aim for the nearest crossing into France. They are trying to get to England, which means they're heading to the coast. We'll find them before they reach it."

"Remember, you are to report to only me," Stadtler reminded the men before they dispersed. "No one else. No Gestapo, no Wehrmacht, no matter their rank. This mission is under the direct authority of SS-Obergruppenführer Rauter and Obergruppenführer Heydrich. I expect absolute discretion. Is that understood?"

"Yes, Sturmbannführer," the men replied in unison, their voices devoid of hesitation.

"Good. We leave in two days, so be sure you have everything in order before we go."

Chapter 65

Two days later, Stadtler, Braun, and Falken arrived at the Wehrmacht base in Bailleul, a French town just over the border with Belgium. Hauser was on his way to the South of France in an attempt to head off Mina Postner, and he'd catch up with the rest once he had her in custody.

After angry phone calls between the camp commander and his superiors in Berlin, Stadtler set up his office in the conference room. The commander had reluctantly placed his men and his equipment at his disposal, and although he hated it, there was nothing the camp commander could do about it.

Stadtler quickly established his base in France, and posted two guards outside the conference room door to stop anyone except himself, Braun or Falken from entering, including the camp commander.

The dusty roads of occupied France bore the weight of Stadtler's relentless pursuit. In Bailleul, the air buzzed with tension as he interrogated local collaborators and Gestapo units, cross-referencing every detail with Kreise's files. The

Evasion

town offered nothing concrete, but each whispered lead nudged him closer to Fernsby and the girl.

On the sixth evening, as Stadtler sat poring over reports in his makeshift office, a knock shattered the stillness. Falken entered, a thin smile tugging at his tired face.

"Erik, we might have something," he said.

Stadtler's cold eyes snapped up. "What is it?"

"I was reading the reports from the Wehrmacht units you sent out after we got here. One of them spoke with a street trader, a farmer who sells his wares at the side of the road several miles west of here."

"I'm all ears." Stadtler knew all about Falken's legendary attention to detail.

"He claims he sold food to a young couple several days ago. He described them as not local."

Stadtler's pulse quickened. *Finally, we might have something on them.*

"Where?" he barked.

"In the middle of nowhere, really. They were headed west and stopped to barter for food. The trader only remembers it because they weren't French."

"Did he say where they were from?"

"The report states he thought they might be British."

Stadtler rose swiftly, grabbing his cap and coat. "Bring him in for questioning."

∾

THE TRADER, a wiry man in his fifties, shifted nervously under Stadtler's piercing gaze. The room felt colder than it should have, as if the man's fear had drawn the warmth from the air.

"They were young," the trader stammered. "The girl

spoke a little French, but when they spoke together, it was in English. I only sold them bread and cheese."

"Did the girl have blonde hair?" Stadtler snapped.

The trader shook his head. "No, she had brown hair, from what I remember."

"She's dyed it then," Stadtler said. "That's good to know."

"If it's them," Falken added.

"Which direction did they go?" Stadtler ignored the intervention.

"Towards the rail lines," the trader replied, his voice trembling.

Stadtler studied the man for a long moment before dismissing him. The details matched Fernsby and the girl too closely to ignore.

The next morning, much to the relief of the camp commander, Stadtler began packing up his maps and equipment. His time in Bailleul had come to an end.

He was convinced Fernsby and Senta were heading west to Boulogne-sur-Mer, which was a port city where they might be able to find a sympathetic fisherman to take them across the English Channel.

Even though there was a heavy German presence in the city, Allied soldiers were still slipping through, albeit in much smaller numbers now they had full control of the area.

Boulogne was, therefore, his next destination, which he hoped would be the one where he'd finally be the man to capture Michael Fernsby.

And the girl, of course.

Falken and Braun were finishing going over the latest reports from France, all of which reached their desks, leaving neither of them with much time to do anything else, such was the volume of reports they had to sift through.

Suddenly, Gerhardt Braun looked up, making a guttural sound in his throat.

"Erik!" he yelled. "We might have something."

Braun jumped up, holding a report in his hand. He rushed to Stadtler, who took the report and read it out loud for all to hear.

"A freight train stopped briefly near Amiens for routine checks. One cart's door was found ajar. Soldiers reported seeing a man and a woman, both around twenty years of age, fleeing the scene. They did not pursue, assuming them to be locals avoiding the fighting."

"Good work, Gerhardt," Falken said. "Now you've found that one, I have another one here somewhere."

Falken flipped through a stack of reports he'd already filed until his fingers stopped at one near the middle.

"I'd discounted this because by itself it meant nothing, but along with yours, it might be what we're looking for."

Falken passed the report to Stadtler, who once again read it aloud.

"Checkpoint inspection, Amiens rail yard, two days ago," he began, his voice clipped and precise. "A freight train was stopped for routine checks. One carriage door was found open, though it had been sealed at departure."

Stadtler paused, his brow furrowing as his eyes flicked down the page.

The carriage was empty. A search of the immediate area revealed nothing unusual, but the soldier noted the open door as peculiar. He filed this report later, stating that it didn't seem significant at the time.

"Do we have the train manifests available?" Stadtler asked. "I want to know if these two reports are about the same train. If so, I want to know what route the train took."

Falken lifted a box he'd already sealed for transportation onto the desk. He broke open the seal and pulled out a thick wad of files. After discarding several of them, he set one down and ran his finger down the list.

"Here it is. The train from Gerhardt's report originated in Lille and passed through Saint-Omer. That was where we think Fernsby and the girl may have caught a train, if indeed that's what they did."

"What about the report you found?" Stadtler asked.

Falken looked at the train details on the report he'd found.

"They match. It's the same train!"

The three men stared at each other.

"It has to be them," Stadtler said. "I just know it. I thought they were trying to get to Boulogne, but I was wrong."

He leaned forward. "Where was this train stopped again?" he asked.

"Amiens," Falken said.

Stadtler looked at the two men.

"We're going to Amiens, gentlemen."

Chapter 66

Five days after their reunion, Jeroen and Mina sat quietly in the back of a delivery truck as it rumbled through the outskirts of Breda. The air inside was heavy with the smell of fresh-cut wood, and the timber was stacked neatly around them, acting as both cargo and camouflage.

Adriaan Westerhout had meticulously arranged their route into France, which neither wanted to take. Mina had barely spoken since hearing about Senta and Michael, and Jeroen was itching to get back to Rotterdam to pick up the pieces of his resistance movement and start again.

Neither spoke, their shared silence broken only by the low hum of the engine and the occasional bump of the uneven road. Mina clutched the strap of her bag, her knuckles white. Jeroen glanced at her, his expression unreadable but his presence steady, a quiet anchor against the tide of uncertainty.

Guilt and sadness tore at his soul. He was the only person she had left in this terrible, dangerous world, and here he was, taking her far away into another country, where she didn't know anyone and couldn't speak the language.

What kind of man am I? How can I do this to her?

And yet, deep down, he knew he was doing the right thing. Mina had plenty to offer the resistance, but she'd be a lot safer doing it far away from Jeroen, who seemed to hold the touch of death for everyone he held dear.

The truck slowed, pulling Jeroen from his thoughts. Adriaan Westerhout's voice came from the front, muffled but firm.

"We're here. Quickly now."

The rear doors creaked open, revealing a narrow bridge arching over railway tracks, flanked by empty fields that stretched over the horizon. The driver climbed out, motioning for them to follow.

A signal box stood close by, its windows faintly glowing against the morning sun.

"This is where we part ways," Westerhout said, his tone brisk, but tinged with something softer. Concern for his old friend, perhaps?

Jeroen nodded. "Thank you, Adriaan. For everything."

Mina looked at Westerhout, her lips trembling as though she wanted to say something. He gave her a small, reassuring nod before turning to the signal box operator.

The operator, a wiry man with grease-stained hands, leaned out of the window and gestured for them to hurry. He held up a pocket watch. "Five minutes," he muttered in Dutch. "Not a second longer."

The low rumble of an approaching train filled the air, and the operator darted back to his post. A sharp whistle pierced the silence, and the train slowed to a halt beneath the bridge.

Two resistance members emerged from the truck,

moving with practised efficiency as they helped Jeroen and Mina clamber into the rear carriage.

Inside, the air was thick with an acrid, musty smell that made Mina grasp her nose. Heavy canvas bags, stacked floor to ceiling, filled the cramped space. The resistance men shoved them into a hollow at the centre and pulled the bags tightly around them.

"The smell will mask your scent," one of them whispered. "Dogs won't track you here."

Jeroen nodded his thanks, his hand instinctively reaching for Mina's. She squeezed it tightly, her eyes reflecting a faint glow of fear and determination.

The train jolted forward, and they were on their way.

Hours passed in a blur of motion and muffled sound. The train's rhythmic clatter against the tracks was their only companion, a steady heartbeat propelling them closer to the border.

Mina shifted uncomfortably in the cramped space, her body sore from the rough ride, but she didn't complain.

Jeroen remained alert as Mina slept, and resisted the urge to comfort her when she awoke. The last thing she needed was his sympathy, so he looked away and focused on his own thoughts.

They stopped in a place called Rumes, where the hiss of steam and the clang of metal announced the engine change. Jeroen remained still, his senses on high alert, his arm brushing Mina's as if to remind her he was there.

"We must be near the border," he whispered. "We'll be in France soon."

Jeroen strained his ears, listening for anything unusual. The faint murmur of voices carried through the air, growing louder and sharper. A chill swept through him as he heard the barking of dogs and the guttural commands of German soldiers cutting through the din.

Mina's pale face got even paler, if that was even possible. She stared at Jeroen, open-mouthed, looking almost resigned to a fate of capture and death.

"Stay quiet," Jeroen whispered, his voice barely audible.

His hand found Mina's in the darkness, their fingers locking in an unspoken pact of silence.

The barking grew closer, punctuated by the thud of boots on gravel. Jeroen tensed, his heart hammering as shadows passed across the small cracks in the carriage's wooden slats.

Doors banged open one by one, the sounds echoing like gunshots. Dogs barked furiously, their claws scratching against the metal steps as they were hoisted into the carriages.

Mina jumped each time a carriage door was slammed open, and as they got nearer, Jeroen could feel the tension rising in her fingers. He squeezed, hoping to provide a small amount of comfort in a situation where their lives were on the line.

The barking was louder now, closer. The clanging of a latch being unfastened sent a bolt of panic through him.

Mina stiffened beside him.

Their door swung open with a metallic screech, and a sliver of daylight spilled into the cramped space. The acrid smell of the cargo masked their scent, but it did nothing to calm the pounding in Jeroen's chest.

A dog leapt up, its front paws landing on the doorway with a dull thud. The handler stood just outside, his rifle slung over his shoulder, waiting.

Jeroen froze, his muscles locked as he heard the dog's nose twitching in the air. As it sniffed, its wet snout quivered as it scanned the cramped, shadowy interior.

Evasion

The dog barked sharply, and Mina flinched, biting her lip to keep from crying out.

Jeroen held his breath, his mind racing. The canvas sacks pressed around them offered scant protection, but he willed himself to lie perfectly still.

Their lives were in the balance, and there was nothing they could do about it.

Seconds dragged into what felt like hours. The dog whined, pawing at the edge of the doorway. Its handler gave a sharp command in German, yanking it back.

"Alles klar," the soldier called out, his tone bored. The door slammed shut, plunging them back into darkness.

The silence was deafening. Neither Jeroen nor Mina moved, as if any motion might still betray them. Only the fading sound of barking dogs and retreating boots convinced them that the danger had passed.

Jeroen exhaled slowly, the sound loud in the enclosed space. Mina mirrored him, her breath shuddering as she wiped at her damp cheeks.

"They're gone," he whispered with relief, though his voice wavered.

The train jolted forward again, its rhythmic motion resuming as it pulled away from Rumes. In the darkness, Mina leaned into Jeroen's shoulder, her body trembling.

Just outside Orchies, France, the train stopped once more. Yet again, the sound of the carriage door sliding open brought a surge of tension.

A voice called out softly in French, the words clear: "La lune brille ce soir."

Jeroen, who could speak French, understood the words: *The moon shines tonight.*

Jeroen stiffened, his grip on Mina tightening. He took a deep breath and gave his response.

"Mais les étoiles sont cachées," which translated said, *but the stars are hidden.*

The door slid wider, revealing two figures cloaked in shadows. One of them, a woman with dark eyes and a steady gaze, motioned them forward.

"It's safe," she said in French, her voice low but firm. "Come with us."

Jeroen and Mina climbed out, the fresh late afternoon air sharp; a blessing after the obnoxious odour in the carriage.

The woman led them to a small, nondescript house nestled in a copse of trees not far from the tracks. Inside, the warmth of a fire greeted them, and the four walls promised safety.

For now, at least.

Two days passed in a blur of quiet conversations and apprehensive waiting. The French resistance woman asked Jeroen and Mina detailed questions about their journey, their connection to Westerhout, and their next steps.

Jeroen answered with precision, his words careful but clear.

The conversations were all in English so Mina could understand, and the French woman, who identified herself as Rose, appeared sympathetic when she heard about Senta and the English spy, Michael Fernsby.

"What am I going to do here?" Mina asked.

"That's up to our leader," Rose replied. "I'm just here to help you settle in and make you feel comfortable."

On the second evening, Rose pulled Jeroen aside and had a conversation with him in French. Mina watched on, her features displaying unease and mistrust as they spoke.

"Don't worry," Jeroen said, noticing the tension in the air. "She's telling me that they've arranged my transportation back to Rotterdam."

Evasion

"Why didn't she say it in English, like the rest of our conversations have been?" Mina didn't believe him.

"Because you've been through so much, Mina." Rose answered for herself. "I wanted Jeroen to tell you himself."

"I've been away too long," Jeroen said, his voice steady but laced with regret. "My place is there, fighting alongside my people. Our work isn't done."

Mina's eyes filled with tears. "But what about you? The Germans? There's a bounty on your head. If they catch you…" She tailed off, leaving the sentence unfinished.

"They won't," he interrupted gently. "And even if they do, it's a risk I have to take. We all have our roles to play, Mina. You're safer here, and you'll make a difference in France."

"When?" Mina asked.

"Tonight," Rose answered.

Soft tears fell down Mina's face, breaking Jeroen's heart all over again.

"I have to go, Mina, just as you have to stay here. I'll be safe, I promise, and when the war is over, well, you know where to find me."

"You're all I have left," Mina said. She closed her eyes and fought back the tears that forced their way through.

Their farewell was brief but heavy with unspoken words. Mina hugged Jeroen one last time.

"Stay strong," he whispered. "For Senta. For Michael, and for yourself."

"I will. And you, Jeroen. Don't be a hero. Stay alive, and we'll meet again when the war is over."

"It's a deal." Jeroen smiled at Mina and hugged her one last time.

"Until then," he said.

Jeroen turned and vanished into the night.

Chapter 67

The following day, Mina was taken to another remote house on the outskirts of another town she didn't know the name of. The journey was long and winding, involving cars, horse-drawn carts, and the last stretch by bicycle.

Rose led her all the way and reassured her that everything was going to be alright and that her leader had plans for her to help the war effort.

As Mina stepped off the bicycle, her legs aching and her mind heavy with uncertainty, a tall, middle-aged man at the door stepped forward, his presence commanding yet calm.

The man's sharp grey eyes immediately caught her attention. They were deep-set and hawk-like, exuding a piercing intelligence that seemed to assess her in an instant.

His gaze softened slightly as he took in her weary appearance, though the hard edges of his expression suggested a man who had long since traded sentimentality for practicality.

"Welcome," the man said in English, his deep, gravelly

voice carrying an unexpected warmth. "I've heard a lot about you. Please, come inside."

Rose stepped beside Mina. "This is Marcel. He's our leader."

Mina nodded hesitantly, her eyes flicking back to Marcel, who inclined his head in acknowledgement.

"You must be tired," he said. "We have much to discuss, but first, you need rest."

As he stepped aside to let them in, Mina couldn't help but feel a mixture of awe and trepidation. She was neck deep in a situation in which she had no control, and she didn't like it.

At least it takes my mind off Senta and Michael.

Mina followed Marcel into the house, with Rose a step behind. He led them into a quaint living room that had a bare stone floor and four chairs surrounding an old wooden table.

Paintings of birds hung on the walls, giving the room an air of rustic charm, though the faded colours and chipped frames hinted at years of quiet neglect.

Mina sat and pressed her fingers together, fidgeting, trying to hold herself together. After all she'd been through, she was surprised at how nervous and uncomfortable she was feeling. This should be a doddle, as Michael would say.

And yet it wasn't.

Marcel must have noticed her discomfort, and he made small talk, while Rose made some hot tea for them all.

Mina relaxed a little, but she couldn't shake the feeling of desperation now that she was completely alone.

"You've been through a lot already," Marcel said after sipping his tea. "From what I heard from Adriaan Westerhout, you've suffered great losses recently."

"No more than others have." Mina took a deep breath.

It was no good feeling sorry for herself. Michael had taught her a long time ago that the only way to defeat the Nazis was to stand up to them, and she wasn't going to wallow in her own misery and allow them to defeat her that way.

No, if the Nazis were going to beat her, they were going to have to do it the hard way, with bullets and bombs.

She sat upright and stopped fidgeting.

"You have a vital role to play," Marcel said, taking note of her new, more confident pose. "The Nazis have taken much from you, but they haven't taken your voice. With it, you can reach places we can't."

Marcel stared into Mina's deep blue eyes. "You'll broadcast the truth about the horrors the Nazis are inflicting on their own people and the world. Your words will cut through their lies, into their own living rooms. Hopefully, it will make a difference."

Mina hesitated, her fingers curling into fists. "I'll try," she said.

She'd done it before, but then she had a bigger incentive to reach out to the world—Michael might be listening, and as long as she held out hope that he'd hear her words, everything seemed possible.

Now he was gone, and she didn't feel his strength pushing her forward.

"You can do it," Marcel replied, his voice unwavering. "And you must. Do it for your sister, and for Michael Fernsby. Do it for your parents, who were taken from you so cruelly. And do it for the countless other families who have lost loved ones at the hands of the Nazis."

Mina took a deep breath and reached deep inside for the confidence she knew was there.

"I'll do it," she said. "I'll do whatever I can to help."

"Good," Marcel said. "That's what I wanted to hear.

You'll stay here while I set up a radio set for you. Make yourself comfortable, but don't wander outside during the day because the Germans patrol the area and we don't want them seeing you and paying us a visit."

I know. I won't. Mina knew the ropes well enough by now.

"By the way, where are we?" Mina asked. "What town is this?"

"Amiens."

Chapter 68

The sound of heavy boots echoed through the street outside Hugo's small house on the outskirts of Amiens, each step pounding like a drumbeat against his nerves.

He'd gone straight there the previous day after the shootout at Edith's farm. Luckily for him, he'd been by the hay cart, and had been lucky enough to survive and live to fight another day.

Only because of the Englishman, Michael, though. If it wasn't for him, Hugo would be dead by now.

He'd sheltered the young couple overnight, with the intention of handing them over to Marcel, who would know how to help them escape to England.

He knows how to help them. Whether he would or not was a whole different story.

He crouched by the window, his breath shallow, his hands trembling as he peeked through the gap in the curtains.

German soldiers were everywhere, and the street was blocked from either direction. It was the same on the other side too, as soldiers and Gestapo officers swamped the area, making it impossible for anyone to come or go.

∼

ACROSS THE STREET, a Gestapo officer barked orders, his leather trench coat gleaming in the faint light of the lamppost. Two soldiers dragged a man from his home, his cries muffled as they shoved him towards a waiting truck. A woman followed, leaving two children behind, their faces streaked with tears.

Hugo let out a cry. The man and his wife were innocent; he knew that much. They were shopkeepers, quiet and kind, who had never given the Germans any reason to suspect them.

None of that mattered now.

He turned away from the window, pressing his back against the wall. His house had been spared so far, but it was only a matter of time as the soldiers moved systematically from door to door.

There was no escape.

Michael and the girl were hidden behind the wood-panelled wall in his small sitting room. It wasn't much, a narrow space barely big enough for one, let alone two, but it had saved his own life more than once. He just hoped it would save theirs, too.

If it did, they'd be even, and Hugo liked that idea.

The knock came suddenly, sharp and commanding. Hugo froze, his heart leaping into his throat.

"Open up!" a voice demanded.

Hugo stood, his legs feeling like lead. He took a deep breath, smoothing his hands over his shirt before unlocking the door.

This is it! This is the end.

Two soldiers stood on the threshold, their rifles slung across their shoulders. Behind them, a Gestapo officer observed the scene with cold, predatory eyes.

"We're searching every house," one of the soldiers said curtly. "Step aside and show me your papers."

Hugo nodded mutely, stepping back as they pushed past him. He passed his identification papers to the Gestapo officer.

"Hugo Tremblay? What work do you do?"

"I-I'm a carpenter," Hugo stammered.

He wasn't faking it. It was the worst fear he'd ever felt. His feet and hands refused to obey his commands, and his knees wouldn't stop shaking.

His palms were slick with sweat as they moved through the small house, opening cupboards, overturning furniture, and poking into every corner. When one of them approached the wall concealing Michael and Senta, Hugo's knees nearly buckled.

"Nothing here," the soldier grunted after a cursory inspection.

The Gestapo officer's eyes lingered on Hugo, his gaze sharp and probing. For a moment, Hugo thought his heart might stop. Then the man nodded, and the soldiers filed out, leaving him standing in the empty doorway.

He closed the door quietly, waiting until the sound of their boots had faded before collapsing into a chair. The adrenaline ebbed, leaving him shaking and weak.

"They're gone," he whispered hoarsely.

The panelled wall creaked open, and Michael stepped out, his face grim. "You all right?" he asked.

Hugo nodded, though the tremor in his hands betrayed him. "They're rounding up anyone they think might be helping us," he said. "It's getting worse."

Evasion

Michael helped Senta from the tiny hole, and they both stretched their muscles that had become stiff from being in such a cramped space.

Chapter 69

The next morning, once the raids had stopped, Hugo made his way to Marcel's hideout outside Amiens, his steps cautious as he navigated the quiet streets of the town.

The tension hung heavy in the air in the aftermath of the Gestapo raids. Every window was shuttered, and every street was bereft of people.

Hugo pedalled steadily along the dirt road, the familiar strain of the bicycle pedals grounding him against the lingering unease in his chest.

The morning sun hung low in the sky, casting long shadows across the endless fields that surrounded him. Rows of wheat swayed gently in the breeze, their golden heads rustling like whispers of reassurance.

It was a calm that belied the extreme tension everyone in France was feeling in those troubled times.

In the distance, Marcel's house came into view, a solitary building amid the sprawling farmland. It was a large stone farmhouse, its weathered walls streaked with ivy, and its slate roof sagged gently under the weight of years.

Evasion

The isolation of the place was its greatest strength. It sat far from prying eyes, and Hugo knew that long before he reached the house, Marcel's men would have spotted him.

As he drew closer, he caught sight of one of the sentries stationed by a hedgerow to the east. The man nodded in recognition, his rifle resting across his knees, eyes scanning the horizon for any sign of danger.

The house itself was surrounded by a modest garden bordered by low stone walls. An old well stood near the front door, its wooden bucket resting on the stone rim.

Beyond it, a small vegetable patch stretched towards the barn, where chickens scratched at the dirt, the faint sound of clucking mingling with the distant hum of insects, providing a deceptive serenity against the tension that lay within.

Hugo dismounted his bicycle and propped it against the wall by the well, straightened his cap, wiping sweat from his brow, and took a deep breath before knocking twice on the old wooden door.

The door creaked open, revealing one of Marcel's men, a wiry, sharp-eyed man named Luc, who gestured for Hugo to enter.

The interior was dim, the only light coming from a small oil lamp on the wall.

The air inside was cool, tinged with the faint scent of damp stone and wood. The floor was bare except for a single worn rug in the centre of the main room.

A sturdy wooden table dominated the space, its surface scarred from years of use. Around it sat the surviving resistance fighters from the battle with the Gestapo, their faces drawn and weary.

To Hugo's right, a fireplace crackled faintly, the embers of an earlier fire still glowing red, and above it hung a faded painting of a fox, its bright eyes incongruous against the muted tones of the rest of the room.

This was Hugo's favourite thing in the house. He loved that painting.

Rose sat closest to the fire, her hands wrapped around a mug of tea. She glanced up as Hugo entered, her dark eyes narrowing slightly before she nodded in greeting.

"Hugo," Marcel said, rising from his chair at the head of the table.

He moved with purpose, his wiry frame seemingly unaffected by the strain of the past days. His grey hair was neatly combed back, but his sharp gaze betrayed the burden of leadership.

Hugo stepped forward, removing his cap. "Marcel. I came as soon as I could."

"I know," Marcel replied softly. "We all did. What happened yesterday was terrible, and believe me, we will get our revenge."

Hugo was comforted by Marcel's words. He always was.

"Please." Marcel gestured for him to take a place at the table. "Sit down. We need to talk."

Hugo took a seat, his eyes scanning the room. The atmosphere was heavy, the air thick with unspoken grief for their fallen comrades. Marcel leaned forward, resting his elbows on the table.

"You were there," Marcel said. "At Edith's farm. Tell me everything. I want to hear it from your perspective."

Hugo recounted the events with precision, his voice steady despite the images still being fresh in his mind. The chaos of the shootout, the bravery of the Englishman, and the quiet strength of the German girl who had stayed hidden in the hayloft.

When he finished, one of the men, a broad-shouldered

fighter named Jacques, spoke up. "And you trust them? The Englishman and the German girl?"

"I do," Hugo said firmly. "The Englishman fought alongside us. He killed several Nazis and saved my life. If it wasn't for him, I'd be dead by now."

He looked Jacques in the eye. "And so would most of you as well," he added. "As for the girl, she stayed hidden, and didn't make a sound. Edith trusted them, and so do I."

Jacques grunted but said nothing more.

Marcel leaned back in his chair, his fingers pushed together under his chin. "The Englishman," he murmured. "You said his name was Michael?"

Hugo nodded. "Yes. That's all I know. He never told me anymore."

Marcel's eyes narrowed, his mind clearly working through the implications.

"What do we do now?" Rose asked, her tone cautious but resolute. "The Gestapo are onto us, and they've found our weapons cache at Edith's farm."

"Poor Edith didn't deserve to die like that," Jacques said. "She was a good woman."

"Indeed, she was, and she won't be forgotten," Marcel agreed. "Her memory is what will drive us forward when things get hard. May her soul rest in peace."

"Amen." Everyone at the table muttered the word at the same time.

"So, what do we do now?" Rose repeated.

"We lie low for a while, until things calm down," Marcel said. "Go about your daily lives and act as though nothing's changed. We'll resume our activities when the time is right. This is going to be a long war, and we have to make sure we live long enough to see it through."

"What do we do with the Englishman and his girlfriend?" Hugo asked. "They can't stay with me for long, and I think they deserve our help in getting out of here."

Marcel's gaze shifted to Rose. "We move them. Tonight. Take them to your house, Rose. I'll meet you there after dark."

Rose frowned, clearly displeased. "And if the Gestapo come knocking? What then?"

"They won't," Marcel said firmly. "Not yet. They've had their pound of flesh for now. But if we wait too long, they'll find their way to Hugo's house. It's only a matter of time."

Reluctantly, Rose nodded. "Fine. But you'd better explain everything when you get there."

Marcel turned back to Hugo. "Can you get them there safely?"

"Yes," Hugo said without hesitation. "I'll make sure they're ready."

He was relieved they wouldn't be his problem anymore.

"Good," Marcel said. "We'll discuss the next steps tonight."

Rose and Hugo were almost out of the door when Marcel pulled them back.

"Have you told the Englishman my name?" he asked.

Hugo shook his head. "No, of course not. I don't tell anyone any of our names unless I have to."

"Good. Keep it that way."

Chapter 70

The cobbled streets of Amiens glistened faintly in the moonlight as Hugo led the way through the winding alleyways, his steps light and deliberate.

Michael and Senta followed close behind, their breaths visible in the cool night air. Shadows stretched long against narrow walls, and the occasional clatter of distant boots sent their hearts racing.

Hugo moved with the ease of someone who knew the streets intimately, slipping from one alley to the next, avoiding the main roads.

Michael kept a hand near the concealed Walther PPK, his eyes scanning every doorway and dark corner.

The trio ducked into a lane where broken crates and empty barrels lined the walls. A stray cat darted past them, its yowl cutting through the silence.

Senta flinched, and Michael placed a steadying hand on her shoulder. She met his gaze briefly, offering a weak but grateful smile.

They crossed a quiet square, its fountain dry and silent, and headed towards the outskirts of the town. The faint hum of voices from an open window made them pause, flattening themselves against the rough stone of a building until the voices faded.

Beyond the town's edge, a dirt road stretched ahead, flanked by fields that glowed softly under the starlight. Rows of wheat swayed gently in the night breeze, the rustle a soothing counterpoint to the tension that gripped them.

"There," Hugo whispered, pointing to a house at the end of a narrow lane.

It stood alone, its stone walls bathed in shadow. A soft light glowed from within, visible through the small windows. The roof sagged slightly in the middle, and a crooked chimney leaned against the night sky.

Hugo knocked twice on the wooden door, the sound sharp in the stillness. After a moment, the door creaked open, revealing Rose's sharp gaze peering out from the shadows.

"Quickly," she said, stepping aside.

Inside, the air was cool, the bare stone floor and sparse furnishings giving the house an austere but homely feel. Four chairs surrounded a wooden table in the centre of the room, their backs worn smooth from years of use.

Michael's eyes caught on the faded bird paintings that adorned the walls, their chipped frames a quiet testament to the passage of time.

Michael stood next to Senta, wanting to protect her from hidden dangers. But there weren't any. Not there, not then.

Temporarily, at least, they were safe. Michael felt it, and he could see that Senta felt it too. They relaxed and stood by the chairs around the table.

The faint creak of a door made Michael turn, his instincts sharpening in the dim light of the room. A figure

Evasion

stepped into the doorway, framed by the soft glow of a single overhead light above him.

All heads turned, and Michael blinked, his breath held as he stared. Once. Twice. Three times.

"Marcel?" he whispered, his voice thick with disbelief.

The man standing there was older, perhaps a touch thinner than Michael remembered, but unmistakably the same Marcel Bertrand who had offered him refuge in Versailles at the beginning of his mission.

Marcel's expression softened with a hint of a smile as he crossed the room in two purposeful strides. He grasped Michael's hand firmly, his grey eyes scanning his face with the intensity of a man sizing up an old ally.

"It *is* you," Marcel said, his voice low but resolute. "I suspected it when Hugo and the others described the firefight at Edith's farm. But now, seeing you, I'm so glad I was right."

Michael returned the handshake, his own mind reeling. "I can't believe it," he said, his voice faltering. "Marcel. Of all the places, all the people. What are you doing here?"

Marcel shifted his attention to Senta, his gaze keen and calculating. Michael felt her tense beside him, and he instinctively stepped closer to her. Marcel's eyes lingered on her for a moment longer, then flicked back to Michael.

"She's the one, isn't she?"

Michael's lips parted to respond, but Rose interrupted, her tone sharp with incredulity. "Wait. You two know each other?"

Hugo stepped forward, equally stunned. "How?"

Marcel let out a faint chuckle, releasing Michael's hand. "Yes. Michael stayed with me in Paris some time ago. A short visit, but memorable nonetheless."

Rose folded her arms, her sharp gaze darting between

the two men. "And now he's here, in France again. Coincidence doesn't seem likely, does it?"

Marcel shook his head. "Not coincidence. Circumstance. I suspected it was him when you told me what happened at Edith's farm, with the Englishman fighting beside you and the girl who stayed hidden. And when you told me his name was Michael—well, I just knew."

Hugo and Rose stared at the two men, wide-eyed in disbelief.

"What are you doing in France?" Rose asked Michael.

"Trying to get back to England."

"What were you doing here?" she pressed.

Marcel intervened, touching Rose's shoulder as if to tell her to stop prying. "He doesn't need to explain further," he said, his tone kind but firm.

"You know, don't you?" Rose asked, glaring at Marcel.

Marcel returned her gaze and remained silent.

"What happened?" Marcel asked quietly. "What went wrong?"

"I could ask the same of you," Michael answered.

"Mine's easy," Marcel explained. "When Paris fell, I returned to my hometown, which is here in Amiens. I know people here, and this is where I can be best positioned to strike back against the Germans."

Michael pursed his lips. "Makes sense. As for us, well, the plane we were on was shot down over Belgium, and since then…" He hesitated for a second. "Let's just say it's been quite a journey."

Marcel gave a small nod, his expression one of quiet understanding. "You've been through hell," he said. "Both of you."

Neither Michael nor Senta responded immediately. The room fell into a contemplative silence, broken only by the faint crackle of the fire.

Evasion

Marcel turned to Hugo and Rose, his voice steady but commanding. "I'll handle this. You've both done enough tonight. Go to my place and wait for me there."

He turned to Rose and gave her a faint sign with his hand. Rose nodded in agreement, and both she and Hugo left the intense gathering, neither believing what they'd just witnessed.

"Can you help us get to England?" Michael asked, renewed hope rising in his chest.

Marcel pondered for a moment before answering. "It's possible," he said. "It will take some time to arrange because the Germans patrol the coast heavily to stop things like this from happening."

Michael nodded. "We understand." Relief washed over him, and for the first time since the Lysander had been shot down, he felt confident that he'd be able to complete his mission.

"There's one more thing," Marcel said. His eyes shifted, glancing behind Michael at the person stood in the doorway.

"What's that?"

"Turn around."

Chapter 71

Michael turned at Marcel's command. Senta too, shifted on instinct, and the sight that met their eyes rooted them both to the floor.

Mina stood in the doorway. Her frame, smaller than Michael remembered, was outlined by the faint glow of the overhead light. Her blonde hair, tangled and dulled but unmistakably hers, fell around her shoulders, and her eyes —those deep, ocean-blue eyes—widened as they locked onto him and Senta.

For a second, time seemed to hold its breath.

Then pandemonium erupted.

"Mina!" Senta's voice cracked as she launched herself forward, her feet barely seeming to touch the ground.

Mina let out a sob that seemed torn from the depths of her soul. "You're alive," she gasped, tears streaming down her face. "I thought… I thought you were dead!"

The sisters collided, clutching each other as if their lives depended on it. Senta buried her face in Mina's neck, her shoulders shaking with uncontrollable sobs. Mina cradled her like a mother would a child, her own tears falling freely.

"I thought I'd lost you," Mina whispered, her voice breaking. "I thought I'd never see you again."

"You didn't," Senta choked out. "You didn't lose me. I'm here."

Michael stood frozen, his heart hammering in his chest. He had imagined this moment a thousand times during their harrowing journey—what Mina might look like, what she might say—but the reality of it left him stunned.

Senta pulled back slightly, her fingers still gripping Mina's arms. "You're so thin," she said, brushing a strand of hair from Mina's face. "Are you all right? Have they been feeding you?"

Mina laughed through her tears, a sound both bitter and sweet. "I've been worse," she said, her voice trembling.

Senta stepped aside, her gaze flicking to Michael, who hadn't moved. Mina's eyes followed, and the room fell silent again as the sisters' connection gave way to something else entirely.

Michael and Mina stared at each other, the air between them crackling with unspoken words and emotions too vast to name.

Mina," Michael whispered, taking a tentative step forward.

Her lips quivered, and she clapped a hand to her mouth, her tears beginning anew. "Michael," she said, her voice breaking on the single word.

Before he could think, before he could plan, he crossed the room in three long strides and pulled her into his arms. Mina collapsed against him, clutching his jacket as if it were the only thing keeping her upright.

"I thought you were dead," she sobbed against his chest. "I thought I'd lost you both."

"Shh," Michael murmured, holding her tightly. He buried his face in her hair, breathing in the faint scent of her, the warmth of her body against his an anchor in the storm of emotions swirling within him.

"I'm here," he said softly. "We're both here. And you're safe now."

Mina pulled back just enough to look at him, her hands moving to cup his face. Her fingers trembled as they traced the contours of his cheekbones and his jaw, as though she needed to feel him to believe he was real.

"Your thinner too," she said, a watery laugh breaking through her tears. "And you look terrible."

Michael smiled, brushing a thumb across her cheek to catch a stray tear. "And you're just as beautiful as ever."

Her laughter turned to a sob, and she pressed her forehead to his, their breaths mingling in the small space between them.

Senta watched them, a soft smile breaking through her tears. "I'll just…" she trailed off, retreating towards the kitchen. "I'm hungry."

Marcel, who'd stood silently watching the emotional reunion, followed Senta into the kitchen.

Neither Michael nor Mina acknowledged their departure. They stayed locked in their embrace, letting the weight of separation, of fear, of longing, finally fall away.

"This is wonderful, Senta, but it's for tonight only," Marcel said, hugging her. "Tomorrow, we must separate you again for security reasons. We have to get you and Michael to England, and we have plans to use Mina as a broadcaster of truth."

Senta gazed at Marcel, a look of deep gratitude in her eyes.

"How?" she asked.

"Coincidence and good fortune," Marcel replied as he walked out of the door. "I'll be back in the morning."

Hours later, the three of them sat around the table, picking at the simple meal Rose had prepared. The fire crackled softly in the background, casting warm light over their tired faces.

They talked, Mina telling them about her escape, her time in hiding, and her regret for leaving Rotterdam in the first place. She told them what Marcel's plans were for her now that she was in France, which met with protests from both Michael and Senta.

Michael recounted the crash, their desperate journey through Belgium, and the Gestapo raid at the farm. He left out certain details, things Mina didn't need to know, focusing instead on their determination to make it back to England.

At one point, Mina reached across the table to grasp Senta's hand. "You're so brave," she said, her voice thick with emotion. "Both of you. I can't believe you made it."

Senta squeezed her sister's hand, a soft smile playing on her lips. "We haven't made it yet. There's a lot that can go wrong between now and us getting to England."

"You know, you can come with us," Michael probed, hoping to hear the words he longed to hear. "I promised Senta I would come back for you once I'd got her to safety. Now you're here, we can all leave together."

Mina's eyes filled again, and she shook her head. "No, Michael. As much as I want to, I'm much more useful here. The Nazis have done too much to my family for me to just hide in England and let others do the fighting for me."

She stroked Michael's hair. "At least now you know where I am, so when you come back, you can find me.

Marcel will look after me, and when the war ends, we will be together."

"I thought you'd say that." Michael understood, but he was disappointed at the same time.

The fire burned lower as the hours stretched on, their voices growing quieter, the silences between their words deeper but more comfortable.

At last, Mina glanced at Senta, something unspoken passing between them. Senta nodded, her smile tinged with understanding.

"I'm going to bed," she said, rising from her chair. "Goodnight, Mina, Michael."

"Goodnight," Mina whispered, her gaze following her sister as she disappeared down the hallway.

Michael watched her go, then turned his attention back to Mina. She was looking at him, her eyes soft and filled with something he couldn't quite name, but felt all the same.

Without a word, he reached across the table and took her hand. Mina stood, her fingers curling around his as he led her up the stairs.

Chapter 72

The commandeered Wehrmacht barracks in Amiens had seen better days. The largest office, now converted into SS-Sturmbannführer Erik Stadtler's operations room, was an austere space, stripped of any personal touches by the furious Wehrmacht commander forced to vacate it.

Stadtler stood by the large desk against the far wall, a grim smile curling his lips as he surveyed the map spread before him. Pins and markings indicated checkpoints, Gestapo activity, and the suspected movements of Fernsby since the plane crash.

The Gestapo chief, SS-Hauptsturmführer Kurt Halbe, entered the room, his boots clicking sharply against the wooden floor. Halbe was a stout man in his mid-forties, with sharp, hawk-like features and an ever-present sneer etched onto his face.

He had little love for the SD's encroachment on his domain, but Stadtler's authority, backed by Heydrich himself, left no room for protest.

"Sturmbannführer," Halbe greeted with a stiff salute.

Stadtler turned to face him, his cold gaze locking onto

the Gestapo officer. "Halbe, have you read the report on the raid at the farm near Amiens?"

Halbe's lips thinned. "I have, Herr Sturmbannführer. A regrettable oversight in allowing those partisan fighters to escape. We were taken by surprise at the level of resistance we encountered."

"But we did recover their weapons cache," he added.

Stadtler waved off the response, his eyes narrowing. "The weapons mean nothing compared to what slipped through your grasp. An Englishman and a girl, likely the same pair I'm hunting, were there. Yet they escaped."

Halbe's jaw tightened. "The chaos of the firefight, Sturmbannführer. My men—"

"Your men failed," Stadtler interrupted, his voice sharp. He gestured to the map. "And now we're left piecing together their trail. They're still here, Halbe, somewhere near Amiens, hidden by the resistance."

Halbe stiffened. "If I were them, I'd be at the coast, probably Dieppe, by now."

"What did you just say?" Stadtler asked.

"I said they're probably somewhere near the coast by now."

Stadtler didn't say anything, but what Halbe said made sense. He too, would probably be at the coast by now if the roles were reversed. Still, he had a job to do, and if nothing else, he was thorough.

"We're visiting the farm," he declared. "Have a vehicle ready in five minutes."

"The Wehrmacht burned it down," Halbe said. "On my orders. The resistance was clearly using it, so we took it away from them."

"We're still going."

Evasion

THE CHARRED REMAINS of Edith's farmhouse loomed before Stadtler as he stepped from the vehicle. Smoke stains blackened the stone walls and shattered windows gaped like hollow eyes. The barn stood nearby, its doors ajar, the faint scent of burned wood lingering in the air.

He approached the barn, flanked by Halbe and two armed Gestapo officers.

"This is where the Englishman came from? The barn?" Stadtler asked.

Halbe nodded reluctantly. "Yes. The firefight started in the yard and spilled into the house. Several of our soldiers were killed, and we killed two of their fighters in return, but the others escaped."

Stadtler took a tour of the barn and the house, noting the positions of the resistance fighters when the soldiers were shot.

Halbe hesitated. "If I may, Sturmbannführer, the locals are tight-lipped. Even under duress, they're unwilling to give up resistance members."

Stadtler rounded on him, his icy stare freezing Halbe in his place. "Then apply more pressure. Increase the searches, triple the interrogations. I want every house, every barn, every shed in a twenty-mile radius of Amiens searched."

Halbe blinked, startled. "That's a large area, Herr Sturmbannführer. The resources—"

"Find the resources," Stadtler snapped. "I don't care if you have to pull men from every nearby Gestapo office. I don't care if you wake every farmer in the region. Find them. And if the locals refuse to cooperate, remind them what happens to those who aid enemies of the Reich."

Halbe saluted stiffly, his face pale but resolute. "Yes, Sturmbannführer."

Stadtler stepped closer, his voice lowering to a

dangerous calm. "This is no ordinary fugitive hunt, Halbe. These two are of utmost importance to the Reich. If they reach the coast and escape to England, it will be on your head. Do you understand?"

"Yes, Herr Sturmbannführer," Halbe replied through gritted teeth.

Stadtler strode back to the waiting vehicle, his mind set on his next move.

Chapter 73

Morning light filtered softly through the thin curtains as Michael stirred, the warmth of Mina's body comforting as she lay next to him. He glanced over at her, nestled against him in the small bed, her blonde hair a tangled halo against the pillow.

For a brief moment, the horrors of the war felt distant, held at bay by the gentle rhythm of her breathing.

The sound of quiet movement in the house brought him back to reality. He gently woke her up, and they held each other for a long moment before heading downstairs.

By the time they joined Senta at the table, Marcel and Rose had already arrived.

Senta glanced at her older sister and stuck out her tongue in a mock reprimand, her eyes sparkling with mischief. Mina's cheeks flushed pink, but she couldn't help smiling as she sat between Michael and Senta, holding their hands firmly.

"Quite the display of unity," Rose teased, her tone light as she leaned back in her chair. "It's sweet, and I envy you. My own lover is somewhere near Paris, probably dodging

German patrols. Romance in wartime has a way of being complicated."

"Thank you, Marcel," Michael said, looking at the resistance leader. "We will never forget this, and we're very grateful that you made this happen."

Marcel cleared his throat, bringing their attention to him. His gaze was steady, the weight of leadership clear in his tone.

"I'm glad you've had this time," he said. "Moments like these are rare, and they remind us of what we're fighting for. But now, we must return to the matter at hand."

The mood shifted instantly. Mina straightened, her fingers loosening their grip on Michael's, though she didn't let go entirely.

"Mina, you're being moved this morning," Marcel continued. "The plan is to keep you away from Amiens, where the Gestapo activity is growing daily. You'll broadcast from various locations, never staying in one place for more than a few days. Your words will reach not just Germany, but the world. What you say matters."

Mina nodded, her expression resolute, though her grip tightened briefly on Michael's hand.

"And what about us?" Michael asked. "Can you get us out?"

"You and Senta will remain here for now," Marcel replied. "Arrangements are being made to get you out of France, but it will take time. The Germans are patrolling the coast heavily. It won't be easy or cheap."

"I have money," Michael said quickly. "Whatever it costs, I'll pay it."

Marcel gave him a nod of approval. "Good. Then we'll proceed as planned. For now, stay out of sight and avoid drawing attention. I'll return when everything is in place."

The reality of the situation settled heavily over the

room. Mina turned to Senta, pulling her into a tight embrace.

"You're my everything," she whispered, her voice thick with emotion. "Stay safe. Promise me."

"I promise," Senta said, her own tears spilling freely.

When Mina pulled back, she turned to Michael, her eyes searching his, as if to memorise every detail of his face. He stood, his heart breaking as he opened his arms. She stepped into them, and for a long moment, they simply held each other, their breaths mingling in the shared space between them.

"I don't want to leave you," she murmured.

Michael pressed a kiss to her forehead. "And I don't want to let you go. But you're right, Mina. You're needed here. Just promise me you'll stay safe, and when this war is over, we can be together."

"We'll find each other," she finished, her voice trembling.

He kissed her, a desperate, passionate kiss that conveyed every unspoken word he couldn't bring himself to say. Her fingers tangled in his hair, her tears mixing with his as the moment stretched into eternity.

Finally, Rose stepped forward, her expression gentle but firm. "It's time, Mina."

Mina nodded, pulling back reluctantly. She glanced at Senta one last time, her eyes filled with love and unspoken promises, before turning back to Michael.

"I'll see you again," she said, her voice steadier than she felt.

"You'd better," he replied, forcing a weak smile.

With that, Mina turned and followed Rose out of the house, her figure disappearing into the morning light. Michael watched until she was completely out of sight, his heart heavy and his arms aching for her return.

Marcel clapped him on the shoulder, his touch grounding. "This is war, Michael, and sacrifices must be made. But we fight so that someday, there will be no more goodbyes like this."

Michael swallowed hard, nodding as Marcel left the room. He glanced at Senta, who reached out and took his hand.

"We'll see her again," she said softly.

Michael nodded, but his gaze lingered on the empty doorway, the echo of Mina's presence still filling the air.

Chapter 74

Hugo stood behind the tattered curtain in his bedroom the following morning in the heart of Amiens, his heart pounding as he watched the streets below. Soldiers swarmed like locusts, moving with ruthless efficiency from house to house.

A truck idled nearby, its bed already packed with pale, terrified faces. A young man was dragged from his doorway, protesting loudly, until the butt of a rifle silenced him.

Hugo's fists clenched. The Gestapo and their Wehrmacht thugs were tearing the town apart, and it was only a matter of time before they reached his place.

The sudden creak of the back door made him whirl around, his heart in his throat. He pointed his pistol at the doorway, ready to open fire at the first sight of a German soldier.

Rose stepped into the dimly lit room, her face flushed and her breath ragged.

"They're searching every house, every building, all across town," she said, her voice low but filled with urgency. "They must be looking for Michael and Senta, because they're pulling out anyone who fits their description."

"Bastards," Hugo exclaimed. "They know these people are innocent."

"The Gestapo don't care," Rose said. "And they'll arrest us if we don't move fast. We need to go. Now."

Hugo nodded, grabbing his coat, and checking his pistol. "You've got the vehicle?"

"Parked in the garage," she confirmed.

"Then let's go."

The two of them slipped out the back, Hugo locking the door behind him out of habit, though he doubted it would slow the Gestapo down.

The narrow alley behind his house offered some concealment, but Hugo's every step felt loud enough to give them away.

Rose led the way, cutting through a gap in a crumbling stone wall and into an overgrown lot where an old garage stood half-hidden by vines and brambles.

The raids hadn't reached that part of town yet, so they hurried to get away before they did.

Rose yanked the doors open, revealing a beat-up Citroën parked inside. "Get in," she ordered.

Hugo slid into the passenger seat, his hand resting on his pistol. Rose started the engine with a low growl, and they pulled out onto a dirt track that wound through the outskirts of town.

"Where are we going?" Hugo asked, though he already knew.

"To my place," Rose replied. "They haven't hit the outskirts yet, but it's only a matter of time. Michael and Senta are still there."

Hugo said nothing, his jaw tightening. He had half a

mind to be angry at the strangers for dragging them into such a mess, but he knew better. None of it was their fault.

The car bumped along the rutted track, the buildings thinning out as they neared Rose's secluded home. She parked the car under a group of trees a short distance from the house, cutting the engine and turning to Hugo.

"Stay here," she said firmly. "I'll get them."

Hugo nodded, watching as Rose disappeared from view. He sat back in his seat, his fingers drumming against his thigh as he kept his eyes on the road behind them.

The minutes dragged on, every sound amplified in the stillness. A distant shout, the faint rumble of an engine, the rustle of wind through the trees. Each one set Hugo's nerves on edge.

Finally, Rose reappeared, leading Michael and Senta towards the car.

Hugo opened the rear door, motioning for them to get in. "Move quickly," he said, his voice low.

Michael and Senta climbed in without a word, their faces tight with tension. As Rose slid back into the driver's seat and started the car, Hugo turned to Michael.

"They're tearing the town apart," he said grimly. "Looking for you. We're heading to the coast. Marcel has a place lined up."

Michael nodded, his expression unreadable. He didn't respond, but instead checked his weapon and tucked his knife in his sock in preparation for whatever lay ahead.

Chapter 75

The hum of typewriters and the occasional sharp bark of orders echoed through the commandeered Wehrmacht barracks in Amiens. Stadtler's office, a stark and functional space dominated by maps and files, was silent but for the ticking of a clock on the wall.

Erik Stadtler leaned over his desk, the faint glow of a desk lamp illuminating his cold, calculating expression. Kreise's files were spread out before him, the dossier on Michael Fernsby open to a rare photograph of the elusive young operative. Stadtler tapped the image thoughtfully, his mind racing.

The image had been distributed throughout the occupied territories, but so far, nothing had come of it. It was as though Fernsby and the girl were ghosts, and yet Stadtler knew deep down in his dark soul that he was on the right track.

They were in his grasp, and all he had to do was play his cards right and they'll fall right into his lap.

The door opened, and Falken and Braun entered. Both men saluted sharply, their faces betraying no emotion.

Evasion

"Gentlemen," Stadtler began without looking up. "We're close, and we're tightening the noose."

Falken and Braun exchanged a glance, stepping forward to stand by the desk. Stadtler gestured to the phone.

"Let me deal with Hauser first. He should have had the sister in custody by now."

He lifted the receiver and dialled, the crackle of the line filling the room. After a moment, Hauser's curt voice came through.

"Sturmbannführer," Hauser greeted. "What can I do for you?"

"What's the status on Mina Postner?" Stadtler got straight to it, his tone sharp and expectant.

"Nothing yet to report, Herr Sturmbannführer," Hauser replied. "We have eyes on the target family, but so far there hasn't been any sign of Mina Postner. But rest assured, if she shows up, we'll have her."

Stadtler's face reddened. "Good. Remain vigilant. If she's heading to that family, she'll arrive sooner rather than later. I want updates every four hours. Am I clear?"

"Crystal clear," Hauser confirmed.

Stadtler hung up and turned his icy gaze to Falken and Braun. "For now, there's nothing on the other sister. Our focus is entirely on Fernsby and the girl."

He paused, jabbing a finger at a map pinned to the wall. "If I were in his shoes, I'd be heading to the coast. Dieppe, specifically. It's one of the most logical points of escape to England."

Falken frowned slightly. "A reasonable assumption, Sturmbannführer. But the coast is heavily monitored. If they're already there, they'll have to be well hidden."

"That's why we're moving to Dieppe," Stadtler said, his voice resolute. "I think they're being helped by the

French, so I want a dozen Wehrmacht soldiers and a half dozen Gestapo agents at our disposal. Arrange for transport and manpower, Falken."

Falken nodded, though he hesitated. "From here, or Dieppe?"

"Take them from here, seeing as they already know what we're trying to do. We'll use the local forces in Dieppe when we get there."

"I can do that, but it isn't going to go down very well with the camp commander or the Halbe."

Stadtler's expression darkened. "If anyone raises a complaint, remind them that this mission has been authorised by Obergruppenführer Heydrich himself. If they still object, refer them directly to me. Do you understand?"

"Yes, Herr Sturmbannführer," Falken said crisply.

Braun, ever the tactician, spoke next. "Speaking of Halbe, will he remain in Amiens during our operation?"

Stadtler smirked faintly. "Halbe has been given another task that will keep him busy for a while. He's going to check every building within twenty miles of Amiens. I'm sure he'll find some resistance fighters, and at least one of them will know where Fernsby and the girl are."

"That's a lot to ask, Erik," Falken said. "He's going to need help."

"He has the Wehrmacht," Stadtler snapped. "And he has the authority to commandeer help from other towns if needed. Halbe failed me once, but I won't tolerate his failure again."

Falken and Braun exchanged a glance, but neither said anything. Stadtler moved to the window, his hands clasped behind his back as he gazed out at the courtyard below.

"Tomorrow morning, we leave for Dieppe. Be ready."

The next morning dawned grey and cold, a light drizzle misting the air as a convoy of vehicles rumbled out of Amiens. Stadtler sat in the lead car, his gloved hands resting on his lap as he stared ahead with grim determination.

Behind him, a truck carried a dozen Wehrmacht soldiers, and a third vehicle held six Gestapo agents, their expressions impassive, their civilian clothes pressed and immaculate.

As the town of Amiens receded into the distance, Stadtler allowed himself a rare moment of satisfaction. The pieces were in motion, and he would not rest until Fernsby and the girl were within his grasp.

Chapter 76

The salty tang of the sea breeze drifted through the cracks in the weathered shutters of the centuries-old smugglers' house, perched atop the white cliffs overlooking the restless waves of the English Channel.

Miles from the nearest town of Petit-Caux, north of Dieppe, the isolated house stood as a beacon to days gone by, its weathered stone walls and sloping roof bearing witness to generations of history.

Michael sat on a low wooden bench near the fireplace, his back against the cool wall. Across from him, Marcel leaned forward in his chair, his grey eyes glinting in the dim light of a single lantern that sat on a wooden table in the middle of the room.

Senta was curled up beside Michael, her hands wrapped around a tin mug of lukewarm tea. Rose sat cross-legged on the floor, tracing patterns in the dust with a finger, her sharp gaze flicking to the door each time the wind groaned against it.

"This house has seen centuries of secrets," Marcel began, his voice low and steady.

Michael raised a brow, intrigued despite the tension that hummed in his veins. His gaze traversed the room—the uneven stone walls, the exposed wooden beams overhead, and the worn furniture that had seen better days.

It didn't seem like much, but Michael trusted Marcel's judgement. If he said the place was safe, it was. At least for now.

"Smugglers?" Senta asked, her tone tinged with curiosity. "Like pirates?"

Marcel's lips quirked into a faint smile. "Not quite. They were mostly locals—farmers, fishermen—men and women trying to make ends meet. This stretch of the Normandy coast has been a haven for smuggling since the seventeenth century. Wine, brandy, lace, whatever they could carry in their boats."

Rose glanced up, her interest piqued. "And the tunnel?" she asked, gesturing towards the fireplace that sat cold and empty. "I've always wanted to know about that."

"That came later," Marcel said, his voice lowering as if sharing a sacred secret. "During Napoleon's time, when the coastal blockades were at their height, they carved it out of the cliffs, a painstaking process, but it was worth it. The tunnel leads directly to the beach below. They were perfect for moving goods without being seen."

Michael leaned forward, the idea of such ingenuity in the face of danger resonating with him. "And now? It's used by the resistance?"

Marcel nodded. "It's one of the safest spots along this coast for smuggling people out of France. The house itself has a few other surprises."

He tapped a foot against the floor and pointed at the walls. "Hidden compartments. False walls. Even if a German patrol found this place, they'd have a hard job trying to get it to give up its secrets."

Senta's eyes widened. "You've used it before?"

"Many times," Marcel replied. "And with success, though I'd prefer not to have to rely on it too often."

Rose tilted her head, her curiosity evident. "Why not?"

"Because if we're here, it means things are desperate," Marcel said simply. "Like they are now."

The room fell silent for a moment, the weight of his words settling over them like a shroud. Outside, the wind picked up, whistling faintly as it swept through the tall grasses surrounding the house.

"When this night is over," Marcel continued, looking straight at Rose. "Once these two are safely away, I don't want you going back to Amiens. It's too dangerous there right now."

"Where to, then?" Rose asked.

"We're going to Grandvilliers, which is about a hundred kilometres from Amiens. We'll be safe there until things quieten down again."

"Then we go back?"

"Then we go back." Marcel bowed his head.

Hugo appeared in the doorway, his silhouette dark against the faint moonlight.

"All quiet," he said. "No sign of patrols so far."

He eyed the lukewarm tea in Senta's hands.

"I can take over for a while," Michael offered. "You can get a cup of tea and warm yourself up a bit."

Hugo glanced at Marcel, but the look on his face told him no.

"Thanks, but I know this coastline better than most. I'll be alright."

Senta handed him her cup of tea. "Here, take this. I can make another one."

"Thank you." Hugo grabbed the tea and ran back outside before Marcel could say anything.

Michael stared at the old stone fireplace. "It must've been something," he said softly, "standing here hundreds of years ago, waiting for a boat just like we are now."

The room fell silent, each lost in their own thoughts. The sound of distant waves filled the silence, a rhythmic reminder of the passage of time.

Marcel leaned back in his chair, his gaze fixed on the shadows dancing across the walls.

"Let's hope," he murmured, "that the sea keeps her secrets tonight."

Chapter 77

The Dieppe Wehrmacht barracks, now commandeered for Erik Stadtler's purposes, exuded the same tension he left in his wake at every military barracks he'd been to.

The largest office, once belonging to the senior military officer in the region, now bore the cold, methodical stamp of the SS. Maps cluttered the walls, pins marking key locations, and dossiers lay open across the central table, their contents meticulously studied and underlined.

Stadtler stood by the window with a cigarette in hand, the soft glow of his desk lamp casting long shadows over his sharply angled features.

He exhaled a thin stream of smoke, watching it dissipate into the dimly lit room. His thoughts churned, every move calculated as he visualised the net closing around Michael Fernsby and the girl.

They were here. He felt it in his bones. All he needed was one break, one slip-up, and they would be his.

The door burst open, and Stadtler turned sharply, his icy glare meeting SS-Obersturmführer Erich Falken's urgent expression. Falken didn't bother with formalities, his efficiency leaving no room for decorum.

"Sturmbannführer," Falken said, holding up a notepad filled with scribbles. "We have something."

Stadtler extinguished his cigarette in the ashtray, his interest piqued. "Go on."

"I've been working through local records and questioning a few French sympathisers." Falken's lips curled slightly at the term. "One of them mentioned an old house near Petit-Caux, north of here. Apparently, it used to be a smugglers' den centuries ago."

Stadtler's expression remained neutral, but his mind raced. "And?"

"It's still in use," Falken continued, his tone firm. "Resistance fighters sometimes use it to smuggle people out of France. It's remote, well hidden, and accessible to the coast. If Fernsby is trying to escape, it's the perfect place to stage his departure."

Stadtler moved around the desk, stopping in front of Falken. "How reliable is this information?"

Falken's jaw tightened. "The sympathiser was given incentives to cooperate. I believe he's telling the truth."

"Believe?" Stadtler repeated, his voice cutting.

Falken didn't flinch. "I'm confident, Sturmbannführer."

Stadtler considered the information, his mind already working through the possibilities. He strode to the map on the wall and placed a finger on Petit-Caux.

"And this house? Exact location?"

"He described it well enough," Falken replied. "It's isolated, a few miles from the town. It's here." He pointed to a spot on the map.

"Find Braun and get him to communicate with the patrols to the north of Dieppe. Tell them to wait for us at this location." Stadtler pointed at a road junction about a mile from the old smugglers' house.

"I want you with me. Bring the sympathiser as well, in case we can't find the house."

"I'll get right on it." Falken turned to exit the room.

"Meet me out front with a vehicle in fifteen minutes," Stadtler shouted after him.

"Yes, Sturmbannführer."

Fifteen minutes later, Stadtler stepped into the chilly night air, the faint drizzle misting his overcoat. A dark Wehrmacht vehicle waited in the courtyard, its engine already running.

Braun was behind the wheel, and Falken sat next to him, with a nervous-looking Frenchman sandwiched between them.

Stadtler climbed into the back seat, his eyes sharp as they caught the frightened gaze of the sympathiser in the rear-view mirror.

"If you've lied to us," he said coldly, "you'll wish you hadn't."

The man nodded frantically, his words tumbling out in broken German. "It's true, I swear it. The house is there!"

Stadtler leaned back, his lips curling into a faint smile. "Fernsby and the girl had better be there as well."

The vehicle roared to life, its tyres spitting gravel as it sped out of the barracks and onto the darkened roads of Dieppe. The journey was silent, punctuated only by the rumble of the engine and the occasional splatter of rain against the windshield.

As they approached the rendezvous point, Stadtler's throat constricted. His entire future, perhaps even his life, was in the hands of a French sympathiser. He gripped his pistol, feeling the raw power in his hands.

Evasion

If the sympathiser was wasting his time, it would be the last thing he ever did

Chapter 78

The wind howled across the cliffs at Petit-Caux, carrying with it a fine drizzle that clung to Hugo's coat and seeped through to his skin. He shifted uncomfortably, tightening his grip on his rifle.

The cold gnawed at him, and the damp air made his bones ache, but he stayed at his post, scanning the darkness with weary vigilance.

Below him, the tide crashed against the rocky beach, the white spray glinting faintly in the dim light of the overcast night. The sound was relentless, almost hypnotic, but Hugo's mind refused to let him relax.

He knew what was at stake.

The old smugglers' house was their last refuge, and the operation was critical. The boat would arrive by one am, and they couldn't afford any mistakes. As he peered into the gloom, everything seemed eerily quiet.

Then he saw it, or thought he did. A flicker of movement near the edge of the lane, barely perceptible. Hugo froze, his pulse quickening. Was it just the wind stirring the

Evasion

undergrowth? He narrowed his eyes, straining to see through the drizzle.

There it was again. A shift in the shadows, like something, or someone, darting between the bushes. Hugo's mouth went dry. His first instinct was to dismiss it as his imagination, but he knew better than to trust complacency.

He crawled forward, trying to keep as low a profile as he could. The wind picked up, masking the sound of his approach as he tried to get a better look.

Halfway to the lane, his heart skipped.

A man. Hugo saw him clearly now, a figure darting across the lane and crouching behind a bush. The outline was unmistakable. This was no trick of the light.

The Germans had found them.

Panic surged through Hugo's mind, but years of intelligence work had taught him to channel that fear into action. He spun around, his knees losing their grip momentarily on the damp ground as he turned back towards the house.

The rifle fell from his hands, clattering to the gravelly ground with an unnatural, agonising sound. Hugo knew he'd blown whatever cover he had.

He rose to his feet and ran, but he wasn't fast enough. A single shot from a rifle cracked in the night air, and a split second later, Hugo crashed to the ground in agony as the bullet tore through his back.

Adrenaline coursed through him as he pushed himself to his feet. He had to warn the others, so, ignoring the intense pain, he forced himself back to his feet and staggered towards the house.

Chapter 79

Hugo stumbled through the doorway, his weight crashing against the frame before he collapsed onto the floor, leaving a dark smear behind him.

The door swung shut behind him, carried by the wind, and Marcel bolted to secure it, the clatter of the heavy lock echoing through the house.

"Upstairs, now!" Marcel barked, his voice sharp and commanding as he turned to Michael and Senta.

Michael hesitated for a moment, glancing down at Hugo, who lay pale and trembling, blood pooling beneath him. Rose was already at his side, her hands pressing desperately against his wound, but there was nothing she could do for him.

"Go!" Marcel snapped, grabbing Michael's arm.

With one last look at Hugo, Michael gritted his teeth and grabbed Senta's hand as they rushed up the stairs behind Marcel. Their footsteps pounded against the wood, mingling with the sound of shouting voices outside and boots hammering towards the house.

In the bedroom at the top of the stairs, Marcel pushed

Evasion

aside an old armoire, revealing a narrow panel in the wall. He yanked it open to reveal a small, dark space behind the plaster.

"Get in," Marcel ordered.

Michael turned to Senta, who was shaking her head, her face ashen. "No, Michael," she whispered. "Not without you."

"There's no time," Michael said, his voice firm but strained. He grabbed her shoulders, steadying her. "You have to. I'll be right behind you."

Marcel gave an urgent nod, stepping aside to let Senta climb into the hidden space. She looked back at Michael, her eyes wide with fear and something unspoken.

"Go," Michael said again, his voice cracking.

Senta ducked inside, and Marcel quickly closed the panel, running his hands over it to ensure it was seamless.

Downstairs, Rose cradled Hugo's head in her lap, her hands trembling as she brushed the damp hair from his brow. His breath came in short, ragged gasps, and his eyes fluttered weakly.

"Hugo," she whispered, her voice breaking. "Stay with me."

He let out a faint, pained chuckle, his lips curling into a weary smile. "Rose," he murmured, his voice barely audible. "There's something I've been meaning to tell you."

"Save your strength," she urged, her tears falling freely now. "You're going to be fine."

"No," he said, shaking his head slightly. "No, I'm not. And that's why I have to say this. I've loved you since the first moment I saw you."

Rose froze, her breath catching in her throat. She let out a soft sob, pressing her forehead against his.

"You fool," she whispered. "You should have told me sooner."

"Would it have changed anything?" Hugo asked, his smile faint but bittersweet.

"Everything," Rose said, her tears falling onto his cheeks. "So don't you dare die on me now, Hugo. You hear me? Don't you dare."

But his eyes were already losing focus, his breathing slowing. His hand twitched, reaching for hers, and she gripped it tightly, pressing it to her heart.

"Hugo?" she whispered, her voice breaking.

He exhaled softly, the light fading from his eyes as his body went still.

The crash of boots against the door shattered the silence. Rose flinched, her grief momentarily overwhelmed by the sudden eruption of violence.

The door splintered inward, and two German soldiers forced their way through as more smashed their way in through the rear of the house.

Michael ran down the stairs towards the sound of breaking wood and shouted orders. Skidding to a halt beneath the stairwell at the rear of the house, he pressed himself into the shadows, his heart pounding as he gripped the Walther PPK tucked into his jacket.

The fight was coming. And he was ready.

Two soldiers smashed their way inside and began clearing the downstairs rooms. One kept watch as the other entered the first room.

The one keeping watch was kneeling down, his rifle aimed and at the ready. His focus was on the corridor ahead, but he constantly moved his head from the corridor to the room his friend was clearing.

Michael waited until his attention was on the room, and then fired a single shot to the head. The soldier immediately fell forward.

Evasion

His comrade screamed, and Michael waited patiently for him to make a move. He couldn't, wouldn't, remain in the room for long, and he was ready for him when he came out.

Shouts, screams and gunshots could be heard coming from the front of the house, and Michael hoped Marcel and Rose had got the better of the soldiers there, or he'd be exposed in his hiding place beneath the stairs.

The barrel of a rifle appeared from the doorway, so Michael took aim and waited. A second later, and the rest of the weapon appeared. The soldier swung it from side to side as he emerged on his belly into the corridor.

The second his head appeared, Michael let off a double tap, killing the soldier instantly.

He waited for a few moments to make sure that no more soldiers were coming in through the back, and happy they weren't, he crawled towards the front of the house, where everything had gone quiet.

Marcel and Rose were unhurt, but the two soldiers were dead. Marcel looked at Michael, who nodded his head as if to tell him the rear of the house was safe, and he pointed upstairs.

Michael understood, and while Rose and Marcel guarded downstairs, he ran to the bedroom to release Senta.

He slid the panel aside, revealing Senta's pale face as she huddled in the small, dark space. Her eyes widened with relief and fear as she scrambled out, clutching his arm.

"Are you alright?" she whispered, her voice trembling.

"I'm fine," he replied, his tone firm but hurried. "But we need to move. Now."

They descended the stairs quickly, watching and listening intently for anything that was out of place. The rooms below were eerily silent after the explosion of violence.

Senta gasped, her hand flying to her mouth. The flickering light from the lamp caught on the shapes sprawled on the floor—two German soldiers laying lifeless, their blood mixing with the dust.

She gasped when she saw Hugo's lifeless body near the door.

Michael placed a steadying hand on her shoulder. "Don't look," he said softly.

"Here," Marcel said, gesturing to the room that held the stone fireplace.

With Michael and Senta present, Marcel reached forward and pressed a hidden mechanism. With a low groan, the rear of the fireplace slid aside, revealing a narrow, shadowy opening.

Marcel grabbed a lantern from a hook just inside the tunnel, lighting it with a practised flick. The flame illuminated the cramped space ahead, the air within thick and musty. He turned back to Michael, Senta, and Rose.

"Inside," he said curtly. "Quickly."

They stepped into the narrow passage, and Marcel pushed the stone door closed behind them. Darkness swallowed them whole, the faint glow of the lantern the only thing keeping the blackness at bay.

"Hold hands," Marcel instructed, his voice low. "The tunnel twists, and you won't see more than a step ahead. Rose, take the lantern and lead the way."

Rose took the lantern in one hand and gripped Senta's hand in the other. Senta grabbed Michael's hand, her grip tight, and Michael grasped Marcel's, forming a chain as they began to move.

The air was stale, each breath carrying the scent of centuries-old oxygen. The walls pressed down from above, the ceiling low so that Michael had to duck slightly.

As the tunnel descended, the height of the tunnel forced them to drop to their knees and crawl through certain sections.

Michael grunted as his rucksack snagged on a protruding rock.

"How short were these smugglers?" he muttered under his breath, earning a faint chuckle from Marcel.

"Resourceful," Marcel replied. "That's all that matters."

The steep incline made their progress slow and arduous. Every movement seemed to echo, the sound magnified in the oppressive silence. The lantern's flame danced with every shift, casting distorted shadows on the rough walls.

Finally, after what felt like an eternity, a faint breeze brushed against Michael's face. It was cool and salty, a promise of freedom after the suffocating confines of the tunnel.

"Fresh air," Senta whispered, her voice tinged with relief.

The tunnel opened up allowing them to stand again, and the sound of waves breaking against rocks reached their ears. Rose stepped out first, the lantern casting light over the pebble beach. Marcel followed, his sharp eyes scanning the shoreline.

Michael stepped into the open air, the breeze chilling his sweat-dampened skin, and for a brief moment, he felt the weight of their plight lift.

He blinked rapidly as he struggled to adjust to the night sky after the oppressive darkness of the tunnel. The drizzle made the pebble beach slick, and the faint light from a crescent moon barely illuminated the scene before him.

Shadows danced across the jagged cliffs, and the crashing waves filled the silence like a distant, ominous drumbeat.

Then he saw them.

Six figures emerged from the shadows near the base of the cliffs. Two soldiers flanked four men in civilian clothes, both of whom aimed their rifles at him as he emerged from the cliffs.

Two others aimed pistols at him, while a frightened-looking man that Michael immediately guessed was a local who'd probably been pressganged into helping them, stood next to a soldier.

It was the man in the centre that grabbed his attention.

The man stood rigid, his form outlined by the faint sheen of moisture on his long coat. Even in the dim light, the sharp angles of his stance and the unmistakable air of authority marked him as someone in charge.

His wide-brimmed hat cast a shadow over his face, adding to the ominous impression as he surveyed the scene with an air of calculated control.

Gestapo or SD.

"End of the line," the man in the centre said, his voice smooth and chilling as he stepped forward. His eyes glittered with cold satisfaction.

"Michael Fernsby. What a pleasure it is to finally make your acquaintance."

Marcel, also exposed in the open, shifted subtly, his stance protective as he stepped closer to Michael. Senta and Rose were still out of sight, hidden behind the rocks at the end of the tunnel.

"Allow me to introduce myself. My name is Sturmbannführer Erik Stadtler of the SD. I'm sure you remember my predecessor, Albert Kreise."

Kreise! Even in death, the man brought anger to Michael's mind and palpitations to his heart.

"I've finally got you, Fernsby. Now, where's the girl? Is she behind you?" He lifted his chin, as if pointing towards the cliffs.

Michael's mind raced, his muscles taut. His gaze flicking between the soldiers and the men stood between them.

Behind him, he hoped Senta and Rose remained out of sight.

Chapter 80

Michael's hands were raised, his body tense and ready despite his apparent surrender. Every fibre of his being screamed to act, but he forced himself to stay calm, to think, to wait.

The air was thick with salt and tension, the crashing waves a distant counterpoint to the chilling voice that addressed him.

Stadtler stepped closer, his boots crunching against the slick pebbles.

"You've been an irritation to the Reich for far too long. They said that you were the greatest threat I would ever encounter, and yet from what I see, you are nothing more than a child who is out of his depth."

Stadtler glared at Michael through the drizzle. "Your luck has run out, Fernsby."

Michael remained silent, his thoughts whirling. Stadtler held all the aces, and for now, he was as helpless as he'd ever been.

He stepped forward with his hands still in the air. Stadtler pointed at Marcel, who followed suit.

Evasion

"Where's the girl?" Stadtler asked. "I won't ask again."

"She's not here," Michael answered. "She's already in England, far away from your clutches."

The barrel of a soldier's rifle twitched slightly in Michael's periphery, its aim shifting from Marcel to him and back again. One wrong word, one ill-timed move, and the entire situation could spiral out of control.

"She'd better still be here," Stadtler continued, his voice sharp with menace. "Because if she isn't, then all of this is going to end very badly. For you, for him." He gestured towards Marcel with a gloved hand. "And for the girl when we do catch her. And we will catch her, Fernsby."

"Your girlfriend sends her regrets that she couldn't be here tonight to witness your downfall," Stadtler continued goading Michael, trying to force him into making a mistake that would give up Senta.

He remained silent.

"Her name is Mina, right? They're sisters. We caught her at her friend's farm, hiding like the vermin she helped to escape."

Stadtler's tone was cold.

"And she will be hurt very badly if Senta doesn't agree to work for the Reich."

Michael knew he was lying, but he remained silent.

Stadtler spoke in a low tone to the two soldiers. The men broke rank and approached Michael and Marcel. When they reached their position, one stood with his weapon pointed at them while the other closed the gap.

Michael yelped in pain as a rifle butt slammed into his stomach, forcing all the air out of his lungs. He dropped to his knees, and as he fell, the soldier kicked him hard in the jaw, sending shards of light through his vision as he fell backwards to the wet stones.

The soldier snatched the Walther PPK from his hand and slammed his rifle butt one more time into his chest.

Michael groaned and curled into a ball to protect his vital organs from the attack. He glanced at Stadtler and the others, who stood by watching the violence unfold.

Marcel got the same treatment, and when he was down and broken, Stadtler stepped towards them.

"You can come out now. I know you're behind those rocks, so come out before these two men are killed."

Out of nowhere, two shots rang out. One was accurate, dropping one of the soldiers with a bullet to the chest. The other was wild, but it ricocheted off the rocks at the side of Stadtler's group, forcing them to instinctively take cover.

Michael reacted instantly. He knew the shots came from Rose and Senta, and he could guess which one killed the soldier, but he didn't have time to ponder.

He rolled towards the safety of the rocks, away from the second soldier, who had thrown himself to the ground and was rolling towards some big rocks.

Marcel was doing the same, and two more shots rang out almost simultaneously. One hit Braun square in the chest, crumpling him to the ground like a rag doll.

Stadtler, Falken, and the Frenchman separated and ran for cover.

The other bullet was from the soldier, and it struck Marcel in his back as he rolled towards cover. He lay there for a moment, before disappearing behind a giant, wet rock.

The French informer saw his chance, and he bolted for the path leading up to the top of the cliffs. Stadtler, from his vantage point, fired off two bullets, dropping the hapless Frenchman in his tracks.

Michael quickly released the backpack from his shoulders and reached inside for his backup weapon. He

Evasion

grabbed it and rolled away, keeping rocks and boulders between himself and the Germans.

The soldier ran from rock to rock towards Marcel, and as Michael continued to move, he heard another gunshot.

The soldier fell.

Stadtler and his last remaining companion were nowhere to be seen, so Michael stopped moving and listened. Even the slightest movement was loud on the stones and pebbles, and he heard crunching sounds from behind a large boulder about twenty feet away.

He headed towards it, trying to keep a large rock between them. When it wasn't possible, he rolled, soaking himself to the skin, to make himself as small a target as possible.

When the rock was less than five feet away, movement above his head made Michael look up while he rolled. Stadtler was halfway up a massive rock, trying to hold on to its slick sides while at the same time reaching for his gun.

Realising Stadtler was off balance, Michael straightened his arm and fired, hitting him somewhere in his side. Stadtler yelled in pain and let go, sliding down the rock to the wet pebbles below.

Michael was on him in a flash. He grabbed Stadtler's gun with one hand and his throat with the other. He was about to shoot him when everything went dark.

Unseen, Falken had crept up on Michael and had used a stone to hit him in the head. He'd lost his weapon somewhere in the slippery melee, so rocks were all he had left to fight with.

Michael groaned and fell to the side of the wounded SD officer. Warm blood ran down the side of his face, mingling with the drizzle and seawater from the wet beach.

Falken went to strike Michael again, but he'd recovered

enough to see it coming. He reached out his arm and blocked Falken's blow with his elbow.

Falken, who was older and slower than Michael, reached back to strike again, but Michael pushed him off and hit him hard in the throat.

Falken gurgled and grabbed at his throat. Then he rolled away, got to his feet, and staggered behind a large rock.

Michael rose unsteadily to his feet, and as Stadtler was lying prone on the ground, he went in search of his new adversary. As he inched around the rock, Falken launched another attack with his fists, but the younger man was far too strong and quick for him.

Michael dropped him like a stone and grabbed him by the hair. He raised Falken's head, but seeing an older, unarmed man, he stopped himself from delivering the fatal blow.

Instead, he drove Falken's head into the stones, smashing it down onto a protruding rock that sliced his head open. Blood poured from the wound, and Falken lay still, unconscious and no longer able to hurt Michael any or anyone else.

A noise behind him made him turn around. Stadtler was sitting up, reaching for his weapon in the pooling water. Michael, who had lost his second weapon in the fight with Falken, threw himself at Stadtler, forcing the air from his lungs. He gasped in agony as Michael landed heavily on top of him.

Michael pinned him down and used his weight to prevent him from moving.

"It doesn't have to end like this," Michael gasped. "Nobody else needs to die tonight. Give up, and I'll let you live."

Stadtler nodded, allowing his body to go limp in

surrender. Michael got to his feet and hauled Stadtler up beside him. He spun him around and started to search him for any more weapons.

In a flash, Stadtler pulled a knife from his belt and arced his arm in a slicing motion as he spun around. Michael leaned back and instinctively turned his body, trying to get away from what he knew was coming.

He screamed in agony as the sharp knife sliced through his clothes, slashing his left shoulder almost to the bone. Blood oozed from the wound, and he almost passed out from the pain.

He lashed out with his right arm, catching Stadtler in the throat.

Stadtler staggered backwards and slipped on the wet stones. Michael leapt forward and pushed him backwards, following him to the ground as he fell.

He landed on top of the angry Nazi, and as soon as they hit the ground, he grabbed a large, jagged stone and struck Stadtler in the head. With visions of Albert Kreise in his mind, he struck him again and again and again, until he knew the SD officer was no longer a threat.

Soaked in salt water and blood, Michael relented and collapsed at the side of the dead Stadtler.

Falken was still alive, so Michael gathered himself, grabbed Stadtler's weapon, and went looking for the older Nazi. He searched everywhere, but he was nowhere to be seen.

Chapter 81

Michael stumbled towards the cliffs to find Marcel and the two girls, his steps uneven as blood seeped from his shoulder. Every breath sent a searing pain through his chest, but he forced himself forward. The salt air stung his wounds, and the distant crash of waves seemed to mock his struggle.

Ahead, Rose knelt on the ground, cradling Marcel's head in her lap. Her sobs were quiet, almost reverent, as though she didn't want to disturb the fragile thread of life still clinging to him.

Senta stood nearby, her face pale and tear-streaked, her hands trembling at her sides. She looked utterly lost, like a child who had wandered too far from home.

Michael dropped to his knees beside Marcel, the impact jolting his wounded body, but he barely felt it. His eyes locked on the older man's face, pale, drawn, and glistening with sweat. Marcel's breathing was shallow, his chest rising and falling in laboured, uneven movements.

Rose's tear-streaked face turned to Michael, her voice breaking. "He can't die," she whispered, almost pleading.

"We need him. He's our leader. We can't go on without him."

Marcel's eyes fluttered open, and a faint, weary smile touched his lips. "You're stronger than you think, Rose," he murmured, his voice barely more than a breath. "You'll lead them now. Amiens needs you. France needs you."

Rose shook her head violently, fresh tears spilling down her cheeks. "No! I can't. Marcel, don't do this to me. Don't you dare."

"You can," Marcel said firmly, his gaze steady despite the shadows creeping into his eyes. "You must."

Michael's throat tightened as Marcel reached out, his trembling hand gripping Michael's firmly.

"Get her out of here," Marcel said, his voice quiet but resolute. "Get Senta to that boat, Michael. The Nazis will be all over this place soon."

Michael swallowed hard, his mouth dry. He nodded, even as a cold dread settled over him. "I will."

Marcel's grip slackened, his hand falling limply to his side. His head tilted back against Rose's lap, his eyes fixed on some distant horizon only he could see.

"Fight for France," he whispered. Then, with a final shuddering breath, he was gone.

Rose let out a broken cry, clutching Marcel's lifeless body to her chest. Her grief was raw and visceral, and it tore through Michael like a blade. Two men had died in her arms tonight, and he felt the weight of their sacrifices pressing down on him.

Senta gasped suddenly, her hands flying to her mouth as she caught sight of Michael's blood-soaked shirt. "Michael! You're hurt!"

"It's nothing," he said, though his voice gave the lie to his statement.

He pushed himself to his feet, swaying slightly.

Rose's head snapped up, her tear-streaked face now hard with anger.

"If you die, then Hugo and Marcel died for nothing!" she snapped, her voice trembling with fury and grief. "Sit down, and don't you dare argue with me."

Michael hesitated, then sank back down onto the rocks. Rose stormed off towards the cliff path that was faster than the tunnel, her figure silhouetted against the faint glow of the moon. Senta crouched beside Michael, her hands fluttering uselessly as she tried to assess his injuries.

"I'm fine," he muttered, though his vision swam with the effort of staying upright. "Really."

Rose returned from the house, carrying a first aid kit and a lantern with green filters. She dropped to her knees beside Michael, her movements brisk and efficient as she opened the kit.

"Senta, hold this," she ordered, thrusting the lantern into the younger woman's hands.

Michael winced as Rose cleaned the wound on his shoulder, the sting of antiseptic nearly sending him over the edge. Senta held his good hand tightly, her fingers cool against his clammy skin.

"This needs stitches," Rose said, her tone sharp but not unkind. "When you get to England, you find someone who knows what they're doing."

"Thank you," he said. "What are you going to do?"

Rose's expression hardened. "My place is here," she said, tying the bandage tightly around his shoulder. "Marcel was right. I have work to do."

Michael didn't argue. He knew better.

A series of red lights flickered out at sea, grabbing their attention. Rose grabbed the lantern and returned the signal with flashes of green light.

Evasion

"That's your boat," she said, standing and brushing the sand from her knees. "Go."

Senta hesitated, tears filling her eyes. "Rose…"

"Go!" Rose snapped, her voice thick with emotion. "I hope saving her was worth it," she said bitterly to Michael. "Because I've lost everyone I care about tonight."

Michael's heart broke, but he said nothing. He couldn't.

Rose turned and walked away, her back straight and unyielding as she disappeared into the shadows without looking back

Michael scrambled to his feet and found his rucksack.

"Ready?"

She nodded, wiping at her tears. Together, they waded into the freezing water, the icy waves biting at their legs as they headed for the waiting boat. Michael didn't look back. He couldn't.

Chapter 82

The grand office in Berlin seemed colder than Erich Falken remembered. Even after years of service to the Reich, standing in the shadow of Reinhard Heydrich's furious presence was a trial few men survived intact.

Falken sat stiffly in a high-backed chair, his bruised ribs protesting against the rigid posture. His head throbbed with every heartbeat, a reminder of his narrow survival on the rocky beach at Petit-Caux.

Across from him, his good friend, SS-Obergruppenführer Hanns Albin Rauter sat equally silent, his usually imperious demeanour diminished in the face of Heydrich's rage.

SS-Obergruppenführer Heydrich paced before them, his movements sharp and volatile, like a predator caged in its own fury. His pale, hawk-like face was flushed with anger, and his sharp eyes darted between Falken and Rauter, daring them to speak.

Neither man ventured to interrupt.

"Idiots," Heydrich hissed, the word slicing through the

tense air like a blade. "Stadtler was a fool. A posturing, incompetent brute who underestimated Fernsby at every turn. How many times did I warn him?"

He slammed a hand against the polished surface of his desk, the sound reverberating in the cold, cavernous office.

Falken kept his gaze forward, his breathing controlled, though his pulse quickened at the mention of Stadtler. The man's arrogance had led them all to ruin, and now Falken bore the burden of his failures as the sole survivor.

"You!" Heydrich's voice snapped, and Falken realised he was addressing him directly. "Your report."

Heydrich seized the document from his desk and waved it like a weapon. "This pathetic debacle is all I have to show for weeks of planning. Do you understand what you've cost the Reich?"

Falken didn't flinch, though his knuckles whitened as he gripped the armrests of his chair.

"Yes, Herr Obergruppenführer," he said, his voice low but steady. "The girl is a valuable asset—"

"A priceless asset," Heydrich interrupted, his voice a venomous growl. "And now she's gone, spirited away to England thanks to your failures."

"And Fernsby!" He spat the name like a curse. "That Englishman has humiliated us once again."

Heydrich's fingers clenched around the report. "Left you for dead," he sneered, quoting Falken's own words. "After beating you senseless. He's younger, stronger, faster. So what? You let that child best you?"

Falken remained silent, his jaw tight. He had described the encounter truthfully, knowing Heydrich valued honesty, even brutal honesty, over flattery. It had been humiliating to write, but it was better than lies that could unravel under scrutiny.

Heydrich's fury seemed to peak, then suddenly dissipate, as if he had willed it into submission. His pacing stopped, and he turned to face Falken, his expression cold and calculating. The predator had regained control.

"Your time in Holland is over," Heydrich said abruptly, his tone flat and absolute. "You are wasted there, Falken. Stadtler's failure was as much Rauter's mistake as his own."

He cast a withering glare at Rauter, who visibly stiffened.

"Herr Obergruppenführer," Rauter began, but Heydrich silenced him with a raised hand.

"Spare me your excuses, Rauter," Heydrich said icily. "Stadtler was a thug, a brute too enamoured with his own reflection to see the enemy before him. I needed someone with intellect, with meticulous attention to detail. I needed a man like Falken."

Falken's head lifted slightly at the unexpected praise, though his face remained neutral.

"You will remain in Berlin," Heydrich said, fixing Falken with a piercing gaze. "I have a new task for you. You will create a department that will answer directly to me. No intermediaries, no bureaucratic nonsense. You will have the authority to pull resources from any branch of the Reich's forces. Do you understand?"

"For what purpose, Obergruppenführer?" Falken asked, his voice steady despite the weight of the moment.

"Have you heard of Unit three one seven?" Heydrich's voice dropped several decibels.

"Only whispers, Obergruppenführer, and even then, only after I was sent to work with Stadtler."

"Your new department will focus solely on eradicating Unit three one seven," Heydrich said. "It's a covert arm of

MI6 for their so-called elite operatives. Fernsby is their star, a menace who has disrupted too many of our operations. He has cost us men, resources, and now the Postner girl. He must be eliminated, as must the rest of his unit."

Falken's heart pounded, though his expression betrayed nothing. "I understand, Obergruppenführer."

Heydrich's lips curved into a cold smile. "Good. Thugs can be found on any street corner, Falken. What you possess—intelligence, discipline, precision—those are rare. You are not a brute, and I do not expect you to fight like one. You will use your mind, your patience, and your attention to detail to outthink and destroy these men."

"Yes, Obergruppenführer," Falken repeated, inclining his head. "I'll do my absolute best, sir."

Heydrich turned his gaze to Rauter. "You are dismissed. Pray you do not disappoint me again."

Rauter stood, glanced at his old friend, and saluted. He left without a word, his boots echoing in the silent corridor beyond. Falken remained seated until Heydrich gestured for him to rise.

"This is your chance to redeem yourself," Heydrich said softly, his tone carrying the import of both warning and promise. "Do not fail me, Falken. Fernsby, and Unit three one seven, must die."

Heydrich paused before continuing. "My secretary has details of your new apartment in Berlin. You have a week to wind up your affairs in Holland, and you will be given your new assignment on your return."

Falken stood, and even though it hurt, he thrust his right arm in front of him.

"Heil Hitler!" he bellowed.

"Heil Hitler." Heydrich returned the Nazi salute.

Falken shuffled out of the office. His limp was

pronounced as he approached the secretary with the echoes of Heydrich's commands ringing in his ears.

This was no longer about survival. It wasn't even about winning the war. For Heydrich, this was about vengeance.

The End

More Books by JC Jarvis

Fernsby's War Series

Ryskamp

Alderauge

Ludsecke

Rotterdam

Evasion

The John Howard Tudor Series

John Howard and the Underlings

John Howard and the Tudor Legacy

John Howard and the Tudor Deception

Get a FREE Book!

Before John Howard found sanctuary on the streets of Henry VIII's London, Andrew Cullane formed a small band of outlawed survivors called the Underlings. Discover their fight for life for free when you join J.C. Jarvis's newsletter at jcjarvis.com/cullane

Please Leave A Review

If you loved Evasion and have a moment to spare, I would really appreciate a short review.

Your help in spreading the word is gratefully appreciated and reviews make a huge difference to helping new readers find the series.

Please click the link below to leave your review:

AMAZON

Thank You!

About the Author

J.C. Jarvis is the author of the breakout Fernsby's War series.

He makes his home at www.jcjarvis.com

Email: jc@jcjarvis.com

Printed in Great Britain
by Amazon